# Identity in Science Fiction

**ALSO AVAILABLE FROM BLOOMSBURY:**

*Introducing Aesthetics and the Philosophy of Art* by Darren Hudson Hick
*Philosophy of Comics* by Sam Cowling and Wesley Cray
*Philosophy through Science Fiction Stories* edited by Helen De Cruz,
Johan De Smedt and Eric Schwitzgebel

# Identity in Science Fiction

## Brain Transplants and Other Misadventures

### Edited by Tom Cochrane

BLOOMSBURY ACADEMIC
LONDON • NEW YORK • OXFORD • NEW DELHI • SYDNEY

BLOOMSBURY ACADEMIC
Bloomsbury Publishing Plc
50 Bedford Square, London, WC1B 3DP, UK
1359 Broadway, New York, NY 10018, USA
29 Earlsfort Terrace, Dublin 2, Ireland

BLOOMSBURY, BLOOMSBURY ACADEMIC and the Diana logo are trademarks of
Bloomsbury Publishing Plc

First published in Great Britain 2025

Copyright © Edited by Tom Cochrane 2025

Tom Cochrane has asserted his right under the Copyright, Designs and Patents Act, 1988, to be identified as Author of this work.

For legal purposes the Acknowledgements on p. ix constitute an extension of this copyright page.

Cover design: Aneeka Makwana
Cover image by Ju-Fang Hsiao and Tom Cochrane

All rights reserved. No part of this publication may be: i) reproduced or transmitted in any form, electronic or mechanical, including photocopying, recording or by means of any information storage or retrieval system without prior permission in writing from the publishers; or ii) used or reproduced in any way for the training, development or operation of artificial intelligence (AI) technologies, including generative AI technologies. The rights holders expressly reserve this publication from the text and data mining exception as per Article 4(3) of the Digital Single Market Directive (EU).

Bloomsbury Publishing Plc does not have any control over, or responsibility for, any third-party websites referred to or in this book. All internet addresses given in this book were correct at the time of going to press. The author and publisher regret any inconvenience caused if addresses have changed or sites have ceased to exist, but can accept no responsibility for any such changes.

A catalogue record for this book is available from the British Library.

A catalog record for this book is available from the Library of Congress.

| ISBN: | HB: | 978-1-3504-9979-9 |
| --- | --- | --- |
|  | PB: | 978-1-3504-9980-5 |
|  | ePDF: | 978-1-3504-9982-9 |
|  | eBook: | 978-1-3504-9981-2 |

Typeset by RefineCatch Limited, Bungay, Suffolk
Printed and bound in Great Britain

For product safety related questions contact productsafety@bloomsbury.com.

To find out more about our authors and books visit www.bloomsbury.com and sign up for our newsletters.

*To Zephram and Karuna*

# Contents

*Acknowledgements* ix

**Introduction** 1

1 **'The Barbie Murders'** *John Varley* 7
   Comment on 'The Barbie Murders' 33

2 **'Marley and Marley'** *J. R. Dawson* 39
   Comment on 'Marley and Marley' 56

3 **'Edward the Conqueror'** *Roald Dahl* 61
   Comment on 'Edward the Conqueror' 78

4 **'Life Sentence'** *Matthew Baker* 85
   Comment on 'Life Sentence' 109

5 ***The Affirmation*** *Christopher Priest* 115
   Comment on *The Affirmation* 125

6 **'Think Like a Dinosaur'** *James Patrick Kelly* 131
   Comment on 'Think Like a Dinosaur' 149

7 **'The Extra'** *Greg Egan* 155
   Comment on 'The Extra' 170

8 ***Sirius*** *Olaf Stapledon* 177
   Comment on *Sirius* 195

## 9 'Through the Window Frame'
*Sean Williams* 201
Comment on 'Through the Window Frame' 219

## 10 'Constitution' *Tom Cochrane* 225
Comment on 'Constitution' 243

## 11 'Social Dreaming of the Frin'
*Ursula K. Le Guin* 251
Comment on 'Social Dreaming of the Frin' 259

## 12 'Remedy' *Claire North* 265
Comment on 'Remedy' 283

*Appendix A: A Guide for Teachers* 289
*Appendix B: Literature and Films on Personal Identity* 297
*Index* 305

# Acknowledgements

When I named my first-born child after a character from *Star Trek*, I thought that my credentials as a science-fiction fan would be firmly established. The Fates demanded more from me, however. It was 2017 when I was preparing to teach a course on personal identity that I wondered if a nice seminar on brain transplants could revolve around Greg Egan's short story 'The Extra'. Might it be possible to find other stories that fit the various issues? I discussed the idea with my colleague Eric Olson, who suggested that it might make a good collection. The idea lingered in the back of my mind for a number of years. It was harder to find a suitable set of stories than I ever suspected, mostly for word-length reasons. Once things finally came together, I workshopped my commentaries with the students in my metaphysics class at Flinders University. Thanks to Lauren Baso, Lilyann Coote, Charles Degrassi, Theresa Ewen, Brodie Manticos, Campbell Mckenzie, Zeph Swain and Rikki Winterburn for a really fun class. Thanks also to Jon Opie, Matthew Tieu, Sean Williams, Craig Taylor, Matthew Nestor and Joshua Tepley for discussions of these issues, as well as the participants of the Uppsala Aesthetics seminar organized by Elisabeth Schellekens. The editors at Bloomsbury, Colleen Coalter and Aimee Brown, have been wonderfully enthusiastic about this project and I appreciate their work in getting this book published.

I feel very proud to reprint stories by the authors in this collection, some of whose works I've been reading since I was a child, and other rising stars whose work I've only discovered in the last few years. I must particularly single out Christopher Priest, who very sadly died while this book was in production. He goes to join the pantheon of writers who have left us a treasure of works that continue to inspire generations, and not a little philosophy.

'The Barbie Murders' © 1978 by John Varley, first appeared in *Isaac Asimov's Science Fiction Magazine*; reproduced with kind permission of the author, and the author's agents, the Virginia Kidd Agency.

## Acknowledgements

'Marley and Marley' © J. R. Dawson, reproduced with kind permission of the author.

'Edward the Conqueror' from *Kiss Kiss* by Roald Dahl (Penguin Books), © The Roald Dahl Story Company Limited, reproduced by permission of David Higham Associates.

'Life Sentence' from *Why Visit America* by Matthew Baker. Copyright © 2020 by Matthew Baker. Reprinted by permission of Henry Holt and Company. All Rights Reserved (America and Rest of the World). Bloomsbury (UK and Commonwealth and South Africa).

Chapter Three from *The Affirmation* © Christopher Priest, reproduced with kind permission of the author.

'Think Like a Dinosaur' © James Patrick Kelly, reproduced with kind permission of the author.

'The Extra' © Greg Egan, reproduced with kind permission of the author.

*Sirius* by Olaf Stapledon (1886–1950) was first published in 1944, Secker and Warburg, London.

'Through the Window Frame' © Sean Williams 2024.

'Constitution' © Tom Cochrane 2024.

'Social Dreaming of the Frin' from *Changing Planes* by Ursula K. Le Guin. Reproduced with permission of the Orion Publishing Group Limited through PLSclear (UK and Commonwealth), Harper and Collins (America and rest of the world).

'Remedy' © Catherine Webb 2024.

# Introduction

Philosophy is about big questions. Is there a God? How did the universe come to be? What makes an action right or wrong? How can I be certain of anything? If you think these questions are worth trying to answer, then you think that philosophy is worth doing.

The desire to answer big questions comes before any rules or methods or traditions in philosophy. We care first and foremost about getting the answers, and in principle, we are open to any means that might effectively get at them. As a result, there remains a fundamental chaos at the heart of our discipline. The methods that we use to approach our questions and the assumptions that we make in so doing are always up for grabs. For instance, although philosophy is different from science, it is not opposed to it. If there are experiments and observations that are relevant to our questions, then we want to know about them! The trouble is that we lack clear scientific ways to provide the answers we seek. We cannot, for instance, find out whether stealing is bad by stealing something a thousand times and then observing the consequences. This is because we'd still have to decide if those consequences are good or bad, or even whether consequences are the only thing that count towards deciding.

Instead, the most characteristic activity of the philosopher is simply to think in a careful and imaginative way, taking into consideration pretty much every single thing that might be relevant. In this manner, a number of schools of thought have slowly emerged that aim to give comprehensive answers to the big questions. But I want to emphasize that the various traditions of philosophy have only the authority of some smart people having spent a lot of time thinking about these issues, and then trying to explain what they've come up with as clearly as they can. If you are not satisfied with the answers they have come up with, you can and should try for yourself.

Let us then consider a big question.

A good one that people ask themselves is – *Who am I?* The idea behind this question is to understand ourselves; to figure out what is characteristic or essential about us. Such a question has intrinsic interest, but it may also have major practical implications if it helps us to live more purposeful and successful lives. Yet philosophers have found that the deep pursuit of that question leads to an even deeper and more perplexing question: *What am I?* Am I even a definite kind of thing? Perhaps it would be more accurate to regard myself as a sort of process, or even a pattern of information. Such alternatives may initially seem to you bizarre, but they each have their defenders (such is philosophy) and the truth of any one of them has major implications for the basic conditions of our existence and the features of us that really matter.

In fact, when we pursue the question of what we are, it turns out to be very tricky. For instance, off the top of my head I might answer – I'm a human being. But that is almost certainly too hasty. For suppose that a scientist was to gradually replace all of my parts, even those inside my brain, with non-organic mechanical components. Would I still exist at the end of that process? If you think that I would still exist, then this suggests that I would not be a human, since a human is a kind of animal, and something with no organic parts is not an animal. Significantly, if I really would still exist in this imagined scenario, then I'm not essentially a human *right now*, before any scientist gets their twitchy little hands on me. That is, if it's even possible for me to undergo such a transformation, then I'm not essentially a human being, because a thing's essential features are what it *must* be, if it exists at all.

Notice what has happened here. I just presented a very brief imaginary scenario to test a philosophical claim; the claim that I am essentially a human. This is what we call a thought experiment, and it is one of the major tools that philosophers use to develop their ideas. Philosophers love thought experiments. They are both fun and informative, and many philosophers have made their names by coming up with really good ones. For instance, René Descartes wondered if an evil demon could be tricking him to think he is experiencing the real world when in fact it's all an illusion. 300 years later, Robert Nozick turned this idea around and wondered if he would want to get into a machine that gave him a lifetime of pleasurable though illusory experiences. Considerable ink has been spilled in consideration of both of these scenarios because philosophers think that by doing so, they can answer important questions about how we know anything and what makes a good life.

This book is all about thought experiments, specifically those that address the question of what we are. I am interested both in exploring the answers to that question, as well as the method of using thought experiments to arrive at an answer.

# Thought Experiments and Science Fiction

It may have crossed your mind that the use of imaginary scenarios to explore big questions is not only something that happens in philosophy books. The kind of scenario that I considered earlier, in which a body is gradually replaced by mechanical parts, is also frequently found in science fiction. In fact, raising deep questions about the nature of reality is one of the special virtues of science fiction. People who love science fiction love this genre because it stretches our imaginations. Great works of science fiction cast off our assumptions about how things have to be or how we have to live. Great science fiction authors offer new and illuminating ways to think about things.

So it seems to me that philosophy and science fiction are natural bedfellows. I do not deny that other genres can present thought experiments. I also do not deny that many science fictions simply delight in wacky cases and don't have much to tell us about things beyond that. Yet because science fiction tends in general to present radical scenarios, it is especially able to stretch our ideas about the world to their breaking point, to the point where we can really see what makes them tick. Meanwhile, when it comes to the question of what we are, the philosopher Tamar Gendler argues that controlled thought experiments *must* depict radical transformations – where we lose, say, everything but our memories or our bodies or our organic make-up. Works that depict such transformations will tend automatically to be classed as science fiction.

Yet how could the imaginings of a science-fiction author, even a very smart one, tell us something informative about what we are? What authority have these authors to guide us through such choppy metaphysical waters? Personally, I agree that we should be cautious when it comes to fictions about fundamental physical forces. For instance, I doubt that science fiction can be very informative about the possibility of backwards time travel. Though some science fictions are usefully informed by contemporary physics, and some authors even have serious scientific qualifications, I've yet to see one that plausibly imagines how backwards time travel could actually be achieved.

However, unlike backwards time travel, the metaphysics of what we are is part of our everyday lives. Here we can usefully make a comparison to ethical thought experiments, in which authors present a moral dilemma, and then consider how their characters should respond. Authors tend to have sufficient real-world moral experience that they can usefully extrapolate how their protagonists make moral decisions. That is, authors can make use of their *intuitions*. Intuitions are quite deeply held ideas we have about how things work that we have gained through everyday experience, perhaps influenced by the very structure of our minds. Similarly, I suppose that science-fiction authors have intuitions about their own nature, informed by their everyday experiences and mental structures. These intuitions can be usefully deployed, along with a bit of reasoning and imagination, to explore what we are. I hasten to add, however, that anything a science-fiction author comes up with still has to be evaluated by the reader, who equally makes use of their intuitions and reason in thinking through the imaginary case.

Here we should also recognize that the way a science fiction explores a philosophical claim is different to the way a thought experiment is likely to go in a philosophy book or paper. First of all, the thought experiments that we find in philosophical works are a lot shorter. They present a scenario as quickly and efficiently as possible so that the author can spend more time reflecting on the philosophical consequences. In this respect, science fiction may have a considerable advantage. A proper literary narrative will immerse us in a world in which the experimental situation could occur. It will take the time to explore little details about how it would come about and its consequences. Many of these details may initially seem accidental, merely adding colour. But as we shall see, often those little details reveal quite interesting implications that get glossed over in the philosophy papers.

On the other hand, science-fiction authors are typically interested in artistic qualities that aren't clearly relevant to answering the philosophical question. First and foremost, the writer of literature wants to engage the reader. Thus the narrative may well have qualities that make it dramatic or funny or moving. These qualities are likely to make the narrative more vivid and memorable, yet philosophers may worry that these qualities are at odds with philosophical goals. For instance, if properly explaining the mechanics of a technological development would be too dry and complex, the science-fiction author is liable to skip over it for the sake of holding the attention of the reader. (Technologies are rarely developed by lone geniuses working overnight in their garages.) Science-fiction authors certainly care about realism (and I think it's safe to say that some deference to technological or scientific realism helps to distinguish science fiction from fantasy), but it won't be the only thing they care about.

On a third hand, when I read the thought experiments presented by professional philosophers, I am often struck by the thought that they haven't taken the time to consider the realism of their imagined scenarios much either. In fact, I'd say science-fiction authors typically do a *better* job than philosophers in this regard, particularly those authors working in what is called 'hard' science fiction. As such, while I think the realism of science-fiction narratives is an important consideration, and one that I will be coming back to throughout this book, I don't think that science fiction is at a disadvantage in this regard.

There's a final worry about thought experiments that I must also mention because it threatens to scupper the whole enterprise from the start. This is the worry that thought experiments can be too leading. That is, they push the reader, by not very rational means, to accept certain philosophical positions or to make certain assumptions. As I noted above, it is typical for metaphysical issues to rely on us carefully weighing up our intuitions. Daniel Dennett uses the term 'intuition pumps' to label the idea that thought experiments may manipulate our intuitions in sneaky ways.

This is certainly a deep worry. In particular, the way in which a scenario is presented will tend to embed certain views right from the start that we fail to notice when evaluating its ideas. Some recent experimental philosophy (that is, where people's philosophical opinions are gauged through psychological surveys) has even found that the order in which certain scenarios are presented can make a difference to peoples' answers.

There are, however, two ways we can respond to this worry. First of all, if one narrative is dubious because it pushes our thinking in a certain direction, then the best remedy to this is not simply to reject the narrative, but to offer up an alternate narrative that pushes us in the opposite direction. That way, we can more clearly see our options and come to some informed opinion of our own. Second, pumping our intuitions, properly conceived, may not be an altogether bad thing. It could help us get out of our cognitive ruts and explore the further reaches of our conceptual schemes. Again, however, this process needs to be balanced with opposing narratives, if we are to get a good mental workout.

Overall, these considerations motivate the present volume. I have carefully selected stories that demonstrate some of the best that the science-fiction genre has to offer in terms of well-thoughtout scenarios that test important claims about identity. Many different views are presented in gripping detail that help us to appreciate the force of certain theories about what we are. At the same time, for these stories to fully function as thought experiments requires that we readers do some evaluative work. Thus following each narrative, I will spell out some of the key ideas that these stories have illustrated and the major philosophical arguments surrounding them. I can't promise to be completely unbiased in my evaluation of these views, but I will make it obvious where I am offering a view of my own. In this way, I hope that the reader will be in an excellent position to make up their own minds one way or another.

# 1

## 'The Barbie Murders'

### John Varley

THE BODY CAME to the morgue at 2246 hours. No one paid much attention to it. It was a Saturday night, and the bodies were piling up like logs in a millpond. A harried attendant working her way down the row of stainless steel tables picked up the sheaf of papers that came with the body, peeling back the sheet over the face. She took a card from her pocket and scrawled on it, copying from the reports filed by the investigating officer and the hospital staff:

> Ingraham, Leah Petrie. Female. Age: 35. Length: 2.1 meters. Mass: 59 Kilograms. Dead on arrival, Crisium Emergency Terminal. Cause of death: homicide. Next of kin: unknown.

She wrapped the wire attached to the card around the left big toe, slid the dead weight from the table and onto the wheeled carrier, took it to cubicle 659A, and rolled out the long tray.

The door slammed shut, and the attendant placed the paperwork in the out tray, never noticing that, in his report, the investigating officer had not specified the sex of the corpse.

\*

Lieutenant Anna-Louise Bach had moved into her new office three days ago and already the paper on her desk was threatening to avalanche onto the floor.

To call it an office was almost a perversion of the term. It had a file cabinet for pending cases; she could open it only at severe risk to life and limb. The drawers had a tendency to spring out at her, pinning her in her chair in the corner. To reach "A" she had to stand on her chair; "Z" required her either to sit on her desk or to straddle the bottom drawer with one foot in the legwell and the other against the wall.

But the office had a door. True, it could only be opened if no one was occupying the single chair in front of the desk.

Bach was in no mood to gripe. She loved the place. It was ten times better than the squadroom, where she had spent ten years elbow-to-elbow with the other sergeants and corporals.

Jorge Weil stuck his head in the door.

"Hi. We're taking bids on a new case. What am I offered?"

"Put me down for half a Mark," Bach said, without looking up from the report she was writing. "Can't you see I'm busy?"

"Not as busy as you're going to be." Weil came in without an invitation and settled himself in the chair. Bach looked up, opened her mouth, then said nothing. She had the authority to order him to get his big feet out of her "cases completed" tray, but not the experience in exercising it. And she and Jorge had worked together for three years. Why should a stripe of gold paint on her shoulder change their relationship? She supposed the informality was Weil's way of saying he wouldn't let her promotion bother him as long as she didn't get snotty about it.

Weil deposited a folder on top of the teetering pile marked "For Immediate Action," then leaned back again. Bach eyed the stack of paper—and the circular file mounted in the wall not half a meter from it, leading to the incinerator—and thought about having an accident. Just a careless nudge with an elbow . . .

"Aren't you even going to open it?" Weil asked, sounding disappointed. "It's not every day I'm going to hand-deliver a case."

"You tell me about it, since you want to so badly."

"All right. We've got a body, which is cut up pretty bad. We've got the murder weapon, which is a knife. We've got thirteen eyewitnesses who can describe the killer, but we don't really need them since the murder was committed in front of a television camera. We've got the tape."

"You're talking about a case which has to have been solved ten minutes after the first report, untouched by human hands. Give it to the computer, idiot." But she looked up. She didn't like the smell of it. "Why give it to me?"

"Because of the other thing we know. The scene of the crime. The murder was committed at the barbie colony."

"Oh, sweet Jesus."

\*

The Temple of the Standardized Church in Luna was in the center of the Standardist Commune, Anytown, North Crisium. The best way to reach it, they found, was a local tube line which paralleled the Cross-Crisium Express Tube.

She and Weil checked out a blue-and-white police capsule with a priority sorting code and surrendered themselves to the New Dresden municipal transport system—the pill sorter, as the New Dresdenites called it. They were whisked through the precinct chute to the main nexus, where thousands of capsules were stacked awaiting a routing order to clear the computer. On the big conveyer which should have taken them to a holding cubby, they were snatched by a grapple—the cops called it the long arm of the law—and moved ahead to the multiple maws of the Cross-Crisium while people in other capsules glared at them. The capsule was inserted, and Bach and Weil were pressed hard into the backs of their seats.

In seconds they emerged from the tube and out onto the plain of Crisium, speeding along through the vacuum, magnetically suspended a few millimeters above the induction rail. Bach glanced up at the Earth, then stared out the window at the featureless landscape rushing by. She brooded.

It had taken a look at the map to convince her that the barbie colony was indeed in the New Dresden jurisdiction—a case of blatant gerrymandering if ever there was one. Anytown was fifty kilometers from what she thought of as the boundaries of New Dresden, but was joined to the city by a dotted line that represented a strip of land one meter wide.

A roar built up as they entered a tunnel and air was injected into the tube ahead of them. The car shook briefly as the shock wave built up, then they popped through pressure doors into the tube station of Anytown. The capsule doors hissed and they climbed out onto the platform.

The tube station at Anytown was primarily a loading dock and warehouse. It was a large space with plastic crates stacked against all the walls, and about fifty people working to load them into freight capsules.

Bach and Weil stood on the platform for a moment, uncertain where to go. The murder had happened at a spot not twenty meters in front of them, right here in the tube station.

"This place gives me the creeps," Weil volunteered.

"Me, too."

Every one of the fifty people Bach could see was identical to every other.

All appeared to be female, though only faces, feet, and hands were visible, everything else concealed by loose white pajamas belted at the waist. They were all blonde; all had hair cut off at the shoulder and parted in the middle, blue eyes, high foreheads, short noses, and small mouths.

The work slowly stopped as the barbies became aware of them. They eyed Bach and Weil suspiciously. Bach picked one at random and approached her.

"Who's in charge here?" she asked.

"We are," the barbie said. Bach took it to mean the woman herself, recalling something about barbies never using the singular pronoun.

"We're supposed to meet someone at the temple," she said. "How do we get there?"

"Through that doorway," the woman said. "It leads to Main Street. Follow the street to the temple. But you really should cover yourselves."

"Huh? What do you mean?" Bach was not aware of anything wrong with the way she and Weil were dressed. True, neither of them wore as much as the barbies did. Bach wore her usual blue nylon briefs in addition to a regulation uniform cap, arm and thigh bands, and cloth-soled slippers. Her weapon, communicator, and handcuffs were fastened to a leather equipment belt.

"Cover yourself," the barbie said, with a pained look. "You're flaunting your differentness. And you, with all that hair . . ." There were giggles and a few shouts from the other barbies.

"Police business," Weil snapped.

"Uh, yes," Bach said, feeling annoyed that the barbie had put her on the defensive. After all, this was New Dresden, it was a public thoroughfare—even though by tradition and usage a Standardist enclave—and they were entitled to dress as they wished. Main Street was a narrow, mean little place. Bach had expected a promenade like those in the shopping districts of New Dresden; what she found was indistinguishable from a residential corridor. They drew curious stares and quite a few frowns from the identical people they met.

There was a modest plaza at the end of the street. It had a low roof of bare metal, a few trees, and a blocky stone building in the center of a radiating network of walks.

A barbie who looked just like all the others met them at the entrance. Bach asked if she was the one Weil had spoken to on the phone, and she said she was. Bach wanted to know if they could go inside to talk. The barbie said the temple was off limits to outsiders and suggested they sit on a bench outside the building.

When they were settled, Bach stared her questioning. "First, I need to know your name, and your title. I assume that you are . . . what was it?" She consulted her notes, taken hastily from a display she had called up on the computer terminal in her office. "I don't seem to have found a title for you."

"We have none," the barbie said. "If you must think of a title, consider us as the keeper of records."

"All right. And your name?"

"We have no name."

Bach sighed. "Yes, I understand that you forsake names when you come here. But you had one before. You were given one at birth. I'm going to have to have it for my investigation."

The woman looked pained. "No, you don't understand. It is true that this body had a name at one time. But it has been wiped from this one's mind. It would cause this one a great deal of pain to be reminded of it." She stumbled verbally every time she said "this one." Evidently even a polite circumlocution of the personal pronoun was distressing.

"I'll try to get it from another angle, then." This was already getting hard to deal with, Bach saw, and knew it could only get tougher. "You say you are the keeper of records."

"We are. We keep records because the law says we must. Each citizen must be recorded, or so we have been told."

"For a very good reason," Bach said. "We're going to need access to those records. For the investigation. You understand? I assume an officer has already been through them, or the deceased couldn't have been identified as Leah P. Ingraham."

"That's true. But it won't be necessary for you to go through the records again. We are here to confess. We murdered L. P. Ingraham, serial number 11005. We are surrendering peacefully. You may take us to your prison."

She held out her hands, wrists close together, ready to be shackled.

Weil was startled, reached tentatively for his handcuffs, then looked to Bach for guidance.

"Let me get this straight. You're saying you're the one who did it? You, personally."

"That's correct. We did it. We have never defied temporal authority, and we are willing to pay the penalty."

"Once more." Bach reached out and grasped the barbie's wrist, forced the hand open, palm up. "*This* is the person, this is the body that committed the murder? This hand, this one right here, held the knife and killed Ingraham? This hand, as opposed to 'your' thousands of other hands?"

The barbie frowned.

"Put that way, no. *This* hand did not grasp the murder weapon. But *our* hand did. What's the difference?"

"Quite a bit, in the eyes of the law." Bach sighed, and let go of the woman's hand. Woman? She wondered if the term applied. She realized she needed to know more about Standardists. But it was convenient to think of them as such, since their faces were feminine.

"Let's try again. I'll need you—and the eyewitnesses to the crime—to study the tape of the murder. *I* can't tell the difference between the murderer, the victim, or any of the bystanders. But surely you must be able to. I assume that . . . well, like the old saying went, 'all Chinamen look alike.' That was to Caucasian races, of course. Orientals had no trouble telling each other apart. So I thought that you . . . that you people would . . ." She trailed off at the look of blank incomprehension on the barbie's face.

"We don't know what you're talking about."

Bach's shoulders slumped.

"You mean you can't . . . not even if you saw her again . . . ?"

The woman shrugged. "We all look the same to this one."

\*

Anna-Louise Bach sprawled out on her flotation bed later that night, surrounded by scraps of paper. Untidy as it was, her thought processes were helped by actually scribbling facts on paper rather than filing them in her datalink. And she did her best work late at night, at home, in bed, after taking a bath or making love. Tonight she had done both and found she needed every bit of the invigorating clarity it gave her.

Standardists.

They were an off-beat religious sect founded ninety years earlier by someone whose name had not survived. That was not surprising, since Standardists gave up their names when they joined the order, made every effort consistent with the laws of the land to obliterate the name and person as if he or she had never existed. The epithet "barbie" had quickly been attached to them by the press. The origin of the word was a popular children's toy of the twentieth and early twenty-first centuries, a plastic, sexless, mass-produced "girl" doll with an elaborate wardrobe.

The barbies had done surprisingly well for a group which did not reproduce, which relied entirely on new members from the outside world to replenish their numbers. They had grown for twenty years, then reached a population stability where deaths equalled new members—which they call "components." They had suffered moderately from religious intolerance, moving from country to country until the majority had come to Luna sixty years ago.

They drew new components from the walking wounded of society, the people who had not done well in a world which preached conformity, passivity, and tolerance of your billions of neighbors, yet rewarded only those who were individualist and aggressive enough to stand apart from the herd. The barbies had opted out of a system where one had to be at once a face in the crowd and a proud individual with hopes and dreams and desires.

They were the inheritors of a long tradition of ascetic withdrawal, surrendering their names, their bodies, and their temporal aspirations to a life that was ordered and easy to understand.

Bach realized she might be doing some of them a disservice in that evaluation. They were not necessarily all losers. There must be those among them who were attracted simply by the religious ideas of the sect, though Bach felt there was little in the teachings that made sense.

She skimmed through the dogma, taking notes. The Standardists preached the commonality of humanity, denigrated free will, and elevated the group and the consensus to demi-god status. Nothing too unusual in the theory; it was the practice of it that made people queasy.

There was a creation theory and a godhead, who was not worshipped but contemplated. Creation happened when the Goddess—a prototypical earthmother who had no name—gave birth to the universe. She put people in it, all alike, stamped from the same universal mold.

Sin entered the picture. One of the people began to wonder. This person had a name, given to him or her *after* the original sin as part of the punishment, but Bach could not find it written down anywhere. She decided that it was a dirty word which Standardists never told an outsider.

This person asked Goddess what it was all for. What had been wrong with the void, that Goddess had seen fit to fill it with people who didn't seem to have a reason for existing?

That was too much. For reasons unexplained—and impolite to even ask about—Goddess had punished humans by introducing differentness into the world. Warts, big noses, kinky hair, white skin, tall people and fat people and deformed people, blue eyes, body hair, freckles, testicles, and labia. A billion faces and fingerprints, each soul trapped in a body distinct from all others, with the heavy burden of trying to establish an identity in a perpetual shouting match.

But the faith held that peace was achieved in striving to regain that lost Eden. When all humans were again the same person, Goddess would welcome them back. Life was a testing, a trial.

Bach certainly agreed with that. She gathered her notes and shuffled them together, then picked up the book she had brought back from Anytown. The barbie had given it to her when Bach asked for a picture of the murdered woman.

It was a blueprint for a human being.

The title was *The Book of Specifications. The Specs,* for short. Each barbie carried one, tied to her waist with a tape measure. It gave tolerances in engineering terms, defining what a barbie could look like. It was profusely illustrated with drawings of parts of the body in minute detail, giving measurements in millimeters.

She closed the book and sat up, propping her head on a pillow. She reached for her viewpad and propped it on her knees, punched the retrieval code for the murder tape. For the twentieth time that night, she watched a figure spring forward from a crowd of identical figures in the tube station, slash at Leah Ingraham, and melt back into the crowd as her victim lay bleeding and eviscerated on the floor.

She slowed it down, concentrating on the killer, trying to spot something different about her. Anything at all would do. The knife struck. Blood spurted. Barbies milled about in consternation. A few belatedly ran after the killer, not reacting fast enough. People seldom reacted quickly enough. But the killer had blood on her hand. Make a note to ask about that.

Bach viewed the film once more, saw nothing useful, and decided to call it a night.

\*

The room was long and tall, brightly lit from strips high above: Bach followed the attendant down the rows of square locker doors which lined one wall. The air was cool and humid, the floor wet from a recent hosing.

The man consulted the card in his hand and pulled the metal handle on locker 659A, making a noise that echoed through the bare room. He slid the drawer out and lifted the sheet from the corpse.

It was not the first mutilated corpse Bach had seen, but it was the first nude barbie. She immediately noted the lack of nipples on the two hills of flesh that pretended to be breasts, and the smooth, unmarked skin in the crotch. The attendant was frowning, consulting the card on the corpse's foot.

"Some mistake here," he muttered. "Geez, the headaches. What do you do with a thing like that?" He scratched his head, then scribbled through the large letter "F" on the card, replacing it with a neat "N." He looked at Bach and grinned sheepishly. "What do you do?" he repeated.

Bach didn't much care what he did. She studied L. P. Ingraham's remains, hoping that something on the body would show her why a barbie had decided she must die.

There was little difficulty seeing *how* she had died. The knife had entered her abdomen, going deep, and the wound extended upward from there in a slash that ended beneath the breastbone. Part of the bone was cut through. The knife had been sharp, but it would have taken a powerful arm to slice through that much meat.

The attendant watched curiously as Bach pulled the dead woman's legs apart and studied what she saw there. She found the tiny slit of the urethra set back around the curve, just anterior to the anus.

Bach opened her copy of *The Specs,* took out a tape measure, and started to work.

*

"Mr. Atlas, I got your name from the Morphology Guide's files as a practitioner who's had a lot of dealings with the Standardist Church."

The man frowned, then shrugged. "So? You may not approve of them, but they're legal. And my records are in order. I don't do any work on anybody until the police have checked for a criminal record." He sat on the edge of the desk in the spacious consulting room, facing Bach. Mr. Rock Atlas—surely a *nom de métier*—had shoulders carved from granite, teeth like flashing pearls, and the face of a young god. He was a walking, flexing advertisement for his profession. Bach crossed her legs nervously. She had always had a taste for beef.

"I'm not investigating you, Mr. Atlas. This is a murder case, and I'd appreciate your cooperation."

"Call me Rock," he said, with a winning smile.

"Must I? Very well. I came to ask you what you would do, how long the work would take, if I asked to be converted to a barbie."

His face fell. "Oh, no, what a tragedy! I can't allow it. My dear, it would be a crime." He reached over to her and touched her chin lightly, turning her head. "No, Lieutenant, for you I'd build up the hollows in the cheeks just the slightest bit—maybe tighten up the muscles behind them—then drift the orbital bones out a little bit farther from the nose to set your eyes wider. More attention-getting, you understand. That touch of mystery. Then of course there's your nose."

She pushed his hand away and shook her head. "No, I'm not coming to you for the operation. I just want to know. How much work would it entail, and how close can you come to the specs of the church?" Then she frowned and looked at him suspiciously. "What's wrong with my nose?"

"Well, my dear, I didn't mean to imply there was anything *wrong;* in fact, it has a certain overbearing power that must be useful to you once in a while, in the circles you move in. Even the lean to the left could be justified, aesthetically—"

"Never mind," she said, angry at herself for having fallen into his sales pitch. "Just answer my question."

He studied her carefully, asked her to stand up and turn around. She was about to object that she had not necessarily meant herself personally as the surgical candidate, just a woman in general, when he seemed to lose interest in her.

"It wouldn't be much of a job," he said. "Your height is just slightly over the parameters; I could take that out of your thighs and lower legs, maybe shave some vertebrae. Take out some fat here and put it back there. Take off those nipples and dig out your uterus and ovaries, sew up your crotch. With a man, chop off the penis. I'd have to break up your skull a little and shift the bones around, then build up the face from there. Say two days' work, one overnight and one outpatient."

"And when you were through, what would be left to identify me?"

"Say that again?"

Bach briefly explained her situation, and Atlas pondered it.

"You've got a problem. I take off the fingerprints and footprints. I don't leave any external scars, not even microscopic ones. No moles, freckles, warts or birth-marks; they all have to go. A blood test would work, and so would a retinal print. An X-ray of the skull. A voiceprint would be questionable. I even that out as much as possible. I can't think of anything else."

"Nothing that could be seen from a purely visual exam?"

"That's the whole point of the operation, isn't it?"

"I know. I was just hoping you might know something even the barbies were not aware of. Thank you, anyway."

He got up, took her hand, and kissed it. "No trouble. And if you ever decide to get that nose taken care of . . ."

*

She met Jorge Weil at the temple gate in the middle of Anytown. He had spent his morning there, going through the records, and she could see the work didn't agree with him. He took her back to the small office where the records were kept in battered file cabinets. There was a barbie waiting for them there. She spoke without preamble.

"We decided at equalization last night to help you as much as possible."

"Oh, yeah? Thanks. I wondered if you would, considering what happened fifty years ago."

Weil looked puzzled. "What was that?"

Bach waited for the barbie to speak, but she evidently wasn't going to.

"All right. I found it last night. The Standardists were involved in murder once before, not long after they came to Luna. You notice you never see one of them in New Dresden?"

Weil shrugged. "So what? They keep to themselves."

"They were *ordered* to keep to themselves. At first, they could move freely like any other citizens. Then one of them killed somebody—not a Standardist this time. It was known the murderer was a barbie; there were witnesses. The police started looking for the killer. You guess what happened."

"They ran into the problems we're having." Weil grimaced. "It doesn't look so good, does it?"

"It's hard to be optimistic," Bach conceded. "The killer was never found. The barbies offered to surrender one of their number at random, thinking the law would be satisfied with that. But of course it wouldn't do. There was a public outcry, and a lot of pressure to force them to adopt some kind of distinguishing characteristic, like a number tattooed on their foreheads. I don't think that would have worked, either. It could have been covered.

"The fact is that the barbies were seen as a menace to society. They could kill at will and blend back into their community like grains of sand on a beach. We would be powerless to punish a guilty party. There was no provision in the law for dealing with them."

"So what happened?"

"The case is marked closed, but there's no arrest, no conviction, and no suspect. A deal was made whereby the Standardists could practice their religion as long as they never mixed with other citizens. They had to stay in Anytown. Am I right?" She looked at the barbie.

"Yes. We've adhered to the agreement."

"I don't doubt it. Most people are barely aware you exist out here. But now we've got this. One barbie kills another barbie, and under a television camera . . ." Bach stopped, and looked thoughtful. "Say, it occurs to me . . . Wait a minute. *Wait a minute.*" She didn't like the look of it.

"I wonder. This murder took place in the tube station. It's the only place in Anytown that's scanned by the municipal security system. And fifty years is a long time between murders, even in a town as small as . . . How many people did you say live here, Jorge?"

"About seven thousand. I feel I know them all intimately." Weil had spent the day sorting barbies. According to measurements made from the tape, the killer was at the top end of permissible height.

"How about it?" Bach said to the barbie. "Is there anything I ought to know?"

The woman bit her lip, looked uncertain.

"Come on, you said you were going to help me."

"Very well. There have been three other killings in the last month. You would not have heard of this one except it took place with outsiders present.

Purchasing agents were there on the loading platform. They made the initial report. There was nothing we could do to hush it up."

"But why would you want to?"

"Isn't it obvious? We exist with the possibility of persecution always with us. We don't wish to appear a threat to others. We wish to appear peaceful—which we *are*—and prefer to handle the problems of the group within the group itself. By divine consensus."

Bach knew she would get nowhere pursuing that line of reasoning. She decided to take the conversation back to the previous murders.

"Tell me what you know. Who was killed, and do you have any idea why? Or should I be talking to someone else?" Something occurred to her then, and she wondered why she hadn't asked it before. "You *are* the person I was speaking to yesterday, aren't you? Let me rephrase that. You're the body . . . that is, this body before me . . ."

"We know what you're talking about," the barbie said. "Uh, yes, you are correct. We are . . . *I* am the one you spoke to." She had to choke the word out, blushing furiously. "We have been . . . *I* have been selected as the component to deal with you, since it was perceived at equalization that this matter must be dealt with. This one was chosen as . . . *I* was chosen as punishment."

"You don't have to say 'I' if you don't want to."

"Oh, thank you."

"Punishment for what?"

"For . . . for individualistic tendencies. We spoke up too personally at equalization, in favor of cooperation with you. As a political necessity. The conservatives wish to stick to our sacred principles no matter what the cost. We are divided; this makes for bad feelings within the organism, for sickness. This one spoke out, and was punished by having her own way, by being appointed . . . *individually* . . . to deal with you." The woman could not meet Bach's eyes. Her face burned with shame.

"This one has been instructed to reveal her serial number to you. In the future, when you come here you are to ask for 23900."

Bach made a note of it.

"All right. What can you tell me about a possible motive? Do you think all the killings were done by the same . . . component?"

"We do not know. We are no more equipped to select an . . . individual from the group than you are. But there is great consternation. We are fearful."

"I would think so. Do you have reason to believe that the victims were . . . does this make sense? . . . *known* to the killer? Or were they random killings?"

Bach hoped not. Random killers were the hardest to catch; without motive, it was hard to tie killer to victim, or to sift one person out of thousands with the opportunity. With the barbies, the problem would be squared and cubed.

"Again, we don't know."

Bach sighed. "I want to see the witnesses to the crime. I might as well start interviewing them."

In short order, thirteen barbies were brought. Bach intended to question them thoroughly to see if their stories were consistent, and if they had changed.

She sat them down and took them one at a time, and almost immediately ran into a stone wall. It took her several minutes to see the problem, frustrating minutes spent trying to establish which of the barbies had spoken to the officer first, which second, and so forth.

"Hold it. Listen carefully. Was this body physically present at the time of the crime? Did these eyes see it happen?"

The barbie's brow furrowed. "Why, no. But does it matter?"

"It does to me, babe. *Hey, twenty-three thousand!*"

The barbie stuck her head in the door. Bach looked pained.

"I need the actual people who were *there*. Not thirteen picked at random."

"The story is known to all."

Bach spent five minutes explaining that it made a difference to her, then waited an hour as 23900 located the people who were actual witnesses.

And again she hit a stone wall. The stories were absolutely identical, which she knew to be impossible. Observers *always* report events differently. They make themselves the hero, invent things before and after they first began observing, rearrange and edit and interpret. But not the barbies. Bach struggled for an hour, trying to shake one of them, and got nowhere. She was facing a consensus, something that had been discussed among the barbies until an account of the event had emerged and then been accepted as truth. It was probably a close approximation, but it did Bach no good. She needed discrepancies to gnaw at, and there were none.

Worst of all, she was convinced no one was lying to her. Had she questioned the thirteen random choices she would have gotten the same answers. They would have thought of themselves as having been there, since some of them had been and they had been told about it. What happened to one, happened to all.

Her options were evaporating fast. She dismissed the witnesses, called 23900 back in, and sat her down. Bach ticked off points on her fingers.

"One. Do you have the personal effects of the deceased?"

"We have no private property."

Bach nodded. "Two. Can you take me to her room?"

"We each sleep in any room we find available at night. There is no—"

"Right. Three. Any friends or co-workers I might . . ." Bach rubbed her forehead with one hand. "Right. Skip it. Four. What was her job? Where did she work?"

"All jobs are interchangeable here. We work at what needs—"

"*Right!*" Bach exploded. She got up and paced the floor. "What the hell do you expect me to *do* with a situation like this? I don't have *anything* to work with, not one snuffin' *thing*. No way of telling *why* she was killed, no way to pick out the *killer,* no way . . . ah, *shit*. What do you expect me to *do*?"

"We don't expect you to do anything," the barbie said, quietly. "We didn't ask you to come here. We'd like it very much if you just went away."

In her anger Bach had forgotten that. She was stopped, unable to move in any direction. Finally, she caught Weil's eye and jerked her head toward the door.

"Let's get out of here." Weil said nothing. He followed Bach out the door and hurried to catch up.

They reached the tube station, and Bach stopped outside their waiting capsule. She sat down heavily on a bench, put her chin on her palm, and watched the ant-like mass of barbies working at the loading dock.

"Any ideas?"

Weil shook his head, sitting beside her and removing his cap to wipe sweat from his forehead.

"They keep it too hot in here," he said. Bach nodded, not really hearing him. She watched the group of barbies as two separated themselves from the crowd and came a few steps in her direction. Both were laughing, as if at some private joke, looking right at Bach. One of them reached under her blouse and withdrew a long, gleaming steel knife. In one smooth motion she plunged it into the other barbie's stomach and lifted, bringing her up on the balls of her feet. The one who had been stabbed looked surprised for a moment, staring down at herself, her mouth open as the knife gutted her like a fish. Then her eyes widened and she stared horror-stricken at her companion, and slowly went to her knees, holding the knife to her as blood gushed out and soaked her white uniform.

"*Stop her!*" Bach shouted. She was on her feet and running, after a moment of horrified paralysis. It had looked *so* much like the tape.

She was about forty meters from the killer, who moved with deliberate speed, jogging rather than running. She passed the barbie who had been attacked—and who was now on her side, still holding the knife hilt almost tenderly to herself, wrapping her body around the pain. Bach thumbed the panic button on her communicator, glanced over her shoulder to see Weil kneeling beside the stricken barbie, then looked back—

—to a confusion of running figures. Which one was it? *Which one?*

She grabbed the one that seemed to be in the same place and moving in the same direction as the killer had been before she looked away. She swung the barbie around and hit her hard on the side of the neck with the edge of her palm, watched her fall while trying to look at all the other barbies at the same time. They were running in both directions, some trying to get away, others entering the loading dock to see what was going on. It was a madhouse scene with shrieks and shouts and baffling movement.

Bach spotted something bloody lying on the floor, then knelt by the inert figure and clapped the handcuffs on her.

She looked up into a sea of faces, all alike.

\*

The commissioner dimmed the lights, and he, Bach, and Weil faced the big screen at the end of the room. Beside the screen was a department photoanalyst with a pointer in her hand. The tape began to run.

"Here they are," the woman said, indicating two barbies with the tip of the long stick. They were just faces on the edge of the crowd, beginning to move. "Victim right here, the suspect to her right." Everyone watched as the stabbing was recreated. Bach winced when she saw how long she had taken to react. In her favor, it had taken Weil a fraction of a second longer.

"Lieutenent Bach begins to move here. The suspect moves back toward the crowd. If you'll notice, she is watching Bach over her shoulder. Now. Here." She froze a frame. "Bach loses eye contact. The suspect peels off the plastic glove which prevented blood from staining her hand. She drops it, moves laterally. By the time Bach looks back, we can see she is after the wrong suspect."

Bach watched in sick fascination as her image assaulted the wrong barbie, the actual killer only a meter to her left. The tape resumed normal speed, and Bach watched the killer until her eyes began to hurt from not blinking. She would not lose her this time.

"She's incredibly brazen. She does not leave the room for another twenty minutes." Bach saw herself kneel and help the medical team load the wounded barbie into the capsule. The killer had been at her elbow, almost touching her. She felt her arm break out in goose pimples.

She remembered the sick fear that had come over her as she knelt by the injured woman. *It could be any of them. The one behind me, for instance . . .*

She had drawn her weapon then, backed against the wall, and not moved until the reinforcements arrived a few minutes later.

At a motion from the commissioner, the lights came back on.

"Let's hear what you have," he said.

Bach glanced at Weil, then read from her notebook.

"Sergeant Weil was able to communicate with the victim shortly before medical help arrived. He asked her if she knew anything pertinent as to the identity of her assailant. She answered no, saying only that it was 'the wrath.' She could not elaborate. I quote now from the account Sergeant Weil wrote down immediately after the interview. 'Victim said, "It hurts, it hurts." "I'm dying, I'm dying." Victim became incoherent, and I attempted to get a shirt from the onlookers to stop the flow of blood. No cooperation was forthcoming.'"

"It was the word 'I,'" Weil supplied. "When she said that, they all started to drift away."

"'She became rational once more,'" Bach resumed reading, "'long enough to whisper a number to me. The number was twelve-fifteen, which I wrote down as one-two-one-five. She roused herself once more, said "I'm dying."'" Bach closed the notebook and looked up. "Of course, she was right." She coughed nervously.

"We invoked section 35b of the New Dresden Unified Code, 'Hot Pursuit,' suspending civil liberties locally for the duration of the search. We located component 1215 by the simple expedient of lining up all the barbies and having them pull their pants down. Each has a serial number in the small of her back. Component 1215, one Sylvester J. Cronhausen, is in custody at this moment.

"While the search was going on, we went to sleeping cubicle 1215 with a team of criminologists. In a concealed compartment beneath the bunk we found these items." Bach got up, opened the evidence bag, and spread the items on the table.

There was a carved wooden mask. It had a huge nose with a hooked end, a mustache, and a fringe of black hair around it. Beside the mask were several jars of powders and creams, greasepaint and cologne. One black nylon sweater, one pair black trousers, one pair black sneakers. A stack of pictures clipped from magazines, showing ordinary people, many of them wearing more clothes than was normal in Luna. There was a black wig and a merkin of the same color.

"What was that last?" the commissioner asked.

"A merkin, sir," Bach supplied. "A pubic wig."

"Ah." He contemplated the assortment, leaned back in his chair. "Somebody liked to dress up."

"Evidently, sir." Bach stood at ease with her hands clasped behind her back, her face passive. She felt an acute sense of failure, and a cold determination to get the woman with the gall to stand at her elbow after committing murder before her eyes. She was sure the time and place had been chosen deliberately, that the barbie had been executed for Bach's benefit.

"Do you think these items belonged to the deceased?"

"We have no reason to state that, sir," Bach said. "However, the circumstances are suggestive."

"Of what?"

"I can't be sure. These things *might* have belonged to the victim. A random search of other cubicles turned up nothing like this. We showed the items to component 23900, our liaison. She professed not to know their purpose." She stopped, then added, "I believe she was lying. She looked quite disgusted."

"Did you arrest her?"

"No, sir. I didn't think it wise. She's the only connection we have, such as she is."

The commissioner frowned, and laced his fingers together. "I'll leave it up to you, Lieutenant Bach. Frankly, we'd like to be shut of this mess as soon as possible."

"I couldn't agree with you more, sir."

"Perhaps you don't understand me. We have to have a warm body to indict. We have to have one soon."

"Sir, I'm doing the best I can. Candidly, I'm beginning to wonder if there's anything I *can* do."

"You still don't understand me." He looked around the office. The stenographer and photoanalyst had left. He was alone with Bach and Weil.

He flipped a switch on his desk, turning a recorder *off*, Bach realized.

"The news is picking up on this story. We're beginning to get some heat. On the one hand, people are afraid of these barbies. They're hearing about the murder fifty years ago, and the informal agreement. They don't like it much. On the other hand, there's the civil libertarians. They'll fight hard to prevent anything happening to the barbies, on principle. The government doesn't want to get into a mess like that. I can hardly blame them."

Bach said nothing, and the commissioner looked pained.

"I see I have to spell it out. We have a suspect in custody," he said.

"Are you referring to component 1215, Sylvester Cronhausen?"

"No. I'm speaking of the one you captured."

"Sir, the tape clearly shows she is not the guilty party. She was an innocent by-stander." She felt her face heat up as she said it. Damn it; she had tried her best.

"Take a look at this." He pressed a button and the tape began to play again. But the quality was much impaired. There were bursts of snow, moments when the picture faded out entirely. It was a very good imitation of a camera failing. Bach watched herself running through the crowd—there was a flash of white—and she had hit the woman. The lights came back on in the room.

"I've checked with the analyst. She'll go along. There's a bonus in this, for both of you." He looked from Weil to Bach.

"I don't think I can go through with that, sir."

He looked like he'd tasted a lemon. "I didn't say we were doing this today. It's an option. But I ask you to look at it this way, just look at it, and I'll say no more. This is the way *they themselves* want it. They offered you the same deal the first time you were there. Close the case with a confession, no mess. We've already got this prisoner. She just says she killed her, she killed all of them. I want you to ask yourself, is she wrong?

By her own lights and moral values? She believes she shares responsibility for the murders, and society demands a culprit. What's wrong with accepting their compromise and letting this all blow over?"

"Sir, it doesn't feel right to me. This is not in the oath I took. I'm supposed to protect the innocent, and she's innocent. She's the *only* barbie I *know* to be innocent."

The commissioner sighed. "Bach, you've got four days. You give me an alternative by then."

"Yes, sir. If I can't, I'll tell you now that I won't interfere with what you plan. But you'll have to accept my resignation."

\*

Anna-Louise Bach reclined in the bathtub with her head pillowed on a folded towel. Only her neck, nipples, and knees stuck out above the placid surface of the water, tinted purple with a generous helping of bath salts. She clenched a thin cheroot in her teeth. A ribbon of lavender smoke curled from the end of it, rising to join the cloud near the ceiling.

She reached up with one foot and turned on the taps, letting out cooled water and refilling with hot until the sweat broke out on her brow. She had been in the tub for several hours. The tips of her fingers were like washboards.

There seemed to be few alternatives. The barbies were foreign to her, and to anyone she could assign to interview them. They didn't want her help in solving the crimes. All the old rules and procedures were useless. Witnesses meant nothing; one could not tell one from the next, nor separate their stories. Opportunity? Several thousand individuals had it. Motive was a blank. She had a physical description in minute detail, even tapes of the actual murders. Both were useless.

There was one course of action that might show results. She had been soaking for hours in the hope of determining just how important her job was to her.

Hell, what else did she want to do?

She got out of the tub quickly, bringing a lot of water with her to drip onto the floor. She hurried into her bedroom, pulled the sheets off the bed and slapped the nude male figure on the buttocks.

"Come on, Svengali," she said. "Here's your chance to do something about my nose."

*

She used every minute while her eyes were functioning to read all she could find about Standardists. When Atlas worked on her eyes, the computer droned into an earphone. She memorized most of the *Book of Standards*.

Ten hours of surgery, followed by eight hours flat on her back, paralyzed, her body undergoing forced regeneration, her eyes scanning the words that flew by on an overhead screen.

Three hours of practice, getting used to shorter legs and arms. Another hour to assemble her equipment.

When she left the Atlas clinic, she felt she would pass for a barbie as long as she kept her clothes on. She hadn't gone *that* far.

People tended to forget about access locks that led to the surface. Bach had used the fact more than once to show up in places where no one expected her.

She parked her rented crawler by the lock and left it there. Moving awkwardly in her pressure suit, she entered and started it cycling, then stepped through the inner door into an equipment room in Anytown. She stowed the suit, checked herself quickly in a washroom mirror, straightened the tape measure that belted her loose white jumpsuit, and entered the darkened corridors.

What she was doing was not illegal in any sense, but she was on edge. She didn't expect the barbies to take kindly to her masquerade if they discovered it, and she knew how easy it was for a barbie to vanish forever. Three had done so before Bach ever got the case.

The place seemed deserted. It was late evening by the arbitrary day cycle of New Dresden. Time for the nightly equalization. Bach hurried down the silent hallways to the main meeting room in the temple.

It was full of barbies and a vast roar of conversation. Bach had no trouble slipping in, and in a few minutes she knew her facial work was as good as Atlas had promised.

Equalization was the barbie's way of standardizing experience. They had been unable to simplify their lives to the point where each member of the community experienced the same things every day; the *Book of Standards* said it was a goal to be aimed for, but probably unattainable this side of Holy Reassimilation with Goddess. They tried to keep the available jobs easy enough that each member could do them all. The commune did not seek to make a profit; but air, water, and food had to be purchased, along with replacement parts and services to keep things running. The community had to produce things to trade with the outside.

They sold luxury items: hand-carved religious statues, illuminated holy books, painted crockery, and embroidered tapestries. None of the items were Standardist. The barbies had no religious symbols except their uniformity and the tape measure, but nothing in their dogma prevented them from selling objects of reverence to people of other faiths.

Bach had seen the products for sale in the better shops. They were meticulously produced, but suffered from the fact that each item looked too much like every other. People buying hand-produced luxuries in a technological age tend to want the differences that non-machine production entails, whereas the barbies wanted everything to look exactly alike. It was an ironic situation, but the barbies willingly sacrificed value by adhering to their standards.

Each barbie did things during the day that were as close as possible to what everyone else had done. But someone had to cook meals, tend the air machines, load the freight. Each component had a different job each day. At equalization, they got together and tried to even that out.

It was boring. Everyone talked at once, to anyone that happened to be around. Each woman told what she had done that day. Bach heard the same group of stories a hundred times before the night was over, and repeated them to anyone who would listen.

Anything unusual was related over a loudspeaker so everyone could be aware of it and thus spread out the intolerable burden of anomaly. No barbie wanted to keep a unique experience to herself; it made her soiled, unclean, until it was shared by all.

Bach was getting very tired of it—she was short on sleep—when the lights went out. The buzz of conversation shut off as if a tape had broken.

"All cats are alike in the dark," someone muttered, quite near Bach. Then a single voice was raised. It was solemn; almost a chant.

"We are the wrath. There is blood on our hands, but it is the holy blood of cleansing. We have told you of the cancer eating at the heart of the body, and yet still you cower away from what must be done. *The filth must be removed from us!*"

Bach was trying to tell which direction the words were coming from in the total darkness. Then she became aware of movement, people brushing against her, all going in the same direction. She began to buck the tide when she realized everyone was moving away from the voice.

"You think you can use our holy uniformity to hide among us, but the vengeful hand of Goddess will not be stayed. The mark is upon you, our one-time sisters. Your sins have set you apart, and retribution will strike swiftly.

"*There are five of you left.* Goddess knows who you are, and will not tolerate your perversion of her holy truth. Death will strike you when you least expect it. Goddess sees the differentness within you, the differentness you seek but hope to hide from your upright sisters."

People were moving more swiftly now, and a scuffle had developed ahead of her. She struggled free of people who were breathing panic from every pore, until she stood in a clear space. The speaker was shouting to be heard over the sound of whimpering and the shuffling of bare feet. Bach moved forward, swinging her outstretched hands. But another hand brushed her first.

The punch was not centered on her stomach, but it drove the air from her lungs and sent her sprawling. Someone tripped over her, and she realized things would get pretty bad if she didn't get to her feet. She was struggling up when the lights came back on.

There was a mass sigh of relief as each barbie examined her neighbor. Bach half expected another body to be found, but that didn't seem to be the case. The killer had vanished again.

She slipped away from the equalization before it began to break up, and hurried down the deserted corridors to room 1215.

She sat in the room—little more than a cell, with a bunk, a chair, and a light on a table—for more than two hours before the door opened, as she had hoped it would. A barbie stepped inside, breathing hard, closed the door, and leaned against it.

"We wondered if you would come," Bach said, tentatively.

The woman ran to Bach and collapsed at her knees, sobbing.

"Forgive us, please forgive us, our darling. We didn't dare come last night. We were afraid that . . . that if . . . that it might have been you who was murdered, and that the wrath would be waiting for us here. Forgive us, forgive us."

"It's all right," Bach said, for lack of anything better. Suddenly, the barbie was on top of her, kissing her with a desperate passion. Bach was startled, though she had expected something of the sort. She responded as best she could. The barbie finally began to talk again.

"We must stop this, we just have to stop. We're so frightened of the wrath, but . . . but the *longing!* We can't stop ourselves. We need to see you so badly that we can hardly get through the day, not knowing if you are across town or working at our elbow. It builds all day, and at night, we cannot stop ourselves from sinning yet again." She was crying, more softly this time, not from happiness at seeing the woman she took Bach to be, but from a depth of desperation. "What's going to become of us?" she asked, helplessly.

"Shhh," Bach soothed. "It's going to be all right."

She comforted the barbie for a while, then saw her lift her head. Her eyes seemed to glow with a strange light.

"I can't wait any longer," she said. She stood up, and began taking off her clothes. Bach could see her hands shaking.

Beneath her clothing the barbie had concealed a few things that looked familiar. Bach could see that the merkin was already in place between her legs. There was a wooden mask much like the one that had been found in the secret panel, and a jar. The barbie unscrewed the top of it and used her middle finger to smear dabs of brown onto her breasts, making stylized nipples.

"Look what *I* got," she said, coming down hard on the pronoun, her voice trembling. She pulled a flimsy yellow blouse from the pile of clothing on the floor, and slipped it over her shoulders. She struck a pose, then strutted up and down the tiny room.

"Come on, darling," she said. "Tell me how beautiful I am. Tell me I'm lovely. Tell me I'm the only one for you. The only one. What's the *matter*?

Are you still frightened? I'm not. I'll dare anything for you, my one and only love." But now she stopped walking and looked suspiciously at Bach.

"Why aren't you getting dressed?"

"We . . . uh, I can't," Bach said, extemporizing. "They, uh, someone found the things. They're all gone." She didn't dare remove her clothes because her nipples and pubic hair would look too real, even in the dim light.

The barbie was backing away. She picked up her mask and held it protectively to her. "What do you mean? Was she here? The wrath? Are they after us? It's true, isn't it? They can see us." She was on the edge of crying again, near panic.

"No, no, I think it was the police—" But it was doing no good. The barbie was at the door now, and had it half open.

"You're her! What have you done to ... No, no, you stay away." She reached into the clothing that she now held in her hand, and Bach hesitated for a moment, expecting a knife. It was enough time for the barbie to dart quickly through the door, slamming it behind her.

When Bach reached the door, the woman was gone.

*

Bach kept reminding herself that she was not here to find the other potential victims—of whom her visitor was certainly one—but to catch the killer.

The fact remained that she wished she could have detained her, to question her further.

The woman was a pervert, by the only definition that made any sense among the Standardists. She, and presumably the other dead barbies, had an individuality fetish. When Bach had realized that, her first thought had been to wonder why they didn't simply leave the colony and become whatever they wished. But then why did a Christian seek out prostitutes? For the taste of sin. In the larger world, what these barbies did would have had little meaning. Here, it was sin of the worst and tastiest kind.

And somebody didn't like it at all.

The door opened again, and the woman stood there facing Bach, her hair disheveled, breathing hard.

"We had to come back," she said. "We're so sorry that we panicked like that. Can you forgive us?" She was coming toward Bach now, her arms out.

She looked so vulnerable and contrite that Bach was astonished when the fist connected with her cheek.

Bach thudded against the wall, then found herself pinned under the woman's knees, with something sharp and cool against her throat. She swallowed very carefully, and said nothing. Her throat itched unbearably.

"She's dead," the barbie said. "And you're next." But there was something in her face that Bach didn't understand. The barbie brushed at her eyes a few times, and squinted down at her.

"Listen, I'm not who you think I am. If you kill me, you'll be bringing more trouble on your sisters than you can imagine."

The barbie hesitated, then roughly thrust her hand down into Bach's pants. Her eyes widened when she felt the genitals, but the knife didn't move. Bach knew she had to talk fast, and say all the right things.

"You understand what I'm talking about, don't you?" She looked for a response, but saw none. "You're aware of the political pressures that are coming down. You know this whole colony could be wiped out if you look like a threat to the outside. You don't want that."

"If it must be, it will be," the barbie said. "The purity is the important thing. If we die, we shall die pure. The blasphemers must be killed."

"I don't care about that anymore," Bach said, and finally got a ripple of interest from the barbie. "I have my principles, too. Maybe I'm not as fanatical about them as you are about yours. But they're important to me. One is that the guilty be brought to justice."

"You have the guilty party. Try her. Execute her. She will not protest."

"*You* are the guilty party."

The woman smiled. "So arrest us."

"All right, all right. I can't, obviously. Even if you don't kill me, you'll walk out that door and I'll never be able to find you. I've given up on that. I just don't have the time. This was my last chance, and it looks like it didn't work."

"We didn't think you could do it, even with more time. But why should we let you live?"

"Because we can help each other." She felt the pressure ease up a little, and managed to swallow again. "You don't want to kill me, because it could destroy your community. Myself . . . I need to be able to salvage some self-respect out of this mess. I'm willing to accept your definition of morality and let you be the law in your own community. Maybe you're even right. Maybe you *are* one being. But I can't let that woman be convicted, when I *know* she didn't kill anyone."

The knife was not touching her neck now, but it was still being held so that the barbie could plunge it into her throat at the slightest movement.

"And if we let you live? What do you get out of it? How do you free your 'innocent' prisoner?"

"Tell me where to find the body of the woman you just killed. I'll take care of the rest."

\*

The pathology team had gone and Anytown was settling down once again. Bach sat on the edge of the bed with Jorge Weil. She was as tired as she ever remembered being. How long had it been since she slept?

"I'll tell you," Weil said, "I honestly didn't think this thing would work. I guess I was wrong."

Bach sighed. "I wanted to take her alive, Jorge. I thought I could. But when she came at me with the knife . . ." She let him finish the thought, not caring to lie to him. She'd already done that to the interviewer. In her story, she had taken the knife from her assailant and tried to disable her, but was forced in the end to kill her. Luckily, she had the bump on the back of her head from being thrown against the wall. It made a blackout period plausible. Otherwise, someone would have wondered why she waited so long to call for police and an ambulance. The barbie had been dead for an hour when they arrived.

"Well, I'll hand it to you. You sure pulled this out. I'll admit it, I was having a hard time deciding if I'd do as you were going to do and resign, or if I could have stayed on. Now I'll never know."

"Maybe it's best that way. I don't really know, either."

Jorge grinned at her. "I can't get used to thinking of *you* being behind that godawful face."

"Neither can I, and I don't want to see any mirrors. I'm going straight to Atlas and get it changed back." She got wearily to her feet and walked toward the tube station with Weil.

She had not quite told him the truth. She did intend to get her own face back as soon as possible—nose and all—but there was one thing left to do.

From the first, a problem that had bothered her had been the question of how the killer identified her victims.

Presumably the perverts had arranged times and places to meet for their strange rites. That would have been easy enough. Any one barbie could easily shirk her duties. She could say she was sick, and no one would know it was the same barbie who had been sick yesterday, and for a week or month before. She need not work; she could wander the halls acting as if she was on her way from one job to another. No one could challenge her.

Likewise, while 23900 had said no barbie spent consecutive nights in the same room, there was no way for her to know that. Evidently room 1215 had been taken over permanently by the perverts.

And the perverts would have no scruples about identifying each other by serial number at their clandestine meetings, though they could do it in the streets. The killer didn't even have that.

But someone had known how to identify them, to pick them out of a crowd. Bach thought she must have infiltrated meetings, marked the participants in some way. One could lead her to another, until she knew them all and was ready to strike.

She kept recalling the strange way the killer had looked at her, the way she had squinted. The mere fact that she had not killed Bach instantly in a case of mistaken identity meant she had been expecting to see something that had not been there.

And she had an idea about that.

She meant to go to the morgue first, and to examine the corpses under different wavelengths of lights, with various filters. She was betting some kind of mark would become visible on the faces, a mark the killer had been looking for with her contact lenses.

It had to be something that was visible only with the right kind of equipment, or under the right circumstances. If she kept at it long enough, she would find it.

If it was an invisible ink, it brought up another interesting question. How had it been applied? With a brush or spray gun? Unlikely. But such an ink on the killer's hands might look and feel like water.

Once she had marked her victims, the killer would have to be confident the mark would stay in place for a reasonable time. The murders had stretched over a month. So she was looking for an indelible, invisible ink, one that soaked into pores.

And if it was indelible . . .

There was no use thinking further about it. She was right, or she was wrong. When she struck the bargain with the killer she had faced up to the possibility that she might have to live with it. Certainly she could not now bring a killer into court, not after what she had just said.

No, if she came back to Anytown and found a barbie whose hands were stained with guilt, she would have to do the job herself.

# Comment on 'The Barbie Murders'

John Varley's story depicts a definite physical possibility. Although it might take more than a couple of days to alter a person's appearance to the exacting specifications he outlines, it could potentially be achieved, even in the near future. With cloning technology, the possibility of creating genetically duplicate humans is also feasible, if ethically fraught. The society depicted in the story also looks physically and psychologically possible. With all the zeal of religious converts (since none of the participants has their belief system handed to them by their parents), members of the Standardist Church make every effort to live as a single person. They avoid talking about themselves as singular individuals, they share information about everything they do and they strive to live generic lives without mark or distinction.

By setting up this society and exploring what happens when a murder is committed within it, it seems to me that Varley makes a very powerful and fundamental claim about personal identity: *you are not your qualities*. You are not your size, your shape, your eye colour, your personality, your race, your gender, your sexual orientation or any one of a thousand other features. All of these qualities are generic. They can be possessed by multiple beings simultaneously. Even a very complex combination of qualities won't necessarily be enough to identify you because this combination could also be possessed by someone else. What makes you *you* isn't sharable in this way.

This is often a point that is hard to convey in the seminar room when students are first presented with the issue of personal identity. Common talk about 'identity' tends to be fixated on qualities like sex and race. These qualities are very important to people. If someone were to deny your sex or your race, for example, it might feel like a deep threat. You might even go so far as to claim that your existence is being denied. But just suppose that you were to lose your sex or your race. Suppose that you underwent the kind of procedure that the barbies undergo in the story, in which your sexual and racial characteristics are radically altered. Does this kill you? It seems clear that it does not. In fact, sometimes people feel the need to change their sexual characteristics precisely for the sake of saving their own lives. This would not be possible if changing their sexual characteristics killed them.

So although racial and sexual qualities are very interesting, philosophers working on identity tend to think about what we are in a more basic way. When we talk about identity, we typically mean *numerical identity* – what makes you one thing, and not two things, or no thing. I realize that this question can seem strangely crude. It's just obvious that I am one thing isn't it? But this is why it's helpful to read a story like Varley's. It helps us to realize that numerical identity can sometimes be confusing. We can read about the Barbie society and genuinely wonder – how many barbies are there? One or many?

The barbies certainly like to think of themselves as a single individual. They are entirely indifferent to which specific 'body' committed the murder and will happily let any member of the society be punished for it. Yet the police take a rather different view of the matter. Lieutenant Bach adamantly refuses to convict the one barbie who she knows did not physically plunge the knife into another barbie's body. It is rather appropriate that the question of numerical identity comes up in the course of a criminal investigation. John Locke, the seventeenth-century philosopher who first established the importance of personal identity, described the concept of a person as a 'forensick term'. He argued that we are interested in personal identity because we want to hold people responsible for their actions. The whole idea of responsibility requires the knowledge that the person we have in front of us is the selfsame one who acted rightly or wrongly.

So is Lieutenant Bach right about identity? The question of numerical identity, it should be emphasized, is very strict. If we have observed things on separate occasions and wonder if they are in fact numerically identical, then it must be shown that literally every single feature possessed by one is also possessed by the other. How could every feature not be shared, if in fact there's just one thing we're talking about? Equivalently, if we can show that our candidates for identity differ in any respect, no matter how trivial, then they cannot be identical.

Thus, despite their strenuous efforts, I think we can conclude that there are many distinct barbies. They differ in lots of ways. Most notably, they are made of different matter and they occupy different positions in space. Is that enough to settle the matter? Maybe not. I can imagine one of the students in my philosophy seminar protesting that a single object can be made of a variety of different stuffs and simultaneously cover a few different locations in space. My chair, for instance, is made of a combination of plastic and metal and cloth and it fills various points in space. My student, if they're clever, may even point out that some single things have their parts scattered about in space rather than joined together. Consider, for instance, a single nation that's made up of a group of islands.

Can we give a more decisive criterion than distinct spatial locations? How about this: you can kill one of the barbies without killing any of the others. That's a pretty decisive difference, it seems to me. It means that each of the barbies has conditions for existence that are strictly distinct from the existence conditions of the others, conditions that are tied not to their qualities, but to the physical stuff they are made of.

But couldn't my clever student object that the individual barbie bodies should be conceived as parts of a larger whole – the collective barbie as it were? If that's the case, then destroying one body without destroying another need not count against there being one big thing that contains all those bodies. Continuing the comparison with my chair, we could chip away at one of legs, destroying that part while leaving other parts intact. Yet this need not mean that the chair isn't one thing.

Here I may admit that *the Barbie society* might be conceived as one thing. But in this respect, the Barbie society is no different from any other society which is identified through the centuries, despite the replacement of its citizens. This society-level perspective fails to mark out the most extraordinary feature of the Barbie society, which is that each body in it is trying to become entirely undistinguishable from each other body. The ideal that the barbies are trying to attain is that each member is interchangeable with any other member *because* there is no real distinction between them. They are seeking identity at the body or mind level. They (as yet) fail to achieve this ideal because very stubborn differences persist.

In this way, Varley illustrates the concept of 'synchronic identity'. Synchronic identity is the subtype of numerical identity which concerns what, at a given time, makes one thing distinct from another thing. Brute physical (or concrete) substance is the most common way to mark out synchronic identity, but when it comes to people, we tend also to appeal to more complex factors. Each barbie has a body which makes up a particular metabolic system. Each barbie can eat independently, excrete independently and be killed independently. It seems that each barbie also has a distinct mind (though it is heavily influenced by the others). For instance, each one has a perceptual experience which is not strictly shared by another barbie. Each can think and feel pain and act independently of the others.

Another claim that Varley's story makes, it seems to me, is that there may be something psychologically incorrigible about individual identity. You can try to suppress it, ignore it or override it, but the truth will out. So part of the drama of the story is that some barbies feel a tremendous pressure to resist their culture's homogeneity (their near *qualitative* identity), despite the fact that they presumably chose at one point to embrace it. The story associates this resistance with the sex drive – an 'individuality fetish', as Lieutenant Bach amusingly calls it. Recall also the way in which a dying barbie gasps, 'It hurts, it hurts … I'm dying, I'm dying.' Her reversion to the personal pronoun indicates that her sense of distinct numerical identity forcefully impresses itself upon her in extremis. In this way, the narrative of the story suggests that the drive for sex and the drive to avoid death are to be found at the root of our individual identities.

This claim embedded in Varley's story is plausible. The sense of individual self seems to be deeply rooted in our psyches. It impresses itself upon us every time we disagree with someone or when one of us feels pain that the other doesn't. Yet it is worth pointing out that the entire notion of a self has been doubted. One of the foundational doctrines of Buddhism is that of *anātman* or 'no self'. It is not terribly clear what is meant by this, and different Buddhist sects maintain different views about it (e.g. sometimes *anātman* is interpreted as the denial of an immortal soul). But one of the major interpretations is that really, there are no such things as selves. There are particular sensations, pains, pleasures, desires and thoughts, but no persisting container or vessel for all those transient things. The self then, is an illusion. A powerful illusion, no doubt. And so in this sense, the Buddhist philosopher may endorse Varley's story. But still, to become enlightened is to learn to see through this illusion and to accept that there is no self at all. We need not incorrigibly believe in the self, even at the point of death.

I find it hard to even explain the no-self position without making reference to what a person thinks about something. That is, it is hard not to imply that there is a subject who is suffering and then trying to overcome the illusion of a self. It is very awkward to write that one conscious thought thinks that a bundle of other thoughts and experiences are not possessed by any larger entity. Do thoughts think? Do dreams dream? Do dances dance? The view seems bizarre. Yet I think the view is worth mentioning as we launch our investigations into personal identity. We should not simply assume that there is such a thing as a self. It would seem to be a simpler or default view that there isn't one, and so some kind of argument should be offered in its defence.

I think the basic argument for a self bears a close relation to the arguments we have already canvassed about what makes one self distinct from another. First, not even the extreme Buddhist denies that there are actions and desires and sensations. Second, many actions, desires and sensations are complex, requiring the combination of distinguishable elements. For example, my experience of drinking lemonade involves a sensation of the liquid, its bubbles, its sweetness, its coldness, the smooth glass touching my bottom lip and so on. Thus, we have direct experience of things combining together to form complex wholes. Third, we can point out that the regular causal interactions amongst actions, desires and sensations seem to form distinct systems. Consider, for example, an ordinary practical reasoning process in which the desire for lemonade combines with the belief that there's some in the fridge, triggering the movement of an arm and hand to open the fridge door. These components interact with a characteristic smoothness that is quite different from the more convoluted process in which the desire for lemonade over here may trigger the movement of a body over there (i.e. when I ask someone to get it for me). The best explanation for these smooth interaction processes seems to be that there are definite entities in which these various components co-occur.

Similarly, what distinguishes one individual from another is that there is a bundle of thoughts, desires and actions that directly interact within them and not directly within the other. Thus, one person can feel sexual desire without that desire directly affecting the actions of her neighbour. Another person can be wounded, causing pain to them and not their neighbour. These are the psychological fundamentals that we have grown used to since we were infants.

So as the great philosopher David Hume pointed out, we may never directly experience the self. We may only experience particular sensations. But still I think we are justified to infer the existence of selves to make sense of how particular sensations interact in the ways that they do. If the thoughts, sensations and actions associated with these different bodies were to start affecting each other more directly, then we might start to doubt that there are distinct individuals. This rather unusual scenario is not depicted in Varley's story so I will leave it aside for now, but I will return to it towards the end of this book.

Overall, I think 'The Barbie Murders' works well as a thought experiment that explores and illustrates some of the most fundamental features of individuality. Ironically, in an introduction written by Varley for a collection of his works, he says that when he originally developed the story in a writers' workshop, one of the best criticisms he received was from fellow author Kate Wilhelm, who said that the story failed to be a 'jumping-off point for a deeper examination of the idea of identity itself'. And yet in its unpretentious, story-focused way, that is precisely what it achieves.

# 2

# 'Marley and Marley'

## J. R. Dawson

I never wanted to turn out like her.

When I met her, I was twelve. There was no one else to take care of me. Before she showed up, she was preceded by this man in a pinstriped suit. A harbinger. He sat me down in his sterile office and he said, "Time Law is not a joking matter." He told me all the horrible things that would happen if I broke any Time Laws. Worlds would collapse. I would turn inside out. Important people would die and important things wouldn't happen. And that's when I first felt that clutching sensation in my chest. Like he had his fingers inside my rib cage and he was squeezing my lungs. Do not fuck this up.

"So are you the one I'm going with?" I asked. Because I was a newly coined orphan and I needed someone.

The pinstriped-suit man shook his head. "No," he said. "The system is hard on children so we've come up with a better option. But you can't go live with her. She must come to you."

Because she lived in the future.

She agreed. She got in the time machine, she met me at the port, and she took me home. She set up shop in Mom's room and she didn't leave until my eighteenth birthday, when, like some sort of Mary Poppins, she up and disappeared back to the future.

She was old, a whole twenty-eight years when she first showed up. She was a disappointment. I asked her where she lived, and she said, "Oh, I live right here in Omaha, just like you." I told her I was going to hang myself that night.

"I'm not going to lie to you about it," she said.

"I'm not going to end up in Omaha," I told her. "I was born here. I'm going to move away."

"Okay," she said, although it sounded like she didn't believe me.

"What happened to you singing in New York?" I said. "I want to be a singer!"

"You're twelve," she said. "When you're nineteen, you'll go to New York on a trip and you'll hate it."

"It doesn't matter if I hate it, it's where I'm going!" I said.

"Aren't you sassy," she said. She started making horrible turkey burgers. Her favorite dish. My least favorite.

"I'm going to New York," I said.

"So go," she said.

So goddamn smug.

"How much of a loser do you have to be in order to spend six years here with me?" I said.

"They're going to send me right back to the day I left," she said.

"You'll be older, though," I said.

"We don't have anyone else, Marley," she said.

We were both named Marley. We were the same person, actually. And it got confusing at times. So she became Old Marley, and I was Little Marley. I hated Old Marley. I swore to never see her in a mirror or a window once she disappeared back to her own time. I would not be her. I would prove her wrong.

But Old Marley was right. When I was nineteen, I went to New York and I hated how crowded it was. Flying back, I felt defeated. No matter what I did, at twenty-eight, I'd have to go be a mother to a little girl. I would be a loser, an angry and sad old woman who ate turkey burgers.

My life was set out for me, with some sort of pinstriped time cops staring through the wrinkles and tears of chronology. I felt like they were watching, making sure things went according to plan. They were the ones who made sure my field trip to New York was horrible.

But there were things Old Marley hadn't told me. There was Jason. And I learned that I didn't like singing parts I had no interest in. Seeing as most parts available for size 14s in New York were scheduled for people with big names and people in ensembles, I didn't feel like eating cardboard dollar pizza the rest of my life. So I bought a house with Jason. It was blue skies on our wedding day. We were happy. While I was in his arms, the time cop man couldn't touch me. We were beyond laws, beyond time, beyond our own selves. She never told me any of that.

She also never told me that he died. She didn't tell me the bank foreclosed on their house and she moved into a one-bedroom apartment close to the cemetery to be nearer to Jason. And she certainly didn't tell me how absolutely horrible it was to wake up in the morning and realize I had to get through a whole twelve hours of sunlight where I was still expected to function.

So when the foster service time cop knocked on my door that day, I didn't adhere to my original plan: rigging up a flame-thrower from my kitchen utensils and laying waste while screaming, "Begone, evil spirits!" No, I let him in.

The man was the same man I'd met when I was little. He was dressed exactly the same, and I realized I didn't know if he was from my time or Little Marley's time or a different time altogether.

"How have you been?" he asked.

"Do you remember me at all?" I asked.

"Yes, Marley, I remember you," he said. "I just met with you a few hours ago—my time, of course." He said this with a little smile that was supposed to be friendly, but I felt that clutching in my lungs. He had said it to remind me where he stood and with what power, and where I stood and with no power.

"You remember how much you needed someone after your parents died," the man sat on the couch and reminded me. Like he had to remind me. Dad died of cancer; Mom hanged herself a year later. I had been alone. Sort of like now, with my husband rotting away in a cemetery down the street and not able to come home. Sometimes I woke up in the middle of the night, sweating from a nightmare where I saw him being picked apart by moles, his jaw now disintegrated, his guts spilling out and into the mouths of rats.

"I hated Old Marley," I told him. "Little Marley doesn't want me."

"It doesn't matter if she wants you," the man said. "There is no one in her time who can care for her. Your little self will end up in the foster system. This is a better alternative. You knew as soon as you were twelve this was inevitable for your adulthood."

"Ah," I said. "So you didn't really give Old Marley a choice to go raise me, did you?"

"Our policy is that it's entirely up to you," the man said.

"Right," I said. That was a lie.

That night, I looked in the mirror. I saw the bags under my eyes, because I'd been crying so much. I saw my glasses. I remembered shouting at Old Marley, "I'll never wear glasses! I'll take care of my eyes or I'll get contacts! You're so ugly! Why did you make us so ugly?"

Old Marley hadn't been old. She'd been twenty-eight. But she seemed so much older.

"Can I ask a question?" I asked him.

He raised one brow, that's it. People in suits barely move their faces. Probably because their bodies are so constricted.

"You work for the Time Law Department," I said.

He nodded, just slightly. "A branch of the TLD—we handle foster services."

"There are a lot of rules, and a lot of surveillance, yes? Things happen for reasons and you make sure of that."

He nodded again.

"So you knew my husband was going to die?"

He did not nod. But he didn't do anything else, either. After a moment of awkward silence, he said, "It's an inopportune time for you to return to the past. We nearly decided against it. We are worried you'll go looking for Jason, or you'll try to twist the events that have already happened in order to save him."

"He's not in the Important People of Interest index," I said. "It wouldn't matter. We're nobodies."

"Time isn't yours to change," he said. "Now, before we let you anywhere near a port, you need to review the relevant Time Laws and sign these documents." He plopped a folder on my coffee table. "We've included a list of individuals from the Important People of Interest index with whom you have come into contact. Your interactions with these people are recorded word for word, action by action, and must not be altered. Now, as for Little Marley, you are not to tell her anything about the future. No lottery numbers, no presidential elections, nothing."

"I know how it works," I said. "I've been through it before."

"You were a child," he said. "A petulant child, from the reports. For your own sake, I would not test the boundaries." Heartless. "You're right, Marley. You are a nobody." Correct. "You keep your head down and fulfill the time loop, that's all you need to do. There are real consequences for everyone, especially you, if you go off-script. Do you understand?"

I did. I understood. I'd always understood. But there was still one question that had always terrified me.

"And you do this a lot, don't you?" I said. "Find foster parents like this?"

"Yes," he said.

"And what happens to the people who do try to change things?" I said.

He stared at me very seriously. "No one ever has."

My life had been controlled by the chronology bogeymen ever since I first saw the Time Law people. They knew everything, they had everything chronicled. Once, I saw a mission statement on some paperwork Old Marley had: "We all play a part in keeping order."

My part was set. No matter what I did, I would never live in New York. I would never have Jason back. I would waste six years with a little girl who hated me.

Maybe I could lie to Little Marley. Maybe I could tell her we grew up and became astronauts.

*

So I packed my things. I showed up in a little wicker brim hat, as a joke. Old Marley was gonna look just like ol' Mary Poppins when she came rolling in. But I knew the joke would be lost, because I didn't remember Old Marley coming in a hat like this and that meant I hadn't been paying attention.

I didn't say goodbye to anyone, mostly because everyone I knew was dead. I traveled to the port station, high above the world—a small white circle spinning around the Earth below—where the pinstriped man helped me prepare. As we orbited, every time we hit the set point below, the whole port exploded with a ringing alarm. I was settled into my pod when the ringing came later that afternoon. The pod stretched, rolled, ceased to exist, and still existed everywhere. In my head, I saw all these moments from all over my timeline. I saw my mother, I saw a trip to the Rockies, and I saw days when a math test was my biggest problem. I smelled my high school gym. I felt the carpet of my old pink bedroom.

And then I was grounded again. With a deep breath, the world pieced me back together and I stumbled out of the pod, in shock. The welcome team was ready, and they wrapped me up in a blanket and gave me hot cocoa. They told me what I was feeling was normal.

"It's like dying," the welcome team lady said. "When I came back, I puked for days."

"Are you going to vomit?" the welcome team man asked.

"No." I vomited.

They rushed me to a recovery room where I slept and watched television. It was relaxing; the robe was comfortable. Then it was time to return to Earth and meet Marley.

*

I remember meeting Old Marley when I was twelve. A non-Time Law social worker picked me up in her car and we drove all the way to the pickup port. I guess the suit man couldn't be bothered. We waited a long time, and I got impatient sitting behind the social worker in the hot car. The thing about social workers was that they meant well, and their hearts were in the right place, but a lot of them didn't have kids of their own and they were ill-equipped to work with a little girl who found her mother dangling from a rope in the bathroom.

I hadn't been a dark kid. My bedroom was pink. But after all of that nonsense, I started writing stories at school about killing myself. No one wants to read that, and my harshest critic was the principal.

When I met Old Marley, she stepped out of the port onto the sidewalk looking refreshed and quite pleased with herself. I hated her on sight because she was fat. I wasn't fat. How did I get fat? I would never be fat.

"You're fat," I told her immediately. Maybe she would glance down at herself and say, "Oh, well, look at that, you're right. I've really let our waistline go. I'll get on that."

But instead she just stared at me, her eyes narrowing the way hawks zone in on little mice. She removed her hat—yes, she did have a hat, I remember now—and she placed it on the empty seat space between us, like a barrier.

"You're a little shit," she said.

Thus our mutual understanding began.

So now, standing at that port in my hat, I knew what was going to happen. I knew what the little shit was going to say. Looking at my waistline, I had to agree with my former self's impending assessment: I was probably a lot fatter than I thought.

I breathed in, seeing the social worker's car drive up to where I stood in my prim boots. The social worker took my bags and I sat in the back seat as if getting ready to take a puppy home for the first time. Although the puppy was taking me back home.

I didn't want to look over at the warm body next to me. She was little, I could tell. I heard her shifting around, unhappy and tired and uncomfortable. She gave out a deep sigh, just like the sigh I give when I'm done with everything.

So I looked at her.

The sensation of looking at yourself is somewhere between finding an old favorite poster from college in a box in the garage and hearing a recording of your own voice.

She was scrawny and haggard. Her skin was soft and smooth. Her hair was unbrushed. Her eyes were strained from squinting so much. She needed glasses. But good God, I had no idea I was ever that skinny.

She stared at me in complete horror.

"You're fat!" she barked at me.

There it was. There was my fear, right there in the open. I'd turned into the woman I hated, and nothing had changed. The next six years would be full of an unyielding current of events.

I set my hat down on the space between us. "You're a little shit."

\*

The house was how I left it. When I turned eighteen and Old Marley disappeared, I tried to keep it up by myself. But I eventually went off to college and had my parents' lawyer sell off the property and everything inside it. My home decomposed and was picked apart while I stayed the hell away from it. But here it was, the everyday humdrum I'd forgotten.

The air conditioner was too loud in the bathroom, and you had to hold the toilet handle down for five seconds for it to actually flush. The kitchen tile looked like instructional footprints for dancing robots. When I was a kid, I'd line my feet up with the blocks and jump forward, then sideways, backward, then forward. The old clunky cell phones sat in their charging stations. And of course, the smell of dog, although Spot Spot was given away years ago.

Or wait, no. At this point it had only been a few weeks.

"Move." Little Marley pushed past me. She couldn't look at me. I remembered I never wanted to see Old Marley because of how old she was. I was terrified of getting old.

Little Marley was only twelve. Spot Spot the dog had only just left. We had only just returned home.

I still had the whole story to plod through.

\*

Before Old Marley came and screwed everything up, I was still a kid and would sit in the corner of my room surrounded by my Barbies and think about all the things I'd be when I got older. I could move to New York and be a singer. I could be a cowboy, although I wasn't sure what a cowboy did other than sit around campfires and play harmonicas. Sounded like a sweet life.

I would be thin and beautiful. I would be smart and have a thousand boyfriends, or maybe just one good guy I loved so much to pick out of everyone. I would travel the world.

But then Old Marley arrived, and I saw no matter what I did, I would wear glasses. I would have a paunch. I would never smile. I would hate myself.

And now I sat across the dining room table, eating wet spaghetti and watching Little Marley pick at it, because we both knew how bad it was.

"I can make something else," I said.

"No," Little Marley said. "Please don't."

"We're not a total loser in the future," I said. "I just can't tell you anything, you know that."

"If the best thing you could do with your time is sit here with me, you're a total loser," Little Marley said.

I put my fork down. "Look, I know the food sucks. I don't make good spaghetti. But you could be a little more grateful. We're all we got right now—"

Little Marley rolled her eyes so hard, I wanted to knock them back into her skull. Little shit. She hadn't helped with dinner. She'd watched TV the whole time.

It wasn't her fault, I tried to remind myself. She was twelve. She was an orphan.

I should have made turkey burgers. I'm better at turkey burgers.

I stopped. I looked to the spaghetti. I laughed. Little Marley stared at me as if I was as stupid as her dinner.

"What?" she said.

"I made spaghetti!" I said. "I didn't make turkey burgers!"

"Okay?"

"Old Marley made turkey burgers for me on the first night!" I howled. "Oh my God, you know what this means?"

"No," she said.

But then I stopped laughing, because I must have been remembering wrong. I remembered Old Marley saying the words I'd just said, laughing for no reason, and I remembered suffering through her spaghetti.

But I thought we'd had burgers.

"Hello?" Little Marley waved at me. "Can we order out pizza?"

My brain scattered from one first dinner to another. Which one had it been?

Spaghetti. It had been spaghetti, although I knew it used to be something else. I'd changed it. Or maybe not.

\*

Little Marley was a pill, but a good amount of her time was spent in school. I had to get up early to drop her off, and I tried to remind her that we were only making it to college if she kept her grades up.

"I'm not an idiot, I know," Little Marley scoffed from the back seat. I was not this horrible when I was a kid.

"No, but I'm telling you, Marley, you need to pay attention in math," I said.

"If I don't do exactly how well you did," Little Marley said, "I'll end up going to a better school than you, and then what? Maybe a piano falls on my head because I happened to be at Yale walking under some dorm room window at the right moment. You could've died if you did better at math."

"I don't know what dorm would have a piano in it," I said.

"If you die," Little Marley said, "I end up in some rotten split-level in Ralston with some construction worker dude and his Avon wife and the other ten foster kids they've got in bunk beds in a room with crappy blue and green wallpaper. And then I die. So no thanks. Rather just suck at math."

She was a smart bugger. She was snappy.

"And besides," she added, grabbing her plastic backpack. A vinyl decal of a vintage cartoon movie's poster was wrapped around the front of it. Toys "R" Us exclusive. It looked brand new. Because it was. It wouldn't be vintage for a long time. "Besides," she said again, "you did all these stupid classes already. Why didn't you just bring like six years' worth of homework and test answers with you?"

"Wasn't on my priority list," I said.

Little Marley snorted. "Goes to show how not-twelve you are."

She slammed the door behind her.

I spent the day trying to figure out what to do in a year I'd already lived. There wasn't much to do but stay out of everyone's way. I decided to look over the Important People index, and I found out that in fifteen minutes, I would meet the President-fifty-years-from-now. She checked me out at the Walmart counter when I went to pick up some Tylenol.

"Hello," she said, tired, not looking at me.

I already had my lines memorized. "Hi," I said, trying not to let her see I was staring at her.

She was just a kid, like nineteen. Her hair was pulled back with little bobby pins. She chewed gum. There were bags under her eyes.

"That's five-fifty," she told me.

I paid it. "Thanks," I said half-heartedly.

"You need your receipt?" she said, handing it to me.

I did want my receipt, but I had to say, "No thanks," and leave at a pace of two steps a second.

I checked the index again. The next Important People index encounter wouldn't be until five months from now.

What makes an Important Person? If the girl at the Walmart had been a rock star or a teacher, would it have mattered if I took the receipt?

What if she had been Jason?

\*

Every day, after Little Marley got off school, we'd eat dinner and go do our own things. She'd curl up and watch television, and I'd walk through the rooms, touching all of the stuff that had been lost throughout the years. Sometimes I'd just sit in my parents' room and do nothing but smell my mother on her clothes. I didn't use the master bath, though. I shared the main bathroom with Little Marley.

She never asked why. She knew why. She asked other things.

"So," Little Marley said one night as we ate ice cream in the den, "you remember how she did it?"

"Yup," I said.

Little Marley poked her ice cream with her spoon and nodded, like we were our own sorority of two, the only ones who could see the same image in our heads. A woman with long, matted hair, her feet dangling above the lime-green-shag bath mat.

"Let's think about something else," I said.

"Tell me how it gets better, then," Little Marley said. "You're depressing. Please tell me you're secretly some CIA agent on a covert mission."

"Nope," I said.

"Well, do we get another dog?"

Old Marley had not gotten me another dog. I shook my head.

"*Could* we get another dog?" Little Marley said.

It had been stupid that Old Marley hadn't let me have a dog. But there must have been a reason, something I wasn't seeing in the space-time continuum of it all. What if I drove us to the pound and killed us both? What if the next John Lennon was supposed to pick out the dog we'd choose and was never inspired to write some ballad that would make him famous?

"I don't know if we can," I said.

"You act like there's some Big Brother watching us all the time." Little Marley scooted up in her La-Z-Boy. "No one is here except us. If we want a dog, we can get a dog."

"How do you even know who Big Brother is?" I said. "You haven't read *1984* yet."

"What are you talking about? It's a TV show," she said.

"Okay." I looked at her. "You know that the pinstripe suit man is tracking us, right? That's still a thing."

Little Marley slowly lost all color in her face. She picked at her melting ice cream. "Yeah," she said. And I knew she felt that clutching sensation, too.

The anxiety. The eyes all around her, peering into our living room. A weight on her shoulders not to step out of line.

And she was already so alone.

I would look like that for the rest of my life. Every time I wanted something, Old Marley would say that's not how it was. I would eventually stop asking and just allow things to happen the way they were supposed to fall.

But not yet. She was still only twelve. And she'd had less time to learn how to be afraid.

"Fuck it," she said, and she set her ice cream bowl on the mantel and bounded up the stairs. "Let's go get a dog."

\*

It occurred to me, after we picked up Rufus the Dog (full name) and no men in black strode out from behind a tree to time-cop arrest me, that maybe the universe didn't care if I had a dog. Nothing changed. Maybe Old Marley had gotten me a dog. Yes, of course she'd gotten me a dog. Little Marley didn't know this yet, but Rufus the Dog would grow up to be three years old and he brought Old Marley and me together. At three, Rufus the Dog had to go away to a rescue because he would be happier with other dogs. It had been the day after my fifteenth birthday and I was devastated. When Old Marley left, I ended up adopting Rufus the Dog the Second, and he'd been a good boy until he died in Jason's and my arms.

Although Old Marley sent him away, if it hadn't been for Rufus, I don't know how Old Marley and I would have bridged the gap at all. And as I watched Little Marley wrap her arms around his scruffy mutt neck and he licked her face, I promised myself I would not send the poor guy away.

Three years passed. Little Marley turned fifteen with a big birthday bash that was part-goth, part pinky ponies. Her best friends came over (I was Aunt Marley, so they weren't my best friends anymore). I bought her a new collar for Rufus the Dog. The little girls went out in the back with the big lumbering galoot. At one point, the nerd had been able to lie on my lap, and now he barely fit on the couch. Then there was chocolate cake for all.

That night, I tucked Little Marley in bed. I kissed her good night even though she was now fifteen. The last three years had their ups and downs, but they were also full of trips across the country, tree climbing, eating pizza for breakfast, and of course the stupid mutt.

"I love you, Old Marley," she said.

"Love you, too," I said.

I went back into the kitchen to feed Rufus the Dog and found him lying on his side, moaning. He didn't need to make a sound for me to know something was wrong. And even before we got to the car, I knew what was going to happen.

Rufus the Dog didn't come back home.

Little Marley woke up, bounding into the kitchen to see her puppy. But the kennel was empty and it was eerily silent. She asked where he'd gone.

I remembered what Old Marley told me.

I understood now.

But Old Marley had been wrong. Little Marley was smart and quick. Little Marley had loved this baby, and now Little Marley would know the truth.

I told her, and immediately saw that my choice this time around was almost as bad as it was the first time.

I told her Rufus was gone. I told her Rufus had gotten into some chocolate cake in the trash can. And she was quiet for three days straight. She woke up screaming in the middle of the night. A week later, she came home and flopped on the couch to watch more television.

"Where are your friends?" I said. "They usually come over on Friday nights. I'm making pizza."

"They're not coming," Little Marley said.

As I watched her on the couch, I recognized that vacant stare. This was the day Heather and Jolie asked if we were going over to my house tonight for dinner with my Aunt Marley. I had said, "No. And I think we should stop doing it forever."

Because mothers die. Dogs die. Friends will die. The only person I knew who would stick around is myself. So best to stay at home with Old Marley and get used to being alone.

Heather and Jolie never did come back to my house. That was the end of our little trio. I missed them. It had been good to see them again, and now I felt a great sadness that we'd hit that mile marker.

"Can I have a list?" Little Marley asked me later that night as we cleaned up the pizza.

"A list of chores? Christmas presents? Cute dudes?"

"No," she said. "People who are going to die."

"I can't do that," I said. "You know I can't."

"I don't have any relatives left," she said. "So what, do you never have a boyfriend? Girlfriend? Nothing? A cat? You're here with me, for six years."

"Yes, and they're sending me right back to when I left," I said.

"Yes, but you still have to live six years without whoever is in the future," she said. "That means there's either no one or there is someone that's dead. I know you, I know us. You ran away from something."

She was too smart. Why had I never realized that?

"Stop," I said. "You want some ice cream? There's no one dead."

"That's a lie," she said. "That's an absolute lie. I'm not a baby, and it's my life, too. I have a right to know."

I left. The puppy trainer taught us that when Rufus the Dog started barking, we should walk away.

But Little Marley just followed me into the kitchen. "There's someone! Who dies! Tell me! Who dies!"

Ah, now I remembered. This fight. I walked away again.

She grabbed my hand. She pulled it to her. I didn't remember that happening. "What are you doing?" I pulled it away.

"I want to see if there's a tan around your ring finger," she said.

"You need to calm down."

"There is a line! There was a ring and now there's not, and it's been three years and it's still there? That means you wear it when you're not around me."

"Other things can happen besides death, Marley."

"But it is death," she said. "I would never marry anyone I could just leave. We're not like that. We would have to really trust someone to be with them."

"What the hell do you know?" I said. "You're a child. I know everything you know, and I know more. I know exactly what is going to happen next, I've known for much longer than you, so don't sit there and tell me what I would do."

Little Marley watched me, her eyes big, her messy hair around her small pale face. She looked like the photographs I'd kept, of a sad, sunken-in child. But there was something the photographs hadn't caught.

When she spoke, she commanded.

"Tell me what I do next, then," she said. "If you know how this all ends, and our life is all figured out, you tell me what I do next."

I did try to tell her. I remembered this fight. Old Marley came up with an excuse about how she was divorced. I told Jason about that when we first met and he just laughed. "Divorced," he said. "Jesus, I hope not."

We almost hadn't married because of it. And we'd always been afraid he'd end up like Rufus. But when someone is alive, you can't imagine them dead.

"I tell you it was a divorce," I say to Little Marley. "You don't want to believe me, but you do, because it's better than the alternative. And then you stomp upstairs and watch some television."

Little Marley nodded. "Well, you're right. I don't believe you. He or she or they dies, right? Fine. Tell me how and I'll stop it."

I shook my head. "No. No, it's against the laws."

"You think every single thing we've done all these years is exactly how it happened before?" Little Marley said. "Who the hell will know what we did? Did we always get a dog, or did we change that? I don't know! But think about it—if I don't leave right now like you say I do, if I stay here instead of watching television, then the past changes, right? Who the hell would know the difference?" She sat down in the middle of the room. "So make this the moment you tell me how they die."

"No," I said. I was shaking. I could feel those pinstriped eyes everywhere; I could feel that rising panic. I could feel the world turning too fast.

"Fine," Little Marley said, tucking her hair behind her ear. "Tell me their name."

I burst into tears.

Little Marley waited. "Fine," she said. "Tell me how you met."

How many things had changed since I'd come back? How many times had we changed the timeline? *Had* we changed anything?

We couldn't change anything.

But then I looked at Little Marley. And I realized she wasn't twelve anymore. And she was alone now, but in only a few years she would go to a college dorm after this house had wandered away from her. She would go to an RA-mandated pizza party, where she would meet the students on the same floor. And that's where she'd see this boy with curly hair and an old popular cartoon on his T-shirt. The same one on her backpack when she was a kid.

"You watch that show?" I asked him, and he nodded.

"Don't care what anyone says," he said. "The old shows are the best. You watch *Saturday Morning Meltdown*?"

"Hell yes, I did," and we sang the main theme: "*Saturday Morning Meltdown*. Four hours of freedom. Come on in and come on down. We're all waiting to begin." It was a stupid song, but it reminded me of early mornings when my dad, in his thick black robe, lounged sleepily on the couch behind me while Mom was in the kitchen, making my cereal.

"We should get dinner sometime," I said. God, I was so outgoing.

He nodded, enthusiastically, more enthusiastically than any other boy I'd spoken to. "I'm Jason. I'm sorry, what's your name?"

And the day we married, it was only us and a piece of paper and two witnesses out at Standing Bear Lake. He held me and there was a boat that went past with people peering out to see our hands in each other's hands and the wind rushed and I looked at him and his eyes were speckled with green and brown and I said, "They look like their own little worlds."

Our marriage was sewn together with cartoon quotes and horrible screechy music from boys with floppy bangs and sad relationships with their suburban parents. We shared books, we popped popcorn and watched our favorite old movies on Friday nights. I could sleep through the night, especially if Jason was there.

Time doesn't heal people. People heal people.

Little Marley still sat in her spot on the floor, watching me like a patient school counselor. And I felt this anger, deep inside, rumbling forward like a train. I saw that man in his pinstriped suit, not moving and not caring when I asked him if it could have been stopped. If Jason could have lived. Because lying on the bed, wrapped in his arms, feeling his heartbeat . . . that man in his suit had deemed it unimportant.

"Jason," I said.

Little Marley nodded. "And how did . . . how will he die?"

"I know what you're thinking. It may not work," I said. "It may make everything worse."

Little Marley shrugged. "Anyone we would marry would be worth the risk."

The way she looked at me, the way she spoke to me, I now realized why I always hated Old Marley with such vehemence. It had nothing to do with New York or her glasses.

She was a coward.

*

Little Marley turned eighteen. I threw her a big party. We ate all of our favorite foods. We watched all of our favorite shows. We got up at six the next morning and made cereal together.

Then the man with the pinstriped suit came to collect me.

He was still sick from his arrival in the past. But although he was completely green, he still barely moved. I couldn't imagine him vomiting.

I hadn't seen him for six years. Maybe nothing had changed. Maybe the Jason secret was the only little wrinkle we could create, or maybe he would stop us.

"Say good-bye," he said to both of us.

"It's cruel to leave her alone so quick," I said.

"If you didn't teach her how to take care of yourself, that is not Time Law's issue," the man said.

Little Marley shoved past the man and said, "I need time with her by myself."

The man waited outside.

"Don't worry," she said. "By the time you get back, I'll have taken care of everything."

"It's too dangerous," I whispered. The man was only on the other side of that door.

"Marley," Little Marley said, "the time cop people don't have anything we don't have. They don't own the cosmos. No one does."

I gave her a hug. "Remember, it's December twenty-fourth and he goes to work in that snowstorm. Slash his tires if you need to. But if you can't stop him," I said, "don't blame yourself."

"Hey, Marley?" she said. She punched me on the arm. "If Jason's alive when you get to the other side, go live in New York."

"We've talked about this," I said. "You take a trip and—"

"And whatever whatever," she said. "It still bothers you that you don't live there. So take Jason and go live in New York. We don't know what's gonna happen to us. You're not that old."

I felt pride. I felt like I couldn't let go of her, like we needed to keep this up for the rest of our lives, me always a couple steps ahead of her and she leaps and bounds beyond us both.

But I left. I returned to the port and got in the pod. I went forward.

I got out, vomited.

"Welcome back," the man in the suit greeted me. It was the same man. It had only been a couple of seconds.

We took a ship back down the Earth. I collected my bags. Jason met me at the pickup curb. It'd been so long since we'd seen each other, and the man in the pinstripes had allowed no correspondence during my time away.

For me, it had been years. For Jason, it had been a couple of hours.

"Do I look old?" I asked. "How old do I look? Don't you dare lie to me."

Jason laughed. "You look beautiful."

"Lies. But thank you."

He put the car into drive. "I'll make you those turkey burgers tonight."

I never heard from the man in the suit again. The loop was done. We were nobodies with no significance. And that was okay. As we pulled into the Lincoln Tunnel, we melted into a million random faces.

"So you didn't ruin the space-time continuum." Jason laughed. "Congratulations."

"You know things can't be changed," I said.

"Yeah, well," Jason said. "It would have been nice to win the lottery. Or meet you when we were younger. You didn't look up my old address while you were there?"

I shook my head. I held his arm and rested my head on his shoulder while he drove in the dark, the lights hitting us one by one in a rhythm while we crossed under the Hudson. It had been a long time since I'd held him. And I knew he wanted me to find him back when we were kids, cross the river and knock on his door and introduce myself. "So we wouldn't have been alone," he said.

But I didn't, because I didn't want to change a thing.

# Comment on 'Marley and Marley'

J. R. Dawson's beautiful and moving story may be better appreciated as an extended metaphor for personal identity than a scientifically plausible take on time travel. As I mentioned in the Introduction to this book, I think that science fiction has little to tell physicists about the fundamentals of time. The mechanism by which Marley travels to the past is highly unspecified. There are also a number of amusing paradoxes in the story whereby Marley's past experiences are causally responsible for bringing about a later action (for her) that lead to those past experiences having never happened. Maybe we could hand-wave these paradoxes away with some sketchy appeal to parallel universes. But as far as I'm concerned, none of that stuff matters, and to worry about it too much interferes with the important ideas in the story. The narrative gives us much food for thought if we don't take it too literally.

The central issue of Dawson's story concerns what is known as 'diachronic identity'. This is the concept of a thing's numerical identity across different times. I think it's safe to say that diachronic identity is one of the most puzzling issues in philosophy. The problem is easy enough to state: we think that things, such as us, persist through time. So, for example, Old Marley should literally be the same person as Little Marley. But people also change, constantly. So how can they literally be the same thing?

Recall that numerical identity is very strict. If two candidates for identity have any differences between them, no matter how small, then they cannot be one thing. Equally, we can reason that if one thing is identical to another, then any feature possessed by one must also be possessed by the other. Now apply this same logic to a being that apparently persists through time, such as the editor of this book. For instance, I want to say that Tom at 9 am is identical to Tom at 10 am; they are the very same person. Yet I may have changed in certain ways. Suppose that I'm cold at 9 am and then after sitting in front of the fire for a while, I'm hot at 10 am. Applying the above logic of identity, if Tom at 9 am is cold and Tom at 9 am is the same thing as Tom at 10 am, then Tom at 10 am *must* also be cold. Yet we've already said that Tom at 10 am is hot. Therefore Tom at 10 am is both hot and cold – a direct contradiction!

Notice also that being cold or hot seems to be a feature that is internal to me. It is not simply that we've moved Tom around and so now he's in a different location, or that the things around Tom have changed. Rather, the *intrinsic* nature of Tom has changed in some way. And, of course, changing from hot to cold is trivial compared to the various other intrinsic changes that we undergo. Consider the basic physical facts: our adult selves are considerably taller and wider than our child selves. In the intervening years, our bodies acquire trillions of new cells, and most of our old cells gradually get replaced – though not, interestingly enough, the neurons in the cerebral cortex (a point we shall return to later in the book). So apart from a few billion cells in our heads, we are made from different stuff.

Despite the preservation of neurons, the mental differences between our adult and child selves are no less dramatic than the bodily differences. This is where the story of 'Marley and Marley' is a particularly striking and psychologically realistic depiction. Old Marley has a lot of memories and knowledge that Little Marley lacks. More than this, their characters are very different. Little Marley is ambitious, obnoxious and angry. In contrast, Old Marley seems to have been rather beaten down by life. She is sad and resigned to her lot. The desires of the two Marleys also differ in various respects and are often in conflict. The two Marleys frequently feel alienated from each other.

There are still some similarities between Old Marley and Little Marley. They both like dogs, for instance. But any two people on earth could share that feature. Some of the connections between Old and Little Marley are more intimate. Old Marley has quite a deep insight into Little Marley's perspective. By the end of the story, Little Marley is also able to assert that Old Marley still secretly wants to live in New York. However, these sorts of intimacies are also possible for close friends.

Thus we get to the central conceit of the story; Old Marley and Little Marley are not in fact one being at all. They are two different beings. By means of the framing device of time travel, Dawson makes it vivid that our old and young selves could be literally distinct beings. The story raises the idea that the way to solve the problem of diachronic identity is to simply give up the claim we are identical over time.

Giving up the preservation of identity raises a couple of problems. One is the problem of intertemporal justice. Often, out of a concern for our futures, we work hard or undergo some painful procedure. Yet if it's true that Old Marley is not in fact Little Marley, it doesn't make much sense for Little Marley to make sacrifices, at least for selfish reasons. Why should Little Marley have to do her maths homework while Old Marley gets to reap the benefits? Of course, in the story it's mostly Old Marley sacrificing her time for Little Marley's benefit (reversing Wordsworth's adage that 'the child is father of the man'). But this sort of sacrifice also happens in regular life. We sometimes labour to fulfil promises made by an earlier self; where they got the benefit of credit and now we have to pay the dues. Consider also how we might blame a past self for staying out late drinking, leaving us with a hangover the next day. In this way, there's a lot of room for grudges to arise between different temporal stages, and potentially the complete breakdown of intertemporal cooperation!

Is intertemporal justice a deep problem? Someone who believes in distinct temporal beings may shrug their shoulders at such moral issues. They might even say that intertemporal relationships *should* be altered. Perhaps we should replace selfish interest with something like concern for others based on our degree of resemblance. On this view, where a person and the stage that follows them one hour later resemble each other very strongly, there's good reason for them to help each other. Meanwhile, the big differences that we observe between Old Marley and Little Marley potentially mean that each has reason to prioritize some other person who resembles them more closely.

I suppose the problem of intertemporal justice isn't that intertemporal grudges are right or wrong. The problem is that it is so contrary to our everyday intuitions. The claim is not that we *should* care about our future and past selves, but that aside from a somewhat dramatic way of interpreting regrets or keeping your promises, that we can't help but do so. That is, the view is implausible because it violates common sense.

Many philosophers are not very troubled by commonsense. Yet I think we can push the issue harder by moving onto the second tricky problem, which is the question of how long these distinct temporal beings are supposed to exist. If the way we solve the problem of diachronic identity is to abandon persistence over time, does this mean that literally every (intrinsic) alteration results in the existence of a new being? Does every tiny movement of a finger belong to a different being, every different thought? Must we not now admit the existence of countless trillions of beings replacing each other at an incredible speed? But now none of these beings seems worthy of being a person. None of them has the mental continuity to sustain a complex thought or to complete an action. Forget about the person who's going to replace you in an hour. The person reading these words won't even survive to the end of this sentence.

On the other hand, if we suppose that a temporal being persists long enough to have a distinct thought, then we run up against the problem of why exactly we drew the line there rather than at some other duration. If we're going to admit that beings can after all persist through some (minor) changes, why not allow that they can also persist through more significant changes?

These are certainly deep problems. But before we throw up our hands in despair, we should consider a suggestion by twentieth-century philosopher David Lewis. Lewis claims that beings at different times are distinct. However, he also has a way of saying that these temporary beings are parts of one person: they are *temporal* parts. The simplest way to make sense of this view is to compare people with events. We commonly divide up events into a beginning, a middle, and an end. For instance, if I host a party, there's the part where I'm setting up, the part where we're all having fun, and then the part where I tidy up. Each of these parts is distinct, but they all join up to make up the event. Similarly, the temporal parts view regards what you are as the one big event of your life, beginning with your birth (or maybe conception) and ending with your death. So strictly speaking, you should not be conceived as a 3 dimensional being with only length, breadth, and width. You are a 4-dimensional being, stretching across a region of space-time like a string of spaghetti.

David Lewis' view is very interesting and we will come back to it at other points in this book. This is because the temporal parts view by itself says little about what we are, other than that we are stretched out 4-dimensionally. As a result, other views about what we are, such as the views that we are minds, animals, or brains, can make use of it to solve problems about persistence (though Lewis himself preferred the view that we are minds). A person need not be distinguished from another person by the material stuff that makes them up so much as the specific history that they have.

However, there's one big issue for the temporal parts view that we must discuss before moving on, which is also relevant to Dawson's story. This is the issue of whether the temporal parts view relies on a controversial theory of time. There's currently a debate raging amongst philosophers between those who believe that all times exist and those who think that only the present exists. Those who think that only the present exists (presentists) argue that they are on the side of everyday experience. After all, all we ever really observe is the present; a present which seems to be constantly changing. In contrast, those who think that all times exist (eternalists) don't think that anything really changes at all. All the events that we call past, present, and future exist eternally in a 4-dimensional block. Moreover, in the most respected version of eternalism, there is no objective 'now' rippling through the block. Every time has an equal right to say that it is 'now', in just the same way as every place in the universe has an equal right to say that it is 'here'.

The idea that all times concretely exist has definite attractions. There are some issues with the theory of special relativity and general relativity that are tricky for presentists to deal with. Eternalism can also potentially allow for time travel, and even meeting ourselves in the past. There's nothing incoherent about one temporal part of Marley being located at the same time as another temporal part of Marley. Marley's temporal parts are simply distributed in an unusual way in the 4-dimensional block, compared to non-time travellers. It's still entirely viable to talk about a person's individual timeline. Note in particular that temporal parts don't really change into each other. It's better to think of them as lined up next to each other. Generally, what makes one temporal part 'older' than another is just that one is a bit more wrinkly, their brain has a bit more information in it, and so on. So these 'older' slices of a person could, in principle, be located at earlier times of the universe.

The eternalist theory of time seems coherent. But that doesn't make it true! So our worry is this: do we have to accept this controversial theory of time in order to accept Lewis' theory of temporal parts? It seems that someone who only believes that the present exists cannot accept that non-present temporal parts exist. A presentist who accepted temporal parts would have to say that we never entirely exist, since only a partial person exists in the present. Yet on the contrary, one of the common-sense intuitions driving the presentist view is precisely that they, a complete person, exists and undergoes changes just as the entire world around them exists and undergoes changes. We are not spread out over times with one part of me at this point in time and another part of me at some other point in time. There are no other points of time. The whole notion of a timeline is just something we make up by remembering and predicting changes. We carry the idea of other times with us, so to speak.

So the presentist is very likely to reject Lewis' view, and they are very likely to reject Dawson's story for the same reasons. It's a mere fiction that people could travel into the past, and equally, it's a mere fiction we are made of distinct beings at different times. The presentist might even say that, if the fiction of time travel is required to demonstrate the idea of temporal parts, then this is evidence that temporal parts are just as fictional. How else, really, are we to give unequivocal evidence that a person is different beings at different times? Absent the device of time travel, we only ever see one person.

So here we have an interesting controversy about the thought experiment of 'Marley and Marley' itself. Dawson's story helpfully illustrates the idea of temporal parts, and as I noted, the conflicts between Little Marley and Old Marley are psychologically realistic. The eternalist philosopher may well embrace it. Yet the presentist philosopher feels resistance. They might admit that it's an attractive story to imagine, but that's what makes it one of those intuition pumps that Daniel Dennett warned us about. It's not a helpful metaphor, but a periously seductive illusion!

# 3

# 'Edward the Conqueror'

*Roald Dahl*

---

LOUISA, holding a dishcloth in her hand, stepped out the kitchen door at the back of the house into the cool October sunshine.

"Edward!" she called. "*Ed-ward!* Lunch is ready!"

She paused a moment, listening; then she strolled out onto the lawn and continued across it—a little shadow attending her—skirting the rose bed and touching the sundial lightly with one finger as she went by. She moved rather gracefully for a woman who was small and plump, with a lilt in her walk and a gentle swinging of the shoulders and the arms. She passed under the mulberry tree onto the brick path, then went all the way along the path until she came to the place where she could look down into the dip at the end of this large garden.

"*Edward!* Lunch!"

She could see him now, about eighty yards away, down in the dip on the edge of the wood—the tallish narrow figure in khaki slacks and dark-green sweater, working beside a big bonfire with a fork in his hands, pitching brambles onto the top of the fire. It was blazing fiercely, with orange flames and clouds of milky smoke, and the smoke was drifting back over the garden with a wonderful scent of autumn and burning leaves.

Louisa went down the slope toward her husband. Had she wanted, she could easily have called again and made herself heard, but there was something about a first-class bonfire that impelled her toward it, right up close so she could feel the heat and listen to it burn.

"Lunch," she said, approaching.

"Oh, hello. All right—yes. I'm coming."

"*What* a good fire."

"I've decided to clear this place right out," her husband said.

"I'm sick and tired of all these brambles." His long face was wet with perspiration. There were small beads of it clinging all over his moustache like dew, and two little rivers were running down his throat onto the turtleneck of the sweater.

"You better be careful you don't overdo it, Edward."

"Louisa, I do wish you'd stop treating me as though I were eighty. A bit of exercise never did anyone any harm."

"Yes, dear, I know. Oh, Edward! Look! Look!"

The man turned and looked at Louisa, who was pointing now to the far side of the bonfire.

"Look, Edward! The cat!"

Sitting on the ground, so close to the fire that the flames sometimes seemed actually to be touching it, was a large cat of a most unusual colour. It stayed quite still, with its head on one side and its nose in the air, watching the man and woman with a cool yellow eye.

"It'll get burnt!" Louisa cried, and she dropped the dishcloth and darted swiftly in and grabbed it with both hands, whisking it away and putting it on the grass well clear of the flames.

"You crazy cat," she said, dusting off her hands. "What's the matter with you?"

"Cats know what they're doing," the husband said. "You'll never find a cat doing something it doesn't want. Not cats."

"Whose is it? You ever seen it before?"

"No, I never have. Damn peculiar colour."

The cat had seated itself on the grass and was regarding them with a sidewise look. There was a veiled inward expression about the eyes, something curiously omniscient and pensive, and around the nose a most delicate air of contempt, as though the sight of these two middle-aged persons—the one small, plump, and rosy, the other lean and extremely sweaty—were a matter of some surprise but very little importance. For a cat, it certainly had an unusual colour—a pure silvery grey with no blue in it at all—and the hair was very long and silky.

Louisa bent down and stroked its head, "You must go home," she said. "Be a good cat now and go on home to where you belong."

The man and wife started to stroll back up the hill toward the house. The cat got up and followed, at a distance first, but edging closer and closer as they went along. Soon it was alongside them, then it was ahead, leading the way across the lawn to the house, and walking as though it owned the whole place, holding its tail straight up in the air, like a mast.

"Go home," the man said. "Go on home. We don't want you."

But when they reached the house, it came in with them, and Louisa gave it some milk in the kitchen. During lunch, it hoped up to the spare chair between them and sat through the meal with its head just above the level of the table, watching the proceedings with those dark-yellow eyes which kept moving slowly from the woman to the man and back again.

"I don't like this cat," Edward said.

"Oh I think it's a beautiful cat. I do hope it stays a little while."

"Now listen to me, Louisa. The creature can't possibly stay here. It belongs to someone else. It's lost. And if it's still trying to hang around this afternoon, you'd better take it to the police. They'll see it gets home."

After lunch, Edward returned to his gardening. Louisa, as usual, went to the piano. She was a competent pianist and a genuine music lover, and almost every afternoon she spent an hour or so playing for herself. The cat was now lying on the sofa, and she paused to stroke it as she went by. It opened its eyes, looked at her a moment, then closed them again and went back to sleep.

"You're an awfully nice cat," she said. "And such a beautiful colour. I wish I could keep you." Then her fingers, moving over the fur on the cat's head, came into contact with a small lump, a little growth just above the right eye.

"Poor cat," she said. "You've got bumps on your beautiful face. You must be getting old."

She went over and sat down on the long piano bench, but she didn't immediately start to play. One of her special little pleasures was to make every day a kind of concert day, with a carefully arranged programme which she worked out in detail before she began. She never liked to break her enjoyment by having to stop while she wondered what to play next. All she wanted was a brief pause after each piece while the audience clapped enthusiastically and called for more. It was so much nicer to imagine an audience, and now and again while she was playing—on the lucky days, that is—the room would begin to swim and fade and darken, and she would see nothing but row upon row of seats and a sea of white faces upturned toward her, listening with a rapt and adoring concentration.

Sometimes she played from memory, sometimes from music. Today she would play from memory; that was the way she felt. And what should the programme be? She sat before the piano with her small hands clasped on her lap, a plump rosy little person with a round and still quite pretty face, her hair done up in a neat bun at the back of her head. By looking slightly to the right, she could see the cat curled up asleep on the sofa, and its silvery-grey coat was beautiful against the purple of the cushion. How about some Bach to begin with? Or, better still, Vivaldi. The Bach adaptation for organ of the D minor Concerto Grosso. Yes—that first. Then perhaps a little Schumann. *Carnaval?* That would be fun. And after that—well, a touch of Liszt for a change. One of the *Petrarch Sonnets.* The second one—that was the loveliest-the E major. Then another Schumann, another of his gay ones—*Kinderscenen.* And lastly, for the encore, a Brahms waltz, or maybe two of them if she felt like it.

Vivaldi, Schumann, Liszt, Schumann, Brahms. A very nice programme, one that she could play easily without the music. She moved herself a little closer to the piano and paused a moment while someone in the audience—already she could feel that this was one of the lucky days—while someone in the audience had his last cough; then, with the slow grace that accompanied nearly all her movements, she lifted her hands to the keyboard and began to play.

She wasn't, at that particular moment, watching the cat at all—as a matter of fact she had forgotten its presence—but as the first deep notes of the Vivaldi sounded softly in the room, she became aware, out of the corner of one eye, of a sudden flurry, a flash of movement on the sofa to her right. She stopped playing at once.

"What is it?" she said, turning to the cat. "What's the matter?"

The animal, who a few seconds before had been sleeping peacefully, was now sitting bolt upright on the sofa, very tense, the whole body aquiver, ears up and eyes wide open, staring at the piano.

"Did I frighten you?" she asked gently. "Perhaps you've never heard music before."

No, she told herself. I don't think that's what it is. On second thought, it seemed to her that the cat's attitude was not one of fear. There was no shrinking or backing away. If anything, there was a leaning forward, a kind of eagerness about the creature, and the face—well, there was rather an odd expression on the face, something of a mixture between surprise and shock. Of course, the face of a cat is a small and fairly expressionless thing, but if you watch carefully the eyes and ears working together, and particularly that little area of mobile skin below the ears and slightly to one side, you can occasionally see the reflection of very powerful emotions. Louisa was watching the face closely now, and because she was curious to see what would happen a second time, she reached out her hands to the keyboard and began again to play the Vivaldi.

This time the cat was ready for it, and all that happened to begin with was a small extra tensing of the body. But as the music swelled and quickened into that first exciting rhythm of the introduction to the fugue, a strange look that amounted almost to ecstasy began to settle upon the creature's face. The ears, which up to then had been pricked up straight, were gradually drawn back, the eyelids drooped, the head went over to one side, and at that moment Louisa could have sworn that the animal was actually *appreciating* the work.

What she saw (or thought she saw) was something she had noticed many times on the faces of people listening very closely to a piece of music. When the sound takes complete hold of them and drowns them in itself, a peculiar, intensely ecstatic look comes over them that you can recognize as easily as a smile. So far as Louisa could see, the cat was now wearing almost exactly this kind of look.

Louisa finished the fugue, then played the siciliana, and all the way through she kept watching the cat on the sofa. The final proof for her that the animal was listening came at the end, when the music stopped. It blinked, stirred itself a little, stretched a leg, settled into a more comfortable position, took a quick glance round the room, then looked expectantly in her direction. It was precisely the way a concert-goer reacts when the music momentarily releases him in the pause between two movements of a symphony. The behaviour was so thoroughly human it gave her a queer agitated feeling in the chest.

"You like that?" she asked. "You like Vivaldi?"

The moment she'd spoken, she felt ridiculous, but not—and this to her was a trifle sinister—not quite so ridiculous as she knew she should have felt.

Well, there was nothing for it now except to go straight ahead with the next number on the programme, which was *Carnaval*. As soon as she began to play, the cat again stiffened and sat up straighter; then, as it became slowly and blissfully saturated with the sound, it relapsed into that queer melting mood of ecstasy that seemed to have something to do with drowning and with dreaming. It was really an extravagant sight—quite a comical one, too—to see this silvery cat sitting on the sofa and being carried away like this. And what made it more screwy than ever, Louisa thought, was the fact that this music, which the animal seemed to be enjoying so much, was manifestly too *difficult*, too *classical* to be appreciated by the majority of humans in the world.

Maybe, she thought, the creature's not really enjoying it all. Maybe it's a sort of hypnotic reaction, like with snakes. After all, if you can charm a snake with music, then why not a cat? Except that millions of cats hear the stuff every day of their lives, on radio and gramophone and piano, and, as far as she knew, there'd never yet been a case of one behaving like this. This one was acting as though it were following every single note. It was certainly a fantastic thing.

But was it not also a wonderful thing? Indeed it was. In fact, unless she was much mistaken, it was a kind of miracle, one of those animal miracles that happen about once every hundred years.

"I could see you *loved* that one," she said when the piece was over. "Although I'm sorry I didn't play it any too well today. Which did you like best—the Vivaldi or the Schumann?"

The cat made no reply, so Louisa, fearing she might lose the attention of her listener, went straight into the next part of the programme—Liszt's second *Petrarch Sonnet*.

And now an extraordinary thing happened. She hadn't played more than three or four bars when the animal's whiskers began perceptibly to twitch. Slowly it drew itself up to an extra height, laid its head on one side, then on the other, and stared into space with a kind of frowning concentrated look that seemed to say, "What's this? Don't tell me. I know it so well, but just for the moment I don't seem to be able to place it." Louisa was fascinated, and with her little mouth half open and half smiling, she continued to play, waiting to see what on earth was going to happen next.

The cat stood up, walked to one end of the sofa, sat down again, listened some more; then all at once it bounded to the floor and leaped up onto the piano bench beside her. There it sat, listening intently to the lovely sonnet, not dreamily this time, but very erect, the large yellow eyes fixed upon Louisa's fingers.

"Well!" she said as she struck the last chord. "So you came up to sit beside me, did you? You like this better than the sofa? All right, I'll let you stay, but you must keep still and not jump about." She put out a hand and stroked the cat softly along the back, from head to tail. "That was Liszt," she went on. "Mind you, he can sometimes be quite horribly vulgar, but in things like this he's really charming."

She was beginning to enjoy this odd animal pantomime, *so* she went straight on into the next item on the programme, Schumann's *Kinderscenen*.

She hadn't been playing for more than a minute or two when she realized that the cat had again moved, and was now back in its old place on the sofa. She'd been watching her hands at the time and presumably that was why she hadn't even noticed its going; all the same, it must have been an extremely swift and silent move. The cat was still staring at her, still apparently attending closely to the music, and yet it seemed to Louisa that there was not now the same rapturous enthusiasm there'd been during the previous piece, the Liszt.

In addition, the act of leaving the stool and returning to the sofa appeared in itself to be a mild but positive gesture of disappointment.

"What's the matter?" she asked when it was over. "What's wrong with Schumann? What's so marvellous about Liszt?" The cat looked straight back at her with those yellow eyes that had small jet-black bars lying vertically in their centres.

This, she told herself, is really beginning to get interesting—a trifle spooky, too, when she came to think of it. But one look at the cat sitting there on the sofa, so bright and attentive, so obviously waiting for more music, quickly reassured her.

"All right," she said. "I'll tell you what I'm going to do. I'm going to alter my programme specially for you. You seem to like Liszt so much, I'll give you another."

She hesitated, searching her memory for a good Liszt; then softly she began to play one of the twelve little pieces from *Der Weihnachtsbaum*. She was now watching the cat very closely, and the first thing she noticed was that the whiskers again began to twitch. It jumped down to the carpet, stood still a moment, inclining its head, quivering with excitement, and then, with a slow, silky stride, it walked around the piano, hopped up on the bench, and sat down beside her.

They were in the middle of all this when Edward came in from the garden.

"Edward!" Louisa cried, jumping up. "Oh, Edward, darling! Listen to this! Listen what's happened!"

"What is it now?" he said. "I'd like some tea." He had one of those narrow, sharp-nosed, faintly magenta faces, and the sweat was making it shine as though it were a long wet grape.

"It's the cat!" Louisa cried, pointing to it sitting quietly on the piano bench. "Just *wait* till you hear what's happened!"

"I thought I told you to take it to the police."

"But, Edward, *listen* to me. This is *terribly* exciting. This is a *musical* cat."

"Oh, yes?"

"This cat can appreciate music, and it can understand it too."

"Now stop this nonsense, Louisa, and let's for God's sake have some tea. I'm hot and tired from cutting brambles and building bonfires." He sat down in an armchair, took a cigarette from a box beside him, and lit it with an immense patent lighter that stood near the box.

"What you don't understand," Louisa said, "is that something extremely exciting has been happening here in our own house while you were out, something that may even be . . . well . . . almost momentous."

"I'm quite sure of that."

"Edward, *please*!"

Louisa was standing by the piano, her little pink face pinker than ever, a scarlet rose high up on each cheek. "If you want to know," she said, "I'll tell you what I think."

"I'm listening, dear."

"I think it might be possible that we are at this moment sitting in the presence of—" She stopped, as though suddenly sensing the absurdity of the thought.

"Yes?"

"You may think it silly, Edward, but it's honestly what I think."

"In the presence of who, for heaven's sake?"

"Of Franz Liszt himself!"

Her husband took a long slow pull at his cigarette and blew the smoke up at the ceiling. He had the tight-skinned, concave cheeks of a man who has worn a full set of dentures for many years, and every time he sucked at a cigarette, the cheeks went in even more, and the bones of his face stood out like a skeleton's. "I don't get you," he said.

"Edward, listen to me. From what I've seen this afternoon with my own eyes, it really looks as though this might actually be some sort of a reincarnation."

"You mean this lousy cat?"

"Don't talk like that, dear, please."

"You're not ill, are you, Louisa?"

"I'm perfectly all right, thank you very much. I'm a bit confused—I don't mind admitting it, but who wouldn't be after what's just happened? Edward, I swear to you—"

"What *did* happen, if I may ask?"

Louisa told him and all the while she was speaking, her husband lay sprawled in the chair with his legs stretched out in front of him, sucking at his cigarette and blowing the smoke up at the ceiling. There was a thin cynical smile on his mouth.

"I don't see anything very unusual about that," he said when it was over. "All it is—it's a trick cat. It's been taught tricks, that's all."

"Don't be so silly, Edward. Every time I play Liszt, he gets all excited and comes running over to sit on the stool beside me. But only for Liszt, and nobody can teach a cat the difference between Liszt and Schumann. You don't even know it yourself. But this one can do it every single time. Quite obscure Liszt, too."

"Twice," the husband said. "He's only done it twice."

"Twice is enough."

"Let's see him do it again. Come on."

"No," Louisa said. "Definitely not. Because if this *is* Liszt, as I believe it is, or anyway the soul of Liszt or whatever it is that comes back, then it's certainly not right or even very kind to put him through a lot of silly undignified tests."

"My dear woman! This is a *cat*—a rather stupid grey cat that nearly got its coat singed by the bonfire this morning in the garden. And anyway, what do *you* know about reincarnation?"

"If his soul is there, that's enough for me," Louisa said firmly. "That's all that counts."

"Come on, then. Let's see him perform. Let's see him tell the difference between his own stuff and someone else's."

"No, Edward. I've told you before, I refuse to put him through any more silly circus tests. He's had quite enough of that for one day. But I'll tell you what I *will* do. I'll play him a little more of his own music."

"A fat lot that'll prove."

"You watch. And one thing is certain—as soon as he recognizes it, he'll refuse to budge off that bench where he's sitting now."

Louisa went to the music shelf, took down a book of Liszt, thumbed through it quickly, and chose another of his finger compositions—the B minor Sonata. She had meant to play only the first part of the work, but once she got started and saw how the cat was sitting there literally quivering with pleasure and watching her hands with that rapturous concentrated look, she didn't have the heart to stop. She played it all the way through. When it was finished, she glanced up at her husband and smiled. "There you are," she said. "You can't tell me he wasn't absolutely *loving* it."

"He just likes the noise, that's all."

"He was *loving* it. Weren't you, darling?" she said, lifting the cat in her arms, "Oh, my goodness, if only he could talk. Just think of it, dear—he met Beethoven in his youth! He knew Schubert and Mendelssohn and Schumann and Berlioz and Grieg and Delacroix and Ingres and Heine and Balzac. And let me see ... My heavens, he was Wagner's father-in-law! I'm holding Wagner's father-in-law in my arms!"

"Louisa!" her husband said sharply, sitting up straight. "Pull yourself together." There was a new edge to his voice now, and he spoke louder.

Louisa glanced up quickly. "Edward, I do believe you're jealous!"

"Oh, sure, sure I'm jealous—of a lousy grey cat!"

"Then don't be so grumpy and cynical about it all. If you're going to behave like this, the best thing you can do is to go back to your gardening and leave the two of us together in peace. That will be best for all of us, won't it, darling?" she said, addressing the cat, stroking its head. "And later on this evening, we shall have some more music together, you and I, some more of your own work. Oh, yes," she said, kissing the creature several times on the neck, "and we might have a little Chopin, too. You needn't tell me—I happen to know you adore Chopin. You used to be great friends with him, didn't you, darling? As a matter of fact—if I remember rightly—it was in Chopin's apartment that you met the great love of your life, Madame Something-or-Other. Had three illegitimate children by her, too, didn't you? Yes, you did, you naughty thing, and don't go trying to deny it. So you shall have some Chopin," she said, kissing the cat again, "and that'll probably bring back all sorts of lovely memories to you, won't it?"

"Louisa, stop this at once!"

"Oh, don't be so stuffy, Edward."

"You're behaving like a perfect idiot, woman. And anyway, you forget we're going out this evening, to Bill and Betty's for canasta."

"Oh, but I couldn't *possibly* go out now. There's no question of that."

Edward got up slowly from his chair, then bent down and stubbed his cigarette hard into the ashtray. "Tell me something," he said quietly. "You don't really believe this—this twaddle you're talking, do you?"

"But of course I do. I don't think there's any question about it now. And, what's more, I consider that it puts a tremendous responsibility upon us, Edward—upon both of us. You as well."

"You know what I think," he said. "I think you ought to see a doctor. And damn quick, too."

With that, he turned and stalked out of the room, through the French windows, back into the garden.

Louisa watched him striding across the lawn toward his bonfire and his brambles, and she waited until he was out of sight before she turned and ran to the front door, still carrying the cat.

Soon she was in the car, driving to town.

She parked in front of the library, locked the cat in the car, hurried up the steps into the building, and headed straight for the reference room. There she began searching the cards for books on two subjects—REINCARNATION and LISZT.

Under REINCARNATION she found something called *Recurring Earth-Lives-How and Why*, by a man called F. Milton Willis, published in 1921.

Under LISZT she found two biographical volumes. She took out all three books, returned to the car, and drove home.

Back in the house, she placed the cat on the sofa, sat herself down beside it with her three books, and prepared to do some serious reading. She would begin, she decided, with Mr. F. Milton Willis's work. The volume was thin and a trifle soiled, but it had a good heavy feel to it, and the author's name had an authoritative ring.

The doctrine of reincarnation, she read, states that spiritual souls pass from higher to higher forms of animals. 'A man can, for instance, no more be reborn as an animal than an adult can re-become a child.'

She read this again. But how did he know? How could he be so sure? He couldn't. No one could possibly be certain about a thing like that. At the same time, the statement took a good deal of the wind out of her sails.

'Around the centre of consciousness of each of us, there are, besides the dense outer body, four other bodies, invisible to the eye of flesh, but perfectly visible to people whose faculties of perception of superphysical things have undergone the requisite development . . .'

She didn't understand that one at all, but she read on, and soon she came to an interesting passage that told how long a soul usually stayed away from the earth before returning in someone else's body. The time varied according to type, and Mr. Willis gave the following breakdown:

| | |
|---|---|
| *Drunkards and the unemployable* | 40/50 YEARS |
| *Unskilled labourers* | 60/100 YEARS |
| *Skilled workers* | 100/200 YEARS |
| *The bourgeoisie* | 200/300 YEARS |
| *The upper-middle classes* | 500 YEARS |
| *The highest class of gentleman Farmers* | 600/1000 YEARS |
| *Those in the Path of Initiation* | 500/2000 YEARS |

Quickly she referred to one of the other books, to find out how long Liszt had been dead. It said he died in Bayreuth in 1886. That was sixty-seven years ago. Therefore, according to Mr. Willis, he'd have to have been an unskilled labourer to come back so soon. That didn't seem to fit at all. On the other hand, she didn't think much of the author's methods of grading. According to him, 'the highest class of gentleman farmer' was just about the most superior being on the earth. Red jackets and stirrup cups and the bloody, sadistic murder of the fox. No, she thought, that isn't right. It was a pleasure to find herself beginning to doubt Mr. Willis.

Later in the book, she came upon a list of some of the more famous reincarnations. Epictetus, she was told, returned to earth as Ralph Waldo Emerson. Cicero came back as Gladstone, Alfred the Great as Queen Victoria, William the Conqueror as Lord Kitchener, Ashoka Vardhana, King of India in 272 B.C., came back as Colonel Henry Steel Olcott, an esteemed American lawyer. Pythagoras returned as Master Koot Hoomi, the gentleman who founded the Theosophical Society with Mme Blavatsky and Colonel H. S. Olcott (the esteemed American lawyer, alias Ashoka Vardhana, King of India). It didn't say who Mme Blavatsky had been. But 'Theodore Roosevelt,' it said, 'has for numbers of incarnations played great parts as a leader of men. . . . From him descended the royal line of ancient Chaldea, he having been, about 30,000 B.C., appointed Governor of Chaldea by the Ego we know as Caesar who was then ruler of Persia. . . . Roosevelt and Caesar have been together time after time as military and administrative leaders; at one time, many thousands of years ago, they were husband and wife . . .'

That was enough for Louisa. Mr. F. Milton Willis was clearly nothing but a guesser. She was not impressed by his dogmatic assertions. The fellow was probably on the right track, but his pronouncements were extravagant, especially the first one of all, about animals. Soon she hoped to be able to confound the whole Theosophical Society with her proof that man could indeed reappear as a lower animal. Also that he did not have to be an unskilled labourer to come back within a hundred years.

She now turned to one of the Liszt biographies, and she was glancing through it casually when her husband came in again from the garden.

"What are you doing now?" he asked.

"Oh—just checking up a little here and there. Listen, my dear, did you know that Theodore Roosevelt once was Caesar's wife?"

"Louisa," he said, "look—why don't we stop this nonsense? I don't like to see you making a fool of yourself like this. Just give me that goddam cat and I'll take it to the police station myself."

Louisa didn't seem to hear him. She was staring open-mouthed at a picture of Liszt in the book that lay on her lap. "My God!" she cried. "Edward, look!"

"What?"

"Look! The warts on his face! I forgot all about them! He has these great warts on his face and it was a famous thing. Even his students used to cultivate little tufts of hair on their own faces m the same spots, just to be like him."

"What's that got to do with it?"

"Nothing. I mean not the students. But the warts have."

"Oh Christ," the man said. "Oh, Christ God Almighty."

"The cat has them, too! Look, I'll show you."

She took the animal onto her lap and began examining its face.

"There! There's one! And there's another! Wait a minute! I do believe they're in the same places! Where's that picture?"

It was a famous portrait of the musician in his old age, showing the fine powerful face framed in a mass of long grey hair that covered his ears and came halfway down his neck. On the face itself, each large wart had been faithfully reproduced, and there were five of them in all.

"Now, in the picture there's *one* above the right eyebrow. She looked above the right eyebrow of the cat. "Yes! It's there! In exactly the same place! And another on the left, at the top of the nose. That one's there, too! And one just below it on the cheek. And two fairly close together under the chin on the right side. Edward! Edward! Come and look! They're exactly the same."

"It doesn't prove a thing."

She looked up at her husband who was standing in the centre of the room in his green sweater and khaki slacks, still perspiring freely. "You're scared, aren't you, Edward? Scared of losing your precious dignity and having people think you might be making a fool of yourself just for once."

"I refuse to get hysterical about it, that's all."

Louisa turned back to the book and began reading some more. "This is interesting," she said. "It says here that Lizst loved all of Chopin's works except one—the Scherzo in B flat minor. Apparently he hated that. He called it the 'Governess Scherzo,' and said that it ought to be reserved solely for people in that profession."

"So what?"

"Edward, listen. As you insist on being so horrid about all this, I'll tell you what I'm going to do. I'm going to play this scherzo right now and you can stay here and see what happens."

"And then maybe you will deign to get us some supper."

Louisa got up and took from the shelf a large green volume containing all of Chopin's works. "Here it is. Oh yes, I remember it. It *is* rather awful. Now, listen—or, rather, watch. Watch to see what he does."

She placed the music on the piano and sat down. Her husband remained standing. He had his hands in his pockets and a cigarette in his mouth, and in spite of himself he was watching the cat, which was now dozing on the sofa. When Louisa began to play, the first effect was as dramatic as ever. The animal jumped up as though it had been stung, and it stood motionless for at least a minute, the ears pricked up, the whole body quivering. Then it became restless and began to walk back and forth along the length of the sofa. Finally, it hopped down onto the floor, and with its nose and tail held high in the air, it marched slowly, majestically, from the room.

"There!" Louisa cried, jumping up and running after it. "That does it! That really proves it!" She came back carrying the cat which she put down again on the sofa. Her whole face was shining with excitement now, her fists were clenched white, and the little bun on top of her head was loosening and going over to one side. "What about it, Edward? What d'you think?" She was laughing nervously as she spoke.

"I must say it was quite amusing."

"*Amusing!* My dear Edward, it's the most wonderful thing that's ever happened! Oh, goodness me!" she cried, picking up the cat again and hugging it to her bosom. "Isn't it marvellous to think we've got Franz Liszt staying in the house?"

"Now, Louisa. Don't let's get hysterical."

"I can't help it, I simply can't. And to *imagine* that he's actually going to live with us for always!"

"I beg your pardon?"

"Oh Edward! I can hardly talk from excitement. And d'you know what I'm going to do next? Every musician in the whole world is going to want to meet him, that's a fact, and ask him about the people he knew—about Beethoven and Chopin and Schubert—"

"He can't talk," her husband said.

"Well—all right. But they're going to want to meet him anyway, just to see him and touch him and to play their own music to him, modern music he's never heard before."

"He wasn't that great. Now, if it had been Bach or Beethoven . . ."

"Don't interrupt, Edward, please. So what I'm going to is to notify all the important living composers everywhere. It's my duty. I'll tell them Liszt is here, and invite them to visit him. And you know what? They'll come flying in from every corner of the earth!"

"To see a grey cat?"

"Darling, it's the same thing. It's *him*. No one cares what he *looks* like. Oh, Edward, it'll be the most exciting thing there ever was!"

"They'll think you're mad."

"You wait and see." She was holding the cat in her arms and petting it tenderly but looking across at her husband, who now walked over to the French windows and stood there staring out into the garden. The evening was beginning, and the lawn was turning slowly from green to black, and in the distance he could see the smoke from his bonfire rising up in a white column.

"No" he said, without turning round, "I'm not having it, not in this house. It'll make us both look perfect fools."

"Edward, what do you mean?"

"Just what I say. I absolutely refuse to have you stirring up a lot of publicity about a foolish thing like this. You happen to have found a trick cat. O.K.—that's fine. Keep it, if it pleases you. I don't mind. But I don't wish you to go any further than that. Do you understand me, Louisa?"

"Further than what?"

"I don't want to hear any more of this crazy talk. You're acting like a lunatic."

Louisa put the cat slowly down on the sofa. Then slowly she raised herself to her full small height and took one pace forward.

"*Damn* you, Edward!" she shouted, stamping her foot. "For the first time in our lives something really exciting comes along and you're scared to death of having anything to do with it because someone may laugh at you! That's right, isn't it? You can't deny it, can you?"

"Louisa," her husband said. "That's quite enough of that. Pull yourself together now and stop this at once." He walked over and took a cigarette from the box on the table, then lit it with the enormous patent lighter. His wife stood watching him, and now the tears were beginning to trickle out of the inside corners of her eyes, making two little shiny rivers where they ran through the powder on her cheeks.

"We've been having too many of these scenes just lately, Louisa," he was saying. "No no, don't interrupt. Listen to me. I make full allowance for the fact that this may be an awkward time of life for you, and that—"

"Oh, my God! You idiot! You pompous idiot! Can't you see that this is different, this is—this is something miraculous? Can't you see *that*?"

At that point, he came across the room and took her firmly by the shoulders. He had the freshly lit cigarette between his lips, and she could see faint contours on his skin where the heavy perspiration had dried in patches. "Listen," he said. "I'm hungry. I've given up my golf and I've been working all day in the garden, and I'm tired and hungry and I want some supper. So do you. Off you go now to the kitchen and get us both something good to eat."

Louisa stepped back and put both hands to her mouth. "My heavens!" she cried. "I forgot all about it. He must be absolutely famished. Except for some milk, 1 haven't given him a thing to eat since he arrived."

"Who?"

"Why, *him*, of course. I must go at once and cook something really special. I wish I knew what his favourite dishes used to be. What do you think he would like best, Edward?"

"Goddamn it, Louisa!"

"Now, Edward, please. I'm going to handle this *my* way just for once. You stay here," she said, bending down and touching the cat gently with her fingers. "I won't be long."

Louisa went into the kitchen and stood for a moment, wondering what special dish she might prepare. How about a souffle? A nice cheese souffle? Yes, that would be rather special. Of course, Edward didn't much care for them, but that couldn't be helped.

She was only a fair cook, and she couldn't be sure of always having a souffle come out well, but she took extra trouble this time and waited a long while to make certain the oven had heated fully to the correct temperature. While the souffle was baking and she was searching around for something to go with it, it occurred to her that Liszt had probably never in his life tasted either avocado pears or grapefruit, so she decided to give him both of them at once in a salad. It would be fun to watch his reaction. It really would.

When it was all ready, she put it on a tray and carried it into the living-room. At the exact moment she entered, she saw her husband coming in through the French windows from the garden.

"Here's his supper," she said, putting it on the table and turning toward the sofa. "Where is he?"

Her husband closed the garden door behind him and walked across the room to get himself a cigarette.

"Edward, where is he?"

"Who?"

"You know who."

"Ah, *yes*. Yes, that's right. Well—I'll tell you." He was bending forward to light the cigarette, and his hands were cupped around the enormous patent lighter. He glanced up and saw Louisa looking at him—at his shoes and the bottoms of his khaki slacks, which were damp from walking in long grass.

"I just went out to see how the bonfire was going," he said.

Her eyes travelled slowly upward and rested on his hands.

"It's still burning fine," he went on. "I think it'll keep going all night."

But the way she was staring made him uncomfortable.

"What is it?" he said, lowering the lighter. Then he looked down and noticed for the first time the long thin scratch that ran diagonally clear across the back of one hand, from the knuckle to the wrist.

"*Edward!*"

"*Yes*," he said, "I know. Those brambles are terrible. They tear you to pieces. Now, just a minute, Louisa. What's the matter?"

"*Edward.*"

"Oh, for God's sake, woman, sit down and keep calm. There's nothing to get worked up about. Louisa! Louisa, *sit down!*"

# Comment on 'Edward the Conqueror'

A story depicting the reincarnation of a long-dead composer in the body of a cat might be considered more fantasy than science fiction. Souls seem to be the province of magic and the supernatural, not the hard-edged technologies that science fiction traffics in. Yet Roald Dahl approaches his fantastic subject matter in a practical, exploratory way that reminds me of the best science fiction. The domestic setting of the story only enhances these qualities. I believe it to be an appropriate and useful thought experiment about what it would take to be convinced of the existence of souls.

The idea of the soul must be one of humanity's oldest theories about what we are. Of course, we commonly appeal to souls to tell stories in which a person survives the death of their body. Yet I think it's plausible that such stories are derivations from the soul's primary function, which is to solve the problem of diachronic identity. Recall the problem that we introduced in the previous chapter was how to explain that we remain one thing, despite the radical changes that we undergo over time. This is a deep intuition we have that seems to defy the logic of numerical identity. The soul theory can potentially solve this issue by pointing to one thing that remains perfectly constant.

What is a soul? A rather tricky question to answer! The soul is not clearly a physical substance. It's also not clear what mental qualities the soul has, if any (we'll come back to this shortly). The soul is frequently believed to have moral qualities. In the ancient Egyptian religion, when Anubis weighs the dead person's soul against a feather, it is the moral qualities that are supposed to make all the difference. This is a common theme in many different religions and speaks once again to the role that personal identity plays in attributing moral or legal responsibility. But apart from all this, my overriding impression is that the soul is supposed to be nothing more or less than a person's *essence*. By a thing's essence, we mean that without which the thing could not exist, and, if present, that which guarantees the thing's existence. A thing's essence is contrasted with its *accidents*; qualities that a thing may happen to have, but do not really define it, and can be lost without undermining existence.

An essence is precisely a solution to the problem of identity through change. Our various physical qualities can be regarded as mere accidents. It does not matter if these are not the same over time. So it does not matter if you gain weight or lose an arm in a threshing-machine accident. It does not matter if you gain new memories or lose the desire to play the bassoon. So long as your soul persists, you persist. In fact, the idea of the soul may precisely be motivated by the intuition that *none* of the mundane features we can point to in ourselves seems very essential. Any of them could be replaced, so something else is required.

Once we come up with the idea of an essence that is unaffected by all sorts of physical changes, it is a relatively small step to suppose that it can survive the death of the body entirely. I should however emphasize here that not every theory of the soul regards it as immortal. For instance, if you read Plato's dialogue *Phaedo*, which depicts the death of Socrates, the main issue that Socrates discusses with his followers is whether or not the soul should be regarded as akin to the tuning of a musical instrument – a harmonious quality that would be destroyed the moment the instrument is destroyed. Yet, so far as the religious idea of the soul is a distinctive answer to the question of personal identity, we'll focus on the indestructible kind here. Later chapters of this book can be considered as explorations of theories of identity that admit the vulnerability of our essence, and thus might be equated with souls in a looser, figurative sense.

So we have a theory on the table: What I am, essentially, is a soul. The question now is, should we believe it? A good way to explore this question is to imagine the conditions that would have to obtain for us to be convinced of the existence of the soul. This is where Roald Dahl's story comes in.

In the story, Louisa comes across a very unusual cat and becomes convinced that it is the reincarnation of the romantic-era composer Franz Liszt. She does not leap to this conclusion. She comes to it as a hypothesis to explain why the cat is so attracted to piano music, and specifically that of Liszt. She goes to the library and tries to find a scholarly work that provides more detail about the hypothesis. She notes that the cat has warts on its face in the same location that Liszt had. She even tests the cat with a piece that Liszt apparently disliked and receives an unequivocal reaction. So the question I would like you to consider is this: if you were in Louisa's situation, making the observations that she makes, would you believe that the cat is the reincarnation of the composer?

Louisa's husband Edward is sceptical. The story encourages us to find him a repellent, dogmatic character. Of course, he's a truly nasty piece of work if he has thrown the cat on his bonfire (or if you prefer, imagine the cat scratched Edward and ran away while Edward was trying to get rid of it). But is Edward wrong to claim that the cat is not Liszt? Despite the man's unpleasant personal qualities, it is often handy to have such a figure in mind when considering difficult philosophical questions. That is, could you convince someone who would take every opportunity to deny the claim? After all, it is truly an extraordinary claim. And as Carl Sagan said, extraordinary claims require extraordinary evidence.

I must admit that I would be pretty compelled by the observations that Louisa makes, despite the fact that I consider myself a 'materialist' philosopher. Each of the individual observations that Louisa makes – the warts, the special liking of one composer and disliking of one piece – might be dismissed as mere coincidences. But the combination of them all makes the claim of coincidence harder to bear. I must note that probability is hard to gauge here. I have literally never heard of a cat being able to distinguish one composer's music from another, let alone showing a special preference for one, so it is hard for me to assign a probability to the case where this happens and the cat is *not* the reincarnation of that composer. I assume, then, that this probability is very low indeed, though not, I think, impossible. Similar considerations concern the special disliking of one piece (though I have to say, I'd want more repetitions of that observation, to be sure that this indeed is what's happening, rather than the cat getting in a bad mood for some other reason). Anyway, I think that this probability should be even lower than the first one, since it is a more specific scenario. Finally, the probability of a cat happening to possess facial warts in the same location as a historical figure would not be so low (cats having warts doesn't sound so strange to me), but still fairly unusual. I then need to multiply the probability of all these observations with each other and arrive at my judgement of the probability that the cat is not the reincarnation of a dead composer, i.e. that it's all a coincidence. All this is very sketchy, but it's going to be an extremely low probability, such as one in a billion. Your judgements may well differ from mine, and as we gather vital scientific evidence about the musical preferences of cats we may arrive at better justified judgements, but let's go with that for now.

The above judgements were pretty hard to make. But here it gets even harder. I need to work out if the one in a billion chance of a coincidence occurring is *lower* than the probability of a cat being the reincarnation of dead composer. If it is lower, then I have reason to believe (not an indisputable reason, but still) that reincarnation has in fact occurred. What I am doing here is comparing the claim with what's called the 'null hypothesis' (that my observations could have happened merely by chance). It is an exemplary way to come to rational conclusions about extraordinary occurrences.

Okay, so how likely is it that people get reincarnated as animals? (I suppose that it being a composer rather than, say, a philosopher, doesn't make much difference, and it being a cat rather than, say, an elephant also doesn't make much difference). My judgement here is going to be pretty close to my judgement about the likelihood of souls in the first place. That is, if there *are* souls that can exist apart from the physical body, then their movement from one body to another doesn't seem so implausible. Similarly, a good reason to believe in the existence of souls is if reincarnation is believed to occur.

I must admit, I am not very sympathetic to the theory of the soul. My main reason for disliking this theory is that I don't know of any reputable physical measurement or observation of a soul (I am aware that people have sometimes claimed to make such measures, but I don't trust them). Moreover, if the soul is supposed to be immaterial (explaining why it can't be physically measured), then I find it even less plausible, because I literally cannot imagine how an immaterial thing can interact with a physical thing (i.e. a person's body). I cannot imagine how an immaterial thing can even be located in physical space. This is the whole problem of souls. When we try to come up with an entity that persists throughout radical physical changes of a person, we simultaneously render that entity less amenable to causal interaction and thereby measurement.

On the other hand, I must also admit that I don't think it's impossible that souls exist. I have read some very spooky reports where the reincarnation of a person (into another human) is claimed to have occurred (see, for instance, the documentary about Scottish boy Cameron McAuley, or the case of Shanti Devi that impressed Mahatma Gandhi enough to launch an official investigative commission). My opinions about physical measurements or interactions might also be wrong somehow (though giving up these views would pretty much upturn my entire understanding of the universe).

Another potential consideration in favour of souls (and reincarnation) might be the fact that millions, perhaps billions, of people believe in them. However, I don't find that this fact moves my needle in favour of souls much. If those millions haven't based their views on either sound reasons or sound evidence, then their opinions are worthless. And if they have, then it's that evidence I need to be directed to, not peoples' opinions about it.

Finally, I might consider the subjective evidence in favour of a soul. Do I *feel* like I have a soul? I certainly feel like I persist through quite radical physical changes. I feel like I am fundamentally the same person as I was when a child (not everyone might feel this, but I do). But I don't have much confidence that what I'm feeling here is a soul. Perhaps it is the result of some psychological function I possess for positing identity or my memories or my animal continuity, as the other theories of identity we'll look at later explore. Those alternative theories seem a bit more respectable to me.

So what probability do I assign to the existence of souls? A very low one indeed, but not as low, I think, as all the coincidences that would have to occur for Louisa's observations to be made. Therefore, if I were in her situation, I would have to grudgingly admit that the cat may indeed be the reincarnation of the composer. At this point, I'd probably try to come up with some explanation of how this could have occurred. I'd generally prefer an explanation that doesn't require me to give up all of my cherished beliefs about the physical universe. For instance, I might suppose that souls are made of some sort of ethereal ectoplasm that science has yet to measure.

Before we move on, there is another philosophical issue to think about. When we consider how the existence of souls could actually be established, the most compelling evidence would be that the subject reports memories from a past life, that they possess information that we believe they could not have gained through ordinary reports or mere guesswork. The alleged real-world cases of reincarnation that I mentioned above were both defended on this basis. Yet when authors depict reincarnation in fiction, they often like to appeal to small physical resemblances such as birth marks (or in Dahl's case, warts). A contemporary person sharing a birthmark with an historical figure is hardly a convincing justification for reincarnation, so generally, such fictions merely stipulate that reincarnation has occurred, and so for my purposes, they are less interesting as thought experiments.

Why do authors like to indicate reincarnation by means of physical resemblances? The reason is that other kinds of evidence are discouraged by the nature of the case. Of course, simple bodily continuity is excluded because of the destruction of the previous body. Meanwhile, it is one of the common claims about reincarnation that we forget our previous lives. Defenders of reincarnation are *forced* to make this claim because reincarnation is supposed to be (near) universal and yet almost no one honestly reports past-life experiences.

But now defenders of reincarnation (and souls) face a dilemma. Either they rule out convincing evidence for souls, or they appeal to memories of past lives. But if they take the second option, we now have an alternate basis for personal identity. We don't *need* to appeal to special ethereal entities. We can simply appeal to memories instead. Indeed, since memories also apply over the course of a single lifetime, and are readily reported, they are a considerably more theoretically attractive basis for personal identity than the appeal to souls.

This was John Locke's reasoning as well. Despite the fact that he was a theist and believed in the existence of souls, he believed that memories were the basis of a far more practical philosophical view of identity, and many philosophers since then have agreed with him. Let us then turn to the memory-based theory of personal identity, allowing that, were memories also established between different lives, this could potentially be combined with a soul view.

# 4

# 'Life Sentence'

## Matthew Baker

Home.

He recognizes the name of the street. But he doesn't remember the landscape. He recognizes the address on the mailbox. But he doesn't remember the house.

His family is waiting for him on the porch.

Everybody looks just as nervous as he is.

He gets out.

The police cruiser takes back off down the gravel drive, leaving him standing in a cloud of dust holding a baggie of possessions.

He has a wife. He has a son. He has a daughter.

A dog peers out a window.

His family takes him in.

Wash is still groggy from the procedure. He's got a plastic taste on his tongue. He's got a throbbing sensation in his skull. He's starving.

Supper is homemade pot pies. His wife says the meal is his favorite. He doesn't remember that.

The others are digging in already. Steam rises from his pie as he pierces the crust with his fork. He salivates. The smell of the pie hitting him makes him grunt with desire. Bending toward the fork, he parts his lips to take a bite, but then he stops and glances up.

Something is nagging at him worse than the hunger.

"What did I do?" he says with a sense of bewilderment.

His wife holds up a hand.

"Baby, please, let's not talk about that," his wife says.

Wash looks around. A laminate counter. A maroon toaster. Flowers growing from pots on the sill. Magnets shaped like stars on the fridge.

This is his home.
He doesn't remember anything.
He's not supposed to.

*

His reintroduction supervisor comes to see him in the morning.

"How do you feel, Washington?"

"Everybody keeps calling me Wash?"

"I can call you that if you'd like."

"I guess I'm not really sure what I like."

Lindsay, the reintroduction supervisor, wears a scarlet tie with a navy suit. She's got a bubbly disposition and a dainty build. Everything that she says, she says as if revealing a wonderful secret that she just can't wait to share.

"We've found a job for you at a restaurant."

"Doing what?"

"Working in the kitchen."

"That's the best you could get me?"

"At your level of education, and considering your status as a felon, yes, it really is."

"Where did I work before?"

Lindsay smiles.

"An important part of making a successful transition back to your life is learning to let go of any worries that you might have about your past so that you can focus on enjoying your future."

Wash frowns.

"Why do I know so much about mortgages? Did I used to work at a bank?"

"To my knowledge you have never worked at a bank."

"But how can I remember that stuff if I can't remember other stuff?"

"Your semantic memories are still intact. Only your episodic memories were wiped."

"My what?"

"You know what a restaurant is."

"Yeah."

"But you can't remember ever having eaten in a restaurant before."

"No."

"Or celebrating a birthday at a restaurant. Or using a restroom at a restaurant. Or seeing a friend at a restaurant. You've eaten in restaurants before. But you have no memories of that at all. None whatsoever." Lindsay taps her temples. "Episodic memories are personal experiences. That's what's gone. Semantic memories are general knowledge. Information. Names, dates, addresses. You still have all of that. You're a functional member of society. Your diploma is just as valid as before. And your procedural memories are fine. You still know how to ride a bike, or play the guitar, or operate a vacuum. Assuming you ever learned," Lindsay laughs.

"Did you do anything else to me?"

"Well, of course, your gun license was also revoked."

Wash thinks.

"Did I shoot somebody?"

"All felons are prohibited from owning firearms, regardless of the nature of the crime."

Wash turns away, folding his arms over his chest, pouting at the carpet.

"Washington, how do you feel?"

"Upset."

"That's perfectly normal. I'm so glad that you're comfortable talking with me about your feelings. That's so important."

Lindsay nods with a solemn expression, as if waiting for him to continue sharing, and then leans in.

"But honestly though, you should feel grateful you weren't born somewhere that still has prisons." Lindsay reaches for her purse. "Do you know what would have happened to you a century ago for doing what you did? The judge would have locked you up and thrown away the key!" Lindsay says brightly, and then stands to leave.

*

Wash gets woken that night by a craving.

An urgent need.

Was he an addict?

What is he craving?

He follows some instinct into the basement. Stands there in boxers under the light of a bare bulb. Glances around the basement, stares at the workbench, and then obeys an urge to reach up onto the shelf above. Pats around and discovers an aluminum tin.

Something shifts inside as he takes the tin down from the shelf.

He pops the lid.

In the tin: a stash of king-size candy bars.

As he chews a bite of candy bar, a tingle of satisfaction rushes through him, followed by a sense of relief.

Chocolate.

Back up the stairs, padding down the hallway, he pit-stops in the bathroom for a drink of water. Bends to sip from the faucet. Wipes his chin. Stands. A full-length mirror hangs from the back of the door. He's lit by the glow of a night-light the shape of a rainbow that's plugged into the outlet above the toilet.

Wash examines his appearance in the mirror. Wrinkles around his eyes. Creases along his mouth. A thick neck. Broad shoulders, wide hips, hefty limbs, and a round gut. Fingers nicked with scars. Soles hardened with calluses. The body of an aging athlete, or a laborer accustomed to heavy lifting who's recently gone soft from lack of work.

He can't remember being a toddler. He can't remember being a child. He can't remember being a teenager. He can't remember being an adult.

He stares at himself.

Who is he other than this person standing here in the present moment?

Is he anybody other than this person standing here in the present moment?

His wife stirs as he slips back into bed. She reaches over and startles him with a kiss. He kisses back, but then she climbs on top of him, and he pulls away.

"Too soon?" she whispers.

Mia, that's her name, he remembers. She has a flat face, skinny arms, thick legs, and frizzy hair cut off at her jawline, which he can just make out in the dark. Her nails are painted bright red. She sleeps in a plaid nightgown.

"I barely know you," he says.

Mia snorts. "Didn't stop you the first time." She shuffles backward on her knees, tugging his boxers down his legs as she goes, and then chuckles. "I mean our other first time."

\*

The restaurant is a diner down by the highway, a chrome trailer with checkered linoleum and pleather booths and ceiling fans that spin out of sync, featuring a glass case of pastries next to the register and a jukebox with fluorescent tubing over by the restrooms. The diner serves breakfast and lunch only. Wash arrives each morning around dawn. The kitchen has swinging doors. He does the dishes, sweeps the floors, mops the floors, and hauls the trash out when the bags get full. Mainly he does the dishes. Dumps soda from cups. Pours coffee from mugs. Scrapes onion rings and pineapple rinds and soggy napkins and buttered slices of toast and empty jam containers and crumpled straw wrappers into the garbage. Sprays ketchup from plates. Rinses broth from bowls. Racks the tableware and sends the racks through the dishwasher. Stacks spotless dishes back onto the shelves alongside the stove. Scours at crusted yolk and dried syrup with the bristly side of sponges. Scrubs skillets with stainless steel pads for so long and with such force that the pads fall apart and still there's a scorched residue stuck to the pans. Burns his hands with scalding water. Splashes stinging suds into his eyes. His shoes are always damp as he drives home in the afternoon. He shaves, he showers, and he feeds the dog, a moody mutt whose name is Biscuit. Then he sits on the porch step waiting for the rest of his family to get home. His house is modest, with small rooms and a low ceiling, and has no garage. The gutters sag. Shingles have been blown clear off the roof. The sun has bleached the blue of the siding almost to gray. Across the road stands a field of corn. Beyond that there's woods. The corn stalks sway in the breeze. The dog waits with him, curled up on the grass around his shoes, panting whenever a car drives past. He lives in Kansas.

Sophie, his daughter, a ninth grader, is the next to arrive home, shuffling off the bus while jabbing at the buttons of a game. Jaden, his son, a third grader, arrives home on the later bus, shouting taunts back at friends hanging out the windows. His wife works at a hospital, the same hours that he does, but she gets home last since the hospital is all the way over in Independence.

Wash tries to cook once, tries to make meatloaf. He knows what a meatloaf is. He understands how an oven functions. He gets the mechanics of a whisk. He can read the recipe no problem. But still the attempt is a disaster. He pulls the pan out when the timer goes off, and the bottom of the meatloaf is already charred, and the top of the meatloaf is still raw. He hadn't been able to find bread crumbs, so he had torn up a slice of bread instead, which doesn't seem to have worked. He samples a bite from the center of the meatloaf, that in-between part neither charred nor raw, and finds some slivers of onion skin in among what he's chewing. When his wife arrives home, she surveys the mess with a look of amusement and then assures him that this isn't a skill he's forgotten. She does the cooking. At home, the same as at the diner, he does the dishes.

Other items that his wife assures him were not accidentally erased during his procedure: the date of her birthday (all he knows is the month, August); the date of their anniversary (all he knows is the month, May).

"Here's a clue. My birthday was exactly a week before you came home. Borrow a calculator from one of your delightful children if you need help with the math," Mia says, dumping a box of spaghetti into a pot of roiling water while simultaneously stirring a can of mushrooms into a pan of bubbling marinara. "If you'd like to know how long you've been married, your marriage license is in the filing cabinet in the basement. In fact, if you're really feeling ambitious, your children have some birth certificates in there, too. Heck, check your immunization record while you're down there, you're probably due for a tetanus shot."

There are moments so intimate that he can almost forget he's living with strangers. His daughter falls asleep on him one night while watching a show about zombies on the couch, her head lolling against his shoulder. His son leans into him one night waiting for the microwave to heat a mug of cider, his arm wrapping around his waist. Late one night after the kids are asleep, his wife hands him a rubber syringe and a plastic bowl and asks him to flush a buildup of wax from her ears, an act that to him seems far more intimate than intercourse.

But then there are the moments that remind him how much he must have lost. One night, during a supper of baked potatoes loaded with chives and bacon and sour cream, his family suddenly cracks up over an in-joke, a shared memory that's somehow related to mini-golf and bikinis. His wife is laughing so hard that she's crying, but sobers up when she realizes how confused he looks.

"Sorry, it's impossible to explain if you weren't there," Mia says, thumbing away tears.

"But he was there, he was the one who noticed," Jaden protests.

"He can't remember anymore, you ninny," Sophie scowls.

And then the subject gets changed.

Wash does know certain information about himself.

He knows his ancestry is part Potawatomi. He knows his parents were named Lawrence and Beverly. He knows his birthplace is near Wichita.

But taking inventory of what he knows isn't as simple as thinking, "What do you know, Wash?"

He has to ask a specific question.

He must know other facts about himself.

He just hasn't asked the right questions yet.

"Wash, were you ever in a fight before?"

"Wash, did you like your parents?"

"Wash, have you seen a tornado?"

He doesn't remember.

He tries asking Sophie about his past one afternoon. Wash is driving her to practice. Sophie runs cross.

"What was my life like before the wipe?" Wash says.

Sophie is a plump kid with crooked teeth, a pet lover, and has a grave demeanor, as if constantly haunted by the fact that not all kittens have homes. She's doing history homework, flipping back and forth between a textbook and a worksheet, scribbling in information. She's got her sneakers propped on the dashboard with her ankles crossed.

"Huh?" Sophie says.

"What do you know about my life?"

"Um."

"Like tell me something I told you about myself before I got taken away."

She sneers at the textbook. Bends over the worksheet, forcefully erases something, and blows off the peels of rubber left behind. Then turns to look at him.

"You never really talked about yourself," Sophie says.

He tries asking Jaden about his past one afternoon. Wash is driving him to practice. Jaden plays soccer.

"What was I like before I went away?" Wash says.

Jaden is a stringy kid with a nose that dominates his other features, a soda junkie, and constantly hyper, regardless of caffeine intake. He's sitting in an upside-down position with his legs pointed at the roof, his back on the seat, and his head lolled over the edge, with his hands thrown across the floor of the truck. He's spent most of the ride listing off the powers of supervillains.

"I dunno," Jaden says.

"You must remember something about me."

"I guess."

"So what type of person was I?"

Jaden plucks at the seatbelt. Frowns in thought. Then turns to look at him.

"A grown-up?" Jaden says.

Wash tries asking his wife, but her taste in conversation is strictly practical, and she doesn't seem interested in reminiscing about his life before the wipe at all. No photos are framed on the counter. No snapshots are pinned to the fridge. If pictures of his family ever hung on the walls, the pictures have long since disappeared.

But other artifacts of his past are scattered throughout the house. In his closet hang flannel button-ups, worn tees, plain sweatshirts, a zip-up fishing vest with mesh pouches, a hooded hunting jacket with a camouflage pattern, a fleece, a parka, faded jeans on wire hangers, and a suit in a plastic garment bag. Who was that person who chose these clothes? In his dresser mingle polished turquoise, pennies smashed smooth by trains, a hotel matchbook lined with the stumps of torn-out matches, an assortment of acorns, ticket stubs from raffles, a pocket knife whose blades are rusted shut, and the marbled feather of a bald eagle. Who was that person who kept these trinkets? There's a safe in the basement where his guns were stored before being sold. He knows a combination, spins the numbers in, and the handle gives. But aside from a bungee, the safe is empty. No rifles, no shotguns, no pistols. Even the ammunition was sold.

Who owned those guns?

And then there are the artifacts of his past that he sees in his family. Sometimes in the driveway, he'll glance up from the car he's washing or the mower he's fueling and see his daughter watching him from the door with an expression of spite. Was he ever cruel to Sophie? Sometimes as he drops his boots in the entryway with a thud or tosses his wallet onto the counter with a snap, he'll see his son flinch over on the couch. Was he ever rough with Jaden? When he sets his cup down empty, his wife leaps up to fetch the carton of milk from the fridge, as if there might be some repercussion for failing to pour him another glass.

He has a beat-up flip phone with nobody saved in the contacts except for his wife and his kids. Were there other contacts in there that were deleted after he got arrested?

At cross meets and soccer matches, the other parents never talk to him. Was that always the case, or only now that he's a felon?

How does he know that trains have cupolas? Where did he learn that comets aren't asteroids? Who taught him that vinegar kills lice?

Wash is at the homecoming football game, coming back from the concession stand with striped boxes of popcorn for his family, when he stops at the fence to watch a field goal attempt. A referee jogs by with a whistle bouncing on a lanyard. Cheerleaders in gloves and earmuffs rush past with pompoms and megaphones. Jayhawkers chant in the bleachers. Wash glazes over, he's not sure for how long, but he's still standing at the fence when his trance is interrupted by a stranger standing next to him.

"You did time, didn't you, friend?"

The stranger wears a pullover with the logo of the rival team. His hair is slicked crisp with mousse. He's got ironed khakis and shiny loafers.

"Do I know you?" Wash says.

"Ha. No. You just had that look. We all get the look. Searching for something that isn't there," the stranger says.

Wash cracks a smile.

The stranger grumbles, "I don't know why people even say that anymore. Doing time. That's not what happens at all. Losing time. That's what happens. Poof. Gone." The stranger glances down and gives the ice in his cup a shake.

"I lost a year. Let's just say, hadn't been totally candid on my tax forms. Couldn't have been worse timing though. I'd gotten married that year. No joke, I can't even remember my own honeymoon. Spent a fortune on that trip, too. Fucking blows." The stranger turns away to watch a punt return, sucks a gurgle of soda through his straw, and then turns back. "How long did you do?"

"Life."

The stranger whistles.

"No kidding? You lost everything? From start to finish? How old were you when you got wiped?"

"Forty-one."

"What'd you do to get life? Kill a cop? Rob a bank? Run a scam or something?"

"I don't know," Wash admits.

The stranger squints.

"You aren't curious?"

"Nobody will tell me."

The stranger laughs.

"To get a sentence like that, whatever you did, it must have made the news."

Wash stares at the stranger in shock. He could know who he was after all. All he'd have to do is get online.

"We don't have a computer though," Wash frowns.

The stranger passes behind him, giving him a pat on the shoulder, and then calls back before drifting off into the crowd.

"Going to let you in on a secret, friend. At the library, you can use a computer for free."

\*

Lindsay, his reintroduction supervisor, is waiting for him at the house when he gets off work the next afternoon. She's wearing the same outfit as before, a scarlet tie, a navy suit. She's sitting on the hood of her car next to a box of donuts.

"Time to check in," Lindsay says through a bite of cruller.

Biscuit stands on the couch, peering out of the house, paws propped against the window.

"Have a seat," Lindsay says brightly.

Wash takes a fritter.

"How are you getting along with your family, Washington?"

Wash thinks.

"Fine," Wash says.

Lindsay leans in with a conspiratorial look. "Oh, come on, give me the gossip."

Wash chews, swallows, and frowns.

"Why'd you have to give me life? You couldn't just give me twenty years or something? Why'd you have to take everything?" Wash says.

"The length of your sentence was determined by the judge."

"Just doesn't seem fair."

Lindsay nods, smiling sympathetically, and then abruptly stops.

"Well, what you did was pretty bad, Washington."

"But my whole life?"

"Do you know anything about the history of prisons in this country?" Lindsay reaches for a napkin, licks some glaze from her fingers, and wipes her hands. "Prisons here were originally intended to be a house of corrections. The theory was that when put into isolation criminals might be taught how to be functional citizens. In practice, however, the system proved to be ineffective at reforming offenders. The rate of recidivism was staggering. Honestly, upon release, most felons were arrested on new charges within the year. And over time the conditions in the prisons became awful. I mean, imagine what your situation would have been, being sentenced to life. You would have spent the next half a century locked in a cage like an animal, sleeping on an uncomfortable cot, wearing an ill-fitting jumpsuit, making license plates all day for far less than minimum wage, cleaning yourself with commercial soaps whose lists of ingredients included a variety of carcinogens, eating mashed potatoes made from a powder and meatloaf barely fit for human consumption, getting raped occasionally by other prisoners. Instead, you get to be here, with your family. Pretty cool, right? Like, super cool? You have to admit. And the wipe isn't simply a punishment. Yes, the possibility of getting wiped is meant to deter people from committing crimes. Totally. But wipes are also highly effective at preventing criminals from becoming repeat offenders. Although there is some biological basis for things like rage and greed and so forth, those types of issues tend to be the psychological byproducts of memories. And a life sentence is especially effective. Given a clean slate, felons often are much calmer, are much happier than before, are burdened with no misconceptions that crimes like embezzlement or poaching might be somehow justified, and of course possess no grudges against institutions like the government or law enforcement or former employers." Lindsay glances over, then turns back toward the road. "For example."

"So I'm supposed to feel grateful?"

Wash didn't mean to speak with that much force.

"Do you even know how much a wipe like yours costs?" Lindsay says, her eyes growing wide. "A fortune. Honestly, most people around here would need a payment plan for a simple vanity wipe. You know, you do something embarrassing at a party, you overhear somebody saying something mean about you that rings a bit too true, so you just have the memory erased. And then there are survivors of truly traumatic incidents, who often have to save up for years after the incident if insurance won't cover the cost of having it wiped. And alcoholics and crackheads and the like have no choice but to shell out, as a selective memory wipe is the only possible cure for addiction. Veterans with post-traumatic stress disorder are generally treated with wipes as well, although those wipes, as was the case with yours, are covered by taxpayers." Lindsay leans back on the hood of the car, propped up on her elbows, and squints into the sun. "It's a better deal for taxpayers anyway. Wiping your memory may have been costly, but was still nowhere near as expensive as paying to feed and shelter you for half a century would have been. That's the problem with prisons. They're overpriced, they underperform."

Wash scowls at the driveway.

"How are you feeling, Washington?"

"Frustrated."

"Tell me more."

"I don't even know what I did to get wiped."

Lindsay smiles. "The less you know about who you were before, the greater your chances of making a successful transition to your new life." Beneath her cheery tone there's a hint of uncertainty. "I would particularly recommend in your case that you avoid asking people about the details of your arrest."

*

Wash has to drive by the local library, a squat brick building with a flag hanging from a pole, whenever he drops off the kids at practice, and he tries to avoid wondering whether whatever he did to get arrested made the news. He notices that other parents stick around during practice, so occasionally he stays, watching Sophie stretching out at the track between intervals, knee braces on, or Jaden dribbling balls through a course of cones, shin guards crooked. Wash likes his kids. He doesn't mind being their parent, but he wants to be their friend, too. To be trusted. To be liked. The desire is so powerful that sometimes the thick fingers of his hands curl tight around the links of the fence out of a sense of longing as he watches the kids practice.

Becoming friends with the dog was simple. Biscuit sniffed him and licked him and that was that. He's the same person he's always been as far as the dog is concerned. The kids are distant, though. He doesn't know how to jump-start the relationships.

On other days he drives home during practice. The wallpaper in the kitchen is dingy, there are gouges in the walls of the hallway, the ceiling fan in the living room is broken, there are cracks in the light fixture in the laundry room, but not until the constant drip from the sink in the bathroom has turned to a steady leak does he actually stop, think, and realize that the house must be in such shabby condition because of how long he was gone, in detention during the trial, when his wife would have been living on a single income. That faucet is leaking because of him.

He knows how to fix a leak. Leaving the light in the bathroom on, he fetches the toolbox from the basement. He's emptying the cupboard under the sink, stacking toiletries on the linoleum, preparing to shut off the water, when his wife passes the doorway.

"What exactly are you doing?" Mia says.

"I'm gonna fix some stuff," Wash says.

She stares at him.

"Oh," she says finally, and then carries on down the hallway, followed by the dog.

By the time the corn in the field across the road has been harvested and the trees in the woods beyond the field are nearly bare, he's got the gutters hanging straight and the shingles patched up again. He takes a day off from the diner to tear out the stained carpeting in the hallway, wearing a dust mask over his face with the cuffs of his flannel rolled. Afterward he's rummaging around the shelf under the workbench in the basement, looking for a pry bar to rip up the staples in the floor, when he notices a quiver of arrows.

Wash tugs the mask down to his neck and touches the arrows. Carbon shafts. Turkey fletching. He glances over at the safe.

Did he have a bow once?

Was the bow sold with the guns?

Turning back to the shelf under the workbench he sees that there's an unmarked case clasped shut next to the quiver.

Wash pops the lid.

Though he doesn't recognize the bow itself, he recognizes that it's a bow, even in pieces. A takedown. A recurve. And before he even has a chance to wonder whether he knows how to assemble a bow, he's got the case up on the workbench and he's putting the bow together, moving on impulse. Bolts the limbs to the riser, strings the bow, and then heads up the stairs with the quiver. Drags a roll of carpet out the back door and props the carpet against a fence post to use as a target. Backs up toward the house. Tosses the quiver into the grass. Nocks an arrow. Raises the bow. Draws the string back toward the center of his chin until the string is pressing into the tip of his nose. Holds. Breathes.

Leaves are falling.

He lets go.

The arrow hits the carpet with a thump.

The sense of release that washes over him is incredible.

Wash is already exhausted from tearing the carpet out of the hallway, but he stands out in the backyard firing arrow after arrow until the muscles in his arms are burning and his flannel is damp with sweat, and arrow after arrow buries deep into the carpet. Fixing leaks, hanging gutters, patching shingles, he can do stuff like that, but the work is a struggle, a long and frustrating series of bent nails and fumbled wrenches. But this is different. Something he's good at. He can't remember ever feeling like this before. The pride, the satisfaction, of having and using a talent. Biscuit watches from the door, panting happily, tail wagging, as if sensing his euphoria.

Wash is scrubbing dishes after supper that night while Mia clips coupons from a brochure at the table.

"I want to go hunting," Wash announces.

"With the bow?" Mia says.

Wash thinks.

"Do you hunt?" Wash says.

"No," Mia snorts.

She sets down the scissors, folds her arms on the table, and furrows her eyebrows together, looking up at him with an inscrutable expression.

"Why don't you ask your children?" Mia says.

Jaden and Sophie are in the living room.

Jaden responds to the invitation by jumping on the ottoman, pretending to fire arrows at the lamp.

Even Sophie, busy working on a poster for a fundraiser to save stray cats from getting euthanized, wants to come along.

"You're okay with killing animals?"

"I only care about cute animals."

"Deer aren't cute?"

"Deer are snobs."

Last weekend of bow season. Hiking off-trail on public land. The dawn is cloudy. Frost crusts the mud. Wash leads the way through a stretch of cedars, touching the rubs in the bark of the trunks, explaining to the kids about glands without knowing where he learned that's why deer make the rubs. Finds a clearing. Sets up behind a fallen log at the edge of the trees, Jaden to this side with a thermos of cocoa, Sophie to that side with a thermos of coffee, whispering insults back and forth to each other. Waits. Snow begins falling. The breeze dies. The kids go quiet as a deer slips into the clearing. A buck with a crown of antlers. A fourteen-pointer. The trophy of a lifetime. The arrow hits the buck so hard that the buck gets knocked to the ground, but just as fast it staggers back up, and then it bounds off into the woods, vanishing. With Jaden and Sophie close behind, he hurries over to where the deer fell. Blood on the snow. Tracks in the mud. Wash and the kids follow the trail through the pines, past a ditch full of brambles, down a slope thick with birches, until the trail disappears just shy of a creek. By then the sun has broken through the clouds. And no matter where he searches from there, the buck can't be found.

He's just about given up looking when he notices some trampled underbrush.

Beyond, on a bed of ferns, the buck lies dead.

Jaden and Sophie dance around the kill, doing fist-pumps and cheering, and that feeling before, shooting arrows into the carpet in the backyard, is nothing compared to the feeling now.

\*

Driveway.

Weekend.

Icicles hanging from the flag on the mailbox.

Jaden, in pajamas, boots, and a parka, is sucking on a lozenge, occasionally pushing the lozenge out with his tongue, just far enough for the lozenge to peek through his lips, then slurping the lozenge back into his mouth, while helping him shovel snow.

Wash chips at some ice.

Jaden starts to wheeze.

Wash glances over.

"What's wrong?" Wash says.

Jaden shakes his head, reaches for his throat, and falls to his knees.

Both shovels hit the ground. Wash grabs him by the shoulders and thumps his back. Jaden still can't breathe. Wash spins him and forces his mouth open in a panic. Sticks a finger in. Feels teeth, a tongue, saliva, an uvula. Finds the lozenge. Claws the lozenge. Scoops the lozenge out with a flick.

The lozenge lands in the snow.

Jaden coughs, sways, blinks some, then looks at the lozenge.

"That was awesome," Jaden grins.

\*

Backyard.

Weekend.

Buds sprouting on the stems of the tree beyond the fence, where a crow is perched on a branch, not cawing, not preening, silent and still.

Sophie, in leggings, slippers, and a hoodie, is helping him to clean rugs.

Wash holds a rug up over the grass.

Sophie beats the rug with a broom.

Dust flies into the air. Coils of hair. Clumps of soil. Eventually nothing. Sophie drapes the rug over the fence, being careful to make sure that the tassels aren't touching the ground, as he reaches for the next rug. Just then the crow falls out of the tree.

The crow hits the ground with a thud.

Wash looks at the crow in shock.

The crow lies there. Doesn't move. Twitches. Struggles up again. Hops around. Then flaps back into the tree.

"Was it asleep?" Wash squints.

Sophie stares at the crow, and then bursts out laughing.

"Nobody's gonna believe us," Sophie says.

\*

Ballpark.

Minor league.

Chaperones on a field trip for the school.

His wife comes back from a vendor with some concessions.

She hands him a frankfurter.

Wash inspects the toppings with suspicion. Rancid sauerkraut. Gummy mustard. What might be cheese.

The meat looks greasy.

"You used to love those," Mia frowns.

She trades him a pretzel.

"Guess that was the nostalgia you were tasting," Mia says.

\*

Basement.

Jaden is hunched in the safe.

Sophie is crouched under the workbench.

Biscuit is leashed to a pipe on the boiler.

Tornado sirens howl in the distance.

"This is taking forever," Sophie says.

"I want to play a game," Jaden whines.

"We should have brought down some cards," Sophie says.

"There's nothing worse than just sitting," Jaden grumbles.

Wash presses his hands into the floor to stand.

"Don't you dare," Mia says.

Wash freezes.

"I'll be fast," Wash says.

And then, after glancing back at his wife at the foot of the stairs, goes up.

Noon, but with the lights off the house is dim, like today dusk came early. Wash hurries down the hallway toward the living room. There's a pressure in the air. In the living room he pinches his jeans to tug the legs up, then crouches over the basket of games, digging for a deck of cards.

Rising back up, tucking the cards into the pocket of his flannel, he glances over toward the doorway.

He can see the door lying in the yard next to a can of paint, where he had been painting the door when the sirens had begun to wail. The windows in the door reflect the clouds above. Through the glass is flattened grass.

The screen door, still attached to the doorframe, is rattling.

Wash crosses the living room.

He stands at the door.

He touches the screen.

Sky a mix of gold and green.

Leaves tearing across the yard in a rush of wind.

He can feel his heart beat.

The screen door opens with a creak.

Wash steps out onto the porch. His jeans snap against his legs. His flannel whips against his chest. Beyond the corn across the road, past the woods beyond the field, a tornado twists in the sky.

\*

The anniversary will be their twentieth, but their first he can remember. Having to plan some type of date makes him nervous. He would just take his wife out to eat somewhere fancy, which he knows is the standard move, but aside from the diner the other restaurants in town are all chains: a burger joint, a burrito joint, a pizza place that doesn't even have tables or chairs. Besides, he feels like this anniversary should be special, something memorable, above and beyond a candlelight dinner. Wash agonizes for weeks, at a loss what to do, worrying that he won't think of anything in time, and then while leaving work after an especially brutal shift the week before the anniversary, he notices a brochure tacked to the corkboard by the door. Wash reaches up, fingers pruny from washing dishes, and plucks the brochure down from the corkboard. The brochure advertises cabin rentals in the state park at El Dorado Reservoir.

His wife looks shocked when he tells her what the plan is, but moments later she's jotting down a list of supplies to buy and gear to pack, which seems like a form of approval.

Sophie gets left in charge of watching Jaden, with cash for emergencies and a fridge full of food, and he and his wife clear out of town. Mia paints her nails teal over the course of the drive, her frizzy hair trembling in the breeze through the windows. Wash stresses, convinced that the cabin won't be as nice as the pictures in the brochure, afraid that his wife might secretly consider the plan too outdoorsy, but the cabin turns out to be just as perfect as promised, and his wife is beaming before the duffels have even hit the floor. He's never seen her like this. At home, she never drinks alcohol, she never plays music, she's stern and practical and tireless, emptying hampers and folding laundry and cleaning the fridge and washing the dog and checking the kids did their homework and helping the kids with their homework and scheduling appointments and reading mail and paying bills and organizing the junk drawer and lugging bags of garbage out to the bin without ever stopping to rest, as if the home, not just the house but the family and the lives contained within, would completely fall apart if she allowed herself to relax for even a moment. But at the cabin she's different, already loosening up, sipping from a can of beer, cranking up the country on the radio, dancing in place at the stove as she cooks up a feast of steak and mushrooms and roasted potatoes crusted with rosemary, giving him a glimpse of who she might have been when he met her twenty years ago, a twenty-year-old girl with a sense of humor and a lopsided smile and few if any responsibilities. He's liked his wife for as long as he can remember, but watching her dance around at the stove makes him feel something new, something powerful, tender, warm. He can tell that the feeling is strong, but even though he knows how strong the feeling is, and though he can't imagine how a feeling could possibly be any stronger, he's not sure whether or not there's still another feeling that's even stronger out there. He can't remember being in love. Has no spectrum to place the feeling on. Doesn't know what the limit for emotions is. Does he like her, or really like her, or really really like her, or really really really like her?

After the meal he leans back with his bare feet flat on the floor and his hands folded together on his gut, stuffed with starch and butter and meat and grease, buzzed from the beer. His wife usually doesn't involve him in parenting decisions, just signs the consent forms and checks the movie ratings herself. But for once she's actually consulting him about the kids, leaning across the table with her chin on the placemat, toying absentmindedly with the tab on a can.

"There are these acne pills Sophie keeps asking to try."

"She gets like a single pimple at a time."

"Should we let her or not?"

"For one zit?"

"So no."

Then:

"Do you think Jaden is getting picked on?"

"What makes you say that?"

"He keeps coming home with ripped clothes."

"He's just wild."

"You're sure?"

Wash feels a flush of pride. He likes when his wife asks his opinion. Maybe it's only because of the anniversary weekend, but he hopes it signals a permanent change.

"I got us something," Mia says suddenly, pushing up off of the table to stand, looking almost giddy. She goes out to the car, pops the trunk, digs under a tarp, and comes back lugging an unmarked cardboard box topped with a silver bow. The present is nearly as long as the table.

Wash takes ahold of the flap and rips through the tape.

Lifts the lid.

A rifle.

"Whoa," Wash says.

The gun lies on a pad of foam. Carbon barrel. Walnut stock. A repeater. A bolt-action. He reaches into the box, but then hesitates, looking to her for permission.

"Take it out," Mia laughs.

The moment he picks up the rifle a sense of relief washes over him. Like having a severed limb suddenly reattached. A natural extension of his body. Automatically he pulls the bolt back to check whether the chamber is empty, then shuts the breech and raises the gun, butt to his shoulder, stock on his cheek, his eye at the scope, testing the sights. The smell of the oil. The feel of the trigger. He can already tell that he's skilled with this thing.

"Are we allowed to have this?" Wash says.

"You're not, but technically I'm the owner, I did all the research, and as long as you don't have access, we're in the clear, so we'll just keep the gun in the safe and if anybody ever asks then we'll say that you don't know the combo. And honestly, on my honor, I did want to have a gun in the house again just in case of intruders. A pistol or a shotgun probably would have been better for that, though. I went with this because of you. You can use it for target shooting out back, even use it for deer hunting if you want. I thought it all through. We'll just be careful. Nobody's going to know."

His chair creaks as she settles onto his lap.

He's overwhelmed.

"I love you," Wash says, without meaning to, the words just coming out.

He sets the rifle onto the table to kiss her, but an expression of alarm flashes across her face, and before he can lean closer she drops her head, with her chin to her sternum. Confused, he waits for her to look back up. Her hands rest on his shoulders. Her ass weighs on his thighs. She's trembling suddenly. No, he realizes, she's crying.

He can't remember ever seeing her cry before.

The sight scares him.

"What's wrong?" Wash frowns.

When she finally responds she speaks in a murmur.

"You're hardly you at all anymore."

"What does that mean?"

"You're just so different."

"Different how?"

Mia goes silent for a moment.

"You never did dishes before."

"Well, it wasn't my job back then, right?" Wash says.

"I mean at home," Mia explodes, shoving him in frustration, startling him.

"But after the meatloaf, you told me that's how things worked, was you doing the cooking and me doing the dishes," Wash says.

"I was kidding, I didn't think you'd actually do them, but then you got up from the table after we finished eating and you just started washing dishes, you'd never washed a dish in that house before in your life, you never used to play games with the kids, you never used to bring the kids along hunting, I always had to nag you to fix things around the house and even after you were done fixing things then you'd get on me for nagging you, I could barely get you to give the kids a ride somewhere without you throwing a fit, all you wanted to do was work and hunt and be alone in the woods, or rant at me about political stuff that there was nothing I could do anything about, we don't even fight anymore, I tried to pretend that you're the same but you're not, you're the same body, you move the same, you smell the same, you talk the same, you taste the same, but the rest of you is gone, you don't remember the tomato juice when I was pregnant with Jaden, you don't remember the fire alarm after I gave birth to Sophie, everything that used to have a secret meaning between us now is just a thing, to you a hay bale is just a hay bale, a batting helmet is just a batting helmet, a mosquito bite is just a mosquito bite, and that's not what they are to me," Mia cries, hitting his chest with her fists, "we lost our past, we lost our history," hitting his chest with her fists, "and you deserved it," a fist, "I didn't," a fist, "not me."

Wash sits there in terror, letting her beat on him, until finally she clutches his tee in her hands and sinks her head into his chest in exhaustion. His skin tingles with pain where the blows landed. His heart pounds from the shock of being struck. Wash glances at the blotchy sunspots on his hands, the faint scars on his fingers, the bone spurs on his heels, the brittle calluses on his soles, relics of years he can't remember living. He's never felt so much like a stranger in this body.

He's almost too shaken to speak.

"Which one do you want?" Wash says.

"Which what?"

"Which me?"

Mia heaves a sigh, then lifts her head, turns her face away, and rises off of him. She shuffles toward the bathroom. "I never would've gotten a gun again if you were the way you used to be."

Midnight. He lies next to his wife in the dark. The sheets are thinner than at home. The pillows are harder than at home. He can't remember ever having spent a night away from home before. He's gotten so used to falling asleep with her nuzzled against him that trying to fall asleep with her facing away from him is intensely lonely. His feet are cold. An owl hoots down by the reservoir.

Does he love his wife?

Did he ever love his wife before?

\*

Lindsay is sitting on the chair in the living room. She's wearing the same outfit as every month. She tucks her hair behind her ears, then bends to grab a toy from the floor, a plastic bone that squeaks when squeezed.

"This is the last time we'll have to meet," Lindsay says.

"We're done?"

Lindsay looks up with a smile.

"Next month will mark a full year since your wipe. By the standards of our justice department, you've been officially reintroduced to your life. Congratulations."

Lindsay tosses the toy down the hallway.

Biscuit takes off running.

Wash thinks.

"There's something I don't understand."

"What's that?"

"What happens if you commit another crime after you've had a wipe like mine? What else could they even do to me if they've already taken everything?"

"They took the memories you had back then. You have new memories they could take."

Wash frowns.

"If you're being sentenced to a partial wipe, a shorter sentence is better than a longer sentence, of course. But for a life sentence, the numbers are meaningless. Is it worse when a sixty-year-old dies than when a six-year-old dies? Of course not. The length of a life has nothing to do with the weight of the loss."

Wash settles back into the couch, folding his arms across his chest, tucking his hands into his pits.

"That's important for you to understand," Lindsay says.

Wash glances over.

"You have another life you could lose now," Lindsay says.

Biscuit drops the bone back onto the floor.

Lindsay reaches down.

"How do you feel, Washington?"

"I feel really good," Wash says.

\*

Mia calls him into the bathroom. She's sitting on the lid of the toilet in drawstring sweatpants and a baggy undershirt. The pregnancy test is lying on the side of the tub.

"We're both going to remember this one," Mia says, smiling up at him.

His kids barge into the bathroom a moment later, already fighting about what to name the baby.

Wash goes shopping for a crib with his family, pushing a cart down the bright aisles of a department store as swing music plays over the speakers.

Wash reclines on a checkered blanket at the park as fireworks burst in the sky above his family, shimmering and fading. Wash hunches over the wastebasket in the bedroom, clipping the nails on his fingers as his wife pops the battery from a watch on the dresser. Wash leans over the sink in the bathroom, tweezing a hair from his nose as his wife gathers dirty towels from the hook on the door. Wash shoots holes into a target shaped like the silhouette of a person as his kids watch from the stump of an oak tree, sipping cans of soda. And wherever he's at, and whatever he's doing, there's something that's stuck in his mind like a jingle, nagging him.

He sits on the porch with the dog. Rain drips from the awning. Silks are showing on the husks of corn across the road. Summer is already almost gone. Behind him, through the screens in the windows, sounds of his family talking drift out of the house.

Sometimes he does want to be alone. Sometimes he feels so lazy that he wants to refuse to help with chores. Sometimes he gets so tense that he has an urge to punch a wall.

But maybe all of that is trivial compared to how he used to be.

Is he a different person now?

Has he been becoming somebody new?

Or does he have some soul, an inborn nature, a congenital personality, that's bound to express itself eventually?

The academic year hasn't started yet, but the athletic seasons have begun. He's on the way to pick up the kids from practice when he passes the library. His eyes flick from the road to the rearview, watching the library fade into the distance as the truck rushes on toward the school.

Knowing who he was might not even be an option. What he did might never even have made the news. And he's already running late anyway. But still his hands clench tight around the wheel.

Swearing, he hangs a u-ey, swinging the truck back around.

He parks at the library.

"I need to use a computer," Wash says.

The librarian asks him for identification, registers him for an account, and then brings him over to a computer. All that time he's thinking, what are you doing, what are you doing, what are you doing, imagining his kids waiting for him by the fence at the school. The librarian heads back to the reference desk.

His hands are trembling as he reaches for the keyboard.

He logs onto the computer, pulls up a browser, and searches his name.

The screen blinks as the results appear.

Nothing. A pop star with his name. A goalie. A beach resort with his name. A monument. He's not there.

He skims through again to be sure, and then laughs out loud in relief.

The temptation was a mirage all along.

Wash swivels on the chair to stand, then thinks of something, and hesitates.

He turns back around.

Puts his fingers on the keyboard.

Tries his name plus his town.

The screen blinks as the results change.

His heart leaps.

He's there.

The list of articles seems to scroll on forever.

The headlines alone are enough to send a beat of rage pulsing through him.

Wash runs his hands over his mouth, glancing at the daylight streaming into the library through the door beyond the computer, trying to decide whether to leave now or to keep reading, flashing through all of the memories he has from the past year that he could lose. Jaden grinning in amazement after choking on the lozenge in the driveway. Sophie cracking up laughing after the crow fell out of the tree. Mia treading water at the reservoir in a white one-piece, glancing at him with a casual expression before suddenly lunging over to dunk him. Jaden lying on the linoleum in the kitchen in cutoff shorts, gripping him by the ankle, begging to be taken to the go-kart track. Jaden whirling around the yard with a lit sparkler. Mia swinging by the diner on a day off from the hospital, hair piled into a bun, trench coat damp with rain, splitting a slice of cherry pie with him while he's on break. Sophie standing under the light in the kitchen in pajamas, holding him by the arm, upset by a dream about a ghost. Sophie singing into a lit sparkler like a microphone. Mia arranging gourds on the porch. Mia brushing icicles from the awning. Mia sweating into a damp washcloth, deliriously rambling about how much she loves him, as he crouches by the bed with the wastebasket, waiting there in case she pukes again. The dog watching a butterfly flutter down the hallway, then turning to look at him, as if waiting for an explanation. His kids dancing around the dead buck, boots tromping through snowy ferns, gloved hands raised in celebration, lit by the dazzling sunbeams spiking through the branches of the trees, and afterward driving back to the house with the deer in the bed of the truck, the mighty antlers rising into the air out the window behind the cab, the kids chattering to each other on the seat next to him, hats both off, hair all disheveled, and later eating bowls of cereal in the kitchen in thermal underwear together as the kids recount the story of the hunt with wild gestures, while his wife sits across the table in a plaid nightgown, smiling over a mug of black tea. The secret experiences that nobody else shared. The joy of discovering the chocolate stash hidden in the aluminum tin in the basement. The habit he's made of visiting the glittering display of chandeliers and pendants and lamps and sconces whenever he goes to the hardware store, marveling at the rich glow of the mingled lights, filtered through the tinted glass and the colored shades. The sense of destiny when a bottle of cola suddenly plunked into the dispenser of a vending machine at the shopping mall as he was walking out of the bathroom. The fear and the awe and the wonder of seeing a monstrous tornado churn in the sky above the town, the funnel spiraling down from the clouds, the tip just about to touch the ground.

Wash sits back in the chair, looking from the door to the computer, biting his lip as he wavers, torn between the possibility of having a future and the possibility of having a past. But only for a moment. Because when he thinks about it, he knows who he is. He already knows what he'll do.

# Comment on 'Life Sentence'

A man commits a serious crime and is sentenced to having all of his episodic memories wiped, from birth until the present day. Our question is simple: Is the being on whom this procedure is performed the same being who emerges afterwards? I'm also interested in the follow-up question: What adjustments to the procedure would be required to get us to change our answer?

Of course post-operative Wash is qualitatively different in lots of ways from pre-operative Wash. For one, post-operative Wash seems to be considerably more agreeable. Major personality changes such as this are often remarked on by saying that they are 'not the same person'. Just so, in Matthew Baker's story, Wash's wife Mia says, 'I tried to pretend that you're the same but you're not, you're the same body, you move the same, you smell the same, you talk the same, you taste the same, but the rest of you is gone.' How literally should we take what Mia says here? When we focus on numerical identity, we commonly allow that a single being can survive quite major changes, such as the loss of a limb or the gain of new religious beliefs. We do not go out of existence when such changes occur, even if the change is sudden. Still, some changes may be radical enough to force us to say that yes, the old being has gone out of existence and has been replaced by a new being. The radical loss of memories may be one such change.

The view that we are identified by our memories is a very popular one in philosophy. One of its earliest defenders was John Locke, as mentioned in the previous chapter. Locke was particularly impressed by the phenomenon of self-consciousness. He believed that this was the most essential feature of a person – to be able to think of yourself as yourself. This is what makes us autonomous, morally responsible beings. Locke moreover thought that some kind of minimal self-consciousness accompanies every experience that we have. For example, right now as I write these words, I am conscious that I am writing. I was similarly self-conscious this morning while I was eating my toast, and many years ago, I was self-conscious when I cried on my first day of school and the teacher sat me on her desk. All of these experiences happened to a person. Memory then allows me to join together these three separate acts of self-consciousness into the thought that I, Tom Cochrane, had all of these experiences. This, in Locke's view, is what makes it true that I am one continuous person who is responsible for all of these different acts, in addition to any other act that I am capable of remembering. Memory enables self-consciousness over time, and thereby the identity of persons over time.

According to Locke then, you are not your body. You are a person. And a person is special kind of psychological process. It might take a body to support the existence of a person, but no particular body is necessary for this. A person such as yourself could, in principle, be swapped into a different body if you could remember experiences had by the earlier body (a scenario we'll explore later in this book). Locke even thinks that a single person could be instantiated by different immaterial 'thinking substances', again so long as one remembers the experiences of the other. In this way, Locke's account could, if we wished, fit with a temporal parts account like David Lewis', where although the stuff doing the remembering can be entirely different from one time to another, the successive acts of remembering form a single continuous being.

Locke's account raises many interesting issues. But right off the bat, one that sticks out is the implication that if I cannot remember some past action that, let's say *this body* undertook, then I am not the person who performed that action, and I cannot be held accountable for it. For example, if this body smashes a shop window while blackout drunk and I fail to retain any memory of doing so (beyond the possibility of recall), then I literally did not do it. The law might take a different view on the matter, but Locke sticks to his guns on this. Equally then, if Wash cannot remember committing the crime for which the person previously known as Washington was convicted, Locke would agree that he is literally not that person. This is why it is fair to allow Wash to go free and live a reasonably pleasant life. The person who committed that crime has effectively been executed. His body is allowed to go free, but this is an admirably precise act of justice, since bodies don't commit crimes, people do.

Yet what is so interesting about Baker's story is that there are all sorts of ways in which Wash maintains continuities with the earlier person, some of which are quite subtle. It is worth considering if any of these continuities implies that the earlier being might not have been destroyed after all. Most notably, only Wash's episodic memory (his recall of first-person experiences) has been wiped, and not his semantic memories (memories of facts) or his procedural memories (learned behaviours). Wash would be reduced to an overgrown infant without these other sorts of memories, which would rather undermine the emotional aims of the story. But does the retention of these memories undermine the thought experiment?

One issue here is whether we can cleanly distinguish these different sorts of memory. Take, for instance, one's knowledge of historical facts such as what happened in New York on September 11, 2001. Such knowledge may well be mixed up with one's episodic memory of witnessing those events. Or consider a skill such as knowing how to make a meatloaf. At least initially, one's awareness of its steps may involve episodically remembering mistakes that one now tries to avoid. I suppose for this thought experiment we'll just have to eliminate vague cases like these, and only retain information that is put into an abstract form, stripped of its experiential first-person details.

Still, some of the procedural and semantic memories that Wash retains express the *character* of the earlier person. Note that we do not all acquire the same set of facts and skills, but a subset that reflects our various opportunities and interests. In Wash's case, this is most vividly illustrated by his knowledge of how to shoot a bow and a gun. Does the fact that post-operative Wash retains this relatively rare skill and interest indicate that he is in fact the same person as pre-operative Wash? Initially we may say no, because it is entirely possible for two distinct people to share such an interest. However, when we look a little deeper into the example, it becomes less clear what we should say.

When two distinct people happen to share a skill, one individual's skill is independent of the other individual's skill. That is, one of them could lose the skill while the other retains it. In contrast, post-operative Wash has his skill because pre-operative Wash acquired it and maintained it. If pre-operative Wash had ever lost the skill, then automatically, post-operative Wash would not possess it either. Even more interestingly, Wash's skill is not a matter of mere information. Wash's body has various characteristics – a certain pattern of muscle development, the calluses on his hands, the organization of his cerebellum – that reflect the life history of the pre-operative person. The things that pre-operative Wash cared about enough to practice day after day are written into post-operative Wash's body. This is a deep continuity. At the very least, it marks a unique connection between pre-operative Wash and post-operative Wash.

It's worth noting here that one of the reasons why philosophers like to appeal to memories as the basis of personal identity is that memories track the things that really matter to us. Memories mark us out as unique individuals who on the basis of our unique experiences have formed various values and concerns. For instance, we sympathize with Wash's wife Mia when she complains how Wash's memory wipe has undermined their shared history. Romantic love is not merely about one's current feelings of attraction towards another person. It includes the sense of accumulating experiences together, which underpins mutual attachment and trust. For the same reason, post-operative Wash fears losing the new memories he has accumulated with his kids. The loss of memories entails the loss of love. We will explore this issue a bit more in the later chapter on self-narratives. But for now, it occurs to me that if the preservation of personal values is why the continuity of memories is so important, then the same consideration should apply to the preservation of bodily skills. Skills are a bodily form of memory that equally encode what matters to a person.

As a result, I'm inclined to think that post-operative Wash's preserved skills are enough to identify him as the same person as pre-operative Wash. Locke might object that when we recall a skill, we don't recall a self-conscious experience. I'm not very convinced that every single experience we have is self-conscious. But supposing they are, the exercise of our skills in the past presumably involved some self-conscious experience. Wash wasn't sleepwalking while he learned to shoot. What's missing in Wash's case is the ability to recall a self-conscious experience of exercising his skill. Yet when we remember a past experience, we don't remember the self-consciousness of that experience so much as what happened at the time. For example, when I remember eating toast this morning, I don't remember thinking to myself, 'I am eating toast now,' I just remember eating toast. By the same criteria, one's recall of a skill should only need to focus on the task and not the self-consciousness of the task. So, even following Locke's account, post-operative Wash's self-consciousness should be sufficient to join up his present possession of the skill with pre-operative Wash's possession of the skill. It does not matter that his memory of the skill fails to pick out a specific event. What matters is that the skill encodes something that he engaged in as a responsible, autonomous person, something that mattered to him, and still does.

If this argument works, I'm inclined to say that post-operative Wash's pattern of semantic memories also makes him the same person as pre-operative Wash. The particular facts that he knows (e.g. his diploma) were equally gained via self-conscious experience, equally reflect his autonomous values, and are equally physically dependent on the structure of pre-operative Wash's brain (specifically his cortex).

Another very important issue for Locke's account was raised by the philosopher Thomas Reid. On Locke's account, if I can remember little Tom's first day of school, then I am numerically identical with little Tom. But my memory is restricted to this dramatic event and I am completely unable to remember what happened the day before my first day of school. This seems to entail then that I am not the person who existed on that day, despite the fact that this person resembled little Tom in many ways. This then raises a serious conundrum. On his first day of school, little Tom most likely remembered what happened the previous day. Therefore by Locke's criterion, little Tom is the same person as little Tom minus one day (let's call him 'littler Tom'). But now we have a potential paradox. I am the same person as little Tom. Little Tom is the same person as littler Tom, but I am not the same person as littler Tom. This violates a logical feature of identity known as 'transitivity'. That is, if A is equal to B, and B is equal to C, then A must be equal to C as well. For instance, if David Robert Jones is David Bowie, and David Bowie is Ziggy Stardust, then David Robert Jones is also Ziggy Stardust. We're only talking about one thing here, no matter how many different names we give him! The same concept is familiar enough from mathematics. If $2 + 2 = 4$, and $3 + 1 = 4$, then $2 + 2 = 3 + 1$.

The way out of this paradox for Locke (and any other defender of the memory criterion) is to allow that a person is identical not just to any person they remember, but also to any person that can be remembered by the persons they remember. In effect, the memory criterion is not a simple relationship between now and all other times, but a chain of overlapping connections. What we are is a *continuity* of self-conscious experiences. I think if Locke had thought it through properly, he would have also embraced this more complex view. His idea was to compare the identity of persons with the identity of plants that persist through the gradual replacement of their parts. Just as life forms a chain of being, so does psychology.

For Baker's story, the implication of this view is that if by continuity of skill, we allow that post-operative Wash is the same person as the pre-operative Wash who learned to shoot (even though of course he lost many of his cherished qualities), then he is also the same person as Wash before he learned to shoot. The chain of psychological connections should encompass every single experience had by persons making use of Wash's body.

How far back exactly this chain of identity goes is a bit vague. The requirement of self-consciousness or autonomy may rule out very young infants, and in all probability rules out the pre-birth foetus. Such a view has potential implications for the issue of abortion that will come up again in the chapter on animalism. For now it seems that if the authorities in Wash's world really wanted to wipe out the person who committed Wash's crimes, then on the basis of the psychological continuity theory, they should have reduced him to the mental capacities of a newborn.

Yet my impression is that the authorities didn't really intend to execute pre-operative Wash. Most of their talk is about the effectiveness of the memory wipe in promoting rehabilitation. And rehabilitation – the sincere renunciation of past crimes and change in a person's moral character – is only possible if, fundamentally, one *is* the person who changes.

# 5

# *The Affirmation*

## Christopher Priest

## Chapter 3

I had imagined myself into existence. I wrote because of an inner need, and that need was to create a clearer vision of myself, and in writing I *became* what I wrote. It was not something I could understand. I felt it on an instinctive or emotional level.

It was a process that was exactly like the creation of my white room.

That had been first of all an idea, and later I made the idea real by painting the room as I imagined it. I discovered myself in the same way, but through the written word.

I began writing with no suspicion of the difficulties involved. I had the enthusiasm of a child given coloured pencils for the first time. I was undirected, uncontrolled and entirely lacking in self-consciousness. All these were to change later, but on that first evening I worked with innocent energy, letting an undisciplined flow of words spread across the paper. I was deeply, mysteriously excited by what I was doing, and frequently read back over what I had written, scribbling corrections on the pages and noting second thoughts in the margins. I felt a sense of vague discontent, but this I ignored: the overwhelming sensation was one of release and satisfaction. To write myself into existence!

I worked late, and when eventually I crawled into my sleeping-bag, I slept badly. The next morning I returned to the work, letting the decoration stay unfinished. Still my creative energy was undiminished, and page after page slipped through the carriage of the typewriter as if there was nothing that could ever obstruct the flow. As I finished with them I scattered the sheets on the floor around the table, imposing a temporary chaos on the order I was creating.

Inexplicably, I came to a sudden halt.

It was the fourth day, when I had upwards of sixty sheets of completed draft around me. I knew each page intimately, so impassioned was my need to write, so frequently had I re-read my work. What lay unwritten ahead had the same quality, the same need to be produced. I had no doubts as to what would follow, what would be unsaid. Yet I stopped halfway down a page, unable to continue.

It was as if I had exhausted my way of writing. I became acutely self-conscious and started to question what I had done, what I was going to do next. I glanced at a page at random, and all at once it seemed naïve, self-obsessed, trite and uninteresting. I noticed that the sentences were largely unpunctuated, that my spelling was erratic, that I used the same words over and over, and even the judgements and observations, on which I had so prided myself, seemed obvious and irrelevant.

Everything about my hasty typescript was unsatisfactory, and I was stricken by a sense of despair and inadequacy.

I temporarily abandoned my writing, and sought an outlet for my energies in the mundane tasks of domesticity. I completed painting one of the upstairs rooms, and moved my mattress and belongings in there. I decided that from this day my white room would he used solely for writing. A plumber arrived, hired by Edwin, and he started to fix the noisy pipes, and install an immersion heater. I took the interruption as a chance to rethink what I was doing, and to plan more carefully.

So far, everything I had written relied entirely on memory. Ideally, I should have talked to Felicity, to see what she remembered, perhaps to fill in some of the minor mysteries of childhood. But Felicity and I no longer had much in common; we had argued many times in recent years, most recently, and most bitterly, after our father's death. She would have little sympathy for what I was doing. Anyway, it was *my* story; I did not want it coloured by her interpretation of events.

Instead, I telephoned her one day and asked her to send me the family photograph albums. She had taken in most of my father's possessions, including these, but as far as I knew she had no use for them. Felicity was undoubtedly puzzled by my sudden interest in this material—after the funeral she had offered the albums to me, and I had said no—but she promised to mail them to me.

The plumber left, and I returned to the typewriter.

This time, after the pause, I approached the work with greater care and a desire to be more organized. I was learning to question my subject matter.

Memory is a flawed medium, and the memories of childhood are frequently distorted by influences that cannot be understood at the time. Children lack a world perspective; their horizons are narrow. Their interests are egocentric.

Much of what they experience is interpreted for them by parents. They are unselective in what they see. In addition, my first attempt had been not much more than a series of connected fragments. Now I sought to tell a story, and to tell it in such a way that there would be an overall shape, a scheme to the telling of it.

Almost at once I discovered the essence of what I wanted to write.

My subject matter was still inevitably myself: my life, my experiences, my hopes, my disappointments and my loves. Where I had gone wrong before, I reasoned, was in setting out this life chronologically. I had started with my earliest memories and attempted to grow on paper as I had grown in life. Now I saw I had to be more devious.

To deal with myself I had to treat myself with greater objectivity, to examine myself in the way the protagonist is examined in a novel. A described life is not the same as a real one. Living is not an art, but to write of life is. Life is a series of accidents and anti-climaxes, misremembered and misunderstood, with lessons only dimly learned.

Life is disorganized, lacks shape, lacks story.

Throughout childhood, mysteries occur in the world around you. They are mysteries only because they are not properly explained, or because of a lack of experience, but they remain in the memory simply because they are so intriguing. In adulthood, explanations often present themselves, but by then they are far too late: they lack the imaginative appeal of a mystery.

Which, though, is the more true: the memory or the fact?

In the third chapter of my second version I began to write of something that illustrated this perfectly. It concerned Uncle William, my father's older brother.

For most of my childhood I never saw William . . . or Billy, as my father called him. There had always been something of a cloud to his name: my mother clearly disapproved of him, yet to my father he was something of a hero. I remember that from quite early on my father would tell me stories of the scrapes he and Billy had been in as children. Billy was always getting into trouble, and had a genius for practical jokes. My father grew up to become a respectable and successful engineer, but Billy had entered into a number of disreputable enterprises, such as working on ships, selling second-hand cars and trading in government surplus goods. I saw nothing wrong with this at all, but for some reason it was considered dubious by my mother. One day, Uncle William turned up at our house, and at once my life was vested with excitement. Billy was tall and sunburnt, had a big curly moustache and drove an open-top car with an old fashioned horn. He spoke with a lazy, exciting drawl, and he picked me up and carried me around the garden upside-down and screeching. His big hands had dark calluses on them, and he smoked a dirty pipe. His eyes saw distance. Later, he took me for a breathtaking drive in his car, whizzing through country lanes at great speed, and honking his horn at a policeman on a bicycle. He bought me a toy machine gun, one which could fire wooden bullets right across the room, and showed me how to build a den in a tree.

Then he was gone, as suddenly as he arrived, and I was sent to bed. I lay in my room, listening to my parents arguing together. I could not hear what they were saying, but my father was shouting and a door slammed. Then my mother started crying.

I never saw Uncle William again, and neither of my parents mentioned him. Once or twice I asked about him, but the subject was changed with the sort of parental adroitness children can never overcome. About a year later my father told me that Billy was now working abroad ("somewhere in the East"), and that I was unlikely to see him again. There was something about the way my father said this that made me doubt him, but I was not a subtle child and infinitely preferred to believe what I was told. For a long time after that, Billy's adventures abroad were a familiar imaginative companion: with a little help from the comics I read, I saw him mountain-climbing and game-hunting and building railroads. It was all in keeping with what I knew of him.

When I grew up, and was thinking for myself, I knew that what I had been told was probably untrue, that Billy's disappearance was almost certainly explicable to the real world, but even so the glamorous image of him remained. It was only after my father died, and I was having to go through his papers, that I came across the truth. I found a letter from the Governor of Durham Prison, saying that Uncle William had been admitted to the hospital wing; a second letter, dated a few weeks later, reported that he had died. I made some inquiries through the Home Office, and discovered that William had been serving a twelve-year sentence for armed robbery. The crime for which he had been convicted was committed within a few days of that crazy, thrilling afternoon in summer.

Even as I wrote about him, though, there was still a powerful part of my imagination that had Uncle Billy away in some exotic place, grappling with man-eaters or skiing down mountain-sides.

Both versions of him were true, but in different qualities of truth. One was sordid, disagreeable and final. The other had imaginative plausibility, in my personal terms, and furthermore had the distinctly attractive bonus that it allowed for Billy to return one day.

To discuss matters like this in my writing I had to be at a stage removed from myself. There was a duplication of myself involved, perhaps even a triplication.

There was I who was writing. There was I whom I could remember. And there was I of whom I wrote, the protagonist of the story.

The difference between factual truth and imaginative truth was constantly on my mind.

Memory was still fundamental, and I had daily reminders of its fallibility. I learnt, for instance, that memory itself did not present a narrative. Important events were remembered in a sequence ordered by the subconscious, and it was a constant effort to reassemble them into my story.

I broke my arm when I was a small child, and there were photographs to remind me in the albums Felicity had sent. But was this accident before or after I started school, before or after the death of my maternal grandmother?

All three events had had a profound effect on me at the time, all three had been early lessons in the unfriendly, random nature of the world. As I wrote, I tried to recall the order in which they had occurred, but this was not possible; memory failed me. I was forced to reinvent the incidents, working them into a continuous but false order so that I could convey why they had influenced me.

Even aids to memory were unreliable, and my broken arm was a surprising example of this. It was my left arm that was fractured. This I know beyond doubt, as one does not misremember such things, and to this day I am slightly weaker in that arm than in the other. Such memory must he beyond question. And yet, the only objective record of the injury was in a short sequence of black-and-white photographs taken during a family holiday. There, in several pictures taken in sunlit countryside, was a mournful-looking infant whom I recognized as myself, his right arm carried in a white sling.

I came across these photographs at about the same time as I was writing about the incident, and the discovery came as something of a shock. For a few moments I was confused and confounded by the revelation, as it seemed to be, and I was forced to question every other assumption I had been making about memories. Of course, I soon realized what must have happened: the processor had apparently printed the entire spool of film from the wrong side of the negative. As soon as I examined the prints more closely—at first, all I had looked at was myself—I saw a number of background details which confirmed this: car registration numbers printed in reverse, traffic driving on the right, clothes buttoned the wrong way round, and so on.

It was all perfectly explicable, but it taught me two more things about myself: that I was becoming obsessed with checking and authenticating what hitherto I had taken for granted, and that I could rely on nothing from the past.

I came to a second pause in my work. Although I was satisfied with my new way of working, each new discovery was a setback. I was becoming aware of the deceptiveness of prose. Every sentence contained a lie.

I began a process of revision, going back through my completed pages and rewriting certain passages numerous times. Each successive version subtly improved on life. Every time I rewrote a *part* of the truth I came nearer to a whole truth.

When I was at last able to continue where I had left off, I soon came across a new difficulty.

As my story progressed from childhood to adolescence, then to young adulthood, other people entered the narrative. These were not family, but outsiders, people who came into my life and who, in some cases, were still a part of it. In particular, there was a group of friends I had known since university, and a number of women with whom I had had affairs. One of these, a girl named Alice, was someone I had been engaged to for several months. We had seriously intended to marry, but in the end it went wrong and we parted. Alice was now married to someone else, had two children, but was still a good and trusted friend. Then there was Gracia, whose effect on my life in recent years had been profound.

If I was to serve my obsessive need for truth then I had to deal with these relationships in some way. Every new friendship marked a moving on from the immediate past, and every lover had changed my outlook for better or worse in some way. Even though there was very little chance anyone mentioned in my manuscript would ever read it, I nevertheless felt inhibited by the fact that I still knew them.

Some of what I intended to say would he unpalatable, and I wanted to be free to describe my sexual experiences in detail, if not in intimate detail.

The simplest method would have been to change names, and fudge around the details of time and place in an attempt to make the people unrecognizable. But this was not the sort of truth I was seeking to tell. Nor could it be done by simply leaving them out; these experiences had been important to me. I discovered the solution at last by use of indirection. I invented new friends and lovers, giving them fictitious backgrounds and identities. One or two of them I brought forward from childhood, so to speak, implying that they had been lifelong friends, whereas in my real life I had lost contact with the other children I had grown up with. It made the narrative more of a piece, with a greater consistency in the story. Everything seemed to have coherence and significance.

Virtually nothing was wasted; every described event or character had some form of correlative elsewhere in the story.

So I worked, learning about myself as I went. Truth was being served at the expense of literal fact, but it was a higher, *better* form of truth.

As my manuscript proceeded I entered a state of mental excitation. I was sleeping only five or six hours a night, and when I woke up I always went directly to my desk to re-read what I had written the day before. I subordinated everything to the writing. I ate only when I absolutely had to, I slept only when I was exhausted. Everything else was neglected; Edwin and Marge's redecoration was postponed indefinitely.

Outside, the long summer was tirelessly hot. The garden was overgrown, but now the soil was parched and cracked, and the grass was yellow. Trees were dying, and the stream at the end of the garden dried up. On the few occasions I went into Weobley I overheard conversations about the weather. The heatwave had become a drought; livestock was being slaughtered, water was being rationed.

Day after day I sat in my white room, feeling the warm draught from the windows. I worked shirtless and unshaven, cool and comfortable in my squalor.

Then, quite unexpectedly, I came to the end of my story. It ceased abruptly, with no more events to describe.

I could hardly believe it. I had anticipated the experience of finishing as being a sudden release, a new awareness of myself, an end to a quest. But the narrative merely came to a halt, with no conclusions, no revelations.

I was disappointed and disturbed, feeling that all my work had been to no avail. I sifted through the pages, wondering where I had gone wrong.

Everything in the narrative proceeded towards a conclusion, but it ended where I had no more to say. I was in my life in Kilburn, before I split with

Gracia, before my father died, before I lost my job. I could take it no further, because there was only here, Edwin's house. Where was the end?

It occurred to me that the only ending that would be right would be a false one. In other words, because I had reassembled my memories to make a story, then the story's conclusion must also be imaginary.

But to do that I should first have to acknowledge that I really had become two people: myself, and the protagonist of the story.

At this point, conscience struck me about the neglect in the house. I was disillusioned by my writing, and by my inability to cope with it, and I took the opportunity to take a break. I spent a few days in the garden, during the last hot days of September, cutting hack the overgrown shrubbery and plucking what fruit I could find still on the trees. I cut the lawn, dug over what remained of the dehydrated vegetable patch.

Afterwards, I painted another of the upstairs rooms. Because I was away from my failed manuscript, I started to think about it again. I knew I needed to make one last effort to get it right. I had to bring shape to it, but to do so I had to straighten out my daily life.

The key to a purposeful life, I decided, lay in the organization of the day. I created a pattern of domestic habit: an hour a day to cleaning, two hours to Edwin's redecoration and the garden, eight hours for sleep. I would bathe regularly, eat by the clock, shave, wash my clothes, and for everything I did there would be an hour in the day and a day in the week. My need to write was obsessive but it was dominating my life, probably to the detriment of the writing itself.

Now, paradoxically liberated by having constrained myself, I began to write a third version, more smoothly and more effectively than ever before. I knew at last exactly how my story must be told. If the deeper truth could only be told by falsehood—in other words, through metaphor—then to achieve total truth I must create total falsehood. My manuscript had to become a metaphor for myself.

I created an imaginary place and an imaginary life.

My first two attempts had been muted and claustrophobic. I described myself in terms of inwardness and emotion. External events had a shadowy, almost wraith-like presence beyond the edge of vision. This was because I found the real world imaginatively sterile; it was too anecdotal, too lacking in story. To create an imagined landscape enabled me to shape it to my own needs, to make it stand for certain personal symbols in my life. I had already made a fundamental step away from pure autobiographical narrative; now I took the process one stage further and placed the protagonist, my metaphorical self, in a wide and stimulating landscape.

I invented a city and I called it "Jethra", intending it to stand for a composite of London, where I had been born, and the suburbs of Manchester, where I had spent most of my childhood. Jethra was in a country called "Faiandland", which was a moderate and slightly old-fashioned place, rich in tradition and culture, proud of its history but having difficulty in a modern and competitive world. I gave Faiandland a geography and laws and constitution. Jethra was its capital and principal port, situated on the southern coast. Later, I sketched in details of some of the other countries which made up this world; I even drew a rough map, but quickly threw it away because it codified the imagination.

As I wrote, this environment became almost as important as the experiences of my protagonist. I discovered, as before, that by invention of details the larger truths emerged.

I soon found my stride. The fictions of my earlier attempts now seemed awkward and contrived, but as soon as I transferred them to this imaginary world they took on plausibility and conviction. Before, I had changed the order of events merely to clarify them, but now I discovered that all this had had a purpose that only my subconscious had understood. The change to an invented background made sense of what I was doing.

Details accumulated. Soon I saw that in the sea to the south of Faiandland there would be islands, a vast archipelago of small, independent countries. For the people of Jethra, and for my protagonist in particular, these islands represented a form of wish, or of escape. To travel in these islands was to achieve some kind of purpose. At first I was not sure what this would be, but as I wrote I began to understand.

Against this background, the story I wanted to tell of my life emerged.

My protagonist had my own name, but all the people I had known were given false identities. My sister Felicity became "Kalia", Gracia became "Seri", my parents were concealed. Because it was all strange to me I responded imaginatively to what I was writing, but because everything was in another sense totally familiar to me, the world of the other Peter Sinclair became one which I could recognize, and inhabit mentally.

I worked hard and regularly, and the pages of the new manuscript began to pile up. Every evening I would finish work at the time I had predetermined on my daily chart, and then I would go over the finished pages, making minor corrections to the text. Sometimes I would sit on my chair in my white room, with the manuscript on my lap, and I would feel the weight of it and know that I was holding in my hands everything about me that was worth telling or that could be told.

It was a separate identity, an identical self, yet it was outside me and was fixed. It would not age as I would age, nor could it ever be destroyed. It had a life beyond the paper on which it was typewritten; if I burned it, or someone took it away from me, it would still exist on some higher plane. Pure truth had an unageing quality; it would outlive me.

This final version could not have been more different from those first tentative pages I had written a few months before. It was a mature, outward account of a life, truthfully told. Everything about it was invention, apart from the use of my own name, yet everything it contained, every word and sentence, was as true in the high sense of the word as truth could attain.

This I knew beyond doubt or question.

I had found myself, explained myself, and in a very personal sense of the word I had *defined* myself. At last I could feel the end of my story approaching. It was no longer a problem. As I worked I had felt it take shape in my mind, as earlier the story itself had taken form. It was merely a question of setting it down, of typing the pages. I only sensed what the ending would be; I would not know the actual words until the moment came to write them. With that would come my release, my fulfilment, my rehabilitation into the world.

But then, when I had less than ten pages to go, everything was disrupted beyond any hope of retrieval.

# Comment on *The Affirmation*

I wish that I could include more of Christopher Priest's novel. The story develops in fascinating and mind-bending ways that, in my opinion, make it one of the best narratives about personal identity ever written. The chapter excerpted here does a fine job of motivating a view of personal identity that is rarely addressed so directly in fiction. I will also describe some of the ways in which this view is deployed as the story continues, but I strongly encourage everyone to go and read the whole thing.

Priest's book is the first-person account of a youngish man who has recently suffered a string of awful luck. His father has died and he lost his girlfriend, his job and his home. Taking up an offer from a family friend, he retreats to a house in the countryside, where he tries to make some sense of his life. He goes about this in a way that many of us will recognize, by organizing the events of his life into a narrative. Such narratives help us to answer questions like, 'How did I get to this point?' and 'How did I come to be me?' Most of us don't go so far as to write this narrative down as a single piece of work. But it is normal to rehearse mini-narratives about our lives in our heads, and when called by social circumstances to introduce ourselves, we are generally able to supply a brief potted history.

Now this mundane mental activity may not seem to have much significance for the metaphysics of identity, but some philosophers and psychologists have been deeply impressed by it. These thinkers claim that we *are* the autobiographical narratives that we tell about ourselves. Here they are picking up on an idea in Locke's psychological theory that current acts of self-consciousness *lay claim* to earlier experiences. In its most radical form, the theory is that there is no self apart from the act of making this claim; in making one's experiences fill out a narrative. In other words, the self is a fiction.

A notable defender of this view is Daniel Dennett. Dennett claims that humans have an evolved tendency to generate autobiographical narratives, the adaptive function of which is to distinguish me and mine from you and yours. For instance, I can tell a story according to which there's a certain car that belongs to *me*: a few years ago, I paid some money for it, and ever since then I regularly drive it around, pay for repairs, keep it next to my house and so on. This narrative about my car allows me to predict that it will be available for me to drive around tomorrow. It also encourages me to take certain responsibilities, such as ensuring that the car won't crash into unsuspecting pedestrians. I can tell a similar story about my body: that I grew up in it, regularly get to move it around, expect to do so again tomorrow and also take responsibility for not crashing it into pedestrians.

All of these beliefs about my car and my body are ways in which I organize information that are helpful but, Dennett says, not objective realities independent of my asserting them and you accepting them. In these respects, the self is like the physicist's idea of a centre of gravity. An object or system's centre of gravity is not a specific bit of matter located near the middle. It is a mathematical abstraction that allows the physicist to make calculations and predictions about gravitational effects. In the same way, Dennett regards the self as a theoretical abstraction and not a material object.

In Priest's novel, Peter Sinclair also adopts the radical narrative view of self. At the beginning of Chapter 3, he writes, 'I had imagined myself into existence. I wrote because of an inner need, and that need was to create a clearer vision of myself, and in writing I *became* what I wrote.' Of course, Peter Sinclair *really is* nothing more or less than the protagonist of a story. Immersing ourselves in the world of the narrative, we are invited to imagine not that Christopher Priest wrote about Sinclair, but that a real person is writing about himself. We have little trouble imagining this.

Sinclair however runs into some difficulties regarding his self-narrative. First, he finds that his memory is fallible and that it is hard to place events correctly. Then he realizes that the point of an autobiography is not just to list things that happened but to impose some order upon them. This ordering process is a matter of selectivity and emphasis. We do not narrate every single thing that happens to us, but only those things that reveal important facets of our characters, the things that we care about and our aims in life. In many respects, this is a matter of subjective interpretation. For instance, I remember as a young child wondering whether the way I see red is the same as the way other people see red. For me, this event is significant because it was one of the first intimations of my lifelong love of philosophy. Yet many children spontaneously engage in philosophical speculations of this sort. Another person could quite easily have had the exact same thought that I had, with no relevance to the life they now lead. As a result, while I include the event in my self-narrative, this other person does not, and may well have forgotten about it completely.

It is the criterion of significance that leads to the peculiarity of Sinclair's narrative. Sinclair becomes convinced that the mundane factual details don't really capture what is essential about him. The more he refines his narrative, the more he finds that metaphor and imagery do a better job. Sinclair describes these as 'imaginative truths'. For instance, he imagines his Uncle

Billy to be a swashbuckling adventurer living in the East, rather than an armed robber who died in prison. Although it is not in fact the case that Uncle Billy was an adventurer, Sinclair believes that his attraction to the imagined figure is important. We may grant him this much, but then Sinclair takes this a stage further. He imagines an entire fictional life for himself, inhabiting an imaginary world that also plays an important role in shaping his identity. Most notably, there is a vast archipelago to the south of his imagined country of origin. Sinclair says that 'for my protagonist in particular, these islands represented a form of wish, or of escape. To travel in these islands was to achieve some kind of purpose.'

The question Priest's novel pointedly raises is this: if the self is a fiction, is Sinclair's narrative any less appropriate than a mundane self-narrative in which one writes down events that actually occurred? Self-narratives seem only to be justified by their pragmatic role in helping us to make sense of our lives and helping us plan our futures. Metaphors and imagery might serve this role just as well.

One difficulty here is other people. The disruption that ends Chapter 3 is the arrival of Sinclair's sister; a prosaic sort of person who is not at all taken in by Sinclair's fantasies and who judges him to have suffered a complete mental breakdown. Yet the pragmatic criterion of success can handle this difficulty. Other people will typically find it easier to cooperate with a narrative that reflects what they independently accept about the world. Thus one's narrative will be more *successful* when it incorporates what other people say about you. Still, truth is relative to use here. We could in principle all agree to a fantasy. In fact, there have been several occasions when cults have grown up around figures who believe themselves to be Jesus Christ. These cults share a certain fictional narrative about their delusional leaders.

Yet in Sinclair's case, his narrative is so divergent from reality that we feel that he will quickly be brought up short. Why, for instance, does he not feel a terrible sense of disorientation when he wakes up in the morning to find that he is not in his imaginary land? According to Dennett, the self only plays a minor organizational role, and so one's everyday navigation of the world might be left untouched. Yet there are all sorts of ways we could push at this claim. For instance, if I convince myself of a narrative according to which I'm invulnerable, I'm liable to act in ways consistent with this story that get me into serious trouble.

The reason I don't construct such a narrative isn't simply because I don't want to get into trouble. More basically, it's because I cannot long sustain an attitude in which I get to *impose* what is true about me onto the world. On the contrary, I am often forced to *accept* what is true about me from the world. For example. I am unable to convince myself that I don't have two hands. This deferential attitude certainly has a pragmatic justification. What *works* helps me to figure out what is *true*. But it must be emphasized that the fundamental pragmatic attitude is the attitude that there's a reality out there independent of what I happen to believe. It is precisely this attitude that underpins my willingness to revise my beliefs when they don't work out.

Priest's novel also puts the self-narrative theory to the test. Following the chapters excerpted here, the novel shifts into the imaginary world that Sinclair has invented. In this world, Sinclair has won the chance to travel to one of the islands of the archipelago, where he will undergo a medical procedure that will make him forever young and healthy. However, a side-effect of the biological renewal of his brain is that his memories will be wiped. The doctors want Sinclair to fill out a detailed questionnaire that will enable them to restore his identity following the procedure. Sinclair wants to use his fictional autobiography.

Priest's novel plays with this scenario in a number of paradoxical, self-referential ways that are hard to summarize. For instance, the breakdown that Sinclair later suffers in which his different realities collide is, on one interpretation, part of the very narrative that Sinclair wrote to define himself. However, consider for yourself the scenario in which a blatantly fictional narrative is called on to restore a person's identity following the complete loss of memory. There is little hope that the amnesiac would interpret the special meanings of this story in the same way as the original person. For instance, the exciting nature of the Uncle Billy character resides in his exotic qualities. But he is exotic in *contrast* to mundane life, which our amnesiac has forgotten. Similarly, the archipelago is evocative of imaginative escape *because* it isn't real, but how is Sinclair to know that without some independent grasp of what is real?

These points lead to a general argument: the identity of a fiction resides in its meaning. The continuity of this meaning relies on the continuity of our understanding over time. This continuity in turn relies on our maintaining some psychological capacities for understanding things. This is where we may argue that the self-narrative view cannot provide sufficient grounds for the continuity of identity. It already relies on the continuity of something else. And if there's already something else that provides continuity, why not ground our theory of identity in that instead?

I think Dennett will agree that brain mechanisms for understanding and interpreting persist through time. What he will argue is that brain mechanisms are not suitable candidates for personal identity. When I declare that I am Tom Cochrane, I am not declaring that certain brain mechanisms are Tom Cochrane. I am referring to the person who owns those brain mechanisms; a centre of first-person experience. As soon as I admit that, Dennett will leap up and challenge me to find that centre of first-person experience. This is what he says is no more real than a centre of gravity. The challenge then is to find a suitable candidate who is the bearer of first-person experience. Later chapters will follow this up.

For now, I think we can conclude that self-narratives need to be at least constrained by reality, which will impose certain truths about us, independent of what we happen to believe. In fact, most philosophers who defend the self-narrative view these days do not treat it as a radical metaphysical thesis in the way that Dennett does. For instance, Marya Schechtman allows that the self is distinct from the *sense of self*, and that self-narratives are the major way in which we develop this sense of self.

In more detail, the sense of self is made up of the various beliefs and attitudes that we carry around which characterize the sort of person we are. This sense of self plays an important role in helping us to understand our lives, to interact smoothly with other people, and to make plans for the future. It is also plausibly something that we gradually construct over time, precisely through the sort of selection and interpretation processes that Peter Sinclair initially engages in. In this respect, the sense of self is like one's character. Character is not quite the same as personality. Personality refers to long-term qualities that we are born with, or which solidify outside of our conscious control. Character refers to those long-term qualities that we endorse and deliberately uphold.

If we make a distinction between the self and the sense of self, we allow that the sense of self can get it wrong. It can fail to track what is true of oneself. For instance, there is important research being done on the ways in which dementia destroys a person's sense of self, where treatment tries to find ways to help a person reconnect with their sense of self, for instance by helping them to recall things that they used to love or things that they are proud of. The condition of schizophrenia can similarly involve a breakdown in the sense of self. Sufferers of this condition frequently report feelings of depersonalization, in which they no longer feel that they properly inhabit their own bodies or minds. Yet in both cases, the loss of the sense of self need not mean that the self has not survived.

In Peter Sinclair's case, it is a fair interpretation of the text that he has developed schizophrenia. This is most clearly evidenced in the descriptions of his white room which, we finally learn, only he can see. It is unclear if Sinclair's experiences of the white room are imaginings or hallucinations, but this is a debate that is also had about schizophrenic delusions. The most important contrast with real-world suffers of schizophrenia is that while Peter Sinclair remains forever defined by the narrative we have been given, the real-world sufferer of schizophrenia can be distinguished from the stories that he or she tells.

# 6

# 'Think like A Dinosaur'

## *James Patrick Kelly*

---

Kamala Shastri came back to this world as she had left it – naked.

She tottered out of the assembler, trying to balance in Tuulen Station's delicate gravity. I caught her and bundled her into a robe with one motion, then eased her onto the float. Three years on another planet had transformed Kamala. She was leaner, more muscular. Her fingernails were now a couple of centimeters long and there were four parallel scars incised on her left cheek, perhaps some Gendian's idea of beautification. But what struck me most was the darting strangeness in her eyes. This place, so familiar to me, seemed almost to shock her. It was as if she doubted the walls and was skeptical of air. She had learned to think like an alien.

"Welcome back." The float's whisper rose to a whoosh as I walked it down the hallway.

She swallowed hard and I thought she might cry. Three years ago, she would have. Lots of migrators are devastated when they come out of the assembler; it's because there is no transition. A few seconds ago Kamala was on Gend, fourth planet of the star we call epsilon Leo, and now she was here in lunar orbit. She was almost home; her life's great adventure was over.

"Matthew?" she said.

"Michael." I couldn't help but be pleased that she remembered me. After all, she had changed my life.

\*

I've guided maybe three hundred migrations – comings and goings – since I first came to Tuulen to study the dinos. Kamala Shastri's is the only quantum scan I've ever pirated. I doubt that the dinos care; I suspect this is a trespass they occasionally allow themselves. I know more about her – at least, as she was three years ago – than I know about myself.

When the dinos sent her to Gend, she massed 50,391.72 grams and her red cell count was 4.81 million per mm3. She could play the nagasvaram, a kind of bamboo flute. Her father came from Thana, near Bombay, and her favorite flavor of chewyfrute was watermelon and she'd had five lovers and when she was eleven she had wanted to be a gymnast but instead she had become a biomaterials engineer who at age twenty-nine had volunteered to go to the stars to learn how to grow artificial eyes. It took her two years to go through migrator training; she knew could have backed out at any time, right up until the moment Silloin translated her into a superluminal signal. It was explained to her many times what it meant to balance the equation.

I first met her on June 22, 2069. She shuttled over from Lunex's L1 port and came through our airlock at promptly 10:15, a small, roundish woman with black hair parted in the middle and drawn tight against her skull. They had darkened her skin against epsilon Leo's UV; it was the deep blue-black of twilight. She was wearing a striped clingy and Velcro slippers to help her get around for the short time she'd be navigating our .2 micrograv.

"Welcome to Tuulen Station." I smiled and offered my hand. "My name is Michael." We shook. "I'm supposed to be a sapientologist but I also moonlight as the local guide."

"Guide?" She nodded distractedly. "Okay." She peered past me, as if expecting someone else.

"Oh, don't worry," I said, "the dinos are in their cages."

Her eyes got wide as she let her hand slip from mine. "You call the Hanen dinos?"

"Why not?" I laughed. "They call us babies. The weeps, among other things."

She shook her head in amazement. People who've never met a dino tended to romanticize them: the wise and noble reptiles who had mastered superluminal physics and introduced Earth to the wonders of galactic civilization. I doubt Kamala had ever seen a dino play poker or gobble down a screaming rabbit. And she had never argued with Linna, who still wasn't convinced that humans were psychologically ready to go to the stars.

"Have you eaten?" I gestured down the corridor toward the reception rooms.

"Yes . . . I mean, no." She didn't move. "I am not hungry."

"Let me guess. You're too nervous to eat. You're too nervous to talk, even. You wish I'd just shut up, pop you into the marble, and beam you out. Let's just get this part the hell over with, eh?"

"I don't mind the conversation, actually."

"There you go. Well, Kamala, it is my solemn duty to advise you that there are no peanut butter and jelly sandwiches on Gend. And no chicken vindaloo. What's my name again?"

"Michael?"

"See, you're not that nervous. Not one taco, or a single slice of eggplant pizza. This is your last chance to eat like a human."

"Okay." She did not actually smile – she was too busy being brave – but a corner of her mouth twitched. "Actually, I would not mind a cup of tea."

"Now, tea they've got." She let me guide her toward reception room D; her slippers snicked at the velcro carpet. "Of course, they brew it from lawn clippings."

"The Gendians don't keep lawns. They live underground."

"Refresh my memory." I kept my hand on her shoulder; beneath the clingy, her muscles were rigid. "Are they the ferrets or the things with the orange bumps?"

"They look nothing like ferrets."

We popped through the door bubble into reception D, a compact rectangular space with a scatter of low, unthreatening furniture. There was a kitchen station at one end, a closet with a vacuum toilet at the other. The ceiling was blue sky; the long wall showed a live view of the Charles River and the Boston skyline, baking in the late June sun. Kamala had just finished her doctorate at MIT.

I opaqued the door. She perched on the edge of a couch like a wren, ready to flit away.

While I was making her tea, my fingernail screen flashed. I answered it and a tiny Silloin came up in discreet mode. She didn't look at me; she was too busy watching arrays in the control room. =A problem,= her voice buzzed in my earstone, =most negligible, really. But we will have to void the last two from today's schedule. Save them at Lunex until first shift tomorrow. Can this one be kept for an hour?=

"Sure," I said. "Kamala, would you like to meet a Hanen?" I transferred Silloin to a dino-sized window on the wall. "Silloin, this is Kamala Shastri. Silloin is the one who actually runs things. I'm just the doorman."

Silloin looked through the window with her near eye, then swung around and peered at Kamala with her other. She was short for a dino, just over a meter tall, but she had an enormous head that teetered on her neck like a watermelon balancing on a grapefruit. She must have just oiled herself because her silver scales shone. =Kamala, you will accept my happiest intentions for you?= She raised her left hand, spreading the skinny digits to expose dark crescents of vestigial webbing.

"Of course, I . . ."

=And you will permit us to render you this translation?=

She straightened. "Yes."

=Have you questions?=

I'm sure she had several hundred, but at this point was probably too scared to ask. While she hesitated, I broke in. "Which came first, the lizard or the egg?"

Silloin ignored me. =It will be excellent for you to begin when?=

"She's just having a little tea." I said, handing her the cup. "I'll bring her along when she's done. Say an hour?"

Kamala squirmed on couch. "No, really, it will not take me . . ."

Silloin showed us her teeth, several of which were as long as piano keys.

=That would be most appropriate, Michael.= She closed; a gull flew through the space where her window had been.

"Why did you do that?" Kamala's voice was sharp.

"Because it says here that you have to wait your turn. You're not the only migrator we're sending this morning." This was a lie, of course; we had had to cut the schedule because Jodi Latchaw, the other sapientologist assigned to Tuulen, was at the University of Hipparchus presenting our paper on the Hanen concept of identity. "Don't worry, I'll make the time fly."

For a moment, we looked at each other. I could have laid down an hour's worth of patter; I'd done that often enough. Or I could have drawn her out on why she was going: no doubt she had a blind grandma or second cousin just waiting for her to bring home those artificial eyes, not to mention potential spin-offs which could well end tuberculosis, famine and premature ejaculation, blah, blah, blah. Or I could have just left her alone in the room to read the wall. The trick was guessing how spooked she really was.

"Tell me a secret," I said.

"What?"

"A secret, you know, something no one else knows."

She stared as if I'd just fallen off Mars.

"Look, in a little while you're going some place that's what . . . three hundred and ten light years away? You're scheduled to stay for three years. By the time you come back, I could easily be rich, famous and elsewhere; we'll probably never see each other again. So what have you got to lose? I promise not to tell."

She leaned back on the couch, and settled the cup in her lap. "This is another test, right? After everything they have put me through, they still have not decided whether to send me."

"Oh no, in a couple of hours you'll be cracking nuts with ferrets in some dark Gendian burrow. This is just me, talking."

"You are crazy."

"Actually, I believe the technical term is logomaniac. It's from the Greek: logos meaning word, mania meaning two bits short of a byte. I just love to chat is all. Tell you what, I'll go first. If my secret isn't juicy enough, you don't have tell me anything."

Her eyes were slits as she sipped her tea. I was fairly sure that whatever she was worrying about at the moment, it wasn't being swallowed by the big blue marble.

"I was brought up Catholic," I said, settling onto a chair in front of her. "I'm not anymore, but that's not the secret. My parents sent me to Mary, Mother of God High School; we called it Moogoo. It was run by a couple of old priests, Father Thomas and his wife, Mother Jennifer. Father Tom taught physics, which I got a D in, mostly because he talked like he had walnuts in his mouth. Mother Jennifer taught theology and had all the warmth of a marble pew; her nickname was Mama Moogoo.

" One night, just two weeks before my graduation, Father Tom and Mama Moogoo went out in their Chevy Minimus for ice cream. On the way home, Mama Moogoo pushed a yellow light and got broadsided by an ambulance. Like I said, she was old, a hundred and twenty something; they should've lifted her license back in the 1950s. She was killed instantly. Father Tom died in the hospital.

"Of course, we were all supposed to feel sorry for them and I guess I did a little, but I never really liked either of them and I resented the way their deaths had screwed things up for my class. So I was more annoyed than sorry, but then I also had this edge of guilt for being so uncharitable. Maybe you'd have to grow up Catholic to understand that. Anyway, the day after it happened they called an assembly in the gym and we were all there squirming on the bleachers and the cardinal himself telepresented a sermon. He kept trying to comfort us, like it had been our parents that had died. When I made a joke about it to the kid next to me, I got caught and spent the last week of my senior year with an in-school suspension."

Kamala had finished her tea. She slid the empty cup into one of the holders built into the table.

"Want some more?" I said.

She stirred restlessly. "Why are you telling me this?"

"It's part of the secret." I leaned forward in my chair. "See, my family lived down the street from Holy Spirit Cemetery and in order to get to the carryvan line on McKinley Ave., I had to cut through. Now this happened a couple of days after I got in trouble at the assembly. It was around midnight and I was coming home from a graduation party where I had taken a couple of pokes of insight, so I was feeling sly as a philosopher-king. As I walked through the cemetery, I stumbled across two dirt mounds right next to each other. At first I thought they were flower beds, then I saw the wooden crosses. Fresh graves: here lies Father Tom and Mama Moogoo. There wasn't much to the crosses: they were basically just stakes with crosspieces painted white and hammered into the ground. The names were hand printed on them. The way I figured it, they were there to mark the graves until the stones got delivered. I didn't need any insight to recognize a once in a lifetime opportunity. If I switched them, what were the chances anyone was going to notice? It was no problem sliding them out of their holes. I smoothed the dirt with my hands and then ran like hell."

Until that moment, she'd seemed bemused by my story and slightly condescending toward me. Now there was a glint of alarm in her eyes.

"That was a terrible thing to do," she said.

"Absolutely," I said, "although the dinos think that the whole idea of planting bodies in graveyards and marking them with carved rocks is weepy. They say there is no identity in dead meat, so why get so sentimental about it? Linna keeps asking how come we don't put markers over our shit. But that's not the secret. See, it'd been a warmish night in the middle of June, only as I ran, the air turned cold. Freezing, I could see my breath. And my shoes got heavier and heavier, like they had turned to stone. As I got closer to the back gate, it felt like I was fighting a strong wind, except my clothes weren't flapping. I slowed to a walk. I know I could have pushed through, but my heart was thumping and then I heard this whispery seashell noise and I panicked. So the secret is I'm a coward. I switched the crosses back and I never went near that cemetery again. As a matter of fact," I nodded at the walls of reception room D on Tuulen Station, "when I grew up, I got about as far away from it as I could."

She stared as I settled back in my chair. "True story," I said and raised my right hand. She seemed so astonished that I started laughing. A smile bloomed on her dark face and suddenly she was giggling too. It was a soft, liquid sound, like a brook bubbling over smooth stones; it made me laugh even harder. Her lips were full and her teeth were very white.

"Your turn," I said, finally.

"Oh, no, I could not." She waved me off. "I don't have anything so good . . ." She paused, then frowned. "You have told that before?"

"Once," I said. "To the Hanen, during the psych screening for this job. Only I didn't tell them the last part. I know how dinos think, so I ended it when I switched the crosses. The rest is baby stuff." I waggled a finger at her. "Don't forget, you promised to keep my secret."

"Did I?"

"Tell me about when you were young. Where did you grow up?"

"Toronto." She glanced at me, appraisingly. "There was something, but not funny. Sad."

I nodded encouragement and changed the wall to Toronto's skyline dominated by the CN Tower, Toronto-Dominion Centre, Commerce Court and the King's Needle.

She twisted to take in the view and spoke over her shoulder. "When I was ten we moved to an apartment, right downtown on Bloor Street so my mother could be close to work." She pointed at the wall and turned back to face me. "She is an accountant, my father wrote wallpaper for Imagineering. It was a huge building; it seemed as if we were always getting into the elevator with ten neighbors we never knew we had. I was coming home from school one day when an old woman stopped me in the lobby. "Little girl," she said, "how would you like to earn a ten dollars?" My parents had warned me not to talk to strangers but she obviously was a resident. Besides, she had an ancient pair of exolegs strapped on, so I knew I could outrun her if I needed to. She asked me to go to the store for her, handed me a grocery list and a cash card and said I should bring everything up to her apartment, 10W. I should have been more suspicious because all the downtown groceries deliver but, as I soon found out, all she really wanted was someone to talk to her. And she was willing to pay for it, usually five or ten dollars, depending how long I stayed. Before long I was stopping by almost every day after school. I think my parents would have made me stop if they had known; they were very strict. They would not have liked me taking her money. But neither of them got home until after six, so it was my secret to keep."

"Who was she?" I said. "What did you talk about?"

"Her name was Margaret Ase. She was ninety-seven years old and I think she had been some kind of counselor. Her husband and her daughter had both died and she was alone. I didn't find out much about her; she made me do most of the talking. She asked me about my friends and what I was learning in school and my family. Things like that...."

Her voice trailed off as my fingernail started to flash. I answered it.

=Michael, I am pleased to call you to here.= Silloin buzzed in my ear.

She was almost twenty minutes ahead of schedule.

"See, I told you we'd make the time fly." I stood; Kamala's eyes got very wide. "I'm ready if you are."

I offered her my hand. She took it and let me help her up. She wavered for a moment and I sensed just how fragile her resolve was. I put my hand around her waist and steered her into the corridor. In the micrograv of Tuulen Station, she already felt as insubstantial as a memory. "So tell me, what happened that was so sad?"

At first I thought she hadn't heard. She shuffled along, said nothing.

"Hey, don't keep me in suspense here, Kamala" I said. "You have to finish the story."

"No," she said. "I don't think I do."

I didn't take this personally. My only real interest in the conversation had been to distract her. If she refused to be distracted, that was her choice. Some migrators kept talking right up to the moment they slid into the big blue marble, but lots of them went quiet just before. They turned inward. Maybe in her mind she was already on Gend, blinking in the hard white light.

We arrived at the scan center, the largest space on Tuulen Station. Immediately in front of us was the marble, containment for the quantum nondemolition sensor array – QNSA for the acronymically inclined. It was the milky blue of glacial ice and big as two elephants. The upper hemisphere was raised and the scanning table protruded like a shiny gray tongue. Kamala approached the marble and touched her reflection, which writhed across its polished surface. To the right was a padded bench, the fogger and a toilet. I looked left, through the control room window. Silloin stood watching us, her impossible head cocked to one side.

=She is docile?= She buzzed in my earstone.

I held up crossed fingers.

=Welcome, Kamala Shastri.= Silloin's voice came over the speakers with a soothing hush. =You are ready to open your translation?=

Kamala bowed to the window. "This is where I take my clothes off?"

=If you would be so convenient.=

She brushed past me to the bench. Apparently I had ceased to exist; this was between her and the dino now. She undressed quickly, folding her clingy into a neat bundle, tucking her slippers beneath the bench. Out of the corner of my eye, I could see tiny feet, heavy thighs, and the beautiful, dark smooth skin of her back. She stepped into the fogger and closed the door.

"Ready," she called.

From the control room, Silloin closed circuits which filled the fogger with a dense cloud of nanolenses. The nano stuck to Kamala and deployed, coating the surface of her body. As she breathed them, they passed from her lungs into her bloodstream. She only coughed twice; she had been well trained. When the eight minutes were up, Silloin cleared the air in the fogger and she emerged. Still ignoring me, she again faced the control room.

=Now you must arrange yourself on the scanning table,= said Silloin, =and enable Michael to fix you.=

She crossed to the marble without hesitation, climbed the gantry beside it, eased onto the table and laid back.

I followed her up. "Sure you won't tell me the rest of the secret?"

She stared at the ceiling, unblinking.

"Okay then." I took the canister and a sparker out of my hip pouch. "This is going to happen just like you've practiced it." I used the canister to respray the bottoms of her feet with nano. I watched her belly rise and fall, rise and fall. She was deep into her breathing exercise.

"Remember, no skipping rope or whistling while you're in the scanner."

She did not answer. "Deep breath now," I said and touched a sparker to her big toe. There was a brief crackle as the nano on her skin wove into a net and stiffened, locking her in place. "Bark at the ferrets for me." I picked up my equipment, climbed down the gantry, and wheeled it back to the wall.

With a low whine, the big blue marble retracted its tongue. I watched the upper hemisphere close, swallowing Kamala Shastri, then joined Silloin in the control room.

I'm not of the school who think the dinos stink, another reason I got assigned to study them up close. Parikkal, for example, has no smell at all that I can tell. Normally Silloin had the faint but not unpleasant smell of stale wine. When she was under stress, however, her scent became vinegary and biting. It must have been a wild morning for her. Breathing through my mouth, I settled onto the stool at my station.

She was working quickly, now that the marble was sealed. Even with all their training, migrators tend to get claustrophobic fast. After all, they're lying in the dark, in nanobondage, waiting to be translated. Waiting. The simulator at the Singapore training center makes a noise while it's emulating a scan. Most compare it to a light rain pattering against the marble; for some, it's low volume radio static. As long as they hear the patter, the migrators think they're safe. We reproduce it for them while they're in our marble, even through scanning takes about three seconds and is utterly silent. From my vantage I could see that the sagittal, axial and coronal windows had stopped blinking, indicating full data capture. Silloin was skirring busily to herself; her comm didn't bother to interpret. Wasn't saying anything baby

Michael needed to know, obviously. Her head bobbed as she monitored the enormous spread of readouts; her claws clicked against touch screens that glowed orange and yellow.

At my station, there was only a migration status screen – and a white button.

I wasn't lying when I said I was just the doorman. My field is sapientology, not quantum physics. Whatever went wrong with Kamala's migration that morning, there was nothing I could have done. The dinos tell me that the quantum nondemolition sensor array is able to circumvent Heisenberg's Uncertainty Principle by measuring spacetime's most crogglingly small quantities without collapsing the wave/particle duality. How small? They say that no one can ever "see" anything that's only $1.62 \times 10^{-33}$ centimeters long, because at that size, space and time come apart. Time ceases to exist and space becomes a random probablistic foam, sort of like quantum spit. We humans call this the Planck-Wheeler length. There's a Planck-Wheeler time, too: $10^{-45}$ of a second. If something happens and something else happens and the two events are separated by an interval of a mere $10^{-45}$ of a second, it is impossible to say which came first. It was all dino to me – and that's just the scanning. The Hanen use different tech to create artificial wormholes, hold them open with electromagnetic vacuum fluctuations, pass the superluminal signal through and then assemble the migrator from elementary particles at the destination.

On my status screen I could see that the signal which mapped Kamala Shastri had already been compressed and burst through the wormhole. All that we had to wait for was for Gend to confirm acquisition. Once they officially told us that they had her, it would be my job to balance the equation.

Pitter-patter, pitter-pat.

Some Hanen technologies are so powerful that they can alter reality itself. Wormholes could be used by some time traveling fanatic to corrupt history; the scanner/assembler could be used to create a billion Silloins – or Michael Burrs. Pristine reality, unpolluted by such anomalies, has what the dinos call harmony. Before any sapients get to join the galactic club, they must prove total commitment to preserving harmony.

Since I had come to Tuulen to study the dinos, I had pressed the white button maybe three hundred times. It was what I had to do in order to keep my assignment. Pressing it sent a killing pulse of ionizing radiation through the cerebral cortex of migrator's duplicated, and therefore unnecessary, body. No brain, no pain; death followed within seconds. Yes, the first few times I'd balanced the equation had been traumatic. It was still . . . unpleasant.

But this was the price of a ticket to the stars. If certain unusual people like Kamala Shastri had decided that price was reasonable, it was their choice, not mine.

=This is not a happy result, Michael.= Silloin spoke to me for the first time since I'd entered the control room. =Discrepancies are unfolding.= On my status screen I watched as the error-checking routines started turning up hits.

"Is the problem here?" I felt a knot twist suddenly inside me. "Or there?" If our original scan checked out, then all Silloin would have to do is send it to Gend again.

There was a long, infuriating silence. Silloin concentrated on part of her board as if it showed her firstborn hatchling chipping out of its egg. The respirator between her shoulders had ballooned to twice its normal size. My screen showed that Kamala had been in the marble for four minutes plus.

=It may be fortunate to recalibrate the scanner and begin over.=

"Shit." I slammed my hand against the wall, felt the pain tingle to my elbow. "I thought you had it fixed." When error-checking turned up problems, the solution was almost always to retransmit. "You're sure, Silloin? Because this one was right on the edge when I tucked her in."

Silloin gave me a dismissive sneeze and slapped at the error readouts with her bony little hand, as if to knock them back to normal. Like Linna and the other dinos, she had little patience with what she regarded as our weepy fears of migration. However, unlike Linna, she was convinced that someday, after we had used Hanen technologies long enough, we would learn to think like dinos. Maybe she's right. Maybe when we've been squirting through wormholes for hundreds of years, we'll cheerfully discard our redundant bodies. When the dinos and other sapients migrate, the redundants zap themselves – very harmonious. They tried it with humans but it didn't always work. That's why I'm here. =The need is most clear. It will prolong about thirty minutes,= she said.

Kamala had been alone in the dark for almost six minutes, longer than any migrator I'd ever guided. "Let me hear what's going on in the marble."

The control room filled with the sound of Kamala screaming. It didn't sound human to me – more like the shriek of tires skidding toward a crash.

"We've got to get her out of there," I said.

=That is baby thinking, Michael.=

"So she's a baby, damn it." I knew that bringing migrators out the marble was big trouble. I could have asked Silloin to turn the speakers off and sat there while Kamala suffered. It was my decision.

"Don't open the marble until I get the gantry in place." I ran for the door. "And keep the sound effects going."

At the first crack of light, she howled. The upper hemisphere seemed to lift in slow motion; inside the marble she bucked against the nano. Just when I was sure it impossible that she couldn't scream any louder, she did.

We had accomplished something extraordinary, Silloin and I; we had stripped the brave biomaterials engineer away completely, leaving in her place a terrified animal.

"Kamala, it's me. Michael."

Her frantic screams cohered into words. "Stop . . . don't . . . oh my god, someone help!" If I could have, I would've jumped into the marble to release her, but the sensor array is fragile and I wasn't going risk causing any more problems with it. We both had to wait until the upper hemisphere swung fully open and the scanning table offered poor Kamala to me.

"It's okay. Nothing's going to happen, all right? We're bringing you out, that's all. Everything's all right."

When I released her with the sparker, she flew at me. We pitched back and almost toppled down the steps. Her grip was so tight I couldn't breathe.

"Don't kill me, don't, please, don't."

I rolled on top of her. "Kamala!" I wriggled one arm free and used it to pry myself from her. I scrabbled sideways to the top step. She lurched clumsily in the microgravity and swung at me; her fingernails raked across the back of my hand, leaving bloody welts. "Kamala, stop!" It was all I could do not to strike back at her. I retreated down the steps.

"You bastard. What are you assholes trying to do to me?" She drew several deep shuddering breaths and began to sob.

"The scan got corrupted somehow. Silloin is working on it."

=The difficulty is obscure,= said Silloin from the control room.

"But that's not your problem." I backed toward the bench.

"They lied," she mumbled and seemed to fold in upon herself as if she were just skin, no flesh or bones. "They said I wouldn't feel anything and here . . . do you know what it's like . . . it's. . . ."

I fumbled for her clingy. "Look, here are your clothes. Why don't you get dressed? We'll get you out of here."

"You bastard," she repeated, but her voice was empty.

She let me coax her down off the gantry. I counted nubs on the wall while she fumbled back into her clingy. They were the size of the old dimes my grandfather used to hoard and they glowed with a soft golden bioluminescence. I was up to forty-seven before she was dressed and ready to return to reception D.

Where before she had perched expectantly at the edge of the couch, now she slumped back against it. "So what now?" she said.

"I don't know." I went to the kitchen station and took the carafe from the distiller. "What now, Silloin?" I poured water over the back of my hand to wash the blood off. It stung. My earstone was silent. "I guess we wait," I said finally.

"For what?"

"For her to fix. . . ."

"I'm not going back in there."

I decided to let that pass. It was probably too soon to argue with her about it, although once Silloin recalibrated the scanner, she'd have very little time to change her mind. "You want something from the kitchen? Another cup of tea, maybe?"

"How about a gin and tonic – hold the tonic?" She rubbed beneath her eyes. "Or a couple of hundred milliliters of serentol?"

I tried to pretend she'd made a joke. "You know the dinos won't let us open the bar for migrators. The scanner might misread your brain chemistry and your visit to Gend would be nothing but a three year drunk."

"Don't you understand?" She was right back at the edge of hysteria. "I am not going!" I didn't really blame her for the way she was acting but, at that moment, all I wanted was to get rid of Kamala Shastri. I didn't care if she went on to Gend or back to Lunex or over the rainbow to Oz, just as long as I didn't have to be in the same room with this miserable creature who was trying to make me feel guilty about an accident I had nothing to do with.

"I thought I could do it." She clamped hands to her ears as if to keep from hearing her own despair. "I wasted the last two years convincing myself that I could just lie there and not think and then suddenly I'd be far away. I was going someplace wonderful and strange." She made a strangled sound and let her hands drop into her lap. "I was going to help people see."

"You did it, Kamala. You did everything we asked."

She shook her head. "I couldn't not think. That was the problem. And then there she was, trying to touch me. In the dark. I had not thought of her since. . . ." She shivered. "It's your fault for reminding me."

"Your secret friend," I said.

"Friend?" Kamala seemed puzzled by the word. "No, I wouldn't say she was a friend. I was always a little bit scared of her, because I was never quite sure what she wanted from me." She paused. "One day I went up to 10W after school. She was in her chair, staring down at Bloor Street. Her back was to me. I said, 'Hi, Ms. Ase.' I was going to show her a genie I had written, only she didn't say anything. I came around. Her skin was the color of ashes. I took her hand. It was like picking up something plastic. She was stiff, hard – not a person anymore. She had become a thing, like a feather or a bone. I ran; I had to get out of there. I went up to our apartment and I hid from her."

She squinted, as if observing – judging – her younger self through the lens of time. "I think I understand now what she wanted. I think she knew she was dying; she probably wanted me there with her at the end, or at least to find her body afterward and report it. Only I could not. If I told anyone she was dead, my parents would find out about us. Maybe people would suspect me of doing something to her – I don't know. I could have called security but I was only ten; I was afraid somehow they might trace me. A couple of weeks went by and still nobody had found her. By then it was too late to say anything. Everyone would have blamed me for keeping quiet for so long. At night I imagined her turning black and rotting into her chair like a banana. It made me sick; I couldn't sleep or eat. They had to put me in the hospital, because I had touched her. Touched death."

=Michael,= Silloin whispered, without any warning flash. =An impossibility has formed.=

"As soon as I was out of that building, I started to get better. Then they found her. After I came home, I worked hard to forget Ms. Ase. And I did, almost." Kamala wrapped her arms around herself. "But just now she was with me again, inside the marble . . . I couldn't see her but somehow I knew she was reaching for me."

=Michael, Parikkal is here with Linna.=

"Don't you see?" She gave a bitter laugh. "How can I go to Gend? I'm hallucinating."

=It has broken the harmony. Join us alone.=

I was tempted to swat at the annoying buzz in my ear.

"You know, I've never told anyone about her before."

"Well, maybe some good has come of this after all." I patted her on the knee. "Excuse me for a minute?" She seemed surprised that I would leave. I slipped into the hall and hardened the door bubble, sealing her in.

"What impossibility?" I said, heading for the control room.

=She is pleased to reopen the scanner?=

"Not pleased at all. More like scared shitless."

=This is Parikkal.= My earstone translated his skirring with a sizzling edge, like bacon frying. =The confusion was made elsewhere. No mishap can be connected to our station.=

I pushed through the bubble into the scan center. I could see the three dinos through the control window. Their heads were bobbing furiously. "Tell me," I said.

=Our communications with Gend were marred by a transient falsehood,= said Silloin. =Kamala Shastri has been received there and reconstructed.=

"She migrated?" I felt the deck shifting beneath my feet. "What about the one we've got here?"

=The simplicity is to load the redundant into the scanner and finalize . . . .=

"I've got news for you. She's not going anywhere near that marble."

=Her equation is not in balance.= This was Linna, speaking for the first time. Linna was not exactly in charge of Tuulen Station; she was more like a senior partner. Parikkal and Silloin had overruled her before – at least I thought they had.

"What do you expect me to do? Wring her neck?"

There was a moment's silence – which was not as unnerving as watching them eye me through the window, their heads now perfectly still.

"No," I said.

The dinos were skirring at each other; their heads wove and dipped. At first they cut me cold and the comm was silent, but suddenly their debate crackled through my earstone.

=This is just as I have been telling,= said Linna. =These beings have no realization of harmony. It is wrongful to further unleash them on the many worlds.=

=You may have reason,= said Parikkal. =But that is a later discussion. The need is for the equation to be balanced.=

=There is no time We will have to discard the redundant ourselves.= Silloin bared her long brown teeth. It would take her maybe five seconds to rip Kamala's throat out. And even though Silloin was the dino most sympathetic to us, I had no doubt she would enjoy the kill.

=I will argue that we adjourn human migration until this world has been rethought,= said Linna.

This was typical dino condescension. Even though they appeared to be arguing with each other, they were actually speaking to me, laying the situation out so that even the baby sapient would understand. They were informing me that I was jeopardizing the future of humanity in space. That the Kamala in reception D was dead whether I quit or not. That the equation had to be balanced and it had to be now.

"Wait," I said. "Maybe I can coax her back into the scanner." I had to get away from them. I pulled my earstone out and slid it into my pocket. I was in such a hurry to escape that I stumbled as I left the scan center and had to catch myself in the hallway. I stood there for a second, staring at the hand pressed against the bulkhead. I seemed to see the splayed fingers through the wrong end of a telescope. I was far away from myself.

She had curled into herself on the couch, arms clutching knees to her chest, as if trying to shrink so that nobody would notice her.

"We're all set," I said briskly. "You'll be in the marble for less than a minute, guaranteed."

"No, Michael."

I could actually feel myself receding from Tuulen Station. "Kamala, you're throwing away a huge part of your life."

"It is my right." Her eyes were shiny.

No, it wasn't. She was redundant; she had no rights. What had she said about the dead old lady? She had become a thing, like a bone.

"Okay, then," I jabbed at her shoulder with a stiff forefinger. "Let's go."

She recoiled. "Go where?"

"Back to Lunex. I'm holding the shuttle for you. It just dropped off my afternoon list; I should be helping them settle in, instead of having to deal with you."

She unfolded herself slowly.

"Come on." I jerked her roughly to her feet. "The dinos want you off Tuulen as soon as possible and so do I." I was so distant, I couldn't see Kamala Shastri anymore.

She nodded and let me march her to the bubble door.

"And if we meet anyone in the hall, keep your mouth shut."

"You're being so mean." Her whisper was thick.

"You're being such a baby."

When the inner door glided open, she realized immediately that there was no umbilical to the shuttle. She tried to twist out of my grip but I put my shoulder into her, hard. She flew across the airlock, slammed against the outer door and caromed onto her back. As I punched at the switch to close the inner door, I came back to myself. I was doing this terrible thing – me, Michael Burr. I couldn't help myself: I giggled. When I last saw her, Kamala was scrabbling across the deck toward me but she was too late. I was surprised that she wasn't screaming again; all I heard was her ferocious breathing.

As soon as the inner door sealed, I opened the outer door. After all, how many ways are there to kill someone on a space station? There were no guns.

Maybe someone else could have stabbed or strangled her, but not me. Poison how? Besides, I wasn't thinking, I had been trying desperately not to think of what I was doing. I was a sapientologist, not a doctor. I always thought that exposure to space meant instantaneous death. Explosive decompression or something like. I didn't want her to suffer. I was trying to make it quick. Painless.

I heard the whoosh of escaping air and thought that was it; the body had been ejected into space. I had actually turned away when thumping started, frantic, like the beat of a racing heart. She must have found something to hold onto. Thump, thump, thump! It was too much. I sagged against the inner door – thump, thump – slid down it, laughing. Turns out that if you empty the lungs, it is possible to survive exposure to space for at least a minute, maybe two. I thought it was funny. Thump! Hilarious, actually. I had tried my best for her – risked my career – and this was how she repaid me? As I laid my cheek against the door, the thumps start to weaken. There were just a few centimeters between us, the difference between life and death. Now she knew all about balancing the equation. I was laughing so hard I could scarely breathe. Just like the meat behind the door. Die already, you weepy bitch!

I don't know how long it took. The thumping slowed. Stopped. And then I was a hero. I had preserved harmony, kept our link to the stars open. I chuckled with pride; I could think like a dinosaur.

*

I popped through the bubble door into Reception D. "It's time to board the shuttle."

Kamala had changed into a clingy and velcro slippers. There were at least ten windows open on the wall; the room filled with the murmur of talking heads. Friends and relatives had to be notified; their hero had returned, safe and sound. "I have to go," she said to the wall. "I will call you all when I land."

She gave me a smile that seemed stiff from disuse. "I want to thank you again, Michael." I wondered how long it took migrators to get used to being human. "You were such a help and I was such a . . . I was not myself." She glanced around the room one last time and then shivered. "I was really scared."

"You were."

She shook her head. "Was it that bad?"

I shrugged and led her out into the hall.

"I feel so silly now. I mean, I was in the marble for less than a minute and then –" she snapped her fingers – "there I was on Gend, just like you said." She brushed up against me as we walked; her body was hard under the clingy. "Anyway, I am glad we got this chance to talk. I really was going to look you up when I got back. I certainly did not expect to see you here."

"I decided to stay on." The inner door to the airlock glided open. "It's a job that grows on you." The umbilical shivered as the pressure between Tuulen Station and the shuttle equalized.

"You have got migrators waiting," she said.

"Two."

"I envy them." She turned to me. "Have you ever thought about going to the stars?"

"No," I said.

Kamala put her hand to my face. "It changes everything." I could feel the prick of her long nails – claws, really. For a moment I thought she meant to scar my cheek the way she had been scarred.

"I know," I said.

# Comment on 'Think Like a Dinosaur'

Teleportation has been a device in science fiction for well over a century. It is most famously used in the TV show *Star Trek*. Inside the transporter room of the *Enterprise*, Captain Picard steps onto a special pad whereupon a beam scans every detail of his body and brain, allowing him to be exactly reconstructed on the surface of a nearby planet a moment later. As a sophisticated citizen of the twenty-fourth century, Picard hardly bats an eyelid at this extraordinary process. We, the audience, are also encouraged to believe that transporter users routinely survive. Barring some unusual accident, the person who steps onto the transporter pad is the same person who appears on the planet shortly afterwards. Both philosophers and science-fiction authors have come to be suspicious about this idea however, even as a fictional device. James Patrick Kelly's story perfectly captures these suspicions.

A crucial detail that *Star Trek* tends to gloss over is whether the teleportation device transmits the physical matter out of which the individual is made, or only a stream of information which serves as a blueprint to reconstruct the individual from local materials. Physically speaking, the latter option is considerably more convenient. After all, one carbon atom is much the same as any other, and in our ordinary lives we constantly gain and lose atoms with no ill effects. So we might suppose that so long as the information that characterizes us is preserved, it does not matter if all of our matter is replaced. Yet the information-only case of teleportation raises deep philosophical worries about survival.

The problem, as Kelly's story points out, is that of potential duplicates. After Kamala Shastri is scanned on the space station in lunar orbit, the teleportation device is then supposed to destroy her before beaming the information to Epsilon Leo. Yet collecting information about a person and then beaming it to some other location seems to be metaphysically independent from destroying the person who is scanned. That is, you are not forced to destroy that person in order to use the information elsewhere. You could just as easily leave the scanned person intact and use the information to create a duplicate. So now we have two people: the Kamala in lunar orbit, and the Kamala on Epsilon Leo. Can we debate which of these is the true Kamala? As Kelly's story depicts, the Kamala remaining in lunar orbit is liable to complain very loudly that it doesn't matter how many duplicates are created, she remains herself. Scanning the position of every atom in her body doesn't change that, for the same reason that taking a photograph doesn't change that.

Yet if that's what we think about the duplication case, we should reconsider the case in which nothing goes wrong. Lunar Kamala gets into the transporter, is scanned, destroyed and the information used to create a being in the Epsilon Leo system. Epsilon Leo Kamala can claim to be the one true Kamala without any annoying objections from competitors. Yet we may still regard the Epsilon Leo individual as a duplicate, and not the original Kamala transported to a new location. Again, this is because the process of constructing Epsilon Leo Kamala is strictly independent from the process of destroying lunar Kamala. The existence of the Epsilon Leo Kamala does not *rely* on the destruction of lunar Kamala in any deep metaphysical sense. In contrast, my existence right now very much depends on what happened to the person sitting in this chair a minute ago, specifically, that they weren't obliterated. This is a basic feature of what it is for a being to persist over time. So, given that this feature of persistence has not been satisfied, Epsilon Leo Kamala should not say that lunar Kamala is their self-same person.

A side note: this argument does not apply if the matter out of which lunar Kamala was made were transmitted to Epsilon Leo. Now there would be a definite causal dependence of one Kamala upon the other. I am however also disturbed by matter transmission varieties of teleportation. Wouldn't smushing up Kamala destroy her, regardless of how that matter is restructured later on? Imagine, by analogy, if we put a Picasso painting in a blender, then poured the resultant mash out onto the floor and laboriously redistributed the atoms of paint so they exactly matched the original. Is this still the original painting? Can an object survive temporary destruction? I'm honestly not sure (and that, to me, suggests that it's a less helpful thought experiment).

Meanwhile, the information-only form of teleportation looks to me like death, and the story does a very effective job of convincing me of this. That is, I do not subscribe to the dinosaurs' cold-blooded way of thinking about identity. Prior to reading stories such as Kelly's, I recall blithely assuming that I'd survive teleportation (no doubt influenced by its depiction in *Star Trek*). Yet I quickly changed my mind once I had been taken through a narrative of the potential consequences. As such, this seems to me an exemplary case in which a science fiction narrative helps us to think more clearly about a metaphysical issue, practically the narrative equivalent of a visual proof in mathematics. Hopefully you agree. Or even if you believe that you would survive teleportation you should at least have a clearer notion of what you are committing to.

The view that teleportation is death also has implications for two other popular science-fiction scenarios. First, it implies that 'mind-swap' cases, in which the pattern of someone's mind is recorded from their brain and then imprinted into another person's brain, are not genuine cases in which a person is transported. Again, all that happens here is that information is duplicated in the way that information always can be. Second, it also implies that 'mind-uploading' is death. This is because mind-uploading, if it deserves the name at all, is a scenario in which information about a person's mental properties is reproduced in a piece of software. That's what normal uploading does. Nothing is physically moved, despite the image of movement that the word 'uploading' suggests. Even worse, mind-uploading doesn't re-instantiate the person's mental information in a definite physical form, since the usual conceit of such stories is that the uploaded person can 'move' between computers. Of course, this isn't to deny that these stories are fun, or worth thinking about. It's just to claim that they stand or fall together with teleportation as tests of personal survival. This is the reason why I don't include stories on these scenarios in this book. If you disagree with my analysis that teleportation is death, you could draw the same conclusion about these other scenarios.

Another scenario that seems to be equivalent, metaphysically speaking, to teleportation, mind-swapping and mind-uploading is, surprisingly enough, the Christian story of bodily resurrection after death. If we suppose that resurrection occurs via the mind of God – that is to say, that God remembers exactly how you were and uses this information to recreate you – then again this is a case in which there is no physical continuity. Alternatively, if God retrieves the particular atoms that made you up, this is equivalent to the smushing version of teleportation. I suppose God would have to use the atoms you had at the actual moment of death, rather than ones from some earlier, healthier stage of life. Otherwise the temporal parts of you following that healthy stage would count as duplicates and things are going to get metaphysically messy again. I assume that God will also have to arrange things so that the atoms making you up aren't needed to make up other people from other points of history.

At any rate, the teleportation thought experiment makes a more general point beyond how we should feel about these various scenarios. The technology involved is, after all, not very feasible. More important is the suggestion that we are not patterns of information. Even if one accepts the psychological view that our mental natures are our essence, it still seems to be important that this mental nature has a specific physical instantiation with a specific concrete history. A pattern of information, in contrast, is an abstract object (or what philosophers call a 'universal'). It can be instantiated in a large variety of ways without being destroyed. So it could be transmitted by telegraph or written out on millions of pieces of paper or captured in the bits of a computer programme. This is the sort of identity that books have (indeed, Dennett explicitly says that his narrative view of identity allows for teleportation). We do not destroy *Moby Dick* by burning one of its copies. We may not even destroy *Moby Dick* by burning all of its copies, given that many people would still remember it. And if all those memories of the book were destroyed as well, would we now have rid the world of *Moby Dick*? Maybe. Or maybe that precise pattern of words still exists as pure potential, waiting to be reinstantiated.

There is another important consideration that we get from Kelly's story, which is also directly relevant to the memory view of personal identity. This is the idea that a person can be wrong about their own identity. At the end of the story, we hear from a Kamala Shastri who has apparently experienced the trip to and from the Epsilon Leo system. She claims to have met Michael before. She regrets what she believes to have been her attitude three years earlier and says, 'I feel so silly now. I mean, I was in the marble for less than a minute and then –' she snapped her fingers – 'there I was on Gend, just like you said'. The story clearly intends for us to regard this Kamala as entirely deceived about what has occurred. She is unaware that what really happened to lunar Kamala is that she was thrown out of the airlock. She also seems to be unaware that she isn't Epsilon Leo Kamala either, but yet another duplicate.

What's nice about Kelly's story is that we can imagine how things seem to new Kamala and why it would be reasonable for her to make the mistakes that she does. Epsilon-Leo Kamala was created with a brain structure that resembles lunar Kamala's brain one minute after being enclosed in the marble. This brain structure encodes lots of information about being in the lunar station and all of lunar Kamala's other experiences. Philosophers have called this information 'quasi-memories' or 'q-memories'. Q-memories are defined as states that *seem* like memories, and refer to *some person's* experiences but do not automatically imply that their possessor is to be identified with that past person. So on the basis of her q-memories, Epsilon-Leo Kamala feels a sense of continuity with lunar Kamala. She *feels* like she is more than a few minutes old. But she is not. The same applies to the new Kamala that appears on lunar station three years later.

So the teleportation thought experiment forces us to refine any theory that relies on memories to define personal identity. It is not enough that it seems to us subjectively as if we have endured over a certain span of time. Our seeming-memories may be deceptive. We have to add a condition that these seeming-memories have the right kind of causal dependence on the person's past experiences. Duplication is not a legitimate kind of causal dependence. A legitimate causal connection is that the actual experience of the event is encoded in one's brain structure, and that brain structure remains physically intact until such point as one reactivates it in recalling the experience. Is this the only legitimate way to have a memory? Well, it is hard to see how any other method avoids the charge of duplication. Suppose, for instance, that I have an experience and write all the details down in my diary that same day. Then suppose that I forget the experience beyond the capacity for recall, but I'm able to use my diary entry to accurately imagine what the experience was like. If we don't admit cases of duplication as genuine, then it looks like this pathway is illegitimate as well.

Overall, Kelly's teleportation story does a good job of clarifying another feature of personal identity, one that is particularly relevant to the memory theory. Memories may seem like just another kind of abstract information that could be physically realized in all sorts of ways, but if they are to do the job of making us what we are, it is important that they retain a link to our concrete individuality.

# 7

# 'The Extra'

## Greg Egan

---

Daniel Gray didn't merely arrange for his Extras to live in a building within the grounds of his main residence – although that in itself would have been shocking enough. At the height of his midsummer garden party, he had their trainer march them along a winding path which took them within metres of virtually every one of his wealthy and powerful guests.

There were five batches, each batch a decade younger than the preceding one, each comprising twenty-five Extras (less one or two here and there; naturally, some depletion had occurred, and Gray made no effort to hide the fact). Batch A were forty-four years old, the same age as Gray himself. Batch E, the four-year-olds, could not have kept up with the others on foot, so they followed behind, riding an electric float.

The Extras were as clean as they'd ever been in their lives, and their hair – and beards in the case of the older ones – had been laboriously trimmed, in styles that amusingly parodied the latest fashions. Gray had almost gone so far as to have them clothed – but after much experimentation he'd decided against it; even the slightest scrap of clothing made them look too human, and he was acutely aware of the boundary between impressing his guests with his daring, and causing them real discomfort. Of course, naked, the Extras looked exactly like naked humans, but in Gray's cultural milieu, stark naked humans en masse were not a common sight, and so the paradoxical effect of revealing the creatures' totally human appearance was to make it easier to think of them as less than human.

The parade was a great success. Everyone applauded demurely as it passed by – in the context, an extravagant gesture of approval. They weren't applauding the Extras themselves, however impressive they were to behold; they were applauding Daniel Gray for his audacity in breaking the taboo.

Gray could only guess how many people in the world had Extras; perhaps the wealthiest ten thousand, perhaps the wealthiest hundred thousand. Most owners chose to be discreet. Keeping a stock of congenitally brain-damaged clones of oneself – in the short term, as organ donors; in the long term (once the techniques were perfected), as the recipients of brain transplants – was not illegal, but nor was it widely accepted. Any owner who went public could expect a barrage of anonymous hate mail, intense media scrutiny, property damage, threats of violence – all the usual behaviour associated with the public debate of a subtle point of ethics. There had been legal challenges, of course, but time and again the highest courts had ruled that Extras were not human beings. Too much cortex was missing; if Extras deserved human rights, so did half the mammalian species on the planet. With a patient, skilled trainer, Extras could learn to run in circles, and to perform the simple, repetitive exercises that kept their muscles in good tone, but that was about the limit. A dog or a cat would have needed brain tissue removed to persuade it to live such a boring life.

Even those few owners who braved the wrath of the fanatics, and bragged about their Extras, generally had them kept in commercial stables – in the same city, of course, so as not to undermine their usefulness in a medical emergency, but certainly not within the electrified boundaries of their own homes. What ageing, dissipated man or woman would wish to be surrounded by reminders of how healthy and vigorous they might have been, if only they'd lived their lives differently?

Daniel Gray, however, found the contrasting appearance of his Extras entirely pleasing to behold, given that he, and not they, would be the ultimate beneficiary of their good health. In fact, his athletic, clean-living brothers had already supplied him with two livers, one kidney, one lung, and quantities of coronary artery and mucous membrane. In each case, he'd had the donor put down, whether or not it had remained strictly viable; the idea of having imperfect Extras in his collection offended his aesthetic sensibilities.

After the appearance of the Extras, nobody at the party could talk about anything else. Perhaps, one stereovision luminary suggested, now that their host had shown such courage, it would at last became fashionable to flaunt one's Extras, allowing full value to be extracted from them; after all, considering the cost, it was a crime to make use of them only in emergencies, when their pretty bodies went beneath the surgeon's knife.

Gray wandered from group to group, listening contentedly, pausing now and then to pluck and eat a delicate spice-rose or a juicy claret-apple (the entire garden had been designed specifically to provide the refreshments for this annual occasion, so everything was edible, and everything was in season). The early afternoon sky was a dazzling, uplifting blue, and he stood for a moment with his face raised to the warmth of the sun. The party was a complete success. Everyone was talking about him. He hadn't felt so happy in years.

"I wonder if you're smiling for the same reason I am."

He turned. Sarah Brash, the owner of Continental Bio-Logic, and a recent former lover, stood beside him, beaming in a faintly unnatural way. She wore one of the patterned scarfs which Gray had made available to his guests; a variety of gene-tailored insects roamed the garden, and her particular choice of scarf attracted a bee whose painless sting contained a combination of a mild stimulant and an aphrodisiac.

He shrugged. "I doubt it."

She laughed and took his arm, then came still closer and whispered, "I've been thinking a very wicked thought."

He made no reply. He'd lost interest in Sarah a month ago, and the sight of her in this state did nothing to rekindle his desire. He had just broken off with her successor, but he had no wish to repeat himself. He was trying to think of something to say that would be offensive enough to drive her away, when she reached out and tenderly cupped his face in her small, warm hands.

Then she playfully seized hold of his sagging jowls, and said, in tones of mock aggrievement, "Don't you think it was terribly selfish of you, Daniel? You gave me your body . . . but you didn't give me your best one."

\*

Gray lay awake until after dawn. Vivid images of the evening's entertainment kept returning to him, and he found them difficult to banish. The Extra Sarah had chosen – C7, one of the twenty-four-year-olds – had been muzzled and tightly bound throughout, but it had made copious noises in its throat, and its eyes had been remarkably expressive. Gray had learnt, years ago, to keep a mask of mild amusement and boredom on his face, whatever he was feeling; to see fear, confusion, distress and ecstasy, nakedly displayed on features that, in spite of everything, were unmistakably his own, had been rather like a nightmare of losing control.

Of course, it had also been as inconsequential as a nightmare; he had not lost control for a moment, however much his animal look-alike had rolled its eyes, and moaned, and trembled. His appetite for sexual novelty aside, perhaps he had agreed to Sarah's request for that very reason: to see this primitive aspect of himself unleashed, without the least risk to his own equilibrium.

He decided to have the creature put down in the morning; he didn't want it corrupting its clone-brothers, and he couldn't be bothered arranging to have it kept in isolation. Extras had their sex drives substantially lowered by drugs, but not completely eliminated – that would have had too many physiological side-effects – and Gray had heard that it took just one clone who had discovered the possibilities, to trigger widespread masturbation and homosexual behaviour throughout the batch. Most owners would not have cared, but Gray wanted his Extras to be more than merely healthy; he wanted them to be innocent, he wanted them to be without sin. He was not a religious man, but he could still appreciate the emotional power of such concepts. When the time came for his brain to be moved into a younger body, he wanted to begin his new life with a sense of purification, a sense of rebirth.

However sophisticated his amorality, Gray freely admitted that at a certain level, inaccessible to reason, his indulgent life sickened him, as surely as it sickened his body. His family and his peers had always, unequivocally, encouraged him to seek pleasure, but perhaps he had been influenced – subconsciously and unwillingly – by ideas which still prevailed in other social strata. Since the late twentieth century, when – in affluent countries – cardiovascular disease and other "diseases of lifestyle" had become the major causes of death, the notion that health was a reward for virtue had acquired a level of acceptance unknown since the medieval plagues. A healthy lifestyle was not just pragmatic, it was righteous. A heart attack or a stroke, lung cancer or liver disease – not to mention AIDS – was clearly a punishment for some vice that the sufferer had chosen to pursue. Twenty-first century medicine had gradually weakened many of the causal links between lifestyle and life expectancy – and the advent of Extras would, for the very rich, soon sever them completely – but the outdated moral overtones persisted nonetheless.

In any case, however fervently Gray approved of his gluttonous, sedentary, drug-hazed, promiscuous life, a part of him felt guilty and unclean. He could not wipe out his past, nor did he wish to, but to discard his ravaged body and begin again in blameless flesh would be the perfect way to neutralise this irrational self-disgust. He would attend his own cremation, and watch his "sinful" corpse consigned to "hellfire"! Atheists, he decided, are not immune to religious metaphors; he had no doubt that the experience would be powerfully moving, liberating beyond belief.

\*

Three months later, Sarah Brash's lawyers informed him that she had conceived a child (which, naturally, she'd had transferred to an Extra surrogate), and that she cordially requested that Gray provide her with fifteen billion dollars to assist with the child's upbringing.

His first reaction was a mixture of irritation and amusement at his own naivety. He should have suspected that there'd been more to Sarah's request than sheer perversity. Her wealth was comparable to his own, but the prospect of living for centuries seemed to have made the rich greedier than ever; a fortune that sufficed for seven or eight decades was no longer enough.

On principle, Gray instructed his lawyers to take the matter to court – and then he began trying to ascertain what his chances were of winning. He'd had a vasectomy years ago, and could produce records proving his infertility, at least on every occasion he'd had a sperm count measured. He couldn't prove that he hadn't had the operation temporarily reversed, since that could now be done with hardly a trace, but he knew perfectly well that the Extra was the father of the child, and he could prove that. Although the Extras' brain damage resulted solely from foetal microsurgery, rather than genetic alteration, all Extras were genetically tagged with a coded serial number, written into portions of DNA which had no active function, at over a thousand different sites. What's more, these tags were always on both chromosomes of each pair, so any child fathered by an Extra would necessarily inherit all of them. Gray's biotechnology advisers assured him that stripping these tags from the zygote was, in practice, virtually impossible.

Perhaps Sarah planned to freely admit that the Extra was the father, and hoped to set a precedent making its owner responsible for the upkeep of its human offspring. Gray's legal experts were substantially less reassuring than his geneticists. Gray could prove that the Extra hadn't raped her – as she no doubt knew, he'd taped everything that had happened that night – but that wasn't the point; after all, consenting to intercourse would not have deprived her of the right to an ordinary paternity suit. As the tapes also showed, Gray had known full well what was happening, and had clearly approved. That the late Extra had been unwilling was, unfortunately, irrelevant.

After wasting an entire week brooding over the matter, Gray finally gave up worrying. The case would not reach court for five or six years, and was unlikely to be resolved in less than a decade. He promptly had his remaining Extras vasectomised – to prove to the courts, when the time came, that he was not irresponsible – and then he pushed the whole business out of his mind.

Almost.

A few weeks later, he had a dream. Conscious all the while that he was dreaming, he saw the night's events re-enacted, except that this time it was he who was bound and muzzled, slave to Sarah's hands and tongue, while the Extra stood back and watched.

But ... had they merely swapped places, he wondered, or had they swapped bodies? His dreamer's point of view told him nothing – he saw all three bodies from the outside – but the lean young man who watched bore Gray's own characteristic jaded expression, and the middle-aged man in Sarah's embrace moaned and twitched and shuddered, exactly as the Extra had done.

Gray was elated. He still knew that he was only dreaming, but he couldn't suppress his delight at the inspired idea of keeping his old body alive with the Extra's brain, rather than consigning it to flames. What could be more controversial, more outrageous, than having not just his Extras, but his own discarded corpse, walking the grounds of his estate? He resolved at once to do this, to abandon his long-held desire for a symbolic cremation. His friends would be shocked into the purest admiration – as would the fanatics, in their own way. True infamy had proved elusive; people had talked about his last stunt for a week or two, and then forgotten it – but the midsummer party at which the guest of honour was Daniel Gray's old body would be remembered for the rest of his vastly prolonged life.

\*

Over the next few years, the medical research division of Gray's vast corporate empire began to make significant progress on the brain transplant problem.

Transplants between newborn Extras had been successful for decades. With identical genes, and having just emerged from the very same womb (or from the anatomically and biochemically indistinguishable wombs of two clone-sister Extras), any differences between donor and recipient were small enough to be overcome by a young, flexible brain.

However, older Extras – even those raised identically – had shown remarkable divergences in many neural structures, and whole-brain transplants between them had been found to result in paralysis, sensory dysfunction, and sometimes even death. Gray was no neuroscientist, but he could understand roughly what the problem was: Brain and body grow and change together throughout life, becoming increasingly reliant on each other's idiosyncrasies, in a feed-back process riddled with chaotic attractors – hence the unavoidable differences, even between clones. In the body of a human (or an Extra), there are thousands of sophisticated control systems which may include the brain, but are certainly not contained within it, involving everything from the spinal cord and the peripheral nervous system, to hormonal feedback loops, the immune system, and, ultimately, almost every organ in the body. Over time, all of these elements adapt in some degree to the particular demands placed upon them – and the brain grows to rely upon the specific characteristics that these external systems acquire. A brain transplant throws this complex interdependence into disarray – at least as badly as a massive stroke, or an extreme somatic trauma.

Sometimes, two or three years of extensive physiotherapy could enable the transplanted brain and body to adjust to each other – but only between clones of equal age and indistinguishable lifestyles. When the brain donor was a model of a likely human candidate – an intentionally overfed, under-exercised, drug-wrecked Extra, twenty or thirty years older than the body donor – the result was always death or coma.

The theoretical solution, if not the detailed means of achieving it, was obvious. Those portions of the brain responsible for motor control, the endocrine system, the low-level processing of sensory data, and so on, had to be retained in the body in which they had matured. Why struggle to make the donor brain adjust to the specifics of a new body, when that body's original brain already contained neural systems fine-tuned to perfection for the task? If the aim was to transplant memory and personality, why transplant anything else?

After many years of careful brain-function mapping, and the identification and synthesis of growth factors which could trigger mature neurons into sending forth axons across the boundaries of a graft, Gray's own team had been the first to try partial transplants. Gray watched tapes of the operations, and was both repelled and amused to see oddly shaped lumps of one Extra's brain being exchanged with the corresponding regions of another's; repelled by visceral instinct, but amused to see the seat of reason – even in a mere Extra – being treated like so much vegetable matter.

The forty-seventh partial transplant, between a sedentary, ailing fifty-year-old, and a fit, healthy twenty-year-old, was an unqualified success. After a mere two months of recuperation, both Extras were fully mobile, with all five senses completely unimpaired.

Had they swapped memories and "personalities"? Apparently, yes. Both had been observed by a team of psychologists for a year before the operation, and their behaviour extensively characterised, and both had been trained to perform different sets of tasks for rewards. After the selective brain swap, the learned tasks, and the observed behavioural idiosyncrasies, were found to have followed the transplanted tissue. Of course, eventually the younger, fitter Extra began to be affected by its newfound health, becoming substantially more active than it had been in its original body – and the Extra now in the older body soon showed signs of acquiescing to its ill-health. But regardless of any post-transplant adaption to their new bodies, the fact remained that the Extras' identities – such as they were – had been exchanged.

After a few dozen more Extra-Extra transplants, with virtually identical outcomes, the time came for the first human-Extra trials.

Gray's parents had both died years before (on the operating table – an almost inevitable outcome of their hundreds of non-essential transplants), but they had left him a valuable legacy; thirty years ago, their own scientists had (illegally) signed up fifty men and women in their early twenties, and Extras had been made for them. These volunteers had been well paid, but not so well paid that a far larger sum, withheld until after the actual transplant, would lose its appeal. Nobody had been coerced, and the seventeen who'd dropped out quietly had not been punished. An eighteenth had tried blackmail – even though she'd had no idea who was doing the experiment, let alone who was financing it – and had died in a tragic ferry disaster, along with three hundred and nine other people. Gray's people believed in assassinations with a low signal-to-noise ratio.

Of the thirty-two human-Extra transplants, twenty-nine were pronounced completely successful. As with the Extra-Extra trials, both bodies were soon fully functional, but now the humans in the younger bodies could – after a month or two of speech therapy – respond to detailed interrogation by experts, who declared that their memories and personalities were intact.

Gray wanted to speak to the volunteers in person, but knew that was too risky, so he contented himself with watching tapes of the interviews. The psychologists had their barrages of supposedly rigourous tests, but Gray preferred to listen to the less formal segments, when the volunteers spoke of their life histories, their political and religious beliefs, and so on – displaying at least as much consistency across the transplant as any person who is asked to discuss such matters on two separate occasions.

The three failures were difficult to characterise. They too learnt to use their new bodies, to walk and talk as proficiently as the others, but they were depressed, withdrawn, and uncooperative. No physical difference could be found – scans showed that their grafted tissue, and the residual portions of their Extra's brain, had forged just as many interconnecting pathways as the brains of the other volunteers. They seemed to be unhappy with a perfectly successful result – they seemed to have simply decided that they didn't want younger bodies, after all.

Gray was unconcerned; if these people were disposed to be ungrateful for their good fortune, that was a character defect that he knew he did not share. He would be utterly delighted to have a fresh young body to enjoy for a while – before setting out to wreck it, in the knowledge that, in a decade's time, he could take his pick from the next batch of Extras and start the whole process again.

There were "failures" amongst the Extras as well, but that was hardly surprising – the creatures had no way of even beginning to comprehend what had happened to them. Symptoms ranged from loss of appetite to extreme, uncontrollable violence; one Extra had even managed to batter itself to death on a concrete floor, before it could be tranquillised. Gray hoped his own Extra would turn out to be well-behaved – he wanted his old body to be clearly sub-human, but not utterly berserk – but it was not a critical factor, and he decided against diverting resources towards the problem. After all, it was the fate of his brain in the Extra's body that was absolutely crucial; success with the other half of the swap would be an entertaining bonus, but if it wasn't achieved, well, he could always revert to cremation.

\*

Gray scheduled and cancelled his transplant a dozen times. He was not in urgent need by any means – there was nothing currently wrong with him that required a single new organ, let alone an entire new body – but he desperately wanted to be first. The penniless volunteers didn't count – and that was why he hesitated: trials on humans from those lower social classes struck him as not much more reassuring than trials on Extras. Who was to say that a process that left a rough-hewn, culturally deficient personality intact, would preserve his own refined, complex sensibilities? Therein lay the dilemma: he would only feel safe if he knew that an equal – a rival – had undergone a transplant before him, in which case he would be deprived of all the glory of being a path-breaker. Vanity fought cowardice; it was a battle of titans.

It was the approach of Sarah Brash's court case that finally pushed him into making a decision. He didn't much care how the case itself went; the real battle would be for the best publicity; the media would determine who won and who lost, whatever the jury decided. As things stood, he looked like a naive fool, an easily manipulated voyeur, while Sarah came across as a smart operator. She'd shown initiative; he'd just let himself (or rather, his Extra) get screwed. He needed an edge, he needed a gimmick – something that would overshadow her petty scheming. If he swapped bodies with an Extra in time for the trial – becoming, officially, the first human to do so – nobody would waste time covering the obscure details of Sarah's side of the case. His mere presence in court would be a matter of planet-wide controversy; the legal definition of identity was still based on DNA fingerprinting and retinal patterns, with some clumsy exceptions thrown in to allow for gene therapy and retina transplants. The laws would soon be changed – he was arranging it – but as things stood, the subpoena would apply to his old body. He could just imagine sitting in the public gallery, unrecognised, while Sarah's lawyer tried to cross-examine the quivering, confused, wild-eyed Extra that his discarded "corpse" had become! Quite possibly he, or his lawyers, would end up being charged with contempt of court, but it would be worth it for the spectacle.

So, Gray inspected Batch D, which were now just over nineteen years old. They regarded him with their usual idiotic, friendly expression. He wondered, not for the first time, if any of the Extras ever realised that he was their clone-brother, too. They never seemed to respond to him any differently than they did to other humans – and yet a fraction of a gram of foetal brain tissue was all that had kept him from being one of them. Even Batch A, his "contemporaries", showed no sign of recognition. If he had stripped naked and mimicked their grunting sounds, would they have accepted him as an equal? He'd never felt inclined to find out; Extra "anthropology" was hardly something he wished to encourage, let alone participate in. But he decided he would return to visit Batch D in his new body; it would certainly be amusing to see just what they made of a clone-brother who vanished, then came back three months later with speech and clothes.

The clones were all in perfect health, and virtually indistinguishable. He finally chose one at random. The trainer examined the tattoo on the sole of its foot, and said, "D12, sir."

Gray nodded, and walked away.

\*

He spent the week before the transplant in a state of constant agitation. He knew exactly which drugs would have prevented this, but the medical team had advised him to stay clean, and he was too afraid to disobey them.

He watched D12 for hours, trying to distract himself with the supposedly thrilling knowledge that those clear eyes, that smooth skin, those taut muscles, would soon be his. The only trouble was, this began to seem a rather paltry reward for the risk he would be taking. Knowing all his life that this day would come, he'd learnt not to care at all what he looked like; by now, he was so used to his own appearance that he wasn't sure he especially wanted to be lean and muscular and rosy-cheeked. After all, if that really had been his fondest wish, he could have achieved it in other ways; some quite effective pharmaceuticals and tailored viruses had existed for decades, but he had chosen not to use them. He had enjoyed looking the part of the dissolute billionaire, and his wealth had brought him more sexual partners than his new body would ever attract through its own merits. In short, he neither wanted nor needed to change his appearance at all.

So, in the end it came down to longevity, and the hope of immortality. As his parents had proved, any transplant involved a small but finite risk. A whole new body every ten or twenty years was surely a far safer bet than replacing individual organs at an increasing rate, for diminishing returns. And a whole new body now, long before he needed it, made far more sense than waiting until he was so frail that a small overdose of anaesthetic could finish him off.

When the day arrived, Gray thought he was, finally, prepared. The chief surgeon asked him if he wished to proceed; he could have said no, and she would not have blinked – not one his employees would have dared to betray the least irritation, had he cancelled their laborious preparations a thousand times.

But he didn't say no.

As the cool spray of the anaesthetic touched his skin, he suffered a moment of absolute panic. They were going to cut up his brain. Not the brain of a grunting, drooling Extra, not the brain of some ignorant slum-dweller, but his brain, full of memories of great music and literature and art, full of moments of joy and insight from the finest psychotropic drugs, full of ambitions that, given time, might change the course of civilisation.

He tried to visualise one of his favourite paintings, to provide an image he could dwell upon, a memory that would prove that the essential Daniel Gray had survived the transplant. That Van Gogh he'd bought last year. But he couldn't recall the name of it, let alone what it looked like. He closed his eyes and drifted helplessly into darkness.

\*

When he awoke, he was numb all over, and unable to move or make a sound, but he could see. Poorly, at first, but over a period that might have been hours, or might have been days – punctuated as it was with stretches of enervating, dreamless sleep – he was able to identify his surroundings. A white ceiling, a white wall, a glimpse of some kind of electronic device in the corner of one eye; the upper section of the bed must have been tilted, mercifully keeping his gaze from being strictly vertical. But he couldn't move his head, or his eyes, he couldn't even close his eyelids, so he quickly lost interest in the view. The light never seemed to change, so sleep was his only relief from the monotony. After a while, he began to wonder if in fact he had woken many times, before he had been able to see, but had experienced nothing to mark the occasions in his memory.

Later he could hear, too, although there wasn't much to be heard; people came and went, and spoke softly, but not, so far as he could tell, to him; in any case, their words made no sense. He was too lethargic to care about the people, or to fret about his situation. In time he would be taught to use his new body fully, but if the experts wanted him to rest right now, he was happy to oblige.

When the physiotherapists first set to work, he felt utterly helpless and humiliated. They made his limbs twitch with electrodes, while he had no control, no say at all in what his body did. Eventually, he began to receive sensations from his limbs, and he could at least feel what was going on, but since his head just lolled there, he couldn't watch what they were doing to him, and they made no effort to explain anything. Perhaps they thought he was still deaf and blind, perhaps his sight and hearing at this early stage were freak effects that had not been envisaged. Before the operation, the schedule for his recovery had been explained to him in great detail, but his memory of it was hazy now. He told himself to be patient.

When, at last, one arm came under his control, he raised it, with great effort, into his field of view.

It was his arm, his old arm – not the Extra's.

He tried to emit a wail of despair, but nothing came out.

Something must have gone wrong, late in the operation, forcing them to cancel the transplant after they had cut up his brain. Perhaps the Extra's life-support machine had failed; it seemed unbelievable, but it wasn't impossible – as his parents' deaths had proved, there was always a risk. He suddenly felt unbearably tired. He now faced the prospect of spending months merely to regain the use of his very own body; for all he knew, the newly forged pathways across the wounds in his brain might require as much time to become completely functional as they would have if the transplant had gone ahead.

For several days, he was angry and depressed. He tried to express his rage to the nurses and physiotherapists, but all he could do was twitch and grimace – he couldn't speak, he couldn't even gesture – and they paid no attention. How could his people have been so incompetent? How could they put him through months of trauma and humiliation, with nothing to look forward to but ending up exactly where he'd started?

But when he'd calmed down, he told himself that his doctors weren't incompetent at all; in fact, he knew they were the best in the world. Whatever had gone wrong must have been completely beyond their control. He decided to adopt a positive attitude to the situation; after all, he was lucky: the malfunction might have killed him, instead of the Extra. He was alive, he was in the care of experts, and what was three months in bed to the immortal he would still, eventually, become? This failure would make his ultimate success all the more of a triumph – personally, he could have done without the set-back, but the media would lap it up.

The physiotherapy continued. His sense of touch, and then his motor control, was restored to more and more of his body, until, although weak and uncoordinated, he felt without a doubt that this body was his. To experience familiar aches and twinges was a relief, more than a disappointment, and several times he found himself close to tears, overcome with mawkish sentiment at the joy of regaining what he had lost, imperfect as it was. On these occasions, he swore he would never try the transplant again; he would be faithful to his own body, in sickness and in health. Only by methodically reminding himself of all his reasons for proceeding in the first place, could he put this foolishness aside.

Once he had control of the muscles of his vocal cords, he began to grow impatient for the speech therapists to start work. His hearing, as such, seemed to be fine, but he could still make no sense of the words of the people around him, and he could only assume that the connections between the parts of his brain responsible for understanding speech, and the parts which carried out the lower-level processing of sound, were yet to be refined by whatever ingenious regime the neurologists had devised. He only wished they'd start soon; he was sick of this isolation.

*

One day, he had a visitor – the first person he'd seen since the operation who was not a health professional clad in white. The visitor was a young man, dressed in brightly coloured pyjamas, and travelling in a wheelchair.

By now, Gray could turn his head. He watched the young man approaching, surrounded by a retinue of obsequious doctors. Gray recognised the doctors; every member of the transplant team was there, and they were all smiling proudly, and nodding ceaselessly. Gray wondered why they had taken so long to appear; until now, he'd presumed that they were waiting until he was able to fully comprehend the explanation of their failure, but he suddenly realised how absurd that was – how could they have left him to make his own guesses? It was outrageous! It was true that speech, and no doubt writing too, meant nothing to him, but surely they could have devised some method of communication! And why did they look so pleased, when they ought to have been abject?

Then Gray realised that the man in the wheelchair was the Extra, D12. And yet he spoke. And when he spoke, the doctors shook with sycophantic laughter.

The Extra brought the wheelchair right up to the bed, and spent several seconds staring into Gray's face. Gray stared back; obviously he was dreaming, or hallucinating. The Extra's expression hovered between boredom and mild amusement, just as it had in the dream he'd had all those years ago.

The Extra turned to go. Gray felt a convulsion pass through his body. Of course he was dreaming. What other explanation could there be?

Unless the transplant had gone ahead, after all.

Unless the remnants of his brain in this body retained enough of his memory and personality to make him believe that he, too, was Daniel Gray. Unless the brain function studies that had localised identity had been correct, but incomplete – unless the processes that constituted human self-awareness were redundantly duplicated in the most primitive parts of the brain.

In which case, there were now two Daniel Grays.

One had everything: The power of speech. Money. Influence. Ten thousand servants. And now, at last, immaculate health.

And the other? He had one thing only.

The knowledge of his helplessness.

\*

It was, he had to admit, a glorious afternoon. The sky was cloudless, the air was warm, and the clipped grass beneath his feet was soft but dry.

He had given up trying to communicate his plight to the people around him. He knew he would never master speech, and he couldn't even manage to convey meaning in his gestures – the necessary modes of thought were simply no longer available to him, and he could no more plan and execute a simple piece of mime than he could solve the latest problems in grand unified field theory. For a while he had simply thrown tantrums – refusing to eat, refusing to cooperate. Then he had recalled his own plans for his old body, in the event of such recalcitrance. Cremation. And realised that, in spite of everything, he didn't want to die.

He acknowledged, vaguely, that in a sense he really wasn't Daniel Gray, but a new person entirely, a composite of Gray and the Extra D12 – but this was no comfort to him, whoever, whatever, he was. All his memories told him he was Daniel Gray; he had none from the life of D12, in an ironic confirmation of his long-held belief in human superiority over Extras. Should he be happy that he'd also proved – if there'd ever been any doubt – that human consciousness was the most physical of things, a spongy grey mess that could be cut up like a starfish, and survive in two separate parts? Should he be happy that the other Daniel Gray – without a doubt, the more complete Daniel Gray – had achieved his lifelong ambition?

The trainer yanked on his collar.

Meekly, he stepped onto the path.

The lush garden was crowded like never before – this was indeed the party of the decade – and as he came into sight, the guests began to applaud, and even to cheer.

He might have raised his arms in acknowledgement, but the thought did not occur to him.

# Comment on 'The Extra'

Greg Egan's story was the one that inspired me to put together this entire collection. It works beautifully as a thought experiment that explores and challenges an important assertion about personal identity. I even think that it succeeds in this way *because* of its qualities as a narrative fiction.

In earlier chapters we explored the memory criterion of personal identity, also known as the 'psychological continuity theory'. The preservation of our psychological qualities is widely believed to be key to our continued existence over time, specifically those qualities that we have gained as self-conscious, autonomous persons. We survive if at least some of these qualities remain, and we die if none of them do. Meanwhile, teleportation stories suggest that concrete physical continuity is required, rather than merely the transference of psychological information. Together, these ideas point us squarely at the brain as the vessel of our persistence over time. Accordingly, most philosophers believe that if you were to have your brain transplanted into another body, you would continue to exist in that other body.

One of the first things that Egan's story points out is that the prospect of transplanting a brain into another body is very far from straightforward. There are a large number of ways in which the brain and body adapt to each other over time. Our neurons send signals to the body via axons, or nerve fibres, the longest of which extends from the base of the spine to the big toe. Severing any of these connections by replacing either the axon or the neuron would require intensive readjustment. Egan plausibly supposes that the more similar the new body is to the original, the more smoothly this process will go. Thus cloned bodies are ideal. However, one is still risking bodily paralysis and death, should the transplanted brain be incapable of keeping up the basic control functions required for bodily survival.

Thus the second suggestion of Egan's story is that doctors do not transplant the entire brain, but only those parts serving the maintenance of personality and memory, and not basic sensory and motor functions. Again a major period of readjustment would be required, but at least the untouched brain areas should keep the new body alive long enough for this to occur. To what extent would the replacement of lower brain functions affect our unique identities? As I explored in response to Matthew Baker's 'Life Sentence', our physical skills contribute to our characters, and it is virtually certain that the specific ways we have learned to use our muscles in the exercise of these skills would be disrupted by a brain transplantation. Yet there is no need to deny that the transplantation process would lead to major changes in one's overall character. The psychological continuity theory is compatible with change. So long as some self-consciously acquired psychological features are preserved, this should be enough for survival.

Of course in Egan's story, the disastrous result of the partial brain transplant is that the being possessing the old body and brain remnants of Daniel Gray continues to think that he is Daniel Gray. The story speculates that he retains aspects of memory and personality, and/or that 'processes constituting human self-awareness were redundantly duplicated in the most primitive parts of the brain'. I take it that this is a possible consequence. It may be unlikely that the remnant brain is capable of the kind of reasoning and memory skills that Egan depicts (depending on how much has been transplanted) but it is hard to resist the idea that a kernel of self-awareness could persist. As a result, we have a dilemma as to whether the old-bodied individual or the young-bodied individual is the true Daniel Gray, if either is.

The reader may be tempted to dismiss this as a botched operation. A more complete transplant would still transplant the person. Yet Egan's story directly tackles one of the major controversies in the philosophy of personal identity. In the 1960s, the philosopher David Wiggins pointed out that, theoretically, we could transplant half a brain into one body and half a brain into another body. By that time, it was already known that splitting the corpus callosum (the band of tissue connecting the two sides of the cortex) was possible, though it created some interesting discontinuities in conscious experience that we will explore in a later story. Even more radically, some people survive hemispherectomies, in which one entire half of the cortex is removed. If half a cortex is enough for survival, then this potentially allows for half-brain transplants. Again, we can expect that the recipients of these brain halves would have impoverished mental characteristics. Still, they may retain enough psychological characteristics, including knowledge and episodic memories, such that each is psychologically continuous with the original.

Now we have a logical problem. According to the psychological continuity theory, the person receiving your left brain (Lefty) is you, and the person receiving your right brain (Righty) is also you. By the transitivity of identity (a necessary feature of identity that we introduced in the chapter on memory), if A is identical to B, and B is identical to C, then A *must* be identical to C. Yet Lefty and Righty are *not* numerically identical with each other. They are two entirely distinct people. Therefore, they cannot both be identical with the pre-transplant original. At the same time, it seems arbitrary to claim that only Lefty, or only Righty, is you, since both seem to retain first-person psychological characteristics of the pre-operative person. This is the same dilemma that Egan's story raises.

This is big trouble for the psychological continuity theory. Numerical identity and psychological continuity have different logical features. Psychological continuity can split into multiple streams while numerical identity cannot. Furthermore, if a varying number of psychological features can be preserved, then psychological continuity can come in degrees, while numerical identity is all or nothing. These considerations led the philosopher Derek Parfit in a famous paper to abandon the idea that numerical identity applies to persons. Parfit cared so much about psychological continuity that he declared that identity does not matter. What matters to us is that there is a being that is psychologically continuous with us, even if in certain scenarios, they are not really us. Parfit took this view to have major ethical implications.

Parfit may have been too hasty here. To the rescue of the psychological continuity theory of identity comes David Lewis' theory of temporal parts. Recall that Lewis proposed that a person should be conceived 4-dimensionally as extending over all the events that make up his or her life. He thought that this model could reconcile the differences between psychological continuity and numerical identity. This is because while psychological continuity is a relationship that glues one temporal part to the next temporal part, numerical identity applies to the whole person – their temporal parts altogether. The fact that psychological continuity has different logical qualities from numerical identity is no more surprising than a river having different logical qualities from wateriness. Wateriness is defined by the way that one water molecule is loosely connected to another. The river is defined by the larger-scale pathway of water molecules.

To clarify: when contemplating split-brain scenarios, Lewis asks us to suppose that a split happening over time is like a split happening in space. Imagine a road that begins in Adelaide and then at some point diverges, one branch going to Sydney and the other branch going to Melbourne. We can say that there are two roads, the one from Adelaide to Sydney and the one from Adelaide to Melbourne, even though these two roads share some parts. Analogously, Lefty is a different person from Righty, even though these two people share some *temporal parts*. Sharing parts is no big deal, metaphysically speaking. For instance, the football team can share parts with the choir, if there are people who belong to both.

Lewis' solution has a couple of unpalatable consequences. First, as we already noted when introducing the view, it seems that you have to buy into a controversial philosophy of time in which all events eternally exist. Second, the view entails that, if a person has divergence coming up in the future, then when we talk to them, we are actually talking to two people. Lewis accepts these consequences. He thinks that when we point to the road from Adelaide pre-divergence, we are pointing simultaneously at the road to Sydney and the road to Melbourne. Alternatively, you may find it more natural to say that we're really pointing at a bit of road, not the whole thing, so equally, we only ever interact with temporal parts, and not whole persons. But it's rather odd to think that we only ever interact with parts of people.

If you're happy with these consequences, then I wish you well in your new theory of personal identity. But let's suppose you are not, or that you're interested in exploring some other options. You could still accept Parfit's view that numerical identity claims should be abandoned. But another way to go is to reject the psychological continuity theory, for reasons that Greg Egan's story also raises.

When I read Egan's story, I'm at least tempted by the idea that the post-operative clone D12 is not Daniel Gray at all, despite the fact that he possesses a big part of Daniel Gray's brain. On the basis of various bits of knowledge or seeming memories, D12 might *think* that he's Daniel Gray, but as we saw when discussing teleportation, that is not a guarantee of identity. It's a consideration certainly, but not a guarantee.

So what about the intuition that we go with our brains in brain transplant scenarios? Well, maybe we should think of brain transplants in the same way that we think of other organ transplants. If I donate a kidney to you, this does not mean that I am transported into your body. It just means that I lose a part and you gain a part. Similarly, maybe I can donate some of my cognitive features to you, perhaps certain bits of knowledge or even personality characteristics (such as Daniel Gray's jaded manner) but that just means that I lose those features and you gain those features.

It's an interesting suggestion, but if D12 is not Daniel Gray, does this mean that old-bodied Gray is instead? There seem to be strong reasons to say yes, he is. First and foremost, old-bodied Gray retains Daniel Gray's living body. The life of this being has remained constant throughout. Old-bodied Gray also retains first-person consciousness. He has lost many of his psychological abilities but the continuity of his consciousness is basically like that of any of us when we go to sleep and wake up again. In Egan's story, old-bodied Gray also remembers many things about Daniel Gray's life. That puts the matter beyond doubt. Yet, I wonder, if old-bodied Gray were *not* to possess any of these memories, were he to lose his bodily skills and knowledge, might he still have a good claim to being Daniel Gray? In particular, if old-bodied Gray were conscious only of the present moment, he would still retain at least one vital continuity with Daniel Gray – the fundamental and pervasive concern for *this living body right here*. This concern is operative every time he feels pain or pleasure or engages in survival responses.

Taking this approach would shift us away from John Locke's view of self, and those following him in the psychological continuity tradition. Recall that in Locke's view, our memories allow our current self-consciousness to lay claim over past experiences; to unify them as belonging to one person. In contrast, a consciousness that only focused on the present moment would make no such claims upon the earlier life of their body. They would not *mentally represent* their continuity. They would simply *have* continuity, and we may think that this is what really matters for survival, not a sophisticated act of mental representation.

Such considerations move us towards the animalist view of identity that we will explore in later chapters. But for now we have to deal with the claims of clone D12. Although it might be *possible* to think of brains transplants like other organ transplants, what reasons have we to deny D12's identity with Daniel Gray? Note that we cannot simply deny their identity because they have different living bodies. That would commit the fallacy of begging the question; it would assume that sharing a body is the criterion of identity, when that is precisely what we are questioning.

Instead, let us try to start from a place where we all agree – that what we are is a thinking thing or conscious being. We can then deny D12's claim by denying that memory and personality are essential to being a thinking thing. Might it not be more accurate to regard memories and personality as *tools* that conscious beings use to achieve certain aims? For instance, my memory of the streets around my house makes it considerably easier for me to navigate them. My memory of my mother similarly makes it easier for me to interact with her. My personality features can similarly be understood as long-term strategies I possess for dealing with other people (e.g. whether I am shy or outgoing) or other sorts of life challenges (e.g. whether I avoid risks or embrace them). All these things are useful but they are not the essence of my consciousness.

Overall, I think there is an argument that Daniel Gray's partial brain transplant leaves him in the same body. And if we endorse this way of thinking about Daniel Gray's case, we may then return to the brain-splitting case of the philosophers with a rather different outlook. If neither Lefty nor

Righty retain the original conscious body, then neither of them are properly continuous with the original being. Instead, two new living beings have gained some cognitive abilities or traits, by means of organic cognitive implants. Meanwhile, the living being who donated the two halves of his cortex may survive if the subcortical regions of his brain are preserved. More likely he would be killed.

What I think is so valuable about Egan's story is that he takes the time to explore the complexities that brain transplantation would plausibly involve. The mordant conclusion in which a rich man's callous treatment of his clones is aptly repaid combines delightfully with the subversion of a philosophical assumption. It forcefully impresses me with the sense that philosophers talking about brain transplants have too glibly assumed that one's consciousness can be moved about, disconnected from the living being it serves. In particular, the brain splitting cases which generate such difficulty for the psychological continuity view demand a distinction between cortical regions and the subcortical regions. But we have very little reason to believe that consciousness can be simply cut adrift from those subcortical regions. Cortical regions are very likely to be involved in consciousness, but they are unlikely to be entirely sufficient for it. As Descartes observed, the mind is not like a sailor in a ship, something that can sit up in the cortex and watch the world go by. The mind is entirely intermingled with all our basic life functions. We shall develop this thought further in the chapters to come.

# 8

# *Sirius*

## *Olaf Stapledon*

## First Meeting

PLAXY and I had been lovers; rather uneasy lovers, for she would never speak freely about her past, and sometimes she withdrew into a cloud of reserve and despond. But often we were very happy together, and I believed that our happiness was striking deeper roots.

Then came her mother's last illness, and Plaxy vanished. Once or twice I received a letter from her, giving no address, but suggesting that I might reply to her "care of the Post Office" in a village in North Wales, sometimes one, sometimes another. In temper these letters ranged from a perfunctory amiability to genuine longing to have me again. They contained mysterious references to "a strange duty," which, she said, was connected with her father's work. The great physiologist, I knew, had been engaged on very sensational experiments on the brains of the higher mammals. He had produced some marvellously intelligent sheep-dogs, and at the time of his death it was said that he was concerned with even more ambitious research. One of the colder of Plaxy's letters spoke of an "unexpectedly sweet reward" in connection with her new duty, but in a more passionate one she cried out against "this exacting, fascinating, dehumanizing life." Sometimes she seemed to be in a state of conflict and torture about something which she must not explain. One of these letters was so distraught that I feared for her sanity. I determined therefore to devote my approaching leave to walking in North Wales in the hope of finding her.

I spent ten days wandering from pub to pub in the region indicated by the addresses, asking everywhere if a Miss Trelone was known in the neighbourhood. At last, in Llan Ffestiniog, I heard of her. There was a young lady of that name living in a shepherd's cottage on the fringe of the moor somewhere above Trawsfynydd. The local shopkeeper who gave me this information said with an air of mystery, "She is a strange young lady, indeed. She has friends, and I am one of them; but she has enemies."

Following his directions, I walked for some miles along the winding Trawsfynydd road and then turned to the left up a lane. After another mile or so, right on the edge of the open moor, I came upon a minute cottage built of rough slabs of shale, and surrounded by a little garden and stunted trees. The door was shut, but smoke rose from a chimney. I knocked. The door remained shut. Peering through a window, I saw a typical cottage kitchen, but on the table was a pile of books. I sat down on a rickety seat in the garden and noted the neat rows of cabbages and peas. Away to my right, across the deep Cynfal gorge, was Ffestiniog, a pack of slate-grey elephants following their leader, the unsteepled church, down a spur of hill towards the valley. Behind and above stood the Moelwyn range.

I was smoking my second cigarette when I heard Plaxy's voice in the distance. It was her voice that had first attracted me to her. Sitting in a cafe, I had been enthralled by that sensitive human sound coming from some unknown person behind me. And now once more I heard but did not see her. For a moment I listened with delight to her speech, which, as I had often said, was like the cool sparkling talk of small waves on the pebbly shore of a tarn on a hot day.

I rose to meet her, but something strange arrested me. Interspersed with Plaxy's remarks was no other human voice but a quite different sound, articulate but inhuman. Just before she came round the corner of the house she said, "But, my dear, don't dwell on your handlessness so! You have triumphed over it superbly." There followed a strange trickle of speech from her companion; then through the gate into the garden came Plaxy and a large dog.

She halted, her eyes wide with surprise, and (I hoped) with joy; but her brows soon puckered. Laying a hand on the dog's head, she stood silent for a moment. I had time to observe that a change had come over her. She was wearing rather muddy corduroy trousers and a blue shirt. The same grey eyes, the same ample, but decisive mouth, which had recently seemed to me to belie her character, the same shock of auburn, faintly carroty hair. But instead of a rather pale face, a ruddy brown one, and a complete absence of make-up. No lip-stick, even. The appearance of rude health was oddly contradicted by a darkness under the eyes and a tautness round the mouth. Strange how much one can notice in a couple of seconds, when one is in love!

Her hand deserted the dog's head, and was stretched out to me in welcome. "Oh well," she said smiling, "since you have nosed us out, we had better take you into our confidence." There was some embarrassment in her tone, but also perhaps a ring of relief. "Hadn't we, Sirius," she added, looking down at the great dog.

Then for the first time I took note of this remarkable creature. He was certainly no ordinary dog. In the main he was an Alsatian, perhaps with a dash of Great Dane or Mastiff, for he was a huge beast. His general build was wolf-like, but he was slimmer than a wolf, because of his height. His coat, though the hair was short, was superbly thick and silky, particularly round the neck, where it was a close turbulent ruff. Its silkiness missed effeminacy by a hint of stubborn harshness. Silk wire, Plaxy once called it. On back and crown it was black, but on flanks and legs and the under surface of his body it paled to an austere greyish fawn. There were also two large patches of fawn above the eyes, giving his face a strangely mask-like look, or the appearance of a Greek statue with blank-eyed helmet pushed back from the face. What distinguished Sirius from all other dogs was his huge cranium. It was not, as a matter of fact, quite as large as one would have expected in a creature of human intelligence, since, as I shall explain later, Trelone's technique not only increased the brain's bulk but also produced a refinement of the nerve fibres themselves. Nevertheless, Sirius's head was far loftier than any normal dog's. His high brow combined with the silkiness of his coat to give him a look of the famous Border Collie, the outstanding type of sheep-dog. I learned later that this brilliant race had, indeed, contributed to his make-up. But his cranium was far bigger than the Border Collie's. The dome reached almost up to the tips of his large Alsatian ears. To hold up this weight of head, the muscles of his neck and shoulders were strongly developed. At the moment of our encounter he was positively leonine, because the hair was bristling along his spine. Suspicion of me had brushed it up the wrong way. His grey eyes might have been wolf's eyes, had not the pupils been round like any dog's, not slits like the wolf's. Altogether he was certainly a formidable beast, lean and sinewy as a creature of the jungle.

Without taking his gaze off me, he opened his mouth, displaying sierras of ivory, and made a queer noise, ending with an upward inflection like a question. Plaxy replied, "Yes, it's Robert. He's true as steel, remember." She smiled at me deprecatingly, and added, "And he may be useful."

Sirius politely waved his amply feathered tail, but kept his cold eyes fixed on mine.

Another awkward pause settled upon us, till Plaxy said, "We have been working on the sheep out on the moor all day. We missed our dinner and I'm hungry as hell. Come in and I'll make tea for us all." She added as we entered the little flagged kitchen, "Sirius will understand everything you say. You won't be able to understand him at first, but I shall, and I'll interpret."

While Plaxy prepared a meal, passing in and out of the little larder, I sat talking to her. Sirius squatted opposite me, eyeing me with obvious anxiety. Seeing him, she said with a certain sharpness fading into gentleness, "Sirius! I tell you he's all right. Don't be so suspicious!" The dog rose, saying something in his strange lingo, and went out into the garden. "He's gone to fetch some firewood," she said; then in a lowered voice, "Oh, Robert, it's good to see you, though I didn't want you to find me." I rose to take her in my arms, but she whispered emphatically, "No, no, not now." Sirius returned with a log between his jaws. With a sidelong glance at the two of us, and a perceptible drooping of the tail, he put the log on the fire and went out again. "Why not now?" I cried, and she whispered, "Because of Sirius. Oh, you'll understand soon." After a pause she added, "Robert, you mustn't expect me to be wholly yours ever, not fully and single-heartedly yours. I'm too much involved in-in this work of my father's." I expostulated, and seized her. "Nice human Robert," she sighed, putting her head on my shoulder. But immediately she broke away, and said with emphasis, "No, I didn't say that. It was just the female human animal that said it. What I say is, I can't play the game you want me to play, not wholeheartedly."

Then she called through the open door, "Sirius, tea!" He replied with a bark, then strode in, carefully not looking at me.

She put a bowl of tea for him on a little table-cloth on the floor, remarking, "He has two meals generally, dinner at noon and supper in the evening. But today is different." Then she put down a large crust of bread, a hunk of cheese, and a saucer with a little lump of jam. "Will that keep you going?" she asked. A grunt signified approval.

Plaxy and I sat at the table to eat our bread and rationed butter and wartime cake. She set about telling me the history of Sirius. Sometimes I put in an occasional question, or Sirius interrupted with his queer speech of whimper and growl.

The matter of this and many other conversations about the past I shall set down in the following chapters. Meanwhile I must say this. Without the actual presence of Sirius I should not have believed the story; but his interruptions, though canine and unintelligible, expressed human intelligence by their modulation, and stimulated intelligible answers from Plaxy. Obviously he was following the conversation, commenting and watching my reaction. And so it was not with incredulity, though of course with amazement, that I learned of the origin and career of Sirius. I listened at first with grave anxiety, so deeply involved was Plaxy. I began to understand why it was that our love had always been uneasy, and why when her mother died she did not come back to me. I began to debate with myself the best way of freeing her from this "inhuman bondage." But as the conversation proceeded I could not but recognize that this strange relationship of girl and dog was fundamentally beautiful, in a way sacred. (That was the word I used to myself.) Thus my problem became far more difficult.

At one point, when Plaxy had been saying that she often longed to see me again, Sirius made a more sustained little speech. And in the middle of it he went over to her, put his fore-paws on the arm of her chair, and with great gentleness and delicacy kissed her cheek. She took the caress demurely, not shrinking away, as human beings generally do when dogs try to kiss them. But the healthy glow of her face deepened, and there was moisture in her eyes as she stroked the shaggy softness under his neck, and said to me, while still looking at him, "I am to tell you, Robert, that Sirius and Plaxy grew up together like the thumb and forefinger of a hand, that he loves me in the way that only dogs can love, and much more now that I have come to him, but that I must not feel bound to stay with him, because by now he can fend for himself. Whatever happens to him ever, I— how did you say it, Sirius, you foolish dear?" He put in a quick sentence, and she continued, "Oh, yes, I am the scent that he will follow always, hunting for God."

She turned her face towards me with a smile that I shall not forget. Nor shall I forget the bewildering effect of the dog's earnest and almost formal little declaration. Later I was to realize that a rather stilted diction was very characteristic of him, in moments of deep feeling.

Then Sirius made another remark with a sly look and a tremor of the tail. She turned back to him laughing, and softly smacked his face. "Beast," she said, "I shall not tell Robert that."

When Sirius kissed her I was startled into a sudden spasm of jealousy. (A man jealous of a dog!) But Plaxy's translation of his little speech roused more generous feelings. I now began to make plans by which Plaxy and I together might give Sirius a permanent home and help him to fulfil his destiny, whatever that might be. But, as I shall tell, a different fate lay in store for us.

During that strange meal Plaxy told me that, as I had guessed, Sirius was her father's crowning achievement, that he had been brought up as a member of the Trelone family, that he was now helping to run a sheep farm, that she herself was keeping house for him, and also working on the farm, compensating for his lack of hands.

After tea I helped her to wash up, while Sirius hovered about, jealous, I think, of my handiness. When we had finished, she said they must go over to the farm to complete a job of work before dark. I decided to walk back to Ffestiniog, collect my baggage and return by the evening train to Trawsfynydd, where I could find accommodation in the local pub. I noticed Sirius's tail droop as I said this. It drooped still further when I announced that I proposed to spend a week in the neighbourhood in the hope of seeing more of Plaxy. She said, "I shall be busy, but there are the evenings."

Before I left she handed over a collection of documents for me to take away and read at leisure. There were scientific papers by her father, including his journal of Sirius's growth and education. These documents, together with a diary of her own and brief fragmentary records by Sirius himself, all of which I was given at a much later date, form the main "sources" of the following narrative; these, and many long talks with Plaxy, and with Sirius when I had learnt to understand his speech.

I propose to use my imagination freely to fill out with detail many incidents about which my sources afford only the barest outline. After all, though a civil servant (until the Air Force absorbed me) I am also a novelist; and I am convinced that with imagination and self-criticism one can often penetrate into the essential spirit of events even when the data are superficial. I shall, therefore, tell the amazing story of Sirius in my own way.

## The Making of Sirius

PLAXY'S father, Thomas Trelone, was too great a scientist to escape all publicity, but his work on the stimulation of cortical growth in the brains of mammals was begun while he was merely a brilliant young research worker, and it was subsequently carried on in strict secrecy. He had an exaggerated, a morbid loathing of limelight. This obsession he justified by explaining that he dreaded the exploitation of his technique by quacks and profit-mongers. Thus it was that for many years his experiments were known only to a few of his most intimate professional colleagues in Cambridge, and to his wife, who had a part to play in them.

Though I have seen his records and read his papers, I can give only a layman's account of his work, for I am without scientific training. By introducing a certain hormone into the blood-stream of the mother he could affect the growth of the brain in the unborn young. The hormone apparently had a double effect. It increased the actual bulk of the cerebral cortices, and also it made the nerve-fibres themselves much finer than they normally are, so that a far greater number of them, and a far greater number of connections between them, occurred in any given volume of brain. Somewhat similar experiments, I believe, were carried out in America by Zamenhof; but there was an important difference between the two techniques. Zamenhof simply fed the young animal with his hormone; Trelone, as I have said, introduced his hormone into the foetus through the mother's blood-stream. This in itself was a notable achievement, because the circulatory systems of mother and foetus are fairly well insulated from each other by a filtering membrane. One of Trelone's difficulties was that the hormone caused growth in the maternal as well as the foetal brain, and since the mother's skull was adult and rigid there must inevitably be very serious congestion, which would lead to death unless some means were found to insulate her brain from the stimulating drug. This difficulty was eventually overcome. At last it became possible to assure the unborn animal a healthy maternal environment. After its birth Trelone periodically added doses of the hormone to its food, gradually reducing the dose as the growing brain approached what he considered a safe maximum size. He had also devised a technique for delaying the closing of the sutures between the bones of the skull, so that the skull might continue to expand as required.

A large population of rats and mice was sacrificed in the attempt to perfect Trelone's technique. At last he was able to produce a number of remarkable creatures. His big-headed rats, mice, guinea-pigs, rabbits, though their health was generally bad, and their lives were nearly always cut short by disease of one kind or another, were certainly geniuses of their humble order. They were remarkably quick at finding their way through mazes, and so on. In fact they far excelled their species in all the common tests of animal intelligence, and had the mentality rather of dogs and apes than of rodents.

But this was for Trelone only the beginning. While he was improving his technique so that he could ensure a rather more healthy animal, he at the same time undertook research into methods of altering the tempo of its life so that it should mature very slowly and live much longer than was normal to its kind. Obviously this was very important. A bigger brain needs a longer life-time to fulfil its greater potentiality for amassing and assimilating experience. Not until he had made satisfactory progress in both these enterprises did he begin to experiment on animals of greater size and higher type. This was a much more formidable undertaking, and promised no quick results. After a few years he had produced a number of clever but seedy cats, a bright monkey that died during its protracted adolescence, and a dog with so big a brain that its crushed and useless eyes were pushed forward along its nose. This creature suffered so much that its producer reluctantly destroyed it in infancy.

Not till several more years had elapsed, had Trelone perfected his technique to such an extent that he was able to pay less attention to the physiological and more to the psychological aspect of his problem. Contrary to his original plan, he worked henceforth mainly on dogs rather than apes. Of course apes offered the hope of more spectacular success. They were by nature better equipped than dogs. Their brains were bigger, their sight was more developed, and they had hands. Nevertheless from Trelone's point of view dogs had one overwhelming advantage. They were capable of a much greater freedom of movement in our society. Trelone confessed that he would have preferred to work on cats, because of their more independent mentality; but their small size made them unsuitable. A certain absolute bulk of brain was necessary, no matter what the size of the animal, so as to afford a wealth of associative neural paths. Of course a small animal did not need as large a brain as a large animal of the same mental rank. A large body needed a correspondingly large brain merely to work its machinery. A lion's brain had to be bigger than a cat's. An elephant's brain was even larger than a much more intelligent but smaller man's. On the other hand, each rank of intelligence, no matter what the size of the animal, required a certain degree of complexity of neural organization, and so of brain bulk. In proportion to the size of the human body a man's brain was far bigger than an elephant's. Some animals were large enough to accommodate the absolute bulk of brain needed for the human order of intelligence; some were not. A large dog could easily do so, but a cat's organization would be very gravely upset by so great an addition. For a mouse anything of the sort would be impossible.

Not that Trelone had at this stage any expectation of raising any animal so far in mental stature that it would approach human mentality. His aim was merely to produce, as he put it, "a rather super-sub-human intelligence, a missing-link mind." For this purpose the dog was admirably suited. Human society afforded for dogs many vocations requiring intelligence at the upper limit of the sub-human range. Trelone chose as the best vocation of all for his purpose that of the sheep-dog. His acknowledged ambition was to produce a "super-sheep-dog."

One other consideration inclined him to choose the dog; and the fact that he took this point into account at all in the early stage of his work shows that he was even then toying with the idea of producing something more than a missing-link mind. He regarded the dog's temperament as on the whole more capable of development to the human level. If cats excelled in independence, dogs excelled in social awareness; and Trelone argued that only the social animal could make full use of its intelligence. The independence of the cat was not, after all, the independence of the socially aware creature asserting its individuality; it was merely the blind individualism that resulted from social obtuseness. On the other hand he admitted that the dog's sociality involved it, in relation to man, in abject servility. But he hoped that with increased intelligence it might gain a measure of self-respect, and of critical detachment from humanity.

In due course Trelone succeeded in producing a litter of big-brained puppies. Most of them died before reaching maturity, but two survived, and became exceptionally bright dogs. This result was on the whole less gratifying than disappointing to Trelone. He carried out further experiments, and at last, from an Old English Sheep-dog bitch, produced a big-brained family, three of which survived, and reached a definitely supercanine level of mentality.

The research continued for some years. Trelone found it necessary to take more trouble about the "raw material" to which his technique was to be applied. He could not afford to neglect the fact that the most capable of all the canine races is the Border Collie, bred through a couple of centuries for intelligence and responsibility. All modern champions are of this breed, and all are descendants of a certain brilliant animal, named Old Hemp, who was born in Northumberland in 1893. The Border Collie of to-day is hardy, but rather small. Trelone, therefore, decided that the best raw material would be a cross between some outstanding champion of the International Sheep-Dog Trials and another intelligent but much heavier animal. The Alsatian was the obvious choice. After a good deal of negotiation with owners of champion sheep-dogs and enthusiasts for Alsatians, he produced several strains, which blended the two types in various proportions. He then applied his improved technique to various expectant mothers of these types, and in due season he was able to provide several of his friends with animals of "almost missing-link intelligence" as housedogs. But there was nothing spectacular about these creatures; and unfortunately all were delicate, and all died before their somewhat protracted adolescence was completed.

But at last further improvements in his technique brought him real success. He achieved several very bright animals with normally strong constitutions, predominantly Alsatian in appearance.

He had persuaded his wife Elizabeth that, if ever he succeeded to this extent, they should take a house in a sheep district in Wales. There she and the three children and the forthcoming baby would live, and he himself would spend the vacations and week-ends. After much exploration they found a suitable old farm-house not far from Trawsfynydd. Its name was "Garth." A good deal of work had to be done to turn it into a comfortable family home. Water-closets and a bathroom had to be installed. Some of the windows were enlarged. Electricity was laid on from the village. An outhouse was converted into a palatial kennel.

Some time after the fourth baby had been born, the family moved. They were accompanied by Kate, the long-established servant, who had somehow become practically a member of the family. A village girl was engaged as her assistant. There was also a nursemaid, Mildred; and, of course, the children, Thomasina, Maurice, Giles, and the baby Plaxy. Thomas took with him two canine families, one consisted of a bitch and four hardy little animals that he intended to train as "super-sheep-dogs." The other family of four were orphans, the mother having died in giving birth to them. They had therefore to be hand-nursed. The brains of these animals were very much bigger than the brains of the other family, but unfortunately three of them were much less healthy. Two died shortly after the removal to Wales. Another was subject to such violent fits that it had to be destroyed. The fourth, Sirius, was a healthy and cheerful little creature that remained a helpless infant long after the other litter were active adolescents. For months it could not even stand. It merely lay on its stomach with its bulgy head on the ground, squeaking for sheer joy of life; for its tail was constantly wagging.

Even the other litter matured very slowly for dogs, though far more rapidly than human children. When they were nearly adult all but one of them were disposed of to neighbouring farms. The one was kept as the family dog. Most of the local farmers had proved very reluctant to take on these big-headed animals even as gifts. But a neighbour, Mr. Llewelyn Pugh of Caer Blai, had entered into the spirit of the venture, and he subsequently bought a second pup as a colleague for the first.

The production of these super-sheep-dogs and others which followed formed a camouflage for Thomas's more exciting venture, of which Sirius was at present the only outcome. The public would be led to believe that super-sheep-dogs and other animals of missing-link mentality were his whole concern. If the little Alsatian really developed to human mental stature, few people would suspect it. Thomas was always morbidly anxious that it should not be exploited. It must grow up in decent obscurity, and mature as naturally as possible.

The super-sheep-dogs, on the other hand, were allowed to gain notoriety. The farmers who had accepted them mostly with great reluctance soon found that fate had given them pearls of great price. The animals learned their technique surprisingly quickly, and carried out their orders with unfailing precision. Commands had seldom to be repeated. Sheep were never hustled, and yet never allowed to break away. Not only so, but Trelone's dogs had an uncanny way of understanding instructions and carrying them out with no human supervision. They attached the right meanings to the names of particular pastures, hill-sides, valleys, moors. Told to "fetch sheep from Cefn" or from Moel Fach or what not, they succeeded in doing so while their master awaited them at home. They could also be sent on errands to neighbouring farms or villages. They would take a basket and a note to a particular shop and bring back the required meat or haberdashery.

All this was very useful to the farmers, and extremely interesting to Trelone, who was of course allowed every chance of studying the animals. He found in them a startlingly high degree of practical inventiveness, and a rudimentary but remarkable understanding of language. Being after all sub-human, they could not understand speech as we do, but they were incomparably more sensitive than ordinary dogs to familiar words and phrases. "Fetch wood from shed," "Take basket to butcher and baker," and all such simple familiar orders could be distinguished and obeyed, as a rule without distraction. Thomas wrote a monograph on his super-sheep-dogs, and consequently scientists from all over the world used to turn up at Garth to be shown the animals at work. Throughout the district their fame was fully established among farmers, and there were many demands for puppies. Very few could be supplied. Some farmers refused to believe that the offspring of these bright animals would not inherit their parents' powers. Naturally, all attempts to breed super-sheep-dogs from super-sheep-dogs without the introduction of the hormone into the mother were a complete failure.

But it is time to return to the little Alsatian, in fact, to Sirius. Trelone was from the first very excited about this animal. The longer it remained a helpless infant, the more excited he became. He saw in it the possibility of the fulfilment of his almost wildest hopes. Discussing it with Elizabeth, he fired her imagination with the prospects of this canine infant, and unfolded his plan before her. This animal must have as far as possible the same kind of psychological environment as their own baby. He told her of an American animal-psychologist and his wife who had brought up a baby chimpanzee in precisely the same conditions as their own little girl. It was fed, clothed, cared for, exactly as the child; and with very interesting results. This, Thomas said, was not quite what he wanted for little Sirius, because one could not treat a puppy precisely as a baby without violating its nature. Its bodily organization was too different from the baby's. But what he did want was that Sirius should be brought up to feel himself the social equal of little Plaxy. Differences of treatment must never suggest differences of biological or social rank. Elizabeth had already, he said, proved herself an ideal mother, giving the children that precious feeling of being devotedly loved by a divinely wise and generous being, yet fostering their independence and making no greedy emotional claims on them. This was the atmosphere that Thomas demanded for Sirius; this and the family environment. And their family, he told her, had taught him a very important truth. Unfortunate experiences in his own childhood had led him to regard family as a hopelessly bad institution, and one which ought to be abolished. She would remember his wild ideas of experimenting with their own children. She had tactfully and triumphantly resisted every attempt to remove her own first two children from her; and before the third was born Thomas was already convinced that a really good family environment was the right influence for a growing child. No doubt she had made mistakes. Certainly he had made many. No doubt they had to some extent unwittingly damaged their children. There was Tamsy's occasional mulishness and Maurice's diffidence. But on the whole—well it would be false modesty and unfair to the children not to recognize that they were all three fine specimens, friendly, responsible, yet independent and critical. This was the ideal social tradition in which to perform the great experiment with baby Sirius. Dogs, Thomas reminded Elizabeth, were prone to servility; but this vice was probably not due to something servile in their nature; it sprang from the fact that their great social sensitivity was forced to take a servile turn by the tyranny of the more developed species which controlled them. A dog with human intelligence, brought up to respect itself, would probably not be servile at all, and might quite well develop a superhuman gift for true social relationship.

Elizabeth took some time to consider her husband's suggestion, for the responsibility would be mainly hers. Moreover, she was naturally anxious about the effects of the experiment on her own baby. Would her little Plaxy suffer in any way? Thomas persuaded her that no harm would be done, and indeed that the companionship of child and super-canine dog must be beneficial to both. With fervour he insisted that the most valuable social relationships were those between minds as different from one another as possible yet capable of mutual sympathy. It is perhaps remarkable that Thomas, who was not himself gifted with outstanding personal insight or sympathy, should have seen intellectually the essential nature of community. It would be very interesting, he said, to watch the growth of this difficult but pregnant companionship. Of course it might never develop. There might be mere antagonism. Certainly Elizabeth would have to exercise great tact to prevent the child from overpowering the dog with its many human advantages. In particular the little girl's hands and more subtle eyesight would be assets which the puppy could never attain. And the whole human environment, which was inevitably alien and awkward for the dog, might well breed neurosis in a mind that was not human but humanly sensitive. Everything possible must be done to prevent Sirius from becoming either unduly submissive or defiantly arrogant in the manner so familiar in human beings suffering from a sense of inferiority.

One other principle Thomas wanted Elizabeth to bear in mind. It was, of course, impossible to know beforehand how the dog's nature would develop. Sirius might, after all, never reach anything like human mental stature. But everything must be done on the assumption that he would do so. Hence it was very important to bring him up not as a pet but as a person, as an individual who would in due season live an active and independent life. This being so, his special powers must he fostered. While he was still, as Thomas put it, a "schoolboy," his interests would, of course, be "schoolboy" interests, physical, primitive, barbarian; but being a dog, his expression of them would necessarily be very different from a real schoolboy's. He would have to exercise them in normal canine occupations, such as desultory roaming and hunting and fighting. But later, as his intelligence opened up the human world to him, he would want some kind of persistent "human" activity; and obviously sheep could provide him with a career, even if he far excelled the typical super-sheep-dog mentality. With this in view, and whatever his destiny, he must be brought up "as hard as nails and fit as hell." This had always been Elizabeth's policy with her own children; but Sirius would some time need to face up to conditions far more Spartan than those of the most Spartan human family. It would not do simply to force him into such conditions. Somehow she must wile him into wanting them, for sheer pride in his own nature, and later for the sake of his work. This, of course, would not apply to his childhood, but in adolescence he must begin of his own free will to seek hardness. Later still, when his mind was no longer juvenile, he would perhaps drop the sheep-dog career entirely and give his mind to more adult pursuits. Even so, the hard practical life of his youth would not have been in vain. It would endow him with permanent grit and self-reliance.

Elizabeth was a good deal more sceptical than her husband about the future of Sirius. She expressed a fear, which did not trouble Thomas, that such a disunited being as Sirius might he doomed to a life of mental torture. Nevertheless, she finally made up her mind to enter into the spirit of the experiment, and she planned accordingly.

## Infancy

WHILE he was still unable to walk, Sirius showed the same sort of brightness as Plaxy in her cot. But even at this early stage his lack of hands was a grave disadvantage. While Plaxy was playing with her rattle, he too played with his; but his baby jaws could not compete with Plaxy's baby hands in dexterity. His interest even in his earliest toys was much more like a child's than like the ordinary puppy's monomania for destruction. Worrying his rattle, he was attentive to the sound that it made, alternately shaking it and holding it still to relish the contrast between sound and silence. At about the time when Plaxy began to crawl, Sirius achieved a staggering walk. His pride in this new art and his joy in the increased scope that it gave him were obvious. He now had the advantage over Plaxy, for his method of locomotion was far better suited to his quadruped structure than her crawl to her biped form. Before she had begun to walk he was already lurching erratically over the whole ground floor and garden. When at last she did achieve the upright gait, he was greatly impressed, and insisted on being helped to imitate her. He soon discovered that this was no game for him.

Plaxy and Sirius were already forming that companionship which was to have so great an effect on both their minds throughout their lives. They played together, fed together, were washed together, and were generally good or naughty together. When one was sick, the other was bored and abject. When one was hurt, the other howled with sympathy. Whatever one of them did, the other had to attempt. When Plaxy learned to tie a knot, Sirius was very distressed at his inability to do likewise. When Sirius acquired by observation of the family's super-sheep-dog, Gelert, the habit of lifting a leg at gate-posts to leave his visiting card, Plaxy found it hard to agree that this custom, though suitable for dogs, was not at all appropriate to little girls. She was deterred only by the difficulty of the operation. Similarly, though she was soon convinced that to go smelling at gate-posts was futile because her nose was not as clever as Sirius's, she did not see why the practice should outrage the family's notions of propriety. Plaxy's inability to share in Sirius's developing experience of social smelling, if I may so name it, was balanced by his clumsiness in construction. Plaxy was the first to discover the joy of building with bricks; but there soon came a day when Sirius, after watching her intently, himself brought a brick and set it clumsily on the top of the rough wall that Plaxy was building. His effort wrecked the wall. This was not Sirius's first achievement in construction, for he had once been seen to lay three sticks together to form a triangle, an achievement which caused him great satisfaction. He had to learn to "handle" bricks and dolls in such a way that neither his saliva nor his pin-point teeth would harm them. He was already enviously impressed by Plaxy's hands and their versatility. The normal puppy shows considerable inquisitiveness, but no impulse to construct; Sirius was more persistently inquisitive and at times passionately constructive. His behaviour was in many ways more simian than canine. The lack of hands was a handicap against which he reacted with a dogged will to triumph over disability.

Thomas judged that his weakness in construction was due not only to handlessness but to a crudity of vision which is normal in dogs. Long after infancy he was unable to distinguish between visual forms which Plaxy would never confuse. For instance, it took him far longer than Plaxy to distinguish between string neatly tied up in little bundles and the obscure tangle which, at Garth as in so many homes, composed the general content of the string-bag. Again, for Sirius, rather fat ovals were no different from circles, podgy oblongs were the same as squares, pentagons were mistaken for hexagons, angles of sixty degrees were much the same as right angles. Consequently in building with toy bricks he was apt to make mistakes which called forth derision from Plaxy. Later in life he corrected this disability to some extent by careful training, but his perception of form remained to the end very sketchy.

In early days he did not suspect his inferiority in vision. All his failures in construction were put down to lack of hands. There was indeed a grave danger that his handlessness would so obsess him that his mind would be warped, particularly during a phase when the infant Plaxy was apt to laugh at his helplessness. A little later she was brought to realize that poor Sirius should not be ragged for his misfortune, but helped whenever possible. Then began a remarkable relationship in which Plaxy's hands were held almost as common property, like the toys. Sirius was always running to ask Plaxy to do things he could not manage himself, such as opening boxes and winding up clock-work toys. Sirius himself began to develop a surprising "manual" dexterity, combining the use of fore-paws and teeth; but many operations were for ever beyond him. Throughout his life he was unable to tie a knot in a piece of cotton, though there came a time when he could manage to do so in a rope or stout cord.

Plaxy was the first to show signs of understanding speech, but Sirius was not far behind. When she began to talk, he often made peculiar little noises which, it seemed, were meant to be imitations of human words. His failure to make himself understood often caused him bitter distress. He would stand with his tail between his legs miserably whining. Plaxy was the first to interpret his desperate efforts at communication, but Elizabeth in time found herself understanding; and little by little she grew able to equate each of the puppy's grunts and whines with some particular elementary sound of human speech. Like Plaxy, Sirius began with a very simple baby-language of monosyllables. Little by little this grew into a canine, or super-canine, equivalent of educated English. So alien were his vocal organs to speech, that even when he had perfected the art no outsider would suspect his strange noises of being any human language at all. Yet he had his own equivalent of every vocal sound. Some of his consonants were difficult to distinguish from one another, but Elizabeth and Plaxy and the rest of the family came to understand him as easily as they understood each other. I described his speech as composed of whimpers and grunts and growls. This perhaps maligns it, though essentially true. He spoke with a notable gentleness and precision, and there was a fluid, musical quality in his voice.

Thomas was, of course, immensely elated by the dog's development of true speech, for this was a sure sign of the fully human degree of intelligence. The baby chimpanzee that was brought up with a human baby kept level with its foster-sister until the little girl began to talk, but then dropped behind; for the ape never showed any sign of using words.

Thomas determined to have a permanent record of the dog's speech. He bought the necessary apparatus for making gramophone discs, and reproduced conversations between Sirius and Plaxy. He allowed no one to hear these records except the family and his two most intimate colleagues, Professor McAlister and Dr. Billing, who were influential in procuring funds for the research, and knew that Thomas's secret ambition soared far above the production of super-sheep-dogs. On several occasions Thomas brought the distinguished biologists to see Sirius.

There was a time when it seemed that these gramophone records would be the sole lasting and tangible evidence of Thomas's triumph. In spite of inoculation, Sirius developed distemper and almost succumbed. Day after day, night after night, Elizabeth nursed the wretched little animal through this peculiarly noisome disease, leaving her own child mainly to Mildred, the nursemaid. Had it not been for Elizabeth's skill and devotion, Sirius would not have come through with his powers unimpaired. Probably he would have died. This incident had two important results. It created in Sirius a passionate and exacting affection for his foster-mother, so that for weeks he would scarcely let her out of his sight without making an uproar; and it bred in Plaxy a dreadful sense that her mother's love was being given wholly to Sirius. In fact Plaxy became lonely and jealous. This trouble was soon put right when Sirius had recovered, and Elizabeth was able to give more attention to her child; but then it was the dog's turn to be jealous. The climax came when Sirius, seeing Elizabeth comforting Plaxy after a tumble, rushed savagely at her and actually nipped her little bare leg. There was then a terrible scene. Plaxy screamed and screamed. Elizabeth was for once really angry. Sirius howled with remorse for what he had done: and actually, out of a sense that retribution was needed, made a half-hearted attempt to bite his own leg. Then matters were made much worse by the family's super-sheep-dog, Gelert, who rushed to the scene of uproar. Seeing Plaxy's bleeding leg, and Elizabeth being very angry with the puppy, Gelert assumed that this was a case for severe punishment, and set upon the abject culprit. Sirius was bowled over and none too gently mauled by the furiously growling Gelert. The puppy's remorse gave place to fright, and his whimpers to screams of terror, to which the weeping Plaxy added screams of fear for her beloved friend. The other children rushed upon the scene, followed by Kate and Mildred with brooms and a rolling pin. Even the infant Plaxy seized Gelert by the tail and tried to drag him off. But it was Elizabeth herself who snatched Sirius from the jaws of death (as it seemed to him) and roundly cursed the officious Gelert.

This incident seems to have had several important results. It made both Sirius and Plaxy realize how much, after all, they cared for one another. It persuaded Plaxy that her mother had not discarded her for Sirius. And it proved to Sirius that Elizabeth loved him even when he had been very wicked. The unfortunate Gelert alone gained no comfort.

The only further punishment inflicted on Sirius was deep disgrace. Elizabeth withdrew her kindness. Plaxy, in spite of her secret knowledge that Sirius was very dear, was filled with self-pity once more when he had been rescued, and treated him with cold self-righteousness. To punish Sirius, Plaxy showed a violent affection for the kitten, Tommy, who had recently been imported from a neighbouring farm. Sirius, of course, was tortured with jealousy, and was afforded good practice in self-control. He succeeded all the better because on the one occasion when he did attack Tommy, he discovered that the kitten had claws. Sirius was very sensitive to neglect and censure. When his human friends were displeased with him he lost interest in everything but his misery. He would not play, he would not eat. On this occasion he set himself to win Plaxy over by many little attentions. He brought her a beautiful feather, then a lovely white pebble, and each time he timidly kissed her hand. Suddenly she gave him a hearty hug, and both broke into a romp. Towards Elizabeth, Sirius was less bold. He merely eyed her askance, his tail timorously vibrating when he caught her glance. So comic was this spectacle that she could not help laughing. Sirius was forgiven.

At a stage in his puppyhood shortly after this incident Sirius conceived a respectful admiration for Gelert. The slightly older and biologically quite adult super-sub-human animal treated him with careless contempt. Sirius followed Gelert about and mimicked all his actions. One day Gelert by great good fortune caught a rabbit and devoured it, growling savagely when Sirius approached. The puppy watched him with mingled admiration and horror. The spectacle of that swift pursuit and capture roused in him the hunting impulses of the normal dog. The scream of the rabbit, its struggle, sudden limpness and hideous dismemberment, shocked him deeply; for he had a sympathetic and imaginative nature, and Elizabeth had brought up her family in a tradition of tenderness towards all living things. But now a conflict arose which was to distress him throughout his life, the conflict between what he later called his "wolf-nature" and his compassionate civilized mentality.

The immediate result was a strong and guilty lust for the chase and an intensified, awed passion for Gelert. He became obsessed by the rabbit-warren. He was for ever sniffing at the entrances to the burrows, whimpering with excitement. For a while Plaxy was almost forgotten. Vainly she tried to win him back into partnership in her games. Vainly she hung about the burrows with him, bored and cross. In her presence he once caught a frog and disgustingly mangled it in an attempt to eat it. She burst into tears. His hunting impulse was suddenly quenched, and horror supervened. He rushed whimpering to his darling and covered her face with bloody kisses.

Many times henceforth he was to suffer the torturing conflict between his normal canine impulses and his more developed nature.

# Comment on *Sirius*

Olaf Stapledon is one of the very few professional philosophers to have become well known as a novelist. He is not celebrated these days as much as he should be. His 1937 novel *Star Maker*, which depicts the development of intelligent beings across the span of the universe, is a masterpiece of speculative fiction. It is clear from both that novel and the novel *Sirius* excerpted here, that Stapledon had a gift for imagining different modes of life. I am not a biologist, but to my mind, his speculations remain plausible, even more than seventy-five years after the book was written.

*Sirius* is unusual in this anthology for focusing not on humans and their possible transformations, but on a dog. Stapledon takes us quite systematically through the various stages of bringing this dog to human-level intelligence. The chapters beyond those excerpted here depict Sirius' maturity, his various struggles and moments of revelation and eventually his death. Throughout the book, we have an overriding sense that Sirius is not just a very clever animal. He is a person.

Of course, Sirius is different from an ordinary human person. His lack of hands make a profound difference to his capacity to engage with the human world. This may even affect how objects appear to him (e.g. as usable or not) in a way that contributes to his sense of alienation from human civilization. Sirius' keener sense of hearing and smell also make an important difference to his psychology and values. His metaphor for spirituality (developed fully later on in the book) as being on the trail of God expresses both his doggish drive to hunt and a conception of the world mediated by his dominant sensory capacity. Yet for all these differences, Sirius' quest for meaning and fulfilment are entirely characteristic of a person, indeed a highly philosophical person.

It is interesting to consider what exactly it takes to be a person. Up to now I have left the matter somewhat vague, but it is high time to consider the issue in more detail. As mentioned in previous chapters, self-consciousness is generally regarded as the core feature. But what is self-consciousness exactly? Consider a key example from the story; the remorse that Sirius feels after biting Plaxy's leg and his consequent attempts to merit forgiveness. Here Sirius displays several key competencies of self-consciousness. First, he projects his existence into the past and future in recognizing that he acted badly in the past and wishes to act better in the future. Second, he displays social awareness in recognizing that a fellow person, his foster sister, is in pain, and that she in turn can make judgements about him. Third, he displays moral responsibility in seeking contrition, thereby displaying the ability to reason about his role in bringing about an outcome, as well as having enough self-control to do what is best for himself and Plaxy over the long term.

The range of features that make up self-consciousness implies that it is complex, relying on a large variety of psychological capacities such as memory, imagination, conceptualization, reasoning and emotional control. All of these capacities are ones that can come in various degrees of sophistication. For instance, we have seen in other chapters how there are several different types of memory and that what we remember often depends on our values. It is quite possible to have some aspects of these capacities and not others, or to be able to use them in some domains and not others. Thus self-consciousness, and thereby personhood, may not be an all-or-nothing matter.

If self-consciousness can come in degrees, this encourages us to consider whether less complex versions of it apply to non-human animals. For instance, in 2022, there was a legal case concerning whether Happy the elephant, captive in the Bronx Zoo, should be legally recognized as a person. Dolphins, whales and great apes such as gorillas and chimpanzees are also considered potential candidates. The orangutan Sandra was initially recognized as a non-human person by an Argentinian judge in 2015, though the decision was later reversed. The arguments that these non-human animals should qualify as persons appeal to their capacities for self-awareness, rationality and complex social ties in just the same way as we form our opinions about Sirius. Some non-human animals have even shown linguistic abilities, the capacity that, in Stapledon's story, the scientist Trelone regards as 'a sure sign of the fully human degree of intelligence'. A number of apes have gained at least the rudiments of sign language and of course many species produce and recognize communicative signals. It is increasingly hard to sustain the claim that the capacities of humans are unique.

Meanwhile, many humans also lack the capacities that we regard as special to persons. This can be due to severe mental disabilities or the onset of diseases such as dementia. Of course, the most common cases are infants, who take a considerable amount of time to show clear signs of self-consciousness. The *potential* of infants to gain the capacities of persons is supposed to be a good justification for their special treatment. Yet if technological developments allow us to raise the intellectual capacities of various non-human animals in the ways depicted by Stapledon, the mere potential for advanced cognition would no longer be an effective way to mark out the specialness of human infants.

Leaving aside ethical issues here, these debates about personhood have clear metaphysical implications that the story of Sirius helps to illustrate. The point is simply this: many non-human animals would be recognized as persons if only their cognitive capacities were a bit more sophisticated. In the same way, many humans gradually become persons as they mature, just as Plaxy does in the story. Stapledon draws a clear parallel between these two kinds of cases. This suggests that a person is not a *thing*, but a kind of quality or property that things can gain or lose (the technical term is a 'phase sortal'). But if personhood is a property, what are the things that gain or lose this property? Perhaps many things could have this property. Perhaps intelligent computers or alien beings made of energy could have the personhood property. But in all the cases that we know about, the things bearing personhood are animals. In fact, so far as we know, personhood is basically a capacity that enables animals to take care of themselves and each other in more effective ways.

This leads us to a new theory of what we are: what we are, essentially, are animals. We animals bear the property of personhood, but that property is not our essence. Personhood is a feature that we can gain or lose. This theory, known as 'animalism', has slowly gained ground over the last few decades. Currently it remains a minority position amongst philosophers, though I believe it should be of at least equal standing with the psychological view.

To explain the animalist view, it is important to see how it opposes the psychological continuity theory. First, animalists and psychological continuity theorists disagree about brain transplants. It seems possible for psychological capacities to be transplanted from one animal's body into another. The animalist will however deny that I can be moved into another animal's body because I am essentially this animal here. As described in the previous chapter, the animalist will regard the brain transplantation scenario as comparable to the transplant of any other organ. They might allow that transplanting my brain would help some other animal to achieve self-consciousness, in the same way that transplanting my lungs would some other animal to breathe. But to think that I would move into the other body confuses the generic ability to be conscious with the unique way that *my* self-consciousness is tied to *my* life. Perhaps if enough of the animal's nervous system or bodily organs were transplanted, the animalist could regard it as a preservation of the animal. However, at that point, the animalist is more likely to say that we give new limbs to the original animal than that we move the animal into a different body.

Another important opposition between animalism and psychological views is that an animal can persist without any of the psychological qualities that the psychological continuity theorist cares about. For instance, some humans end up through disease or accident in persistent vegetative states, in which cortical functions are irreparably destroyed, though basic life functions remain, including breathing, chewing and the wake–sleep cycle. Here consciousness is lost but animal life is preserved. Those who identify themselves with their conscious minds typically regard these conditions as equivalent to death and as a result, are commonly indifferent to whether the persisting body is kept alive or not. An animalist is likely to feel differently about this scenario, however. They are more apt to say that we survive if we fall into a persistent vegetative state. The animalist may still agree that the qualities that really matter to them are lost, and so would prefer a dignified death, yet there remains an important distinction between losing one's mind and death.

Similarly, at the beginning of life, the animalist disagrees with the psychological continuity theorist. Animals start out as unthinking embryos, while psychological qualities like self-consciousness turn up a lot later. Thus the animalist will say that we exist much earlier than the psychological continuity theorist allows. And if one is willing to accept that one existed as an embryo, even if one wasn't yet a person, this could potentially affect one's opinion about abortion.

Thus in a variety of scenarios, the view that we are essentially animals has major implications for our survival conditions that differ from the view that we are essentially persons. Why then, should we think it is true? So far, the main argument I have raised is the idea that personhood is a property that comes in degrees rather than a thing. We might deny that we are things. We might instead embrace the idea that we are a special kind of property. Yet a number of previous chapters in this anthology have offered reasons for tying our identity to our material nature; for thinking that we are things. Patterns of information or complex combinations of properties can be duplicated indefinitely, while we, in contrast, are unique. The animal body can supply this unique material nature. Recall for instance how in the chapter on memory loss, we explored how our unique histories, and the values expressed by those histories, are written into our bodies.

Another argument for animalism comes from thinking about sleep. Although dreams seem to qualify as conscious experiences, there are various periods of sleep in which we are entirely unconscious. We do not think that we go out of existence during these periods, so in what sense are we still ourselves? The psychological continuity theorist is forced to say that we maintain psychological properties if we have the *potential* or capacity to regain self-consciousness. But what is the actual state of us when we have this potential? What makes that potential real and not just speculation? It seems to be the state in which we remain living animals.

A third argument comes from the definition of personhood. Earlier we defined personhood in terms of self-consciousness and then we saw how Sirius' self-consciousness was expressed in his sense of moral responsibility. But notice now that all the characteristics of self-consciousness rely on assumptions about what a self is. To be self-conscious assumes that I have an idea of a self that persists through time, that this self is distinct from other selves and that there are particular ways for this self to be affected or for it to bring about effects. So if I try to define what I am – what my self is – in terms of being a person, my definition is circular. That is, if a self is a person and a person is a self-consciousness thing and being a self-conscious thing relies on what the self is, then a self relies on what a self is. We haven't explained anything. The circularity of 'self' and 'self-consciousness' suggests that we need an independent concept from which to ground our accounts of both. The animalist can supply that independent concept. That is, we define the self in terms of being an animal, and then specify that when we become conscious of this animal's persistence through time, its relationships to other animals and its responsibility for its actions, it becomes self-conscious.

Last, but not least, there is a brutally simple argument for animalism that we get from the philosopher Eric Olson. This argument involves three premises, each of which is hard to deny. Premise one: I am sitting here and thinking. Premise two: There is an animal sitting here and thinking. Premise three: There is only one being sitting here and thinking. It follows logically from these premises that I am numerically identical with the animal.

Can any of these premises be denied? It is hard to deny that I am sitting here thinking. Everyone talking about personal identity seems to agree that we identify ourselves with the thinking thing. Animalists may ultimately allow that there are states of me in which I am not thinking (e.g. if I fall into a persistent vegetative state), but right now, I am able to identify myself as the thinking thing. My sense of self seems to be at least this accurate.

How about the second step – could we deny that the animal is sitting here and thinking? One move might be to deny that there's really an animal here. Biologists are unlikely to be happy with this move. They will say that the thing in this chair is comparable to billions of other animals on this planet in its fleshy characteristics. Okay, but is the animal really thinking? Setting aside my first-person perspective, the evidence that could be given for this animal thinking (by just observing its behaviour from the outside), seems just as good as the evidence we have for all the other animals thinking. The only reason it seems one could try to deny that the animal thinks is if thinking is somehow disconnected from animal bodies in general. One way to do this is to identify thinking only with brains and not the animals containing those brains. We already looked at reasons to doubt that claim in the previous chapter. Another way is to claim that minds are immaterial entities that only interact with animal bodies. Yet as I discussed in the chapter on souls, if minds are not material, it is baffling how they even have physical location, let alone the force to make a material body do anything, or indeed to be affected by material bodies.

So what about the third step? Can we deny that there is one being sitting here and thinking? This may seem like a very strange move to make. It suggests that every person is accompanied by a thinking animal. Do they occupy the same region of space? If so, how do we tell which is which? Surprisingly, this turns out to be the most promising way to reject, or at least modify, the animalist theory. Some philosophers argue that we are *made* of animals, but are not strictly identical to them. Because this is fairly complicated to explain, I will examine this theory in detail in Chapter 10.

For now, a number of considerations converge on the claim that we are essentially animals. As such, I must admit that I am very attracted to the animalist theory of identity. In some ways, it even feels like the common-sense view, though I've been studying this area for so long that I fear my common sense has become completely scrambled.

# 9

# 'Through the Window Frame'

## Sean Williams

*Monday's child is full of grace.*
*Wednesday's child is fair of face.*

## March 1

Jay wakes with three scratches on the soft skin above his elbow, on the inside of his left arm. They're deep, and he's bled enough to stain the sheets, so he runs a wash before starting his chores. It isn't the first time something like this has happened. Not long ago, he found scratch marks behind his ear. The time before that they were on his leg, including one that was long and curved like a hook leading up to his groin. Neither of those times did he bleed, though, so this time feels different. Significant, in a way he can't define.

Because of the wash cycle, he's late for his session with Dr Warner, which displeases her. He mentions the scratches, and she tuts as she takes a look at the fresh injury through a magnifying lens.

"It's nothing," she says, returning to her seat and jotting a note before moving the conversation onto his homework, an essay on Eugene O'Neill, which is also running late.

"Are you sure?" he presses her, ignoring her signal that the conversation is over. "I'm hurting myself in my sleep—what if it keeps happening?"

"File your nails more thoroughly, or wear gloves."

"Are you joking?"

"Do I ever joke?"

"No," he admits, sagging into himself.

She tuts again. "Any unusual dreams, memories, or headaches?"

"None."

Noticing him rubbing at the scabs on his arm, she puts down the pen of her tablet, the one labelled "SPP" even though they are not her initials, and he retreats a minute distance into his chair, aware that he is annoying her.

"You haven't mentioned," she says, "that it's the first day of the month. And it's an *odd* month."

He feels like a fool.

"Well, that explains that, I suppose," he says. Odd months are always more difficult than even. The blood on his sheets caused him to forget, though, which isn't like him.

"Yes," she says, "I think it does. May we move on?"

Dr Warner picks up her pen and resumes her interrogation. He answers her questions as he always does, honestly and with good faith. Their routine is familiar and exact, like every day that passes in his lifetime of confinement. The ritual brings him some relief, as does the proposed explanation of the mystery, but the knot of unease remains in his belly. Something new has entered his world.

Dr Warner knows him better than anyone: of the few people who share his existence, she is his constant, the anchor and chain pinning him to the seabed of his imprisonment. When waves toss him, she holds fast. But she herself might miss something that is surfacing from his mind unbidden.

Perhaps, he wonders, the long-locked memories of his crime will come with it.

He will, therefore, start monitoring the appearance of the scratches to see if they coincide with odd months. If they do, mystery solved, and he need say no more about them.

"Homework completed by tomorrow," Dr Warner instructs him at the end of their session. "Without fail. Exercises and meals as normal."

Obediently, he nods, glad he won't be on a restricted diet for making her impatient. The exercise he doesn't care about. His muscles hurt so often, no matter what he does or doesn't do with them.

"Dismissed, then." She waves him away, and he leaves the anteroom where they usually meet. It is a small room, empty apart from two steel chairs facing each other across a short distance. There are two sturdy doors, one through which he retreats now, to his rooms; the other he has never even seen through. Only one sense has penetrated the barrier surrounding him. Occasionally, Dr Warner brings a scent of the outside on her hair or clothes. He has no words for what those smells might be, although he knows the words for many smells, from books he has read.

Similarly, Jay knows the word "horizon" but has never seen it. The closest he's come is the changing view through his skylight. Clouds are common; occasionally he sees stars, and on three occasions the moon. His rooms' one other window is painted over on the outside, a tromp l'oeil of a sunlit garden, vegetables and flowers under a low-draping willow. If he presses his ear against the cool glass, he hears nothing but the double whirr of air-conditioning and blood in his veins.

## March 3–17

The next day, and over the five odd-numbered days following, more scratches appear. It doesn't matter what side he goes to sleep on, or if he sleeps on his stomach or back. He tries putting his hands in socks at night (not wanting to bother Dr Warner again by asking for gloves) but they slip off overnight and, sure enough, by morning a new batch of scrapes have appeared: on his hip, along one protruding rib, even on his toes. Not once does he catch himself doing it, which doesn't entirely surprise him, since he is a very deep sleeper; his nightly medication ensures that it takes more than a scratch to disturb his slumber.

Whatever he's been doing to himself, despite doing it with some determination, he does it without conscious awareness.

Although he's not telling Dr Warner, he does keep a mental tally of the occurrences in case he needs it later for later reference. Arm, ear, leg, hip, toe, rib . . . Even as he works on his homework (the essay is finished at last; now he's studying algebra problems) and grudgingly goes about his regular chores, a rhythm develops. Connections form. Strange, he thinks, how the names of the sites where scratches appear are all three letters long . . .

One morning, he finds a new set overlapping a site that was previously scratched, and two things become immediately apparent.

The first is that the number of scratches is the same: there are three of them, on his leg, just above where the hem of his sagging, grey cotton shorts hang.

The second is that the scratches in this instance are the same shapes as the previous: one curved, one straight, and one something that might be a circle.

Perhaps, if the white scars of the earlier scratches had completely faded, he might have doubted these conclusions, but there they undeniably are: ghostly, film-negative shadows of this fresh insult to his skin; incontrovertible evidence that this isn't random.

A very odd month, he tells himself.

## March 19

The next day, another scratch, same number as before, same shapes as before, but all different to the previous day, the previous place. He commits them even more firmly to memory, these patterns that have formed with some emphasis now on his arm and his leg. Each shape is different from the others around it, yet emphatically the same as the one inscribed before, and as inscrutable.

They remind him of mathematical symbols, but that's just the maths homework speaking, probably.

## March 21

This time, on his hip. The algebra puzzles are getting tricker, so he can do little more than memorise the marks and get on with his chores, which are never-ending, a constant source of irritation and distraction. Dr Warner is watching him closely, he can tell. There will be no repeat of his earlier tardiness. The assignment will be delivered on time today, or else, he fears, punishment will be severe.

## March 23

The next day, he wakes with bloodstains on his pillow. Leaping from bed, he pulls back his right ear, contorting himself as he does so, and sees crimson trickling steadily from deep cuts. Steadily and *emphatically*, he thinks. Where repetition failed at whatever purpose these scratches serve, his subconscious has resorted to brutality.

Dabbing with a tissue and squinting as closely as he can, he confirms that his initial impression is correct: these new scratches trace paths etched before. But there is more to be gleaned this morning. Each of the individual symbols—one straight line, one cross, and one open-ended triangle—has occurred before, not just behind his ear, but on his leg, arm, and toe.

Algebra is still echoing in his mind. Nine symbols in previous days. Three more today, scattered among the previous nine. A thought nags at him like the itches on his healing skin. For now, however, he cannot pursue it, needing to do another load of laundry to clean the sheets, and then to begin the day's usual routine. He will not mention this puzzle to Dr Warner, because she will have a new homework assignment for him, and puzzles only go one way in their strict relationship. He will, however, tell her that the scratches continue, and he will continue to ponder their meaning in the interstices of his life.

Only much later, as he gathers himself up in his freshly cleaned sheets, feeling the fog of his evening medication beginning to descend, does one possible solution occur to him from the meandering of his thoughts.

Three symbols each on his leg, arm, hip, rib, and ear. Three letters in the name of each site. The last three symbols appearing once on each of the previous sites.

The symbols dance in his mind, and the words join them: leg, arm, hip, rib, and ear, in threes first, but then breaking into individuals, cavorting and spinning, breaking apart and reforming, sometimes in the same patterns, sometimes in new ones. The letters line up with the symbols and dance in a double spiral, linking metaphorical arms and—

It comes to him in a flash.

The three repeating symbols align with three repeating letters—yes! The "e" in leg, the "a" and "r" in arm, and none from hip—combined to form "ear."

*The scratches are a code.*

Then the tide of irresistible nighttime rolls over him in a wave, and he is asleep.

# March 25

He wakes in a highly confused state, splayed out in bed under sweat-stained sheets. The lights are down, but his body is alive with sensation, none of it pleasant. He feels as though he's been wrestling with the darkness as though it is a living beast. His heart pounds loudly in the silence.

Then the world lurches and suddenly he is sitting up, rubbing at his temples—but it's not him doing it. He's the puppet of an invisible, irresistible will. He tries to scream and makes no sound. His throat, mouth and lips—his entire body—is not his to control.

His entrapment is complete. Bad enough to be confined to one small set of rooms—but to now lose command of his body as well. It's a nightmare.

His hands cease their vigorous rubbing. There's a sobbing sound.

*The Night Hag*, he tells himself, not a nightmare. Either way, he's dreaming, just dreaming.

"Is that you?" The sound of his whispering voice is odd when he is not the one speaking. "Are you there now?"

*I'm always here*, he wants to cry back, but the darkness is thickening around him, growing heavier, dragging him back onto the bed.

And then the nightmare ends, if that is what it is, and he is back in control. He tests his arms, his legs, his neck, and all is as it should be. He can tell it's morning because the skylight is open, letting in the first hint of natural daylight. The sky that day shines pale, washed-out blue.

His left big toe is sticky and stings when he rubs at it with the next toe along. More bloody scratches, he assumes, the dream clinging to him like tar, making him feel strange and dissociated, but the lights haven't come on yet, so he can't check. He wonders what they will look like today . . . and it is then he remembers the insight that came to him the night before. If the "e" in "toe" aligns with the same symbol in "ear" and "leg", he will feel justified in his conclusion that the scratches form a simple substitution cypher. One symbol per letter—and he has collected thirteen of them, like a child might collect stamps or marbles. That's half the alphabet.

What could one write with these letters? *Import*, he thinks. And *Gambit*. Then *Bagel*, because he is hungry for breakfast. *Glib Metaphor* contains all of them, and so does *Hot Pig Ambler*.

Finally, the lights come on, and he has halfway convinced himself that he's imagined a fine diversion that is killing some time, but has no further significance than that. Until he confirms that his toe is indeed scratched, and the symbols do align.

When he meets with Dr Warner, he is going to tell her all about it, but before he can do so she asks about dreams, and instead of revisiting the Night Hag, that horrible feeling of not being himself, or at least not belonging to his body, he tells her about another one he remembered while struggling through his chores that morning. He can't remember if it happened before or after the other one, but there had been a woman standing at the end of his bed—or was it a cot?—reciting that old rhyme about the days of the week. There had been a child . . . or was he the child? But he was *seeing* the child, so how could he be the child as well? Perhaps there were *two* children . . .

In the dream, the woman looked like Dr Warner, except her hair was black, not grey, with a white streak leading back from her left temple. A young Dr Warner, perhaps—and therefore an image he cannot in theory consciously access. Is this a memory, poking through the layers of psychic block that lie between him and his crime? Perhaps the curtains are parting and he will remember why he has been imprisoned. That, she has always told him, would be an absolutely devastating impediment in his quest for atonement. Unless she is convinced that that knowledge—and the urges that lie behind it—has been entirely and permanently erased, he will never be released.

Dr Warner, upon hearing about this dream, becomes fiercely fixated on the image of the two children—*boys*, she calls them, although he didn't actually say they were boys or girls—and the rhyme.

"That's definitely the version you remember?" she asks. "'Monday's child is full of grace / Wednesday's child is fair of face'—those words exactly?"

"Of course," he says. "That's how it goes. Isn't it?"

She frowns, and he wonders why they've gone down this unusual alley. It's so trivial and simple to prove wrong, like telling her there's a wheel of cheese in his pocket or her shirt is green instead of blue.

Wanting to change the subject, he says, "I scratched myself, again. My toe, again, and—"

"To the devil with your scratches. Cut your toenails. Didn't I tell you this already?"

"Not exactly. You said fingernails—"

"One more word, and I'm taking away your reader for a week."

He falls instantly silent.

"It's late." The heel of her right shoe taps a brisk rhythm on the floor. "You're under stress. Take the night off and watch something, if you want. I'll add a movie to the folder. A couple came from Editing this week."

All his media is closely monitored for content that might trigger his suppressed memories. Sometimes words are erased from the speech of the actors or blurred out in signs and on newspapers, and sometimes, too, the text in his reader parses oddly, as though it has been censored as well. He wonders what will happen when—*if*—he is released and all those hidden words are revealed to him. Perhaps they are introduced slowly, one at a time, to test the resilience of the blocks formed by medication and his therapy sessions with Dr Warner. And maybe that—yes, surely that—is what is happening to him now.

It's entirely possible Dr Warner's indifference to the scratches is feigned. It could be a test. A test he can either ignore or pursue with increased diligence—and it is too late to ignore it, beyond feigning indifference right along with her . . .

So.

That night, after lights-out, he bites an edge off one of his fingernails and carefully but quickly, before the medication kicks in, inscribes the symbols for *Hello* on the shelf of his pelvis, just above the line of his pubic hair. It hurts, but he grits his teeth. Test or not, he must know the answer.

A trickle of blood snakes across his pale skin as he falls back onto the mattress and lets unconsciousness consume him.

## March 25–29

He wakes feeling like a fridge has fallen on him. Every joint aches, and the symbols he carved tug at him, crusty with dried scab. He rolls with significant effort out of bed and inspects himself in the mirror, front and back. There are, disappointingly, no new symbols in evidence: just what looks like a mosquito bite in the hollow of his armpit and several bruises across his shoulders and thighs. Is this some further attempt by his subconscious to awaken something in him, or to punish him?

The aches and pains ease somewhat with the passing of the day, and he goes to bed feeling little more than stiff with healing, and glad that the worst is behind him.

The next day, though, the pains are back, and while the first set of bruises have turned yellow with age, there is a new set marbling his skin, dark and angry. Around his left wrist he sees lines that can only be from fingers gripping tightly. When he attempts to align his right hand along those marks, he can't do it: the angle is all wrong. Could someone have attacked him while he slept?

Dr Warner dismisses the bruises in her pursuit of further dreams. There have been none. She persists, however, and he wonders again why she seems so unsatisfied by his answers. What is she looking for?

The third morning after scratching *Hello*, he wakes with a terrible ache in his temples and a roiling, turning stomach. He barely makes it to the metal toilet, where he vomits noisily and messily, ejecting a churn of brownish chunks that resembles nothing he put down his throat the night before.

Gasping, he releases the bowl and flops onto his side on the cool, tiled floor, curled in a foetal position, clutching his aching stomach.

Only then does he realise that, under a new set of throbbing bruises, is the persistent sting of sweat getting into a set of fresh scratches.

He uncoils slightly to look.

*Hello*, he wrote four days ago. Overlaying those fading symbols are a set that match perfectly, spelling out the same word. And below them, another set that spells a different word entirely, one he failed to tease out of the letters.

*Hello. Brother.*

He stares, not entirely sure he isn't hallucinating. *Brother?* The word heralds a whole new kind of madness.

Or is it hinting at the possibility that he literally *had* a brother, once . . . a brother he *killed*?

He shivers, feeling the space between his shoulder blades as he never has before. Its vulnerability, its fragility. If someone—or something—were to touch it now, he knows he would scream.

Don't be silly, he tells himself. There's no vengeful ghost. It's just a fiction.

But the scratches . . . *They* are real. Even the ones that have faded to blurred lines of scar tissue.

He stays on the bathroom floor, too weak to move, until an orderly comes to check on him. They get him up on rubbery legs and call for the medical bed to be brought to the interview room. There, he is put on a drip and examined closely. Dr Warner watches from one corner of the room, expression unreadable: her features are triangular, suggesting worry, or some other emotion that he has never seen before. The orderly is blank faced, as always. Jay has learned never to address them.

As his vitals are taken, he keeps one hand over the marks on his stomach, so no one will see. This is between him and himself, now, him and his reflection, his echo, his . . . *brother*.

After an hour, they move him to his bed, where he stays all day, chores thankfully suspended while he recovers. The cause of his sickness is not explained to him; perhaps they don't themselves know the cause, these people who simultaneously care for and contain him. He drifts in and out of sleep, playing with letters and symbols in his mind, trying out combinations and permutations for size. Thirteen letters is not enough for what he wants to say. He needs more.

Dr Warner herself comes to give him his medications that night, and she watches closely while he takes the tablets into his mouth and swallows with an audible gulp. She waits as the fog enfolds him. She is the last thing he sees, sitting on the edge of his bed with her hands folded tightly in her lap.

If she is watching for anything out of the ordinary, she is too late. He has marked himself already, etching himself with symbols kept carefully out of sight. The words they spell will trigger a reaction, surely, as maybe the word *Brother* was intended to do.

*Help. Me.*

Help him what? He doesn't know, any more than he knows what *Brother* means. The act of communication is what matters.

## March 31

Everything is different. The old cups and plates are gone, replaced with ones that look the same but are obviously different—and new, furthermore, rather than scuffed and scratched by repeated cycles of use and cleaning. The clothes in his small wardrobe are new too, and they smell of the outside in ways he can't describe. Even the walls are different, freshly painted in patches and swathes to cover new dents and scrapes that he can feel with his fingers. The air itself feels disordered, shaken as though by an eruption that has somehow come and gone without him noticing.

Whatever happened while he slept left its mark on his body, too. He is covered with small marks—bruises, yes, as before, but more than that. These marks are like the scratches from before, but they are singly or in pairs, and they don't align with any of the others he has memorised. But if they aren't words, what are they?

It is as though the explosion of thoughts in his mind found their way out, like a poltergeist, and turned his small world upside-down.

No one tells him anything when they come to check on him, and his tongue stumbles over the questions he wants to ask. He staggers through his morning routine, body aching inside and out, mind deeply fogged with what feels like medication, a new kind that leaves him awake but barely capable of connected thought. Restricted to reactions and sporadic impulses, he fumbles through chores even more half-heartedly than usual and is monosyllabic when interviewed by Dr Warner. She seems curiously satisfied with his state, and expresses only distracted approval that he no longer feels nauseous. His sickness has indeed passed completely, as though it never happened.

"Today is the last day of the odd month," she tells him at the end of session. "You'll be glad when everything is back to normal."

He nods and shuffles back to his rooms, there to eat a bowl of listless noodles and stare at the reading he has been set for homework, an essay on the platypus. On the back of the thumb holding his spoon, he has one of the mysterious scratches. It's a half-circle with a faint line across it, and it too is like a letter missing the rest of its word. If it, like the previous words he's deciphered, spelled the name of the part of him it was carved into, then . . .

He almost slaps his forehead. *Thumb* has five letters. Four of them are known to him. The missing symbol must be the fifth, the "u".

If someone was trying to complete the alphabet for him, they might do it precisely this way.

He gets up and undresses. Whoever's watching will accept that he's getting into his pyjamas. It's not weirdly early, and Dr Warner knows that he is in a fog. That fog has parted now, but he is careful not to give a clue revealing his newfound alertness. He moves slowly, tracing the new symbols on his body and the letters they represent with only his eyes.

The letter "w" is on his elbow. *Knee* gives him "k" and "n". *Wrist*—there's the "s".

Slowly, methodically, he mentally fills the gaps in his body's alphabet—all except "z", "q" and "j"—and then covers it all up again, just as methodically, with his pyjamas and goes back to his e-book. Lying on the couch and turning the pages without absorbing a word on them, he begins composing a reply.

*Who are you?*

*Friday's child's a-flood with woe.*
*Sunday's child has far to go.*

## Monday (21 days ago)

"Who is he?"

Dr Warner ignores him, as she always does when Cully interrogates her, instead of the other way around.

"I'll tell you about my dreams if you tell me who he is."

"You will tell me about your dreams or I'll reduce your meal allowance."

She's a robot, Cully decides, with nothing inside her. An automaton programmed to ask certain questions and deliver certain responses. It must infuriate her when he refuses to follow her script, but there's no sign of that emotion or any other on her face. She even looks like a robot.

"Is *he* your captive, too?"

Finally, she gives up trying to get what she wants from him. She leaves, and two orderlies come in to shave his scalp and face, as they do every day, to trim his finger—and toenails, then to enforce an exercise regime that leaves him exhausted: punishment for his intransigence, along with the threatened snap diet. His homework (a short work of harmonic counterpoint) and regular chores he does willingly, afterwards: who wants to live in a swamp? (It's amazing how quickly dust forms on every horizontal surface in his tiny world.) He is as fastidious as he is observant. In the act of closely inspecting everything, he might find another clue.

The first came a week ago in the form of a curled-up fragment of dried two-minute noodle tucked into the corner of the kitchen. It wasn't there the day before; he's sure of it. Although there are packets of noodles in the cupboard, he never eats two-minute noodles because they're too salty.

Someone has been in the kitchen, eating: someone who wasn't as tidy as him.

But who?

And when?

The only possible time is when he was asleep, bombed out on the chemical cocktails Dr Warner makes him take every night. A dozen orderlies could eat saucepans of noodles and he wouldn't know.

That was his first thought—the orderlies. But why? They have the whole world to eat in, when he just has his tiny apartment, with its single, narrow skylight and the window painted with images of a world he has never seen. So that doesn't help him with *who*?

The next question really stumped him, though: what to do about it?

What *could* he do about it?

He might have convinced himself he was imagining things—filling up the futile emptiness of his life with stories to make it seem interesting—were it not for the pubic hair he later found clinging to the wall of the shower like a slug or an alien invader in a horror movie. Not one of his own, because he assiduously wipes down the shower after every use.

Someone else, he realises, has been using his bathroom, as well as his kitchen.

Why would they do such a thing?

The answer, when it comes to him, is surprisingly simple: *Because they live here too.*

## Wednesday (20 days ago)

He has a nagging feeling all day that someone is watching him. It's just the cameras, he tells himself: there's one in each room, including the bathroom. He can usually ignore them, but today the sensation is acute, like a ghost is peering at him from behind the furniture, under the bed, out of the gap between fridge and wall, through the skylight, when it is open during the day, letting in narrow glimpses of the sky.

It unsettles him, undermines his ability to resist Dr Warner's steady interrogation.

"What's the worst crime you can imagine?" she asks him.

"Being a robot pretending to be a human."

"Pretending to be something or someone you're not. . ." She takes his barb seriously. "Does that truly bother you?"

"Shouldn't it?"

"It depends on one's frame of reference. A spy, for example, pretends to be someone else in service of a greater good."

"How can they be sure of good or bad when they themselves are living a lie?"

She smiles, thinly. "How do *you* imagine they do that?"

Cully can never get past her, no matter how he tries. Always, she finds a way to turn the conversation back to him. Probing, dissecting, analysing. Isn't *he* supposed to be the victim, here, hidden from a catastrophic childhood about which he has no memories?

"You tell me" he fires back at her.

"Imagine you're a spy infiltrating the Gestapo, in order to bring them down. Can you picture the things you would have to do to get away with it?"

"I couldn't."

"How do you know? Wouldn't you want to?"

He feels physically ill. Again, she has trapped him. "Is that the kind of person who's looking for me? Is that why I'm in danger from them?"

"Are you?"

"Why won't you just tell me?" He is on his feet now, shaking with emotion. "What exactly was done to me?"

"What do you think was done to you?"

Cully collapses back into his chair with such violence that it rocks back on its legs and threatens to tip. He catches himself in time, unclenches his fists.

"I would remember something like that," he says. "I'm sure of it."

Again, that thin smile painted on a mouth of steel. "One never knows what one is capable of," she tells him, "until one makes the sincere attempt."

\*

That night, after he has taken his medication, Cully stays awake as long as he can. Perhaps, if he tries hard enough, he will see who has been sneaking into his room and using his stuff. If it's one of the orderlies, he'll report them to Dr Warner, who will deal with it promptly, he's sure. She isn't the type to tolerate any kind of rule-breaking.

He pinches himself. Bites his tongue. Holds his eyelids open. Anything that won't show up on the cameras watching him in infrared. The tide is relentless. He has never prevailed against his medication so long, and his heart races with the effort. The utter darkness of his room begins to swirl with colourless shapes, as though ghosts are crowding around him. No, not ghosts: doppelgangers. They move through his rooms, picking things up and putting them back down in different places. They lean over the bed to examine him, like he is some kind of freak on display. But they are him, and he is them.

Desperate not to lose the war with sleep, he digs his fingernails into his arm so deeply he is afraid of scratching himself. What would happen, he wonders in a fever of possibilities, if he smashed his hand so hard against the wall that he broke a bone? Would the pain override the medications and allow him to remain conscious?

He's aware he's not thinking in a straight line. His mind is slipping. The doppelgangers are dancing now, assuming strange, twisted shapes that bear little resemblance to humanity. He feels a crisis approaching, and he shivers uncontrollably, all over. He's losing sense of skin, of limbs, of self. He's becoming one of the doppelgangers—disappearing—disintegrating—

And then he's back, in body and mind, intact, and the darkness is nothing but darkness. He fumbles about him, feels sheet, mattress, pillow, wall exactly where they ought to be, if maybe not where they *used* to be. There's a musty smell of sleep, and he understands that time has passed, perhaps the whole night. He must have succumbed without knowing. The medication won, after all.

Did he learn anything, though?

Maybe. The shadows looked like him. What if the person moving through his room at night is *actually* him? Sleepwalking.

But he is watched every moment of his existence. Why would the orderlies let him do this?

And then there's the hair. It's the same colour as his own: that narrows down the suspects—but who could it have come from, if they didn't live here too?

He feels equal parts frustrated and energised. He's close to something, he can feel it. Like he's knocking on a door, waiting for an answer . . .

*A door.*

When the lights come on and he goes to the bathroom, he looks in the mirror at his reflection and thinks: *Time for a sincere attempt of my own.*

## Friday (19 days ago)

That morning, during his session with Dr Warner, he is unresponsive. She asks questions; he doesn't answer. She tries to draw him out; he remains silent. She threatens him with every punishment at her disposal, and some he hasn't heard of before. With every appearance of sullen rebelliousness, he stares back at her, mute.

Inside, he is a roil of alertness and anxiety, making him regret eating breakfast because now he feels like might throw it back up. It's all he can do to avoid looking directly at the other door, the one leading away from his rooms, while at the same time focussing every iota of his attention on it through the corner of his eyes—because what if he's been lied to and it doesn't lead outside at all, but to another bedroom like his—inhabited by someone whose hair is the same colour as his, and who uses Cully's kitchen and bathroom while Cully is sleeping in drugged oblivion?

*Roommate*, he thinks. *Brother. Fellow prisoner . . .*

Finally, Dr Warner has had enough. She calls for an orderly and the door opens inward a crack. Cully is already moving, slipping the fingers of both hands into that crack and wrenching with all his strength so the handle on the other side yanks free of the orderly's grip. Then he's dropping, rolling, jabbing an elbow into the orderly's knees as he goes past, scrabbling across floorboards that look the same as those in the room behind him—and in his rooms, too—but are lined in ways he hasn't traced with his gaze a million times, nails he hasn't counted ten thousand times, scuffs he hasn't added to a thousand times before.

A corridor. There are more doors. Two to his left, one to his right. He plunges through the first one, and it's empty apart from a long wooden table and ten wooden chairs. Ducking and weaving, he avoids the grasping hands of a shouting orderly, runs around the table and exits the room.

Back in the corridor, he sees that the other doors are open now. Startled people peer through them, eyes wide. None of them look like him or are even the same size as him. They gape at him, and he stares past them, hunting for any signs of permanent inhabitation, but sees nothing, just offices, desks, glowing computer screens, chairs, a sign on one wall with curling letters spelling the initials "SPP" and a string of words that comes into focus as he lunges—

*Society for Practical Philosophy*

Two arms wrap around him from behind. He is pulled bodily to the floor and feels a piercing pain in his arm. The sedative works dizzyingly fast, throwing his consciousness into a spin.

Dr Warner appears in his view, scowling, furious. It's the most intense emotion he has ever seen her display.

He closes his eyes and lets the darkness claim him.

*

They keep him drugged until the following day, but his awareness comes and goes. He remembers this from the only other time they sedated him: he was seven years old and was scared of the orderly wanting to move the razor from his scalp to his chin. He thought they were going to kill him, not shave him. Then, as now, he found himself in a drugged state that was neither sleep nor waking. Occasionally, he rose to a confused half-awareness, before sinking back down again.

This time, older by nearly a decade, and expecting it, he takes note of what he experiences in that twilight state.

He dreams of being in his tiny apartment, going about his life as though nothing has changed. But when Dr Warner summons him for his interview, she calls him by another name.

## Sunday (18 days ago)

Dr Warner's pen taps a fast tattoo on the face of her tablet.

"Why did you do it?"

"I wanted to know what's out there."

This is the first truth he has told in the entire interview. His head is still spinning from the after effects of the sedative and from what he learned during his brief excursion through the doorway. Perhaps she sees some of the latter in his expressions—and why not? She knows him better than anyone, which is why has to be so careful around her.

"Did anything you saw trigger any specific thoughts or emotions?"

Of course it did, he wants to say. Only a machine wouldn't be triggered by the revelation that there is nothing on the other side but strangers and their offices. No other bedrooms like his. As far as he knows, he is the only person living in the entire building.

"Cully?"

He sighs. This is even more like an interrogation than usual.

He paints a picture of confusion and fear that is built on reality in ways he hasn't until this instant acknowledged to himself. The other side of the door is a strange and alienating prospect, he tells her. He doesn't belong there. He won't try again.

There are no other bedrooms there. He is the only tenant.

Or is he?

"I want to believe you," she says.

"Why would I lie?"

She gives him a long, assessing look, and he wonders what she sees in him.

*

Later that night, in bed, hungry from restricted diet and sore from enforced exercise, he scratches his first mark upon his body, somewhere *they* won't see. The letter J.

*Tuesday's child is loving living.*
*Thursday's child has some misgivings.*

What is this?

I'm you, but at the same time not you.

How?

We're awake.

We're seeing each other.

We're seeing through them, at last.

I think this an experiment.

So the questions . . .

Seeing if we know anything about each other.

I thought I'd done something wrong.

There's nothing wrong with us.

I'm just . . .

. . . incomplete

Two minds in the same body.

How could we not know?

Our realities are edited.

> The odd months, the even months.

The medication to make me sleep ...

> ... while I was awake.

And vice versa.

> We overlap now.

> But it's hard, resisting the tablets.

I'm sorry if I made you sick.

> Don't be sorry.

> This is better, being awake.

> Life makes sense now.

Yes.

> I dreamed of you, but I never suspected, not like you did.

I was slow.

> I was slower!

No roommate, no twin.

> Just us.

> Two pieces of a puzzle we didn't know we were part of.

> I thought I was going out of my mind—

When it was the exact opposite.

> How could they do this to us?

*The child born on a Saturday*
*Is last, to keep the bad at bay.*

My name is Cully.                                           My name is Jay.

> I want to see the horizon.

# Comment on 'Through the Window Frame'

Philosophical thought experiments are often rather callous. It's somewhat inevitable when one is dealing with matters of life and death. In Sean Williams' eerie tale, the Society for Practical Philosophy has come up with a particularly sinister experiment. They have apparently placed two people into the same body. How could they have done that?

In the 1930s, a surgical procedure was developed to treat severe epilepsy by cutting the corpus callosum – the band of nerve fibres connecting the two cerebral hemispheres. Cutting these fibres prevents seizures from spreading across the entire brain. Following the operation, patients are able to live normally (e.g. they can walk and talk and drive a car). However, the left hemisphere is receptive to information from the right visual field and the right side of the body, while the right hemisphere is receptive to information from the left visual field and left side of the body. Furthermore, in most people, the capacity to produce speech tends to be localized in the left hemisphere. Hence, in the early 1960s neuroscientists Roger Sperry and Michael Gazzaniga found that if a word is presented only to a patient's left visual field, the patient reports seeing nothing, because the left hemisphere responsible for speech fails to read this word. Yet surprisingly, the patient is still able to pick out the proper corresponding object with their left hand, because the right hemisphere controlling that hand has read the word. It seems that the left brain doesn't know what the right brain knows.

Does splitting the brain cause a split in consciousness? Maybe not. Note that the cerebral hemispheres remain connected to the subcortical regions beneath them. These unified regions might enable a unified consciousness, even if the person's consciousness fluctuates between the two fields of information in other respects. Alternatively, it may be that only the verbal left hemisphere is conscious. Although the right hemisphere is responsive to information, and can even react emotionally to wrong guesses by the left hemisphere, we have other evidence that quite complex actions can be performed unconsciously. Yet another alternative is that there are two streams of consciousness, but they partially overlap such that some aspects of experience belong simultaneously to both.

It should be emphasized that split-brain patients are for the most part mentally integrated (very occasionally, the two sides may seem to tussle, e.g. there was one case in which the patient's left hand appeared to be hostile to the patient's wife). The disassociations are typically generated under controlled conditions, in which information is prevented from being available to both visual fields (whereas both eyes can normally sense both visual fields merely by swivelling from side to side). As such, we might think that the person's consciousness only temporarily splits. Yet the experimental procedure involves merely flashing up information briefly enough that there's no time for an eye saccade. Could this really be enough to split human consciousness? It seems more probable that whatever is happening to consciousness in the experiments is happening all the time, even when the patient's mind appears integrated.

The problem is that we do not yet know how the brain generates consciousness. It may be that lots of independent processes generate the consciousness of specific qualities and then these are all combined to form the unified field of qualities that we normally enjoy. Or it may be that consciousness is generated by a single global mechanism in the first place. Yet split-brain experiments show conclusively that the brain hemispheres are independently capable of responding sensitively to information. At the very least, these cases raise the definite possibility that two entirely distinct streams of consciousness could be realized within a single human body. For example, even if the consciousness-making mechanism relies on subcortical regions, it could be that one hemisphere is kept asleep while the other hemisphere gets to use them.

In an interesting recent paper, the philosopher Mark Reid develops precisely this scenario. Reid argues that by means of careful sedation, two surgically separated hemispheres could alternate in consciousness over many years, developing their own distinct streams of memory, skills and personality features. In this way, two entirely distinct persons could be generated within the same body.

It was Reid's suggestion that I presented to Sean Williams, whose twisted imagination then produced the story that you've just read. By means of alternate neural sedation, Jay and Cully grow up in the same body. Both are equally capable of controlling that body, such that one can move about while the other is asleep. Both lead apparently independent lives. Jay works on his algebra homework on the odd numbered days while Cully concentrates on harmonic counterpoint on the even numbered days. Jay and Cully also have somewhat different personalities. Jay seems fairly timid while Cully is more defiant. Jay is a bit of a slob while Cully cleans his room carefully. All of these differences demand that Jay and Cully possess a range of distinct capacities for memory, reasoning, emotion, planning and communication. It also means that Cully can be morally responsible for an action, such as attacking a guard, of which Jay is entirely innocent.

Last, but by no means least, Jay and Cully seem to have different survival conditions. Although both of them rely on the same body, it looks like we could end Jay's existence by removing the hemisphere that he uses, while Cully survives. Cully could similarly be destroyed while Jay survives. Thus the distinction between the two is based upon a clear material difference.

This imaginary scenario is significant for our investigations into personal identity because it raises a powerful objection to the animalist theory. Recall that the animalist says that I am identical to the animal whose body I inhabit. One good way of justifying this claim is by noting that I am the being sitting in this chair and thinking, while the animal is equally sitting in this chair and thinking. But now imagine Jay and Cully making this claim. Jay claims that he is numerically identical to the animal that is thinking his thoughts, and so does Cully. There is only one human animal that they are both referring to, yet Jay and Cully are not numerically identical to each other. This is a violation of the transitivity of identity. One thing cannot be identical to two different things. Thus we have a vivid counter-example to the animalist claim that we are identical with our animal bodies.

It is worth pointing out that this counter-example to animalism is stronger than some comparable cases. For instance, a common trope in fiction is the multiple personality, more formally known as Dissociative Identity Disorder (DID). Fictions tend to exaggerate how cleanly DID personalities are distinct from each other. Usually DID is the result of trauma, where a person generates an alternate personality in order to disassociate themselves from horrible experiences. In extreme cases, there can also be amnesiac barriers between personalities (though sometimes the sufferer will report one personality watching another). Yet the split in DID seems to be an intense form of compartmentalization that many people perform where, for instance, they are a ruthless manager at work but set all that aside when they come home and play with their kids. Mark Reid also points out that therapy can enable a DID sufferer to eliminate a distinct personality. In contrast, it generally takes a lot more than simply talking to a person to destroy them. Overall, the DID sufferer is arguably not two different people, but only two different sets of attitudes that get triggered in different contexts.

Another real life case that raises a comparable challenge to animalism is that of Abby and Brittany Hensel. Abby and Brittany are dicephalic parapagus conjoined twins. Their bodies are fused such that they appear to have two heads upon a single body. The twins have separate spinal cords, hearts and stomachs, but a single reproductive system, large intestine and liver. Their small intestine is partially fused, as are their medial lungs. Each twin controls one half of the body, but they are able to cooperatively engage in normal behaviours such as driving and playing the piano. Although their speech sometimes overlaps, their independence of thought conveys a strong sense of two different people. At the same time, given the fusion of their digestive, circulatory and reproductive systems, there is some reason to think that they have a single animal body.

Still the animalist may wriggle out of this case. It is not entirely clear that the Hensel twins count as one animal, rather than two animals that overlap in some respects. One reason for thinking that they may be two animals is that each twin's brain controls a variety of functions in her half of the body. If that twin's brainstem were to be removed, the organs on her side of the body would fail and her limbs would become paralyzed. This would look a lot like the death of that side, despite the remaining twin's heart and lungs continuing to supply oxygenated blood. As such, it's at least debateable that we have two animals, with different survival conditions, to go along with two people. And if we have two animals, there's no violation of the animalist theory of numerical identity.

So one real-life case is not convincingly two people and another real-life case is not convincingly one animal. This is why it helps to construct an imaginary case of two persons in one animal. It is also the reason why the case needs to be as realistic as possible, to prevent the animalist from dismissing it as mere fantasy. As we saw when discussing brain transplants, we cannot draw simplistic conclusions when brains are handled realistically. This is why when Mark Reid writes about such cases, he is at some pains to show that current medical science allows one hemisphere to be anaesthetized while the other is awake.

I am satisfied enough by the realism of the case. But there's another requirement for us to draw philosophical conclusions from thought experiments. How much the animalist should worry about this imaginary case depends on how *transferrable* our conclusions about the thought experiment are to the identity of non-split beings. The case of Jay and Cully most directly addresses the question of synchronic identity: What makes one being distinct from another? When we ask what makes Jay and Cully distinct beings, we think that it cannot be that they are different animals. Thus some other criterion for their identity must be supposed instead. Yet why can't the animalist claim that, while admittedly Jay and Cully aren't identical to the animal, we still are? That is, why can't the animalist simply chalk it up as an exception that proves the rule (where the exception is not in effect, the rule is)?

The objection to animalism seems to be that whatever identity conditions we come up with for Jay and Cully should also be applied to regular people. That is, if we allow that *some* human people are not identical with animals then *no* human person is identical with an animal. Yet I wonder if the animalist could, at least in this specific case, deny this. Maybe Jay and Cully's conditions for identity do not apply to non-split people.

To explain: suppose we start out by saying that Jay and Cully are identical with their continuous psychologies. As we have seen in previous chapters, we need to interrogate that claim a bit more. What actually are those psychologies? The best evidence for Jay and Cully's distinct minds is that each can live a fully independent life while the other is asleep. And to do that, each of them requires not just a cerebral hemisphere but a brain stem and a living body. In fact, by means of eating and breathing, each of them keeps the other's hemisphere alive while it is sedated, a bit like how a mother keeps a foetus alive. The organic distinction between Jay and Cully is actually rather subtle, but it seems fair to suppose that Jay's physical existence is distinct from Cully's physical existence. When we argued earlier that Jay can be killed without Cully being killed, we implied that a certain brain hemisphere is an essential basis for Jay's existence, but not Cully's.

Once we consider these physical details, it looks like Jay is identical with a large part of an animal, while Cully is identical with another large part of an animal. These two animal parts overlap a great deal, but so long as there is some material distinction between them, they are strictly distinct beings. I suppose if Jay and Cully always alternate in their use of the body, we might also say that they are identical to different temporal parts of an animal.

At any rate, what generalization can we make from this case? Is the conclusion supposed to be that all of us are really identical with large parts of an animal, just like Jay and Cully? It is true that ordinary non-split people *could* satisfy these identity conditions. We know that a person *could* survive the removal of an entire hemisphere of their brain, just as they could survive the removal of a limb. Yet it is strange to imply that when these things haven't happened – when we have more complete bodies and brains – that our limbs or brain hemispheres aren't part of what we are. All of our parts contribute some function. Even a single skin cell contributes to blocking out germs from the environment. Thus it is much more attractive to say that what we are is *all* the organic components that make us up at any given time, not just our brains, or part of our brains.

Of course, the problem that animalists have is that it's hard to say that any of our organic parts are essential. That's the whole issue with living bodies: they change constantly and none of their parts necessarily persist for the animal's entire existence. Some psychological continuity theorists appeal to the brain instead, in part because that is more permanent. But as we shall see in the next chapter, there's reason to think that neural structures could be gradually replaced as well. None of the actual physical stuff seems to be essential across a person's entire life. The animalist needs to explain how we can have different parts at different times while still basically persisting.

The alternative is that we identify only with some deeper essence, specifically, some part that is immediately responsible for what makes us a person. Thus, some philosophers have suggested that we only identify with our brains because those are what allow us to have self-conscious thoughts. Yet as we have already seen, self-consciousness is complex. There might be one circuit in the brain responsible for one kind of self-conscious thought, while another circuit in the brain is responsible for another self-conscious thought. Insisting that we are only those bits of us that are immediately responsible for self-consciousness will lead to the conclusion that we are in fact a collection of thousands of distinct beings. Similarly, those self-conscious beings won't be the beings that walk and talk and have sex, because some other animal functions are required for those capacities. And even then, which bits of the animal are strictly required for those functions? As Eric Olson points out, perhaps some water molecules in our foot are required for walking where others aren't.

Overall, my sense is that worrying about which particular bits are directly responsible for personhood is the wrong approach. The animalist philosopher won't identify us with a lump of flesh, or many such lumps of flesh at different times, but the overall living function, which imposes a certain organization upon the comings and goings of fleshy matter. This is a thought that we shall explore further in the next chapter.

Meanwhile, it looks like when Jay and Cully finally become co-conscious, the barrier between their minds starts to break down and their identities begin to fuse. Poor old Dr Warner is going to have to find another child for her gruesome experiments. The Society for Practical Philosophy will not be deterred!

# 10

# 'Constitution'

## Tom Cochrane

---

I resurface slowly, at first only a dark, dull throbbing in the pit of my stomach. Gradually, the rest of my body returns to me with a hollow jaggedness. I become self-conscious –

Ugh, still alive.

I'm going to have to open my eyes at some point, but I'm afraid this will only make things worse. I linger in the penumbra for a while, until the irritating sounds of bustling and curtains being opened force me to take stock. A quiet muttering – yes this is the one – and then the unmistakable consciousness of someone hovering over me.

I open my eyes. A doctor with a neatly clipped goatee and delicate eggshell nostrils is looking down at me.

"It's not going well is it?" he says.

I close my eyes again.

He reels off, "James Bronowski, male, 25, admitted 11.45pm for barbiturate overdose, stomach pump administered, no further complications. History of major depressive yadda yadda … Tested for yadda yadda yadda … Patient also possesses a J60 artificial limb, left arm. Now *that's* interesting."

"What do you want?" I murmur.

The doctor leans over me until I'm forced to open my eyes again.

"You're going to get well James."

"I don't want to get well. I want to die."

"Oh come on now. If you really wanted to kill yourself you'd have thrown yourself off a bridge. Instead, you overdose on the Hammersmith and City line. No, not a serious attempt *at all*."

"Sorry – do better next time."

"You could James. If you've a mind to, we could hardly stop you ... But what if instead you could be happy again? I mean a genuinely, happy, person?"

There's a hard look in his eyes.

"... Excuse me *who* are you?"

"Ah yes, I'm Dr Gerard Manley." He holds out his hand, and when I do nothing, awkwardly returns it. "I'm a researcher at the Taviton institute attached to University College Hospital. I've been looking out for someone just like you James."

"Dr Madly –"

"Manley"

"Dr ... *I'm in pain.*"

Manley takes a small paper cup from a trolley and hands it to me. "Here, you're allowed two of these." He fills a glass a water, then sits on the side of the bed and holds it out to me. I stare at the blank little pills in the paper cup. Then with a sigh, I place them in my mouth and chug as much water as I can stand. As dry as my throat is, there's not the slightest feeling of refreshment.

I rest my head back on the pillow. "What's so special about me?" I ask.

"It's that prosthetic of yours ... May I?"

I allow him to take my left hand. He cups it delicately.

"This is a beautiful bit of kit." He lightly strokes the palm and I involuntarily clench. "You get full sensation don't you? Fine motor control too." He tuts, chiding my selfish attempt to waste such an investment. "How long have you had it?"

"They've been upgrading me since I was a kid." I flash on the old accident, metal, mangled flesh, screaming – not mine.

"You must have had significant neurosurgery." Manley glances up at my scalp. "These things connect all the way up to your somatosensory cortex. That, plus your ... problem, makes you an ideal candidate."

"... to be happy."

"Yes!" he says, dropping my hand. "I can get to the root of it!"

"I've tried a lot of drugs" I say.

"Pah! No more drugs! I'm talking about an implant, a replacement really. I want to rebuild that sad brain of yours. Your prosthetic control system – that's our bridgehead."

"You want to replace my brain? ... *My brain?*"

"Oh, there's no need to be so dramatic. Just a little piece of it. A crucial piece, no doubt, but still ..." Manley frowns and strokes his silly beard. "You see, James, your problem is that the bit of you that sees the attraction of things, the zest, the zing of things has gotten well . . . let's say it's gotten all burnt out. Your previous medications were designed to stimulate that part of you but, for some people, we believe it does more harm than good, and so . . ." he gestures around the antiseptic hospital room. "This is where it gets you."

I follow his gaze around the room, and suddenly the enormity of it all hits me again, knocking the breath right out of me. The utter, utter despair and horror of a nightmarish world that made me unable to face another day. I grasp the bedsheets white knuckle tight and tears stream out of me.

Dr Manley looks uncomfortably around for help. He pats my arm. "Come on now."

Finally, with a gasping intake of air I say, "It's not my fault?"

Manley shakes his head pityingly. "It was never your fault."

\*

Dr Manley leaves me some reading material and says he'll come back tomorrow. I'm all set to be committed for 28 days to Lambeth Psych, with its grilled windows and lumpy, sweat stained mattresses. But Manley says if I agree to the procedure, I'll be transferred to his clinic instead. The brochure shows tastefully decorated rooms and handsome, ethnically diverse people brimming with renewed confidence and not at all thinly veiled terror and psychosis.

From the consent document I learn that Manley wasn't exaggerating about rebuilding a part of my brain. The diagram shows clusters of artificial neurons to be implanted in three distinct areas, projecting nanoscale fibres that will ultimately develop into tens of thousands of tendrils to form a 'feel good' circuit. There's some technical stuff about synchronization patterns and gamma range vectorwaves that I don't fully grasp. But the overall message is clear enough: this is how my stupid meat brain *should* be working.

I lie back and stare up the ceiling, studying the pale squares of the ceiling tiles in their aluminium frames. I feel calm now. Mentally I survey the last few days: that idiotic phone call to Mara, the senseless walking around until I ended up sleeping rough on Hampstead Heath. Then getting beaten up by those drunks. Then tramping back to my shitty flat to find the electricity had been disconnected. The begging phone call to my mum that ended in yet another argument. All the usual shabbiness. None of it means a thing to me anymore. Maybe I've passed through something.

Then I realize, this calm, this is as good as it's going to get. At best I'm as pale and uninvolved as these ceiling tiles. I try to remember being happy. I can remember *doing* things alright. I can remember eating and drinking and dancing and having sex. But I can't remember any of that feeling good. I'm no longer sure it even felt good at the time.

I raise up my prosthetic arm, stretching and bunching my fingers. So apparently this thing could save me. I've never much liked it. That at least I'm sure of. It's a tool, nothing more. But that's also true of my other arm isn't it? And my feet. And my dick. And my tongue. And my fat head.

*

"Yes, it's true that we've not performed the surgery on humans yet" says Dr Manley the next day. "But our confidence is high. I can show you some extremely contented chimpanzees."

"So actually there are major risks" I say.

"Of course there are risks!" says Manley. "But in your case, well . . ." he struggles to find the right words.

"– You're banking on me having nothing to lose."

Manley smiles grimly.

"That doesn't mean I have to go along with you" I say.

He's about to say something but I hold my hand up "– Whatever. There's something you need to explain first. If this thing is so very sophisticated, I mean, just like a real brain circuit and everything, how do you know it's going to make *me* happy? How do you know it won't just make . . . itself happy?"

"That's a strange question James – the device isn't conscious!" Manley lets out a little barking laugh. "But I'd have thought that you of all people could appreciate how a prosthetic system can become part of you. This arm – you feel like it's your arm don't you? I mean, I see you using it just as automatically as your organic one. That's the beauty of neural connectivity."

"I suppose so. I don't know. This thing you're planning seems deeper."

"True, true. But I can assure you, the neural mechanics are comparable."

"But to actually replace so much of my brain. Can't you do it more gradually – see how it goes?"

"Oh of course!" says Manley grinning. "We could replace your whole brain neuron by neuron."

"Really?"

"Yes, let's see, one per minute would be a realistic rate. It would only take. . ." He taps on his tablet. ". . . about 190 thousand years."

"Oh."

"Give or take a few hundred."

"I see."

Manley leans forward. "Look James. People are always losing and adding bits of their brains. Not this particular bit admittedly. But there's no reason to think it will be any different."

"But how do you *know*?"

"Well, only you will really *know* James. You'll be the first to tell us what it's like! Doesn't that sound exciting?"

I sigh. "No."

"Well, it will James." Manley pats my arm reassuringly. "It will."

\*

I'm being prepped for surgery. Manley's research assistant takes me through a long, familiar checklist. Her name is Dr Jess Carraway. She has a nose ring, and tracing all the way up her arm are tattoos of little birds flying off into the distance.

"Are those crows?" I ask, looking at her arm.

Jess nods "Uhuh."

"Omens of death and transfiguration" I say.

She raises an eyebrow. "I wouldn't read too much into it."

Manley breezes in wearing a blue surgical hat and gown, holding his gloved hands up artificially in front of his chest. "All ready then? Excellent! We're going to screw your head right back on James – ha ha!" And he shoulders his way into the operating theatre.

Jess sees my grimace. "Don't be nervous. I know Gerard's annoying. But he's kind of a genius actually."

"I'm not nervous." I feel closer to tears.

Jess smiles at me encouragingly. "Good luck champ."

I'm awake throughout the surgery. Manley needs to make sure he's not damaging anything as he inches his way around the crevices of my brain. Occasionally he applies a little electrode and asks me if I sense anything. I get flashes of tessellated patterns, more felt than seen, and one time a strong impression of my mother's face.

"Hmm. And how does that make you feel?"

"Desperately sad" I say.

"Interesting. We could excise Freud at a stroke!"

After two hours of them digging around in my head, they close me up. Manley is exhausted but jubilant.

"I think we did it James. I really do. Time will tell!"

He strides out of the operating theatre, singing to the heavens. "I love brains!"

\*

For a week, I feel nothing but a persistent itch where my scalp was sewn up. The clinic treats me like an honoured guest. I get three meals a day, and a wide selection of books, films, and games consoles. Most of it is left untouched. I wear a fluffy white dressing gown with a pair of matching slippers, and when I can't sleep anymore, I go out into the courtyard behind the clinic. There's a bench where I can sit and watch the clouds go by, and a basketball hoop I occasionally throw at. I feel like a rather disappointing pet. Still, the quiet atmosphere of the place does me a kind of good. I don't have to deal with the world, or all the terrible things I've done.

Every day either Dr Manley or Jess comes to check on me. They show me pictures of rolling landscapes and sandy beaches, witty cartoons, exotically dressed women, laughing babies. I have to rate them on a seven point scale, from neutral to ecstatic delight.

". . . This?" says Jess.

"1."

"This?"

"1."

"This?" It's a picture of a golden retriever, almost exactly the same as the one I had as a kid.

". . . 1."

"This?"

"1."

"Seriously!?" says Jess. "She's smoking hot."

"Alright . . . 2."

Jess lights up. "Really? Shall I put 2 down?"

"No."

Jess gives an exasperated little snort.

A few days later I'm out in the courtyard shooting basketball. Generally I stand about five feet away and bounce the ball off the backboard. I prefer to have it bounce right back to me if at all possible. Thud, swish, bounce, catch. Thud, swish, bounce, catch. Thud . . . the ball awkwardly catches the rim and bounces away. Sighing, I trudge after it, pick it up, and with an angry little impulse, heft it overarm at the hoop.

To my surprise, the ball goes in and bounces obediently right back to me. I grab it and immediately throw it back, twisting my body with a grunt. I know as soon as I shoot that it's going in and I run up underneath the net to catch it before it bounces and score another. As the ball falls into my hands a third time, I stop, breathing heavily. Ok, that was unusual. Am I imagining things or do I feel . . . switched on? My arms and legs feel tight, springy. The dimples of the basketball excite my fingertips.

I bounce the ball experimentally a few times. Its thudding rings in my ears, making me feel a bit woozy. Then I slowly dribble to the back corner of the courtyard, turn, and chuck the ball. It bounces on the rim, once, twice, then drops in.

Then it's like a nuclear blast roars through me. My knees go to jelly and I stagger wildly across the courtyard. I manage to steady myself at the bench. But when I see the ball rolling innocently by, I feel a crazed impulse to chase after it like a puppy. I sit down on the bench and check myself. I'm shaking like a leaf. Ok, I'm ok.

After a few minutes, I decide I ought to experiment again. I retrieve the ball and take up a relatively difficult angle towards the hoop. My heart is pumping hard. I aim, shoot, and the ball flies right over the backboard. Of course it does. My next three shots are duds too. But at least, well, at least I'm interested in trying. I keep thinking I should retreat to my room, but as soon as the ball drops I grab it again. Is that me, or the implant talking?

Finally, I try another overarm rainbow shot and the ball drops into the net with a perfect swish. For a moment I can't believe it, and then I'm hit by the nuclear blast again, exactly as intense as before. This time I fall to my knees, but I have the presence of mind to note that the blast cuts off as suddenly as it begins. It's like a foghorn in my body. Is that supposed to be pleasure? It's been a while I admit, but that's not how I remember it.

Dr Manley is very excited when I tell him.

"Wonderful James, wonderful! This is just what I was expecting."

"But what I felt. . . I don't think that was pleasure."

"Let's not get ahead of ourselves James. The implant still needs to fully mesh with your cortical systems."

Manley rolls his chair over to his computer and brings up a display of my brain. "Too intense yes? Well we can adjust that." He starts tapping the keys.

"What are you doing?"

"I have bluetooth access to the implant of course."

"Wait, what?"

Manley looks at me quizzically. "I must make adjustments. It was all detailed in the consent form."

I'm stunned. "Really? I don't remember that at all . . . I don't think I'm okay with that."

Manley waves this off. "Don't worry about it James. By the way, were you using one particular arm when the effect occurred?"

I'm knocked back again. "Huh. Now you mention it, I suppose they were left-handed shots."

"Fascinating!" says Manley. "Yes, perfectly in line with predictions."

\*

Later in the evening, I sit up in bed, experimentally throwing screwed up balls of paper into the wastepaper basket across the room, triggering my implant over and over again. I no longer get a blast when I succeed, but it makes my body vibrate like an alarm clock. It's odd. I'm certain pleasure never felt like this. In fact, I don't believe pleasure was ever such a distinct sensation. Wasn't it always just a matter of liking that sweet taste, that soft touch, that fluid stroke? Not this drumming down my spine, and never so gated, never so reliable.

Still, there's something compelling about it. A taste I'm willing to acquire perhaps.

A while later, it occurs to me that the sensation does remind me of something after all. It reminds me of when I was a kid and I figured out how to masturbate. The first few times I had an orgasm, it too was a strange white-hot sensation, unlike any pleasure I'd ever felt before. Before long I was overflowing with the milk of human kindness every chance I got. But at least that was a natural pleasure, something that my body was built for. This is something else.

More tests in the morning. The pictures still aren't doing anything for me. But Jess has me playing computer games and sometimes, these too trigger the vibration. And then, a most interesting new wrinkle. I'm rounding the last corner in a racing game, pretty sure of a win, when I start to anticipate the implant. I find myself imagining the buzz running through my body – not as obvious as the thing itself – but increasingly vivid as I near the finish line. And this time, when it hits, the thrill joins seamlessly with my anticipation, lingers briefly, then smoothly tapers off.

I sit back with a sigh. On the screen my little character is waving its arms in jubilation.

"You look satisfied" says Jess.

I snap out of my reverie. "It wasn't as strong that time. But it felt . . . a lot more natural. This time I could feel it coming. I could ride with it."

Jess nods. "This was never about imposing something against your will. Pleasure is conscious if anything is. It needs your acceptance, even your deliberate employment to work right. Just like with your arm, it's a prosthetic that you're slowly learning to use."

"I don't remember having to learn to feel pleasure."

"Do you remember learning to see or hear? No, right? Still, there's all sorts of ways that those fundamental capacities get shaped by your knowledge of how things are supposed to look and sound. Same with pleasure. There's all sorts of ways we curl around the things we enjoy."

"So I have to learn to pleasure myself?"

Jess says, "I'm here to help."

I raise an eyebrow. Jess blushes. "I mean, we can calibrate the implant until it snugly fits your motivational systems."

Can it be so easy I wonder? Can I simply choose to like things?

Can I choose to like Jess?

\*

Over the next few days I make steady progress. I can't deploy my implant at will. But I can sort of lean into it when I know it is likely to operate and this allows me to shape the overall experience. It has a way of reinforcing my willingness to continue whatever it is that I'm doing. Dr Manley is, however, increasingly insufferable. Every time I report a new extension, his mouth twitches in a smug way and he says 'very good James' like I'm a performing dog.

"I'm sick of these pictures Dr Manley. They never do any good."

"It's not enough for task success to please you James. We've got to invigorate your sense of the world."

"But all this fluffy sunny shit. I was never into that."

"Well that's precisely the problem isn't it?"

"Couldn't we at least have some different pictures?"

"What do you have in mind?"

I cough, embarrassed. "I was wondering if maybe, you could put some pictures of Jess in."

Manley grins at me.

"Forget it" I say.

"James" says Dr Manley in a sing-song voice. "This is serious science. Do you like Dr Carraway?"

"I don't know." I say, irritated. "Maybe."

Manley twitches his mouth.

"– That doesn't mean it was your fucking implant. I did have feelings before I came to you!"

"When you came to me, you were in a state of despair." Manley strokes his beard. "At any rate, I think it would be interesting to present you pictures of various people in your life, which could include myself and Dr Carraway."

\*

The next day, I'm rating pictures again with Jess, having scraped my social media for images of relatives and friends. I say friends. As each is presented to me, the only thing that comes to mind is some incident when I said something hurtful and stupid. Their blank faces arouse nothing in me but self-loathing. Eventually my ex – Mara – comes up.

"She's cute." Jess suggests.

"Minus infinity" I say.

The next picture is of Jess. I focus all of my attention upon it, studiously avoiding the real Jess's gaze. In the picture she has the barest hint of a smile. I can see the shadows of suffering in her eyes. I can see her defiance and her tenderness. I keep staring, trying to summon the vibration, but nothing comes.

Even so, I turn to her ". . . I'll rate that picture a 5."

Her mouth parts with a little O. Neither of us says anything. My heart is pounding. Then she touches my hand, her cold fingers gently resting on my own. And now the vibration hits me hard, filling up my chest and shooting tingles down into my arms and legs. I cannot help but smile, and she smiles back at me!

Before I can tell her how I feel, Dr Manley strides in. "Going well? Any progress?"

Jess straightens up professionally. "I think we might be getting somewhere."

"Very good James." Manley says patronizingly. "Ha ha! Yes. Let's try my picture."

Jess brings up the picture of Dr Manley. It's some kind of publicity shot, soft autumnal background, chunky knit sweater – the brave visionary looks off into the distance.

And for once a picture has a definite effect on me. Quite unexpectedly, the vibration builds in my belly. I'm disoriented. For a moment I feel like I'm going to be sick and it occurs to me that I'm going to puke directly onto Manley's picture. I turn to Dr Manley and see the same expectant grin he always has. There's something so perfectly obnoxious about him. Instead of bile, a wave of hilarity vomits out of me. I laugh in Manley's face.

"Dr Manley. You are, without a doubt, a complete tit."

Manley's grin stays rigidly fixed. Another wave of hilarity hits me.

Manley clears his throat and lifts his chin. "Be that as it may James, that's the first time we've seen you laugh."

\*

At last, three weeks after my operation, they're letting me out into the world. I'm to report back every few days, but otherwise entirely free to ruin my life again. I step out onto the windy street rather shocked by the harsh vividness of it all. November has become December and the streets are glistening with frost. Now what?

I make my way to the tube station in a bewildered state. Am I seriously going to have to pick up the threads of my old life? I want to go back to my room in the clinic and play video games. I want to stay with Jess.

As I get on the train I realise that the last time I was on one of these I tried to kill myself. I remember collapsing to the floor, dribbling, dimly conscious of the people asking me if I was alright before I blacked out. I wonder what would happen if I threw myself on the floor again. Maybe I could do it better this time.

I'm hit by a vibrating wave of amusement, and a laugh escapes me before I can suppress it. Ever since that time with Manley's picture I've been prone to these attacks. And now, looking around me, it's starting to make sense. The world is just as desperate, just as mired in shit as it always was, but I don't believe in it anymore. I study the other people on the train, all wrapped up in their own bubbles, frothy, evanescent, ready to burst.

I get back to my flat. At least the fee I got from the experiment allowed me to pay off my electricity bill. But when I switch on the light, it's a sorry sight. I survey with disgust the dirty clothes, the grimy plates, the stained carpet. Just what kind of animal lives here? Oh yes, me. Another wave of hilarity shakes me. I'm about ready to set a match to the whole thing. But I'm curious if I can put my new capacities to productive use. I pick up a dirty glass and take it to the sink. Then, breathing deeply, I start to wash it, imagining a buzz of triumph. The cold water hits my hand, and it reminds me of Jess's touch. Maybe if I cleaned this place up, I could show her how much I've progressed? I hold up the clean glass and, yes, there's a tiny thrill of satisfaction, all mingled up with my mental image of Jess.

In this manner I manage to clean up quite a bit of my flat. 2 hours later, sweaty, my back aching, I survey the results. Yep, still a shithole. I laugh and laugh.

\*

There's something I need to do. I'm all bundled up, standing outside Mara's office, my breath steaming in the frigid morning air.

At last Mara rounds a corner, looking every inch the cool-headed professional. I may be the only one who knows any different. She tenses up when she sees me.

"Mara" I call.

She approaches, wary. "What are you doing here?"

"I thought it would be less creepy if I tried to catch you here."

Mara looks around as people pass on both sides, streaming into the building. "I need to get to work James."

"I'll only be a second . . . I just wanted to say I'm sorry . . . you know, for fucking everything up."

She winces. "Is that it? Are you done?" she says.

"Yes, that's it."

"For fuck's sake James . . ."

"– I won't bother you again."

"Really."

My head feels hot, and I remove the beanie I've been wearing. Mara looks up and sees the scar running across the length of my scalp.

"Oh my God, what have you done to yourself?"

I stroke my head. "I had surgery . . . I'm getting better."

"Surgery!? For what?"

"To stop me being such an awful person."

She laughs a bit at that. And I laugh too, a bit too hard. The tall buildings around are making me feel dizzy. She frowns. "Seriously. What was it for?"

"You know there was something deeply wrong with me right?"

"Are you kidding me?"

"No."

". . . And so what, now there isn't?"

I smile, broad and sincere. "Only what's wrong with everyone else." I laugh again.

Mara looks a bit afraid. "I'm not dealing with this. I'm going to work."

"Ok, see you around!"

She walks quickly into her building, glancing back only as she pushes the revolving door. I wave and think about the child that was never born. That will never love and never suffer and never die. I used to think the ledger was in their favour. Now I think the idea of a ledger is absurd. There's no profit, no loss. Just a dance of joy and sorrow.

Amazing cure for depression this. Now I can properly regret my past mistakes!

I grin. My body starts to shake. And there in front of my ex-lover's building, I guffaw until I can hardly breathe. The arriving lawyers give me a wide berth. I sit on the curb, clutching my chest. Eventually a porter comes and shoos me away.

\*

I'm back at the clinic. I'm excited to see Jess again and report my progress. I feel witty and ebullient. I'm going to ask her out today.

"... yes I'd certainly say the world has come alive for me in a way it wasn't before, like things call out to me where before they were cut off? I'm not saying I'm completely comfortable, like maybe things seem messy or I'm messy but that doesn't bother me so much. Anyway I was able to clean my flat and pay off my bills so that's good right?"

Jess looks up from her notes. She smiles at me. "Yes that's good. It can't have been easy going back to your old life."

"Oh before it would have been impossible! I literally could not pick up a dirty plate. It was like there was some massive gravitational force pinning it down, pinning me down. I think NASA should investigate really, ha ha, do you think they'd be interested? No maybe not. Did you see that new image from the James Webb telescope?"

"... what?"

"It was just in the news today. Oh amazing. Just thinking about it I get tingles. That's what it's all about isn't it? Us monkeys flying through space on this big ball of mud." I laugh to myself, and half push myself out of my chair.

"You seem a bit hyper James."

I stand up. My heart is beating hard. My arms and legs feel all tingly and electrical. I sit down again.

"Listen Jess. I was wondering ... would you like to go out to lunch with me after this?"

Jess frowns and bites her lip.

"There's a Thai restaurant round the corner that looks pretty good" I say. "Do you like Thai food?"

"James" she says. "er ... I don't think ...." I can hardly hear what she's saying the blood is thumping so hard my ears. "I think professionally, that would be inappropriate. Of course, you're a lovely person."

"Ok, no worries. It's fine, it's fine. You don't have to worry about me. No, yes you're right. I can see that."

"Sorry."

And now again I see the funny side of it. James Bronowski, the doofus, puts his foot in it once again. Oh man what an idiot! This is excruciating. Poor Jamesy-wamesy, nobody loves him ha ha. I see stars and galaxies in my mind, and here's the saddest speck of dust in the universe. My body is rippling. The room starts spinning. I clench my teeth but a giggle builds in me until I'm convulsing with it.

I hear Jess's voice. "Are you okay James?"

I can't stop myself shaking. It's incredible and horrific. Tears stream from my eyes. You stupid sad fuck! You know how to impress them!

I dimly hear Jess calling for help. Dr Manley comes rushing in. I'm unable to sit in my chair. I think... yes! I'm going to wet myself. Oh this is wonderful ... And then as the warmth spreads across my crotch, I feel a needle going in my arm and I black out.

*

I awake from troubled dreams to find myself in my old room at the clinic. I feel unrested. My nerves are jangling and even this beige room seems to me lurid and uneven. I hold up my hands. My prosthetic is fine, but my right hand is shaking. Giggles escape me like hiccups. Am I going mad? Is this what madness feels like?

Eventually Dr Manley comes to see me. He pulls up a chair close to the bed.

"How are you feeling now James?" he asks.

I'm afraid he's going to set me off again. It's all I can do to put my hands over my mouth and shake my head.

"Still the hysterical mood yes?"

He's going to stroke his beard again. I can feel it. I close my eyes tight.

"I believe I know what's wrong James" he says. "Every measure we've taken indicates that the implant is working perfectly. It is stimulating pleasure and enlivening your sense of the world in just the way I predicted. However, what I did not predict was the chaotic way your remaining organic affective systems would interact with it."

I manage to crack open my eyes. I've got to concentrate on this.

Manley continues. "I believe you're still a depressed person James. We cured your anhedonia alright, but the system for tracking the painful and unpleasant aspects of experience remains hyperactive, perhaps even exacerbated by your restored capacity for pleasure. Thus, we get this combined effect – things still seem awful to you, but your pleasure tells you not to take it seriously. The result: you find everything funny."

I clench my teeth. "I think you've hit the nail on the head Doc. Horrifying and silly. That's how it is."

Manley stands up and paces about. "James. I *cannot* remove the implant without plunging you back into suicidal despair. I'm certain you would not last a week. However, I have, alongside the pleasure implant, developed an implant for tracking and regulating negative affect."

Manley turns to me with wide eyes. "I propose that we replace your organic system with this, and thereby create a more harmonious affective whole."

I feel a wave of desperation. "Haven't you already made me enough of a machine?"

"We're all machines" Manley says, placidly.

"I don't feel like I'm a machine!"

"But consider what is telling you that! A complex neural system for tracking your identity over time. It's as replaceable as every other system in your body."

Manley starts stroking his beard. Oh God I'm about to start laughing again. I clamp my hands back over my mouth. This is hellish!

"Look James. You've already taken the biggest step" Manley says. "The only real question to ask yourself is whether your current prosthetics – your arm, your pleasure – are part of you or not. Decide that and you'll know what to do. I'll leave you to think about it."

I spend the next hour just trying to think straight. In the end all I can decide is that I want to see Jess. Despite my embarrassment and my jangling nerves I must see her. Breathing carefully, I get dressed and knock on the door of her office. When she sees me she smiles, but it's full of pity. That's not what I want from her.

"Did Manley tell you what he thinks is wrong?" I ask. "What he wants to do?"

"Yes" she says quietly.

"And do you agree?"

"Oh James . . . Maybe . . . I don't know."

"There is something you can do for me" I say. "I want you to touch my prosthetic hand, just like you did my other one that time."

She blushes.

"Please" I say. "I need to know if this is me." I sit down next to her and hold my left hand out.

She appraises me for a second. "Alright" she says, "close your eyes."

I close them, my every sense alert, waiting. And then, so softly, I feel her fingertips stroking my palm. I open my eyes and she looks directly into mine. Then she gently lifts my hand and rests her cheek against it.

"What do you feel?" she whispers.

I feel music and fireworks and angels singing. If this isn't me, it surely beats the hell out of me.

\*

I resurface slowly, at first only a dark, dull throbbing in the pit of my stomach. Gradually, the rest of my body returns to me with a hollow jaggedness. I become self-conscious –

God, I'm hungry.

I push the call button and request breakfast. The nurse arrives with a tray loaded with toast and scrambled eggs and bacon and hot coffee. I eat ravenously. Everything is delicious. I literally cannot remember enjoying food so much. It's not until I'm rounding off my second cup of coffee that I spare much thought for yesterday's operation.

It's all pretty hazy. My hysterical mood meant that I had to be quite heavily sedated. I was still just about conscious, but I couldn't cooperate much with Manley's explorations. Anyway, thank God the constant ticklish sense of hilarity seems to have disappeared. I can remember *thinking* that it was hellish, but right now I struggle to recreate what it was like. How can laughter have felt bad? In fact, now that I mention it – how can anything feel bad? Interesting. I suppose it will take a while until the negative affect implant goes online.

At any rate, I'm very plainly still here. My heart is still pumping – good ol' heart! My stomach still gurgles – good ol' stomach! My muscles still stretch and contract . . . It occurs to me that I'd rather like to play some basketball.

I get dressed and bound down the back steps of the clinic three at a time. The ball is resting patiently in the middle of the courtyard, as if it's been waiting for me. Hello Mr Ball! I grab it and spin it and loop it round my waist. I'd forgotten how good I am at this game. I run at the hoop, jump high, and dunk that fucking ball like it deserves. It pounds the pavement and I imagine the crowd cheering. Bron-ow-ski! Bron-ow-ski! Yaaay!

Funny though – I don't feel the vibration I used to get. I was looking forward to that.

Later on Manley says the sense of distinct feeling may have been an artefact of the conflict with my organic neural systems. Since I'm clearly able to enjoy things he declares the entire experiment a resounding success.

"So what about my negative feelings?" I ask.

"Small steps on that James. Very small. In the meantime I suggest you make the most of your positive mindset."

"Thanks Doc" I say "you're the best" and draw him into a big hug. I see a little tear in his eye when I pull back. Now it all makes sense. The guy doesn't get hugged enough!

\*

It's a whole glorious week before any negative feelings come back to me. After an incident in which I scalded myself in the shower, not realising that the hot water was supposed to feel painful, they've had to keep a close eye on me. Nobody minds this particular duty, however. I've become the most popular person in the clinic.

Small steps, like Manley said. First they're teaching me to feel itchiness again. I mean, not just that my skin scratches, but that I don't want it to. Very carefully, they adjust the new implant while scratching my thigh. Even so, I almost bite my own leg off the first time I feel irritated. And when, the second time, they hold me down, I burst into tears. It takes considerable repetition before I'm inclined merely to jump out of my chair.

\*

The world still seems to me a sunny place when a couple of days later Jess comes to see me looking very frowny-faced, and not at all chilled out.

"James" she says. "I've just learned something very disturbing."

"Oh?" I say, smiling.

"I don't how to tell you this James, but Gerard . . . Dr Manley, I think he was activating and manipulating your pleasure implant without your consent."

"Hmm" I say, trying to copy the frown on her face.

"You remember that time you laughed at his picture?" Jess says. "Lots of other times too. It's all in the programme logs."

"Ok."

"Don't you see!? Your whole hysteria may be because he was pushing you too hard! And everything that came after . . ."

"It all turned out for the best though right?"

"It's a total violation of your autonomy!" she thunders. "I knew Gerard was obnoxious, but I can hardly believe he would do this."

She continues, stammering. "And it's not just that . . . it's . . . James . . ." Her eyes are glistening. "He told me to encourage you, you know, to get the new implant . . . And that's what I did, didn't I!"

Her cheeks are flushed. She looks incredible.

Then I see a new angle on the situation. "Yes Jess, I see what you mean. It's very serious isn't it?"

"I'll say!" she says, wiping her eye.

"But do you think you can help me?" I hold out my hand for hers.

She holds my hand and I feel quite wonderful. "Yes of course I'll help you" she says.

"Great! We need to think carefully about what to do. Best not around here either" I say, looking around with exaggerated suspicion. "How about we get a coffee round the corner and go over everything?"

"Ok, sure!" she says.

As I walk with Jess down the corridor of the clinic, I feel a tremendous surge of optimism. The clinic has been decorated for Christmas and all the tiny lights dance in my eyes. Like Manley said, I've already taken the biggest steps. There's really no limit to what I can do with my body now. My pleasures and pains are pristine, and my left arm is top of the line. So why not the rest of me? Why not indeed? In time my organic body will break down, but that's an opportunity, not a limitation! There are artificial hearts and artificial livers. There are mechanical eyes and mechanical ears. I must ask Manley about other aspects of my brain. Didn't I read something the other day about artificial reasoning implants? They said it was no different in principle to working things out with paper and pencil. But stronger, faster, better . . .

Jess and I reach the entrance of the clinic and I dash ahead a little to hold the door open for her. As she passes me with a smile, a fly, fat and old, lands with a buzz on my outstretched right arm.

Quick as a flash I slap my arm, and the ugly thing falls down dead.

# Comment on 'Constitution'

Our question is one that I briefly touched on in the introduction to this book: would I still exist if my body – including my brain – were to be gradually replaced by machine parts? I think this is the question about identity that I find most fascinating. As a consequence, when I was building this collection, I had exacting standards for how a story should address it. I found several good stories, but none that completely satisfied me. It then occurred to me that I could turn an obstacle into an opportunity and explore the persuasive impact of a thought experiment from the writer's perspective.

Most people I have asked think that we can survive gradual bionic replacement. They know that the cells in our bodies get replenished over time and suppose that, as long as the functional roles are maintained, machine parts could do this job just as well. Yet it is not so commonly known that most neurons in our brains do not get replaced. This adds an interesting wrinkle. Is there a special reason why neurons endure, connected in some way to our identity? I find it quite plausible that the permanence of our neurons plays a role in the preservation of our memories, for example.

But we can take the science a step further. It is even less commonly known that cell homeostasis implies that the molecules that make up our individual cells, including our neurons, are also gradually replenished. A neuroscientist colleague tells me that when a protein that say, acts as a receptor for a neurotransmitter, starts to degrade, it gets tagged by quality control machinery in the cell, and the amino acids that make up the protein are recycled. If this isn't done, the individual becomes susceptible to disorders such as Parkinson's disease and Alzheimer's disease. Whether the entire neuron will be gradually replenished over time is a probabilistic matter. But the basic fact of cell homeostasis entails that a neuron can maintain its connections to other neurons while its constituent molecules are replaced.

Of course, these biological routines are different from replacing a brain with machine parts. We don't know exactly how neurons contribute to the realization of experience. It is most likely that information is captured by patterns of neuronal firings, but exactly how this works might rely on organic properties that are hard to replicate. I think a thought experiment on this subject has to simply assume that a functionally equivalent device is invented. This is a possible weakness.

The other big problem is how one could replace each and every neuron in a person's brain. Our brains contain over 100 billion neurons, each possessing thousands of synaptic connections to other neurons. I can think of no realistic way for neurons to be replaced one by one in a feasible amount of time. This then led to my first insight in trying to write a narrative for myself. Once you start thinking about how brain replacement could actually be done, instead of retreating to vague claims about cell replacement, you realize the enormous complexity of the task. Science fiction gives us a great deal of latitude in describing technologies, but I wanted to resist handwavy appeals to nanotechnology.

It then occurred to me that our minds can be divided up into a number of different abilities, and that it may be possible to replace the neural machinery serving these abilities chunk by chunk. For instance, there has already been some success in replacing sensory inputs. Cochlear implants allow deaf people to gain hearing, although current devices do not achieve the full nuance of the biological cochlear. Motor outputs have also been artificially extended, enabling brain activity to trigger prostheses. I do not see a major conceptual difficulty with the replacement of these inputs and outputs. But what about our higher cognitive functions, such as reasoning or memory recall? It seems to me that we already use external resources to support these functions (such as doing long-division on a piece of paper or keeping a diary to support our memories). So the more complete handling of these functions by machines does not seem impossible. Are there any abilities that are harder to replace? Digging deeper, we come to capacities that seem core to our everyday sense of being alive: emotions, pain, pleasure. It seems to me that if even these could be replaced, then this would offer sufficient 'proof of concept' that any part of our brains could be replaced.

From this thought, the basic premise of the story and much of the narrative action quickly followed. Why would a person want to replace their affective capacities? Most likely because they suffer a life-threatening affective disorder, such as depression. But would it really work? This I did not want to assume. I wanted to use the writing of the story to explore that question, and I held off supplying a definite answer for as long as possible.

As I was writing, there were other fictional cases on my mind. There is an excellent story by Greg Egan called 'Learning to be Me', which coincidentally replicates similar ideas in a story by Daniel Dennett called 'Where am I?' (Dennett got there first, but Egan's version is more narratively compelling.) Both stories imagine a device placed in the brain that learns to perfectly track neuronal activity to the point when it can predict exactly how the brain will behave next. One day the device is allowed to take over from the organic brain. The person appears to behave just as they usually do. Yet both Dennett's and Egan's stories suggest that the person is replaced by a replica. If we have any intuitions that our brains play a necessary role in the preservation of our identities, then this is not survival. A mechanical copy is not me.

From the Dennett/Egan scenario, a challenge is raised: if sudden replacement is not survival why should gradual replacement be any different? While writing, the following response occurred to me: James Bronowski survives even when he lacks the capacity for pleasure entirely. He doesn't have a good life, but he survives. More generally, complex beings like us can survive the loss of a few parts. So we have a principled way to distinguish gradual from sudden replacement. Unlike taking away a single part, sudden replacement takes away all of a thing's parts, and so the thing does not endure. The vital next step is then whether a new part can become genuinely integrated within the complex being. If it can, then this new whole being can again survive the loss of one its parts. The replacement process can iterate indefinitely.

Now an animalist philosopher may deny that artificial parts would genuinely be integrated. Eric Olson supposes that gradual replacement would just be a matter of the original animal growing smaller and smaller as the machine grows larger and larger. Admittedly, the animal won't immediately die when a single part is replaced, but it won't be entirely maintained either. Consider what happens when we replace a limb with an artificial prosthetic. It seems that the animal learns to interact with a new tool, not that the prosthetic is now part of the animal. Similarly, as the brain is replaced, Olson would say that the animal interacts with a sophisticated prosthetic, but this prosthetic is never part of the animal. Artificial prosthetics are not part of the animal's metabolic system; they are not part of the animal's life.

These considerations were on my mind as I was writing the story. It seemed to me that at least from James' perspective, what would matter was whether he felt like he was interacting with a tool when using the pleasure implant, or whether it would feel as seamless and transparent as using any other part of his body and brain. The case of cochlear implants also inspired me to consider how at least initially, people would find these devices rather clunky. It did however make sense that over time, use of the implant would come to feel more 'natural'. Thus, James may be persuaded. Yet recall that the sense of self is not the self. James might *feel* like his implant is genuinely part of him, but he could be wrong. There could even be a sense in which the implant is manipulating his judgement, in service of the nefarious schemes of Dr Manley.

This brings up another issue that writing the story made very clear to me. There is a strong artistic urge to make a story dramatic. It would never do, for instance, to write a story in which someone replaces their parts and everything goes exactly as planned. The writer wishes to intrigue their readers, and to intrigue themselves. Thus at various stages in the process, the writer will wonder: what is the less obvious choice here? These decision points should not be forced, they should make sense within the story world that has developed. Thus there is a special way that a writer can genuinely experiment with a scenario. However, as readers of science fiction thought experiments, we must be aware that artistic narratives will tend towards the exceptional, and not the mundane. This means that artistic narratives best function as stress tests of the ideas that they focus on.

The question we arrive at then is this: Does replacement count as survival, even if James might be deceived by those around him, and even if his implants may be affecting how he thinks about them? Once I got to the end of my story, I felt persuaded that replacement had indeed passed that stress test. James will survive even if he ultimately replaces his entire brain and body with inorganic parts.

Then a few months later, I changed my mind! I realized that my earlier conclusion was betraying the narrative voice of the story. This narrative is telling us that James has been tricked. He has gotten deceived into embracing the machine and neglecting the call of his animal body. So much for writer's insight. I had to become a better reader of my own story before I could understand what it was arguing.

My opinion now is that the case depends on the details of the replacement, and we need to do some careful philosophy if we're going to sort it all out. In particular, we need to introduce another important theory of personal identity.

Suppose for the time being that machine replacement counts as survival. What does this say about what we are? The standard interpretation is that if it's even possible to exist without any organic parts, then we cannot essentially be animals. I can continue existing while the animal goes out of existence entirely. However, the view also allows that sometimes I have animal parts, and at other times I don't. This idea is explained by what is called 'constitution theory'.

A prominent defender of constitution theory is Lynne Rudder Baker. Baker claims that we are not essentially animals, but we are *constituted* by animals. For one thing to constitute another is for those two things to be spatially coincident (i.e. they take up the same exact space) but not identical. They are not identical precisely because one could be replaced while the other endures.

The classic example of a constitution relationship is the relationship between a statue and the lump of clay it is made of. Shaping the clay in the right way brings the statue into existence. There are two things – the statue and the lump of clay – that spatially coincide. Yet the statue and clay are not identical. This is because you could destroy the statue by squashing it, while the clay survives. You could also repair damage to the statue with a new bit of clay, maintaining the statue, but changing the clay. Baker also adds that constitution relationships require the right circumstances. The existence of a statue requires an environment in which statues are recognized and appreciated. The right environment allows the statue to do things that a mere lump of clay cannot. For instance, given an art world, the statue can win a prize, or inspire other artists.

Baker applies these same considerations to people. Baker claims that we are made of animals, but we are not animals. Essentially, we are persons, which Baker defines in terms of self-consciousness. Like the statue, Baker claims that persons can be maintained while the animal is destroyed (i.e. in the thought experiment we are considering). Like the clay, the animal can also remain in existence while the person is destroyed (e.g. if we fall into a persistent vegetative state). Baker also points out that people have casual powers that mere animals lack, such as having a legal status. Like statues, these causal powers depend on the right circumstances.

So what would Baker say about Olson's thinking animal problem? Recall that Olson argues that I am sitting here thinking and so is the animal, and since there's only one being here, I must be identical to the animal. Baker's view is that although the animal is thinking, it is doing this in a merely derivative sense. The animal is only thinking (or more exactly, being self-conscious) in virtue of constituting a person, and it is only the person that is thinking in a non-derivative sense. Similarly, Baker will say that I am sitting, but only in a derivative sense, in virtue of being constituted by an animal that is non-derivatively sitting.

This takes us back to the issue we had in the last chapter about what is directly involved in realizing a self-conscious thought, or any other human function. It is not very intuitive to say that I only derivatively sit, or that the animal only derivatively thinks. Baker also refuses to break down the crucial feature of a person – their self-consciousness – into component skills or mechanisms. She attributes self-consciousness only to the person as a whole. It cannot be reduced any further than that. The person is a new thing, brought into being by an animal in the right circumstances, but strictly distinct from it.

Influenced by examples such as Sirius, I am less inclined to think that persons are things, and less inclined to sharply distinguish the animal thing from the person thing. *Personhood* is rather a complex property that animals can have to a greater or lesser degree. Animals are not passive lumps of clay but intelligent, autonomous, valuing things. They move their bodies around and they think. Sometimes they think by moving their bodies around.

Baker wants to distinguish the person from the animal precisely because of thought experiments like the one we have presented here. She thinks bionic replacement can only mean that the person and animal must be distinct. But maybe there's another way we could interpret bionic replacement cases. Maybe they don't distinguish the person from the animal it is made of, but the living thing from the flesh that it is made of.

We already know from cell replacement that any bit of flesh is fungible. What endures is the living being as a kind of dynamic functional organization. Similarly, I'm inclined to think that in the story, James endures if he is still alive after a given replacement. This is why he is reassured after his second operation that his heart is still pumping and his stomach is still gurgling.

Yet James then contemplates replacing those parts of his body too. Could that work? If our key distinction is between flesh and life, could machine parts still constitute a person's life? The question here is effectively what makes something alive. Not an easy question to answer. However, it looks like living has something to do with the way a being collects resources from the environment that it uses to sustain itself or to prevent itself from falling apart at the cellular level. Every cell in our bodies, including our neurons, relies on the supply of oxygen and nutrients as well as the avoidance of various forces that cause cells to be destroyed such as excessive heat, germs, and sharp bits of metal. The trillions of cells that make up our bodies, including our neurons, are constantly engaged in this collective task.

Could machine parts then become part of this task? Certainly an artificial heart helps to deliver blood that keeps the cells alive. But could an artificial heart also itself be *sustained* by such a task? This is not a feature of current technology and it is reason for thinking that artificial parts are not yet at the point at which they are fully integrated within us. We should not however rule out the possibility of such technology being developed in the future. Or more abstractly, we should not rule out the possibility that the project of sustaining a body, even at the cellular level, could have artificial analogues. A machine could be made of vulnerable parts that need constant upkeep, and organic and inorganic parts could work together to achieve this. That is, machine parts could *constitute* a living thing.

Overall, I think that bionic replacement of a living being is possible, but only if those bionic parts are integrated into the function of collective maintenance. I don't think Dr Manley has created parts like this, so I don't think these parts are genuinely part of James. In other words, James' implants do not (partly) constitute him.

In some ways this is a disappointing result. Bionic replacement is not the key to immortality. The replacements would have to resemble the organic components too closely to count as a genuine change in our physical nature. Yet in terms of figuring out what we are, it does seem to me that we have reached a more refined answer. I am neither essentially my flesh nor essentially my memories. I am the *life* that this flesh, and these memories preserve; the living organization if you like. This living organization is not some abstract pattern that can float free of the stuff that makes it up. It is precisely the collective activity of all that stuff. I am like a society that my cells sustain.

# 11

# 'Social Dreaming of the Frin'

## Ursula K. Le Guin

*Note: much of the information for this piece comes from An Oneirological Survey on the Frinthian Plane, published by Mills College Press, and from conversations with Frinthian scholars and friends.*

ON THE FRINTHIAN PLANE, dreams are not private property. A troubled Frin has no need to lie on a couch recounting dreams to a psychoanalyst, for the doctor already knows what the patient dreamed last night, because the doctor dreamed it too; and the patient also dreamed what the doctor dreamed; and so did everyone else in the neighborhood.

To escape from the dreams of others or to have a private, a secret dream, the Frin must go out alone into the wilderness. And even in the wilderness, their sleep may be invaded by the strange dream visions of lions, antelope, bears, or mice.

While awake, and during much of their sleep, the Frin are as dream-deaf as we are. Only sleepers who are in or approaching REM sleep can participate in the dreams of others also in REM sleep.

REM is an acronym for "rapid eye movement," a visible accompaniment of this stage of sleep; its signal in the brain is a characteristic type of electroencephalic wave. Most of our re-memberable dreams occur during REM sleep.

Frinthian REM sleep and that of people on our plane yield very similar EEG traces, though there are some significant differences, in which may lie the key to the Frinthian ability to share dreams.

To share, the dreamers must be fairly close to one another. The carrying power of the average Frinthian dream is about that of the average human voice. A dream can be received easily within a hundred-meter radius, and bits and fragments of it may carry a good deal farther. A strong dream in a solitary place may well carry for two kilometres or even farther.

In a lonely farmhouse a Frin's dreams mingle only with those of the rest of the family, along with echoes, whiffs, and glimpses of what the cattle in the barn and the dog dozing on the doorstop hear, smell, and see in their sleep.

In a village or town, with people asleep in all the houses around, the Frin spend at least part of every night in a shifting phantasmagoria of their own and other people's dreams which I find hard to imagine.

I asked an acquaintance in a small town to tell me any dreams she could recall from the past night. At first she demurred, saying that they'd all been nonsense, and only "strong" dreams ought to be thought about and talked over. She was evidently reluctant to tell me, an outsider, things that had been going on in her neighbors' heads. I managed at last to convince her that my interest was genuine and not voyeuristic. She thought a while and said, "Well, there was a woman—it was me in the dream, or sort of me, but I think it was the mayor's wife's dream, actually, they live at the corner—this woman, anyhow, and she was trying to find a baby that she'd had last year. She had put the baby into a dresser drawer and forgotten all about it, and now I was, she was, feeling worried about it—Had it had anything to eat? Since last year? Oh my word, how stupid we are in dreams! And then, oh, yes, then there was an awful argument between a naked man and a dwarf, they were in an empty cistern. That may have been my own dream, at least to start with. Because I know that cistern. It was on my grandfather's farm where I used to stay when I was a child. But they both turned into lizards, I think. And then—oh yes!" She laughed. "I was being squashed by a pair of giant breasts, huge ones, with pointy nipples. I think that was the teenage boy next door, because I was terrified but kind of ecstatic, too. And what else was there? Oh, a mouse, it looked so delicious, and it didn't know I was there, and I was just about to pounce, but then there was a horrible thing, a nightmare—a face without any eyes—and huge, hairy hands groping at me—and then I heard the three year-old next door screaming, because I woke up too. That poor child has so many nightmares, she drives us all crazy. Oh, I don't really like thinking about that one. I'm glad we forget most dreams. Wouldn't it be awful if we had to remember them all!"

Dreaming is a cyclical, not a continuous activity, and so in small communities there are hours when one's sleep theater, if one may call it so, is dark. REM sleep among settled, local groups of Frin tends to synchronise. As the cycles peak, about five times a night, several or many dreams may be going on simultaneously in everybody's head, intermingling and influencing one another with their mad, inarguable logic, so that (as my friend in the village described it) the baby turns up in the cistern and the mouse hides between the breasts, while the eyeless monster disappears in the dust kicked up by a pig trotting past through a new dream, perhaps a dog's, since the pig is rather dimly seen but is smelled with great particularity. But after such episodes comes a period when everyone can sleep in peace, without anything exciting happening at all.

In Frinthian cities, where one may be within dream range of hundreds of people every night, the layering and overlap of insubstantial imagery is, I'm told, so continual and so confusing that the dreams cancel out, like brushfuls of colors slapped one over the other without design; even one's own dream blurs at once into the meaningless commotion, as if projected on a screen where a hundred films are already being shown, their soundtracks all running together. Only occasionally does a gesture, a voice, ring clear for a moment, or a particularly vivid wet dream or ghastly nightmare cause all the sleepers in a neighborhood to sigh, ejaculate, shudder, or wake up with a gasp.

Frin whose dreams are mostly troubling or disagreeable say they like living in the city for the very reason that their dreams are all but lost in the "stew," as they call it. But others are upset by the constant oneiric noise and dislike spending even a few nights in a metropolis. "I hate to dream strangers' dreams!" my village informant told me. "Ugh! When I come back from staying in the city, I wish I could wash out the inside of my head!"

Even on our plane, young children often have trouble understanding that the experiences they had just before they woke up aren't "real." It must be far more bewildering for Frinthian children, into whose innocent sleep enter the sensations and preoccupations of adults—accidents relived, griefs renewed, rapes reenacted, wrathful conversations held with people fifty years in the grave.

But adult Frin are ready to answer children's questions about the shared dreams and to discuss them, defining them always as dream, though not as unreal. There is no word corresponding to "unreal" in Frinthian; the nearest is "bodiless." So the children learn to live with adults' incomprehensible memories, unmentionable acts, and inexplicable emotions, much as do children who grow up on our plane amid the terrible incoherence of civil war or in times of plague and famine; or, indeed, children anywhere, at any time. Children learn what is real and what isn't, what to notice and what to ignore, as a survival tactic. It is hard for an outsider to judge, but my impression of Frinthian children is that they mature early, psychologically. By the age of seven or eight they are treated by adults as equals.

As for the animals, no one knows what they make of the human dreams they evidently participate in. The domestic beasts of the Frin seemed to me to be remarkably pleasant, trustful, and intelligent. They are generally well looked after. The fact that the Frin share their dreams with their animals might explain why they use animals to haul and plow and for milk and wool, but not as meat.

The Frin say that animals are more sensitive dream receivers than human beings and can receive dreams even from people from other planes. Frinthian farmers have assured me that their cattle and swine are deeply disturbed by the visits of people from carnivorous planes. When I stayed at a farm in Enya Valley the chicken house was in an uproar half the night. I thought it was a fox, but my hosts said it was me.

People who have mingled their dreams all their lives say they are often uncertain where a dream began, whether it was originally theirs or somebody else's; but within a family or village the author of a particularly erotic or ridiculous dream may be all too easily identified. People who know one another well can recognise the source dreamer from the tone or events of the dream, from its style. Still, it has become their own as they dream it. Each dream may be shaped differently in each mind. And, as with us, the personality of the dreamer, the oneiric I, is often tenuous, strangely disguised, or unpredictably different from the daylight person. Very puzzling dreams or those with powerful emotional affect may be discussed on and off all day by the community, without the origin of the dream ever being mentioned.

But most dreams, as with us, are forgotten at waking. Dreams elude their dreamers on every plane. It might seem to us that the Frin have very little psychic privacy; but they are protected by this common amnesia, as well as by doubt as to any particular dream's origin and by the obscurity of dream itself. Their dreams are truly common property. The sight of a red-and-black bird pecking at the ear of a bearded human head lying on a plate on a marble table and the rush of almost gleeful horror that accompanied it—did that come from Aunt Unia's sleep, or Uncle Tu's, or Grandfather's, or the cook's, or the girl next door's? A child might ask, "Auntie, did you dream that head?" The stock answer is, "We all did." Which is, of course, the truth.

Frinthian families and small communities are close-knit and generally harmonious, though quarrels and feuds occur. The research group from Mills College that traveled to the Frinthian plane to record and study oneiric brain-wave synchrony agreed that like the synchronisation of menstrual and other cycles within groups on our plane, the communal dreaming of the Frin may serve to establish and strengthen the social bond. They did not speculate as to its psychological or moral effects.

From time to time a Frin is born with unusual powers of projecting and receiving dreams—never one without the other. The Frin call such a dreamer whose signal is unusually clear and powerful a strong mind. That strong-minded dreamers can receive dreams from non-Frinthian humans is a proven fact. Some of them apparently can share dreams with fish, with insects, even with trees. A legendary strong mind named Du Ir claimed that he "dreamed with the mountains and the rivers," but his boast is generally regarded as poetry.

Strong minds are recognised even before birth, when the mother begins to dream that she lives in a warm, amber-colored palace without directions or gravity, full of shadows and complex rhythms and musical vibrations, and shaken often by slow peaceful earthquakes—a dream the whole community enjoys, though late in the pregnancy it may be accompanied by a sense of pressure, of urgency, that rouses claustrophobia in some.

As the strong-minded child grows, its dreams reach two or three times farther than those of ordinary people, and tend to override or co-opt local dreams going on at the same time. The nightmares and inchoate, passionate deliria of a strong-minded child who is sick, abused, or unhappy can disturb everyone in the neighborhood, even in the next village. Such children, therefore, are treated with care; every effort is made to make their life one of good cheer and disciplined serenity. If the family is incompetent or uncaring, the village or town may intervene, the whole community earnestly seeking to ensure the child peaceful days and nights of pleasant dreams.

"World-strong minds" are legendary figures, whose dreams supposedly came to everyone in the world, and who therefore also dreamed the dreams of everyone in the world. Such men and women are revered as holy people, ideals and models for the strong dreamers of today. The moral pressure on strong-minded people is in fact intense, and so must be the psychic pressure. None of them lives in a city: they would go mad, dreaming a whole city's dreams. Mostly they gather in small communities where they live very quietly, widely dispersed from one another at night, practicing the art of "dreaming well," which mostly means dreaming harmlessly. But some of them become guides, philosophers, visionary leaders.

There are still many tribal societies on the Frinthian plane, and the Mills researchers visited several. They reported that among these peoples, strong minds are regarded as seers or shamans, with the usual perquisites and penalties of such eminence. If during a famine the tribe's strong mind dreams of traveling clear down the river and feasting by the sea, the whole tribe may share the vision of the journey and the feast so vividly, with such conviction, that they decide to pack up and start downriver. If they find food along the way, or shellfish and edible seaweeds on the beach, their strong mind gets rewarded with the choice bits; but if they find nothing or run into trouble with other tribes, the seer, now called "the twisted mind," may be beaten or driven out.

The elders told the researchers that tribal councils usually follow the guidance of dream only if other indications favor it. The strong minds themselves urge caution. A seer among the Eastern Zhud-Byu told the researchers, "This is what I say to my people: Some dreams tell us what we wish to believe. Some dreams tell us what we fear. Some dreams are of what we know though we may not know we know it. The rarest dream is the dream that tells us what we have not known."

Frinthia has been open to other planes for over a century, but the rural scenery and quiet lifestyle have brought no great influx of visitors. Many tourists avoid the plane under the impression that the Frin are a race of "mindsuckers" and "psychovoyeurs."

Most Frin are still farmers, villagers, or town dwellers, but the cities and their material technologies are growing fast. Though technologies and techniques can be imported only with the permission of the All-Frin government, requests for such permission by Frinthian companies and individuals have become increasingly frequent. Many Frin welcome this growth of urbanism and materialism, justifying it as the result of the interpretation of dreams received by their strong minds from visitors from other planes.

"People came here with strange dreams," says the historian Tubar of Kaps, himself a strong mind. "Our strongest minds joined in them, and joined us with them. So we all began to see things we had never dreamed of. Vast gatherings of people, cybernets, icecream, much commerce, many pleasant belongings and useful artifacts. 'Shall these remain only dreams?' we said. 'Shall we not bring these things into wakeful being?' So we have done that."

Other thinkers take a more dubious attitude towards alien hypnogogia. What troubles them most is that the dreaming is not reciprocal. For though a strong mind can share the dreams of an alien visitor and "broadcast" them to other Frin, nobody from another plane has been capable of sharing the dreams of the Frin. We cannot enter their nightly festival of fantasies. We are not on their wavelength.

The investigators from Mills hoped to be able to reveal the mechanism by which communal dreaming is effected, but they failed, as Frinthian scientists have also failed, so far. "Telepathy," much hyped in the literature of the interplanary travel agents, is a label, not an explanation. Researchers have established that the genetic programming of all Frinthian mammals includes the capacity for dream sharing, but its operation, though clearly linked to the brain-wave synchrony of sleepers, remains obscure. Visiting foreigners do not synchronise; they do not participate in that nightly ghost chorus of electric impulses dancing to the same beat. But unwittingly, unwillingly—like a deaf child shouting—they send out their own dreams to the strong minds asleep nearby. And to many of the Frin, this seems not so much a sharing as a pollution or infection. "The purpose of our dreams," says the philosopher Sorr-dja of Farfrit, a strong dreamer of the ancient Deyu Retreat, "is to enlarge our souls by letting us imagine all that can be imagined: to release us from the tyranny and bigotry of the individual self by letting us feel the fears, desires, and delights of every mind in every living body near us." The duty of the strong-minded person, she holds, is to strengthen dreams, to focus them—not with a view to practical results or new inventions but as a means of understanding the world through a myriad of experiences and sentiences (not only human). The dreams of the greatest dreamers may offer to those who share them a glimpse of an order underlying all the chaotic stimuli, responses, acts, words, intentions, and imaginings of daily and nightly existence.

"In the day we are apart," she says. "In the night we are together. We should follow our own dreams, not those of strangers who cannot join us in the dark. With such people we can talk; we can learn from them and teach them. We should do so, for that is the way of the daylight. But the way of the night is different. We go together then, apart from them. The dream we dream is our road through the night. They know our day, but not our night, nor the ways we go there. Only we can find our own way, showing one another, following the lantern of the strong mind, following our dreams in darkness."

The resemblance of Sorrdja's phrase "road through the night" to Freud's "royal road to the unconscious" is interesting but, I believe, superficial. Visitors from my plane have discussed psychological theory with the Frin, but neither Freud's nor Jung's views of dream are of much interest to them. The Frinthian "royal road" is trodden not by one secret soul but by a multitude. Repressed feelings, however distorted, disguised, and symbolic, are the common property of everybody in one's household and neighborhood.

The Frinthian unconscious, collective or individual, is not a dark wellspring buried deep under years of evasions and denials, but a kind of great moonlit lake to whose shores everybody comes to swim together naked every night.

And so the interpretation of dreams is not, among the Frin, a means of self-revelation, of private psychic inquiry and readjustment. It is not even species-specific, since animals share the dreams, though only the Frin can talk about them.

For them, dream is a communion of all the sentient creatures in the world. It puts the notion of self deeply into question. I can imagine only that for them to fall asleep is to abandon the self utterly, to enter or reenter the limitless community of being, almost as death is for us.

# Comment on 'Social Dreaming of the Frin'

Group mindedness, or the mental fusion of individuals, is an ancient fantasy. Plato's dialogue *The Symposium*, which is all about love, includes a memorable description. In the dialogue, the playwright Aristophanes recounts a myth that humans were once paired creatures, with two heads and eight limbs, tumbling hand over foot. For fear of their power, the Gods split them into two, and ever since then, individual humans have been searching for their other halves. Aristophanes then imagines the god Hephaestus asking a pair of lovers if they wish to be fused once again into a single being with a single soul. Since Hephaestus is the god of metallurgy, who we can suppose would use mechanical means to achieve this fusion, we can take this 2,500-year-old story to be one of the first ever hints of science fiction.

Ursula Le Guin offers a modern take upon this idea, with her charming anthropological study of a human-like species who experience mental fusion while they sleep. Thematically, it is significant that these people only share their dream lives. Social dreaming is a clearly a metaphor for the ways in which people can share their ideals. The notion of strong minds that inspire people with a common dream reminds us of the way a great work of literature can articulate our common values. Yet, like all great science fiction, Le Guin is also interested in exploring the scenario for its own sake. She imagines how social dreaming would affect babies and animals, or the difference between living in the city and living in the countryside. There are many delightful and unexpected ways that social dreaming would impact society.

So far as the mechanism of mental fusion is concerned, Le Guin is content to gesture vaguely at brainwave synchrony. We can however think of ways that mental fusion could be practically brought about. As we have already explored in this book, the 300 million or so nerve fibres in the corpus callosum are sufficient to allow consciousness to be shared between the two hemispheres of the brain. Accordingly, it is possible that if a comparable number of signals were exchanged between the neurons of separate brains, then consciousness could be sharable between those brains. In fact, there is a real-life case of brain connection in the world today. Tatiana and Krista Hogan are a pair of conjoined twins with a unique neural bridge connecting the thalamic regions of their brains. The apparent consequence is that the twins share emotions, as well as sensations of pain, vision, touch and taste.

A crucial point when considering mental fusion is to distinguish it from mind-reading or telepathy. Many writers depict group-mindedness rather like a mass conversation happening inside everyone's heads. This is not very philosophically interesting, in my opinion, because it still preserves the distinction between speaker and hearer. If I hear your thoughts, we have not overcome the division between us in any deep sense. It would still be me interpreting your thoughts, and I could still fail to understand things in the same way that you do. In contrast, mental fusion should be an extension of the way that the large network of neurons within a single brain manages to generate a unified experience. As much as possible there should be one experience, or one inner monologue, happening in many heads. Thus the Hogan twins are marvellous because they seem to literally experience one pain between the two of them.

Le Guin describes mental fusion in the true sense. Although she allows that one individual may sometimes be discerned as the source of a certain image or thought, the Frin experience their dreams not as individuals receiving images from one another other, but as a group collectively generating images that they collectively enjoy.

It is when experiences are shared in this way that a question is raised about personal identity. Throughout this book we have defined personhood in terms of the possession of self-consciousness. The radical sharing of self-conscious thought might therefore be regarded as a sharing of personhood. This will raise a similar argument against animalism that the brain bisection case raised: I identify myself with the bearer of my self-conscious thoughts, but the bearer of my self-conscious thoughts is not a distinct animal. What makes me distinct is not the same as what makes the animal distinct. Therefore, I am not identical with an animal.

The animalist response to this problem need not be the same as it was for brain bisection cases. In that case, it seemed that the animalist could accept that bisected people are not identical with the entire animal, but it was an exception that proved the rule. Here I think the animalist could deny that I would be identical with any group mind that I participate in, although they could allow that the group is a person in their own right.

First, it is important to clarify the thought experiment. The idea that dream sharing depends on how close the dreamers are in space throws up an interesting issue. If we each share the dreams happening within a 100-metre radius, then if you sleep near the boundary of my range, you can share dream contents with both me and someone else who is not in my range. Le Guin's story does not suggest that everything I receive in my dreams must be transmitted to everyone with whom I overlap. Rather, each dreamer's contribution carries a certain distance. This entails that the combined set of dream elements that I experience may be quite different from the combined set of dream elements that you experience. This could profoundly alter the overall character of our dreams. For instance, one of us could combine a walk in the forest with a squirrel where the other combines it with a snake, with very different emotional consequences.

Thus in any community with a radius above 100 metres, we cannot simply identify the group as one self-conscious individual. We can distinguish many individuals in virtue of their different sets of dream elements. In fact, it makes more sense to identify people with the animals at the centre of their range, plus their contributing mental environment. This is analogous to the way we each stand at the centre of a perceptual environment which overlaps with other peoples' perceptual environments. The difference is that the vehicle of one person's consciousness can include another person's brain activity. Note also that the neural base of a dreamer's experiences will shift over time both as they move between sleeping and waking and as they sleep in different locations. As a result, to reliably remember dream contents over time will rely on the individual animal carrying around a copy within their own brains. So I'd be inclined to define the individual almost entirely in terms of the animal at the centre, simply adding that this animal receives a lot of the information making up their mental lives from their neural environment.

Of course we can purify the case so that it makes a more definite counter-example to animalism. Let us suppose that every animal stays within the transmission range of every other animal. Furthermore, let there be no distinction between waking and dreaming life. Sharing is thus complete and enduring. Do we still have a distinct individual associated with the distinct animal?

The answer is unclear. Suppose that I live twenty years as an ordinary person and then join a group mind. It seems odd to say that I die in this scenario. The animal body that kept me alive for the last twenty years remains, and all the memories that I acquired over that period would also be preserved and accessible to the group mind. In addition, if the group mind were to disband, I would be returned to my previous condition. I may well remember certain aspects of my time within the group mind, specifically those aspects that made use of my brain and which my brain has stored, but much of the wider experiences of the group mind would be lost. It seems that this situation is just a more intense version of joining any group. In the same way that I do not stop existing when I join a cricket team, I do not stop existing when I join a group mind.

On the other hand, it does seem that the group is an individual person in its own right and not merely the aggregate of all of its members. Consider the way that the group will be capable of thoughts and experiences that are inaccessible to any of its members individually. For example, the group mind could directly experience the contrast between a shade of red in one brain's visual field and a shade of red in another brain's visual field. Even if the conceptual understanding of that contrast is physically realized in only one of its brains, the complex experience itself requires the combined neural vehicle. There may be many complex experiences of this sort of which the group is capable. Imagine it flexing all of its animal bodies at once, feeling its group strength. This would be a form of self-consciousness. Imagine its experience of raising a barn roof, or staging a mass protest, or performing a symphony.

Here it is worth noting that even apart from group consciousness, many philosophers have been impressed by the idea of group agents. Philosophers such as Margaret Gilbert and Raimo Tuomela have argued that groups can have their own beliefs and desires and intentions to act. When an orchestra performs a symphony, they say, we should not analyse this as me intending to play the oboe part plus you intending to play the cello part and so on. Those individual intentions only make sense if there is first an overarching intention by the group to play the symphony. This collective intention does not belong to any of the individual members on their own. No member of the group is able to decide whether or not the symphony is performed. Even orchestras led by dictatorial conductors still require the consent of the musicians. It is only the *agreement* between the various group members that has power to bring about the group action and this only exists at the group level.

This is not to say that the collective intention is a magical non-physical mental state that floats above the group members. The collective intention still very much relies on the brain states of the individual members and the ways these members interact with each other. This is why the theory of collective intentions is still controversial. Some philosophers prefer to analyse the intention to perform the symphony as a set of interlocking individual mental states. They regard it as fanciful that the group has a mental state in its own right. In particular, it is reasonable to doubt that a group can have a mental state if the group can't also be conscious of this mental state. The situation however may be different in the sort of scenario of Le Guin describes. If the group can genuinely be conscious, a key doubt of the philosophers would be eliminated.

Meanwhile, the other vital feature of the group mind is that it can survive independently of the existence of any of its members. If one of the humans contributing to it dies, the consciousness of the group will endure, in the same way that a normal human's consciousness endures despite the loss of some brain cells after a night of heavy drinking. As such, I find it highly plausible that a group mind would be a definite person.

Back to our original question then: if I join a group mind, do I persist as an individual human person, or do I become one with the group? My impression is that points about constitution introduced in the previous chapter do an excellent job of making sense of this case. I think we should say that the group person is constituted by animals in just the same way that the animal is constituted by its cells. In both cases one can exist without the other, and in both cases the larger entity gains causal powers that its constituents lack. At the same time, however, the individual animal's property of personhood is radically transformed. The individual animal's capacity for consciousness is given over to the group, generating a larger consciousness and a larger, perhaps more sophisticated form of personhood. This would have definite moral and legal implications. For instance, we should not blame the individual human for any crime committed while it was under the control of the group mind. The individual human is no longer a responsible agent in its own right. Only the group is.

What really keeps me up at night is whether it would be a good idea to become part of a group mind. Unlike all the other transformations that I've considered in this book, this one genuinely attracts me. Of course, joining a group mind would totally destroy my privacy and autonomy. We might even say that it destroys my individual personhood. Yet in the same moment, it would destroy my individual isolation and frailty. Most of all, I wonder if the group mind would allow me to escape the death of my body. If my consciousness is fully absorbed in the consciousness of the group, and if I never revert back to individual consciousness, the group person need not despair the death of this human body. There might even be a way to back up the memories of this human, perhaps by getting the group mind to rehearse those memories and distribute their storage.

In some ways, joining a group mind even strikes me as an ideal solution to the problem of death. Individual immortality or extreme longevity raises problems of overpopulation and eventual boredom. But the group mind would not add to the number of mouths to feed, and it would be continually invigorated by the influx of new members. Of course, life need not be completely rosy for the group mind. It could still suffer, and it could still potentially die. Yet it seems more robust than the individual human, in just the same way as the human is more robust than the individual cell. The group mind feels to me like the next level in the development of life.

But would it still be *me*? Would I survive if the group mind endures while my body dies? Ultimately, I think I must say no. I cannot be strictly identical with a group if other, distinct individuals, would have the same grounds for saying they are identical with that group. But besides this logical problem, the science fiction odyssey that we've gone on convinces me that I am essentially this living being here. I am the product of my cells working together to produce a complex, dynamic system that interacts with the environment to preserve its complex, dynamic, systematic nature. Call this animal autonomy. While this animal autonomy persists, I persist, even though my thoughts may be fused with others and my personhood may be lost. As soon as this animal autonomy is destroyed, I no longer exist.

Interestingly, the view that identifies me as an autonomous animal also denies that I persist while my body endures but is biologically fused with other autonomous animals (i.e. our metabolisms are shared). My body and many of my capacities would endure as *parts*. But the autonomous organization would be lost. The group biology has a different autonomy, in which concern for this body here is replaced by a concern for a very different organization of matter.

There is potentially some ambiguity here. I should be able to absorb other organisms (such as single cells) while maintaining autonomy. More generally, my biological organization should be able to change gradually. At what exact point biological fusion breaks the continuity of an animal's autonomy is an open question. Linking up blood streams doesn't seem to be enough. But what level of fusion would be? And what about the role that our psychologies play in the preservation of animal autonomy? The reader may further consider the very ordinary process of pregnancy and birth and how the autonomous animal view should deal with this case.

Overall, I think the group mind must be a new being. But this is not to deny that the group mind may still be desirable for us all too vulnerable humans. If my consciousness were to be absorbed into the group mind, I may not even notice my own physical decline, because this human animal would not be self-conscious in its own right. Meanwhile, certain things that matter to me might be preserved. Some of the skills and experiences that I've accumulated could perhaps be passed on. Given that the group mind can recall some of my conscious experiences, it might also feel a certain amount of continuity with me, even if not strict identity. The group could remember what it was like to be me.

# 12

# 'Remedy'

## Claire North

---

Seven years after Edward last left his flat, they re-wired his brain.

"You gonna give me an IQ of Einstein, doc?" he joked, as they removed the consent forms from his clammy, shaking hands, his last chance to say no, his last moment of freedom, pulled from pale bloated digits that could barely hold the pen.

"I am sure you are already very smart," the doctor replied, and he knew she didn't think that at all, because no one could look at him and think that he was anything other than broken, disgusting, a fool.

"Hey – give me some of those Casanova skills, won't you?" he said to the nurse, who was a creature barely old enough to grill her own cheese toastie, and yet who now was somehow trusted with needles thick as jousting lances and shoving catheters up men's bits with the same perpetual expression of mild not-quite-tea-break-time. He wanted to wink at her, to make her blush, to make her smile. He didn't tell them how scared he was. He didn't know how.

"There it is, there's the beastie," he mumbled, trying to make his voice big, roll back his shoulders into the raised bolsters of his bed, as they reverentially removed the machine from its box.

Remedy, they called it.

A simple solution; a last resort.

In the end, of course, he did cry.

He cried as the nurse shaved the thin whips of dark hair from his small, yellowing head, but he was still joking with her as she did, though again, she didn't seem to find it funny.

He cried, as they attached the machine to his skull, though it didn't hurt when it engaged.

He cried in hope, for this was truly his last chance to be alive.

He cried in fear, for despite their repeated reassurances as to the non-intrusive nature of the proceeding, this was still brain surgery, and no consent form is complete without listing Every. Possible. Side effect.

He cried for loss. Loss of time, loss of choice, loss of everything, anything, everything.

Mostly, however, he cried because this was something unknown, and the unknown, it turned out, had always terrified him.

\*

Dr Hester sat on the end of the great, yellow-stained bed that had become his whole world, a tablet in one hand, stylus in another, making little notes on a digital screen, while the nurse daubed the tears away from the corners of his eyes. She wore a grey suit cut entirely from triangles, and a necklace of polished cerulean sea glass.

"The human mind exists in a constant tug between two states. On the one hand, you are always receiving new sensory input. Light, colour, smell, touch – the human experience is a constant barrage of new data, demanding to be processed. It is too much, and most brains exclude the vast majority of this input, ignore it, if you will, in order to stay focused on the task at hand. This exclusion saves time and sugar. You are not constantly having to burn glucose in an effort to process the great ocean of sense data coming upon you, whatever form that may take. At the same time, the brain forms predictions. It creates expectations, of everything from what to expect when crossing the road – imagine how exhausting it would be if you had to work that out every single time – whether to fear a tiger, to how other people are likely to behave in a social or professional situation. Studies patterns. Learns behaviours. These behaviours can also be time-saving, sugar-saving. As a woman, I predict that if I walk alone down an alley at night, I will be murdered. The statistical odds of this happening are next to none – most murder happens in the kitchen – but it is a prediction my brain has created from various cultural inputs, in order to keep me safe. Thus, I see an alley at night: I feel fear. I make a prediction, and I change my behaviour. These behaviours protect us, keep us safe. They allow us to make quick, occasionally life-saving decisions. Your predictions, however, have become flawed."

She had given this speech many times before, he could tell. The tears did not seem to stir her. His terror was a familiar, *predictable* thing; it did not move her now.

"Your mind has tried to protect you. It predicts that if you step outside, you will experience awful things. There is no shame in this. You have experienced pain. That pain created expectation. That expectation has become reinforced. Too much so. A feedback loop has been created between mind and body. You now think of stepping outside, and your heart beats fast; your body interprets this as terror, associates that terror with stepping outside, your heart beats faster and so on. It is natural; how we are designed. This is nothing to be ashamed of; it is simply human."

Countless therapists have tried to tell him this, and they are wrong, and he is broken past all repair, and he knows it. No fucking point trying. No fucking point any more. And he is ashamed.

"That's all very well, Dr Hester," he said, "But I don't think any tiger would dare take you on if it met you in a dark alley."

She smiles, and has heard something like this before, and doesn't find it amusing.

*

He had said no, the first three times his therapists suggested Remedy.

His entire support team had queued up around him, their murmurings beginning with compassion – so good for you, such a revolutionary procedure, hope, liberation, only wanting the best – before escalating to a declaration of: you are going to die here, in this room.

You are going to die here.

"Well I hope I go watching Match of the Day," he'd replied, though he could hear the trembling in his voice. "Someone's gotta pop it, way Spurs have been playing."

Brian, the mental health nurse who always brought his own teabags when he came to visit, had been the most honest. Perhaps it was because everyone said he was a man in a woman's profession; perhaps that gave Brian a different perspective, made him fearless, stripped away certain illusions about what mattered, what didn't in his line of work.

Edward, he'd said. No one can force you to live. But I think they might just try.

It was that, more than the fear of death, which made Edward agree to the procedure. The idea of them going to court, of people arguing over his capacity, his sanity, his failures

failure, failure, failure

of him being *dragged* there, hauled out in an extra-large wheelchair, strapped into it perhaps, put, screaming, into the back of the police van – they'd never fit him in one of those small cars, not these days – and hauled around in public, a monster on display, a beast to be pointed and laughed at while lawyers argued over his state of mind, his shame, his deficiency – it was too much.

So he consented, even though he knew that under these circumstances, it wasn't consent at all.

*

They lightly sedated him for the procedure, just to keep him calm. No painkillers required.

The entire thing was run off Dr Hester's tablet – a thing that seemed far too small, far too meagre to be editing his brain. She'd even asked if there was wifi in the flat when she'd arrived, struggled to connect to it. What kind of machine could this be, if it couldn't even connect to iPlayer? (What kind of machine, if it could? Was Dr Hester just watching old series of Dr Who, while Edward's mind was re-written?)

Afterwards, the nurse said he'd feel tired, and he did.

He tried to make one of his usual jokes, and found he couldn't be bothered.

Tried to say that at least it was an early finish for the day, her boyfriend would be happy to see her home, and the words were grey cobwebs in his mouth.

She gave him a packet of tablets – more tablets – to take, one twice a day for seven days.

On the eighth day, she said they'd be back.

*

They started him in the back garden.

He hadn't been in it for five years – no, four – there had been that awful night when Mr Lichtarowicz' supper caught fire in the basement flat and the fire brigade had dragged him, weeping, begging, outside in his pyjamas while they extinguished the blaze, just to be safe while they checked the pipes, they'd said, just to make sure.

This time, they said he could take his time. "Sure," he grumbled, "I've just had brain surgery!"

Bluster, terror-as-laughter, usually came so easy to him. Yet this time, he found himself rehearsing his lines before the physio arrived, running over and over through his mind, trying different variations, and in the end, when he delivered it, his voice sounded utterly feeble, child-like in its pity, and it didn't make the damnest difference at all.

He ground his jaw so hard he thought he might crack a tooth when they loaded him into his chair, but did not beg. Did not implore them to have mercy, did not claw at the bed covers as they manoeuvred his swollen body, squeezed him, marbled flesh and creaking wheel, through the door and out onto the little patio out back.

The sun hurt his eyes, and he shielded them.

His heart thundered – nothing new there – he gasped for breath – but it was different this time, he could still breathe. Was still breathing. Wasn't about to pass out, fall to the floor in a pool of blackness. What had Dr Hester said? That they were breaking the feedback loop. Dialling things down a little.

The wind stirred the sweat on his skin, and it was . . .

. . . something new.

A thing of fresh touching, soft and kind. On the surface cooling, but below the wind raised some blood to his skin, warm-and-cold all at once, cause-and-reaction, a stirring, a kind of singing without music – it was hard to explain. A thing that was at once familiar and alien, into which, for just a moment, he found himself resting.

Before his slippered feet, an English summer garden. Slightly overgrown soft green grass – a green unlike any green he had seen before. Had green ever glistened, had it ever been so bright, so full of myriad qualities? Had he ever studied green, had he ever fallen into it, fallen into every part of it, into a depth unfathomable?

Rehearsed lines died on his lips.

His heartbeat – so slowly – slowed.

Edward did not weep, did not scream, did not laugh, did not show any sign of reaction other than the straining of his wide-open eyes, the turning of his head to hear the call of birds, the distant grumble of the main road and hiss of the closing doors of the 259 bus.

Then time had passed and the physio said: "Shall we go back inside?"

And he said yes, because that was what he always said, had always said, an ancient habit that rose unstoppable to the tip of his tongue; but as he said it, the sound seemed strange on his lips, as if he had never shaped syllables like it before.

*

After that the physio came three times a week.

Dr Hester had booked this without checking, so confident she was of her treatment.

Edward puffed and wheezed and sweated and groaned with the effort, limbs that hadn't stretched and bent for so long, creaking under the medic's ministrations. He knew that he was ashamed of his body, of himself, of having let himself get to this place. He didn't dare say it out loud – to say it might have been to crack, to split asunder, to fall apart, but after, when the physio was gone and Brian came for his usual PG Tips, milk-no-sugar catch-up, he said: "Poor bloody girl. Having to put up with a whale like me."

Brian held his mug in both hands, blew steam off the top with puckered pink lips. Edward knew that Brian had had a dog – he'd seen the white hairs sometimes clinging to his coat – and that in recent weeks, the dog had been put down. Grown old, Brian had said. Old and blind and confused and sad and he widdled everywhere. That's no life for an animal. Do I feel sad about it? No, not really. It was sadder watching him suffer, than letting him die.

"Poor bloody girl," Edward added, because his words had sounded hollow even to him, and when you find yourself with hollow words, you must add more, make more until the sound is complete, until people look at you and know you've done it right, said the right thing. "Poor bloody girl."

These sounds did not seem to offer meaning. Did not seem to fill the space.

"Do you feel . . . different, when you do physio?" Brian asked.

Different as in before, as in the time before Remedy, all those abortive efforts with PTs and OTs and CBTs and social workers and support workers and specialists and . . .

"I think I'm gonna piss myself in front of her every time she comes, and when she touches me I say sorry 'cos she has to touch my flesh."

"And is that different?" he repeated, grey eyes glinting over a Spurs mug with a long-lost, fallen-behind-the-fridge handle.

"I . . . I let her in," Edward answered. "This time. I let her in."

*

Amber came to visit, while Hailey and the kids were at junior taekwondo.

He had lost many friends, in the last seven years.

Some had tried to save him, and when they couldn't, their egos had felt hurt, because they fancied themselves the saving sort, the kind of people who made things right, and they couldn't quite cope with this not being true.

Others had been too uncomfortable. Found the stink of his flat, the soft, warm perforation of his bed sores and hint of ulcerating pus oozing from the sheet beneath him too much. Some primal part of their brains that saw danger in the poisonous, in the unclean, in the unknown had triggered a deep response of disgust, and their visits had grown less.

"Another life-saving prediction," Dr Hester had mused, when he'd tried to explain this in his pre-op interviews. "Disgust is the brain's mechanism of keeping us away from things that we fear may harm us. As with all predictions, it can become overly potent and keep us, from say, eating our broccoli."

Amber was one of the very few who'd stuck with him. She still opened the windows when she arrived, even in November, and sometimes even mumbled half-apologetic excuses for it; but he didn't care. She'd stayed around when very few others did, even though her seemingly endless-pregnancies, even when breast-feeding Hailey and Devon and PJ – he'd been so grateful for that, even though the kids had screamed – so grateful that she was willing to let her kids see him like this – and now, she sat in her usual seat by his bed and said: "You're looking good, Ed. This thing. You're looking real good."

"I mean it. You should be proud of yourself. Of what you're accomplishing here."

"Yeah," he mumbled. "Yeah." And because he couldn't find anything else to say, anything that seemed real, that seemed true: "Yeah."

And they sat there a while, awkward – when had they last been awkward together? – until Amber suggested they put Masterchef on the TV.

*

The first time Edward stepped outside of his front door in seven years, unaided save for a pair of walking sticks, he felt the urge to run back inside.

"I thought I wouldn't feel this," he stammered. "I thought it would be fine."

"It's ok," Jo, the physio replied. "You're still going to feel all the feelings. You're going to feel all of it. But before, when you felt these things, you predicted that you would fail. You predicted that there was no point trying. That's no longer the case. You can make new predictions now. You are still yourself. But you can start again. Make something new."

Edward made it all the way to the post box and back, swaying, stumbling, confident he'd fall. "Wouldn't believe how much . . . a second class stamp . . ." he gasped, but the joke died on his lips, was meaningless, empty, he stopped before it was finished, because what was the point? What exactly was he trying to prove, and who would even believe a moment of it, this gasping, vast, weak, weary man sweating and shaking his way down the street? What was it all even for?

"You're doing well," Jo said. "Slow and steady. Slow and steady."

He'd thought he'd fall for so many years. So many years of not daring to stand for knowing that he'd fall, and the physios had always said: if you fall, we'll help you back up again, and he'd known they were lying, known they were wrong, and now . . .

. . . those thoughts were still there, but he just wasn't quite as sure of it, anymore.

Afterwards, he bawled like a child.

Not when Jo was there, of course.

It wasn't proper to weep in front of a woman. It wasn't right. It wasn't who he was.

And yet, when she was gone, he wailed so loud that Mrs Lichtarowicz came to knock on the door to see if he was alright, and through the closed door he blubbered that yes, yes, everything was fine, thank you but yes, but no, but yes it's all fine, nothing to worry about Mrs Lichtarowicz, nothing at all, thank you, thank you, goodbye, yes.

He thought the pity of his neighbours would make it worse. That he would die from shame. But strangely, once she was gone, he just kept on crying for his own reasons, the old reasons, and fairly quickly forgot about her knocking on the door.

*

Two weeks later, he picked up his sticks, and walked to the corner shop.

No Jo, no Brian, no Amber or the hawk-eyed Dr Hester watching.

He'd thought about doing it, lay awake, staring at the ceiling, running every possible fantasy through his mind – making it, not making it, falling, being hit by a car, being mugged by kids, being laughed at, pointed at, everyone seeing him what he was – shame, shame, shame! But these notions seemed, for the first time in ... he did not know how long ... distant. Detached, almost. As if a voice were telling a story and the audience of his mind was raising its hand going, "yeah, but is it though?"

And so, he made it to the corner shop.

The young man behind the counter, as he bought a pint of milk – he didn't want a pint of milk, but he had to buy something, had to make this journey normal, a casual, simple thing, instead of the breaking-apart-and-coming together of his universe – didn't even look at him as he handed over his change. He was watching something on his phone out of the corner of his eye, which was far more interesting than Edward, as he shuffled back to his flat.

*

"Drive you?" Amber said. "Drive you where?"

"The bank?" he said.

"The bank? You sure?"

"Yes please," he replied. "Time to ... money-grabbing ... my savings account... I'd ... it'd mean a lot to me, you know, but only if the kids aren't ... I mean, if you've got ...."

"I'll pick you up after Devon's swimming club."

*

The journey was a heart-thundering, rib-shaking terror.

Amber drove slowly and safe, but the world was still full of mad idiots swerving, it seemed, to try and kill them; cyclists with a death wish, pedestrians walking out into the middle of the road, eyes fixed on their mobile phones. Edward gasped a couple of times at a threat only he could see, and he knew it annoyed Amber, who drove with quiet precision and perfect calm, and he wondered how he could explain this to her.

I am still scared, he wanted to say.

I am still petrified.

But something in me has changed. This thing, it is still there, but it is lesser. It is not so strong that I cannot try.

The streets of the city were a zigzag, saw-toothed, sandpaper-on-skin, dreamscape of overwhelming new. Had the sign on the newsagent always been so blue, the red of the post boxes so vibrant, the grey of the tarmac so jewelled with hues of gold and silver where the light hit the afterglow of rain? It was too much – all of it, too much – so much he thought he might drown in it, nearly cried out to Amber to stop the car, squeezed his eyes shut and yet, at the same time, could not look away.

Afterwards, when they were back at his flat and his heart no longer thumped in his ears, he realised something was different about Amber too.

"New . . . lipstick?" he tried.

No, it was not new lipstick.

"New haircut?"

She'd had the ends tidied up, but it was still basically the same.

He knew he was not supposed to say anything about a woman's weight, but . . . "You're looking . . . healthy."

Amber gave him the look of one who knows precisely what this word means, precisely what is implied, and is both disappointed that it is being deployed, and pleased with its context.

"I got my nails done," she said.

\*

"There was something . . . different," Edward mumbled, as he sat on the edge of the park with Brian. He knew that he would go into the park one day; knew he was probably ready to try it today, even though the grass rolled down to a view of endless sky, endless tower block and terraced house and falling city, too much, too many details, too much to see, impossibility, overwhelming, body-squeezing, brain-crushing in its majesty. But Brian said he was confident Edward was getting there; that it wasn't a setback to take things slow.

Shame, shame, shame, whispered the drumbeat of Edward's heart, but even that seemed lessened these days. So many things that had been so fundamental to who he was, seemed lessened, leaving only . . . what?

What was left, when the drumbeat of his life was just a whisper?

"She didn't seem how I remembered her."

"Well, that's not a surprise," Brian declared, breezy as if he had been told that toenails grow, scalps flake. "You have these ideas of who she is, of what her behaviours will be. Those ideas will have been altered too. You will have to re-learn your predictions of Amber, just as she is probably re-learning her predictions of you."

"I think she's the most incredible Mum and friend there is," Edward said, and it was true – that was what he had thought for years. But it tasted wrong, saying it with his new lips.

\*

The next time he saw her, he tried to tell her about Brian, about their conversations on the edge of the park, and she said: "A male nurse? Really? Doesn't he want to be a doctor?"

Amber was buying Halloween decorations. She wanted his opinions – she didn't want his opinions, she wanted someone to validate her own, he knew that instinctively, marvelled that he had never thought it before. Red leaves or orange pumpkins? Witches hats or fairy wands? Spider webbing or slime mould? He said he wasn't sure. He didn't know she cared so much.

"I don't care," she replied lightly. "But it's important for the kids."

Edward retreated from the subject, mumbled that no, Brian did not want to be a doctor. He was happy as he was.

"My my," Amber mused. "A man who wants to be a nurse. Fancy that."

Automatically, Edward reached for the old jokes. Something about Brian being gay, perhaps? Or no, that wasn't right, not because Brian wasn't gay – Edward didn't think he was, but then, his idea of what gay looked like didn't really seem to count any more, gay was everywhere it turned out, there were even footballers, even boxers these days, and you wouldn't have thought . . .

. . . alright, something else. A . . . Mummy's boy, a . . . something about colorectal investigations, about . . .

But the more he reached, the more the words seemed . . . unnatural.

Strange.

Distant.

Lost.

He knew he was meant to say something, that he was behaving . . . that he kept saying things that were putting her on edge. That challenged her *predictions*. In the past he would have breezed straight on by, but now the asymmetry of it grated against his teeth, rattled up his spine, made him want to tug at the soft folds of skin around his belly that were more and more holding in nothing but air, the place where old flesh had used to be. "Why's that strange?" he blurted, and was astonished to hear him ask it. "A man being a nurse?"

Amber looked at him sideways, and the look seemed to him laced with a kind of pity that she hadn't shown when he was stuck in that bed, in that flat, in that body, and it shocked him to his core. "I mean . . . it's not strange, I suppose. It's just that. You know. Men tend not to be the caring type."

"What does that mean?"

"There's no need to get . . . you know. It's just . . . I mean, isn't it? Women just are. And men are – obviously they offer so much, I'm not saying they don't feel, it's just different for men and women. It just is. That's just how it is, isn't it?"

*

There was an interview on the TV.

A young woman with long, mousy hair and a red sweater, staring off to one side of the camera, towards an unseen, sympathetic interviewer. "I thought if I'd eat, I'd be disgusting. All I could picture was the fat inside me. Just yellow rolls of fat, liquid, swilling around in me. The doctors said I was going to die. Remedy changed that. I still . . . struggle. Every day is still hard. But now when I eat, it's as if it's all been . . . dialled back. The fear is still there, but I know it's not . . . it's not real. Or it's real. But it's not my world."

Edward lent closer to the screen, his baked beans on toast suddenly forgotten.

"I couldn't talk in public," the man said. "I couldn't do it. I felt sick. I just knew everyone was going to laugh at me. But now I feel that, I picture that . . . and then I let it go."

And there, inevitably of course, was Dr Hester.

"We are in the business of saving lives," she declared. "The human brain is a beautiful, fantastic thing. It seeks to protect the body, any way it can. Sometimes that protection is too much. When it is – as a last resort – we step in."

"She's just different now," said another man, an older man, a man in a green cardigan with a white badge that probably meant something – Edward didn't know what. "I'm happy, of course, so happy that she's doing better. But also. She's different."

"How different?" asked the interviewer.

"I don't know. She's still the same person, she just . . . doesn't jump on things as much, you know? Doesn't get so angry, doesn't get so sad. But also doesn't get so excited by things, you know? It's like the things that used to make her happy ... now she doesn't expect as much from them, and so maybe, like, maybe 'cos she doesn't expect it, it doesn't happen, you see?"

Dr Hester, of course, refuted these claims.

"We turn down old predictions," she exclaimed. "We do not prevent the mind from forming new predictions of its own."

\*

"Of course I'll come visit," Edward's brother said, and Edward knew he would not. Richard had long since joined the cohort of friends and family who found it uncomfortable, distasteful even, to gaze upon the decaying mortality, the wretched disappearance of flesh that had been Edward Abelman's last seven years.

"I'm doing better now," he tried to explain. "I'm doing much better."

"Of course, of course! Although you don't sound ... you know. Quite yourself."

"What do I sound like?"

"I don't know. Bland? Anyway, don't even think about it, I'll check with Kim, see if I can get some time off from the kids, we're going to Dublin for holidays actually, then driving around Ireland, it's going to be a lovely trip...."

People liked to talk about nothing, Edward knew, when they thought there was a possibility that they might have to talk about things that made them sad. No one wanted to feel sad; it just wasn't an acceptable thing to be.

\*

"There's a men's group, meets down the local park," Brian said. "Cheaper for the NHS to prescribe than ketamine."

They planted carrots and potatoes and cabbages and talked in the quiet voices of loss and shame of marriages disintegrated, children unseen.

"I don't feel like a real man any more," said Nick, as they carried fresh compost to the herb patch. "I don't do the things a man is meant to do."

"What does that mean?" Edward blurted, soil under his nails, soft and warm and astonishing, as so many things in this world seemed to always be. "What is a man meant to be?"

"You know," Nick replied, and it was the same thing Amber had said. "You get it."

Edward thought about it, and realised, with a sudden start of surprise, that he did not.

\*

One evening, he sat in the park beneath the leaves of a red maple tree, and marvelled that he had never looked at it before.

He had seen it of course, a thousand times, but never looked. Never just stopped to bathe in its wonder.

*

"You're different," Amber said.

"Good."

"I mean . . . not just . . . all this, which is incredible, by the way, incredible, I'm so happy for you, I really am. But like . . . also different."

"In what way?"

"I mean, like that, right there. 'In what way.' You'd never have spoken like that before. You'd have made some joke or something, you'd have laughed it off, you'd have been . . . not always appropriate, mind, not always actually as funny as you thought you was, but . . . there'd have been something there, you know. Something . . . different. It's hard to explain, sorry."

She was growing distant from him, he knew, even as he was coming back to life.

*

"You're a good listener," Gary from the men's group said. "You don't ever judge."

He was right, Edward realised with a start.

Whatever people told him, whatever they said, his response seemed to be . . . curiosity. A kind of blank fascination, learning, listening. Never saying what he thought, mostly because . . . he didn't seem to think very much about much of all this at all.

*

That night, he went home, and stood in front of the mirror, unaided, and looked at himself for the first time.

Not the first time. The first time. Not the first time.

This moment, this him, always seemed these days to be something new. Someone new. Here: work jeans, many sizes too large, held up with a cheap belt, stained with soil. He didn't see the point of buying new clothes until the old ones wore out, even though people said Ed, seriously, Ed, your body is changing shape, you don't have to dress like . . . you know. You know.

You know, you know.

Everyone seemed to say that all the time. Seemed to assume there was a thing he knew, a great unspoken contract, a truth universal.

He had tried to fathom it out.

You know . . . how women are.

You know . . . how men are.

You know . . . what people are like.

What *other* people are like.

What people say.

In a purely abstract sense, he understood what everyone was getting at. Women were supposed to behave in a certain way; men in another. But the more time he spent looking – actually looking – the more it seemed to him that no one actually did. That the expectations everyone had were, in point of fact, bollocks.

He tried explaining this to Gary. "Yeah, I guess you're right," Gary replied, but that evening he still invited Ed to go down the pub to watch the football and Ed went because it was important to make friends and he really did like Gary, but everyone got hammered really fast and he didn't care about the teams playing and when people said you just need to get into the spirit of it, come on! he felt suddenly small, and sad, and desperately alone. And on the way home, a group of kids started shouting at him, started swearing and laughing and calling him names – just because they could, because they were bored, because they were trying to show off to each other – and he looked at them and didn't think it likely they were going to hurt him, and felt merely . . .

. . . curious.

At this strange thing they did.

At this odd performance they put on for each other, to obtain some sort of social status, in which his participation was barely required at all.

So he kept on walking, while they jeered and threatened to throw bricks at him and didn't because fundamentally they were afraid more than they were boisterous, and eventually they went home shouting 'faggot' and 'nonce' at him because these were the insults their fathers had used to belittle their children, and so they were the insults that the children then used to belittle others, because that was where safety lay. In being the belittler; not the belittled.

Edward felt a pang of sympathy for them then, but he contacted the cops anyway, just because it seemed likely they'd harass someone else too, and the next person they went after might be desperately, desperately upset by it all. They might experience this thing and conclude that going outside was a terrifying thing, impossible, frightening, that round every corner of every street there was a gang of youths laughing and prancing and getting their tackle out, and then they might leave their flat less and less and might become small and shrunk within their souls and well.

Well.

Edward knew what that was like, and it wasn't proper to wish that on anyone.

\*

"Well yes," his therapist said. "All a judgment is, is a kind of prediction. A strongly held, snap opinion that you can reach for without even trying. You might have lost a few of those."

"That sounds good," Edward replied. "That sounds . . . healthy."

"Yes. I suppose in many ways it is," she mused, and there was something in her voice which implied she instinctively felt it was not.

\*

He got a job. Before, in the then-times, he had been a caretaker at a local college. Now he wrapped baked goods in the backroom of the supermarket.

His colleagues were Carly, 18, and Dev, 20.

Carly did almost no work, but sat in front of her phone preening for the camera, and snapped if asked to help by anyone except her boss, in front of whom she was a model of good behaviour.

"Who are you talking to?" Edward asked one day, as she fluttered her eyelashes, pouted her lips.

"It's for Insta," she replied. "I'm building a following."

"But . . . following what?"

"Following me."

"I see." He did not. And then, the actual question, the one that had burned inside him ever since he'd first seen her practice her liquid-gel cat-eye technique and book her first eyebrow lamination: "It makes you . . . happy?"

"What the fuck kind of question is that?" she blurted. "What the fuck kind of fucking question even is that?"

Which Edward thought was no kind of answer at all.

\*

Brian visited less and less.

"You're not an acute case anymore," he explained. "I've got a lot of mad mums that need support."

Edward was grateful for Brian's honesty. Other people might have tried to brush it over, slip away politely, oh, no, sorry, can't do next Tuesday, but let's keep in touch? Brian set clear deadlines. Didn't leave Edward wallowing in doubt and uncertainty as to when, what, when, what. Edward hated not having clear answers to these things. People seemed to assume that everyone else understood their schedules, that you could just 'feel' out a date for meeting, that something would arise naturally – but it never did. Not for Edward. Not, as far as he could tell, for anyone else.

"I feel . . . lost," he said, and Brian blew the steam off his cup of tea, waited, as all good mental health professionals always seemed to do. "I feel . . . I don't know what I'm meant to say to people. I don't know what I'm meant to say."

"Ok. Does that matter?"

"I . . . yes? I think it does. There are things you're meant to say, but they seem . . . before, I was funny, you know? I think I was funny. Only I don't think I actually was. But like, I was solid. I was solid. There was a solid me. I liked the things I liked. I hated the things I hated. I knew you held the door open for women and offered to carry their shopping even if they objected; I knew that men watched footie on a Sunday and cracked on with things. I knew that I was a man. I was a man. So that's what I did. And now. I don't know. Any of it. Any of it. I think I am lost."

Edward thinks he should be crying while saying this, but he does not.

These things are fact, a thing that is worth saying.

They are neither good nor bad, there is no law against these feelings, it is simply the truth.

"Dr Hester said that after my predictions were altered . . . I could still form new predictions. That I'd learn to expect something more. How to feel again. How to . . . I know it sounds bloody naive when I put it like this, but . . . how to fall in love again. I didn't think I ever could, thought I was too far gone, but now, because I look . . ."

Normal, is the word, but Edward find it sticks on his tongue.

". . . like this. People ask me. If I'm looking for someone. And I say I don't know. I don't know what love is. I don't know if I can do it. What if Dr Hester took that from me too? What if, along with the fear, she took all the other things that are big?"

"Remedy dials down the strength of your physiological responses," Brian conceded. "Instead of paralytic terror, it's just a knot in your stomach. The fear is still there, but the feedback loop is broken."

"Does that mean I'll never . . . feel like me . . . again?"

"A different you," he conceded. "A different kind of feeling. You are going to have to learn all your new predictions for yourself. When you're a child, it's easy. You copy your parents' behaviours. Their beliefs are your beliefs. Their failures become your failures. It takes time to become something new. These things are harder, when you're already someone else." Then: "Do you regret it? Remedy?"

"No. No! I was dying. And I thought . . . well, maybe that was ok. Maybe that was proper. I thought that, I did. Sometimes I still think . . . but now I'm useful. It's important to me to be useful, to say thank you for all those people who tried so hard with me. What's the point if I can't be . . . the group, going back to work, it is . . . if I wasn't useful, then I think sure, maybe you should have just shot me, maybe that would have been kind, but this . . . ."

"Are you happy? You don't have to be," Brian added. "A lot of people put far too much value on the idea of 'happiness' like it's some kind of fucking euphoria. Content. Are you content?"

"I think . . . I think I am. I have my routines, my structure, I like people, they seem to mostly like me, or at least, don't mind my company. I find them hard to read. I wonder if all along I was doing it right."

"But you still feel lost."

"Yeah. I feel like, when I'm with people . . . they're just so solid. All the things they say and do, they really believe them, you know? There's so much going on there, and it's all true to them, you know? Like, they really believe in the things they believe in, the things that go all the way down, the deepest of all things, even when it's bollocks, even when it's bigotry, when it's toxic bullshit about how other people should be, or like, even how they should be themselves you know? Like Amber, she drives those kids so hard, all the time, taekwondo, swimming, Mandarin, music – 'cos she's gotta be a proper Mum. And she's doing so well, and those kids are beautiful, they really are, but Amber just doesn't let go. Doesn't ever stop. And I'm like . . . Amber . . . can't you see? Can't you see what this is doing? To you? To Hailey, to Devon, can't you just . . . take a breath? But she believes she's doing right, and people have to believe they're doing right, and if you take that away from them – if you break them down then build themselves back up – I guess that's what Remedy is. Cleansing. Of everything you believed to be true."

Sometimes, recently, Brian has bought half a packet of Rich Tea biscuits, which he delicately dunks, just for a moment, in his tea, before nibbling around the edges. Since his dog died, he's been dressing a little smarter, a grey shirt and a pop of colour beneath it, trying to impress the ladies he says, trying a little harder now he doesn't smell of Jack Russell half-breed, trying to get the attention of a certain type. Edward isn't sure if it's going well. Knows it isn't appropriate to ask. Cannot for the life of him fathom why.

"Have you said any of that to Amber?"

"God no. You're not meant to say these things. It is . . . something fundamental. What is left, if you take these things away?"

"You are. You're what's left," Brian said, and when Edward shot him a look, Brian shrugged. "I just drop the pearls of wisdom. Can't help it if they look like turds."

\*

And one day, at work, Edward tried saying to Carly:

"I think most people are at their most beautiful when they don't feel the need to try. When they're happy in themselves. When they're no longer trying to be someone they're not. Someone they think they're meant to be. When they just see themselves for beautiful."

And Carly said: "Whatever, piss off granddad."

*

And one day, at the men's group, Edward tried saying: "I do enjoy listening, I really do, but also, there are things I think I want to say. Things that I think are important. I think that vulnerability, over time, can become an identity. That we get so used to being vulnerable, feeling safe being that person, that we don't go to the next step. Because here we are safe. But what if we had to be someone else – someone new – who wasn't? What if that's what's next? I suppose what I want to ask is: what's next?"

And everyone applauded, and quickly moved on.

*

And one day, while helping Amber tidy the kitchen after another mud-pie incident with Devon:

"You know, I don't think Hailey wants you to throw her a party, you know. I mean, she understands how nice it is, really, she knows what an incredible Mum you are, how much you care . . . but actually she was saying, there's this K-pop gig and Rachel's sister got her tickets and they'd go together, and I know they're still quite young but her sister is 19 and maybe . . . ."

And Amber screamed: "WHAT THE FUCK DO YOU KNOW ABOUT IT THEY'RE MY KIDS I'M THEIR MUM I'M THEIR MUM I'M THEIR MUM I'M THEIR FUCKING MOTHER!"

And he apologised, and let himself out of the flat, and though he kept on apologising and they texted a bit, they never really spoke again.

*

I am lost, said Edward Abelman.
    I am lost.
    These things that I believed
        these terrors that were my life
            I am lost

*

Ten years after Edward decided never to leave his flat again
    three years after the doctors re-wired his brain
        he sat beneath a maple tree with crimson leaves in his local park, and stared through its bowers towards the summer sky as if he had never seen such a wonder upon this earth before.

# Comment on 'Remedy'

A man undergoes a procedure that is initially subtle yet has far reaching implications for his nature. The goal of this procedure is to weaken his expectations. For years, Edward has been stuck in his house, unable to face the outside for fear of catastrophe. Following the procedure, Edward still feels fear, but he is no longer overwhelmed by expectations of failure. He still imagines being pointed at and laughed at, but these imaginings are no longer emotionally compelling. Slowly, but surely, he is able to change his ways.

The narrative reveals further changes to Edward's psychology that his doctor seems not to have anticipated. Along with his expectations goes Edward's sense of how things should be – his sense of social norms. These norms inform not only what sort of person Edward takes himself to be and how he is supposed to behave, but also what men and women in general are supposed to be like, or what children and their parents are supposed to be like. When the grip of these norms is loosened, Edward becomes socially awkward. Yet he is also in a position to detect the arbitrariness and falseness of certain stereotypes.

The ramifying effects of Edward's operation go further. He no longer feels willing to make snap judgements about what's good and bad, generating a noticeably mindful and receptive state of mind. Most delightfully, Edward's sense of the natural world is vivified. For we not only have generalized ideas about what people are like. We also have generalized ideas about what grass is like, and what trees are like. In our everyday lives, we may recognize the things around us under categorical labels like 'grass' or 'tree', and in so doing pay little attention to their rich individual features. In this way, our generalized notions can function like barriers between us and our environments. With this barrier weakened, Edward experiences rawer confrontations with reality.

So Edward changes a great deal over the course of the narrative. And much of the appeal of the story lies in its rich description of what it's like to undergo a profound change. But so far as the basic question of numerical identity goes, there is really no doubt that Edward survives his procedure. The Edward of the narrative's end is both psychologically and organically continuous with the Edward of its beginning. As a way to save his life, Edward has clearly made the right decision. But if that's true, why does Edward feel lost? Why does he no longer feel 'solid', as he puts it?

Edward's state of mind does not seem to me an implausible consequence of the way his expectations have been undermined. Losing one's sense of the sort of person one is could certainly be disorienting. In my commentary on Christopher Priest's chapter, I mentioned the phenomenon of depersonalization, whereby a person can lose the sense of their own reality or feel detached from themselves. Some of the things that Edward says suggest this. But I don't think that Edward is experiencing depersonalization. It's not like he feels a floaty sense of alienation from his own mind or body. Instead, what Edward is detached from is a certain constructed image of himself – his persona.

Edward's persona was, by the looks of it, very bad for Edward. It kept him in a state of decay. It even encouraged him to think that it was 'proper' for him to die, given what he believed to be his repulsive and shameful condition. To destroy this persona is a liberation for Edward. Edward's nurse Brian makes the key point, I think. Edward asks, "What is left, if you take these things away?" and Brian replies, "You are. You're what's left." So just as Edward is invited to see trees and grass as if for the first time, unmediated by generic concepts, he is also invited to see himself as if for the first time, unmediated by the persona he has been carrying around for so long. This raw confrontation with the reality of his self promises to be more disturbing than any confrontation with the outside world.

There is a concept that philosophers have reflected on over the last couple of hundred years that is relevant to what is going here. This is the concept of authenticity. One of the first philosophers to think about this was Jean-Jacques Rousseau, who observed how living in a society, and wanting the esteem of others, can lead us to neglect our inner, 'natural' selves. Certainly we can think of examples in which following a social norm can come into conflict with a deep desire. For instance, one may grow up in a society in which homosexuality is considered perverse, and yet still feel a powerful and enduring sexual desire for people of one's own sex. Attempts to suppress or deny one's sexual orientation may be considered a kind of inauthenticity. This can result not just in unhappiness but a disorganized personality, in conflict with itself. Nor is it easy to say that one should just shrug off the social restriction. Well-being also depends upon one's social standing, and in some cases, threats to one's safety make 'coming out' a genuine risk.

The harms of inauthenticity suggest that we should organize our society in a liberal way that allows people to live in accordance with their deepest desires. However, there is clearly a balance to be struck here. What if someone deeply desires to hurt others? Do we want authentic serial killers? Getting along with each other requires that we have a few strong social norms. Another issue is that a society can embrace divergent lifestyles and end up generating yet more social norms to go with them. For instance, there are social norms for what a homosexual person is supposed to like that can be just as rigid and inauthentic as the heterosexual norm. Or consider how Edward says to his men's group how vulnerability can become an identity. The emergence of such norms seems inevitable. Social norms define societies. Wherever we identify a community or sub-community, we can expect social norms to follow. Navigating social norms is very much a part of communal life.

The fact that humans virtually always live in societies structured by social norms raises another question that gets at the heart of personal identity. Isn't living in accordance with social norms part of our nature? How really do we justify a distinction between the authentic 'natural' self and the constructed social self? Above, I supposed that a conflict can arise between a social norm and a deep and pervasive desire. But why should we say that deep and pervasive desires are those closest to our true selves? We might establish that some of our desires are innate, though that is no easy task beyond the most animalistic functions. But it is also very much part of human nature to learn and adapt and to question how things are. So we could alternatively argue that our 'truest' desires are those that come from sustained reflection on how we want to live. Innate or instinctive desires aren't very important to our special uniqueness as persons.

Here I should discuss another important philosopher – Jean Paul Sartre. Sartre argues that there is no way that humans are naturally supposed to be. When we say that we *should* live in a certain way, we are saying that it is *good* to live in a certain way. But Sartre thinks that value is something that we do, not something that we discover. In other words, values come from our own interpretation of things. As a result, it is always an option to value things in a different way than we have done up to now. We can always question what sort of person we should be, and no particular answer is guaranteed to be more correct than any other.

Sartre has a notion of 'bad faith' that is closely related to the idea of inauthenticity. One important kind of bad faith is to suppose that one has no choice about the kind of person one is. Sartre has a famous example in which he observes a waiter at a café behaving in a rather robotic manner. The man's job is to be a waiter, but it is not his essence to be a waiter and he does not have fixed 'waiterly' properties. He seems to be pretending to have waiterly traits that determine his behaviour. In the same manner, we may imagine ourselves to be a certain kind of person, and that our behaviour flows from this nature in a way we cannot choose. But this is bad faith. We are denying our constant capacity for choice.

Why would we deny our capacity to choose? Because it can be hard to choose! Because sensitivity to our freedom raises constant doubts and anxieties. We have to choose to return to our jobs on Monday, and not to throw ourselves out of the window. We have to be constantly responsible for what we are like, and we cannot offload this burden onto some fixed nature. Sartre doesn't have much time for the idea of authenticity in the end. But it does seem that for him, being true to ourselves requires that we acknowledge or accept that our values and meanings can always be questioned.

When I read Claire North's story in light of these ideas, it seems to me that Edward is something of a Sartrean hero. Following the destruction of his previous expectations, and the radical change in his lifestyle, it should have been possible for Edward to develop a new set of predictions about how things are supposed to be, and how he is supposed to be. This at least is what Dr Hester seems to think will happen. But this is not what happens. Three years after his operation, Edward still maintains his state of wonder. My impression is that he still hasn't settled into any new persona and remains open to possibilities.

Just how radical is this openness? One of Sartre's slogans is that 'existence precedes essence'. That is, our bare existence comes before any essential function or quality. This volume has been a quest to identify our essential natures; are we essentially souls, minds, brains, animals, or what? So is Sartre denying that there is an answer to that question? I don't think so, because Sartre makes claims about human nature, that we are beings for whom radical freedom is possible, for one. Sartre also does not deny that we have minds and bodies that have persisted for a certain amount of time. He is more concerned about the significance or meaning of what we are. This is what he thinks is always open to interpretation.

Does our metaphysical essence have any definite implications for our significance, or for the way we should live? Or is it the case that no matter what we are, how to live is always optional? On the face of it, it seems like it could make quite a bit of difference. For instance, if we are immortal souls then this may recommend a rather different way of living than if we are mortal animals. One's fear of death would very likely be impacted, for example, with various other knock-on effects. Or consider the various decisions that the protagonists in our stories have made, usually under some conception of the sort of thing that they are.

One of the key ideas in philosophy is that you can't get an 'ought' from an 'is'. So, even if it *is* the case that we have immortal souls, this does not entail that we *ought* to act as if we have immortal souls. Maybe for various moral and prudential reasons we'd better off if we acted like we didn't. At the very least, before we draw any evaluative conclusions, we need first to introduce some evaluative premises. For instance, it is given the premise that we'd like to survive that our metaphysical identity becomes relevant to our decision-making.

Of course, sometimes people don't want to stay alive. A person's will to live can vary in strength. They can be more or less willing to endure suffering or ill health for the sake of living longer. Still, I would like to finish this set of commentaries by suggesting that it is intrinsic to what we are that *we are valuing things*, even if that valuing is entirely destructive in character. This is because it is an intrinsic feature of being alive and having a mind that we engage in preferential interactions. For example, animals will automatically tend to regulate their body temperature and blood sugar levels by means of various interactions with the world. Psychological creatures will automatically tend to regulate their beliefs – preferring to pay attention to some things rather than others and preferring to imagine some things rather than others.

Our metaphysical nature informs these evaluative processes. It seems to me that it is because I am essentially an animal that I evaluate the world in the way that an animal does, in terms of its relevance for my animal nature. It is because I am an animal that I pay attention to the overall organization of my body and not very much the living and dying of individual cells. In Claire North's story, it is because Edward has the body that he does that the world comes across as a threatening or welcoming place to him. If we had different natures – if we were made of steel and copper wires for instance, I think we would evaluate the world in a way relevant to that. If we were essentially narrative entities, and not material beings, then it is the coherence of our narratives and not our bodily constitutions that would direct our thinking.

This is to say that while I may agree with Sartre that value is something that we do, I don't think that the manner in which we value is entirely optional. It is constrained by our nature. I invite the reader to reflect on how their evaluation of things is guided by what they are, just as how they imagine is guided by what they are.

# Appendix A: A Guide for Teachers

This collection stems from my teaching of an upper-level undergraduate class at Flinders University. Students would read one story prior to each two-hour seminar. We would then usually begin with an open discussion of the story's merits, especially its realism, before I presented any formal philosophical content. Because we have very little teaching of metaphysics at my institution, one of my aims was to use identity to introduce a variety of metaphysical concepts and problems. At the same time, one of the great things about teaching identity is that it can connect to virtually every area of philosophy, including ethics, politics, aesthetics, epistemology and the philosophy of the mind. Teachers can tailor the depth and complexity of the issues they introduce with these stories to suit the interests and level of the students they teach. I will also gladly share my reading lists and slides with anyone who writes to me.

## Week 1: Thought Experiments

It is good to begin with a general introduction to metaphysical questions and the great difficulty we have in reaching answers. I recommend then surveying a few thought experiments with the aim of comparing their success in different areas. Teachers may wish to begin with some of the famous thought experiments in science such as Galileo's differently weighted balls or Maxwell's demon, before moving onto classic philosophical thought experiments such as Judith Jarvis Thompson's people seeds (ethics of abortion), Goldman's fake-barn case (analysis of knowledge) or Harry Frankfurt's Jones and Black case (free will). The opening chapter of Tamar Gendler's *Thought Experiment: On the Powers and Limits of Imaginary Cases* (2000) provides a straightforward characterization of thought experiments and is suitable for students.

## Week 2: Numerical Identity (Story: 'The Barbie Murders')

The main aim is to clarify the distinction between numerical and qualitative identity. This is a good launching pad for the distinction between substance and qualities. Teachers may wish to introduce the basic problem of what a substance is apart from its qualities, the identity of indiscernibles (e.g. Max Black's two iron spheres example) or Platonist versus nominalist accounts of universals. Another approach is to introduce theories about how proper names refer, contrasting Russell's description theory with Kripke's causal theory. Teachers may wish to think more about sexual and racial qualities and how these relate to survival. It is always an option to consider what a certain theory of universals will say about socially important qualities. However, theories about the social construction of certain qualities are best saved for a later session.

## Week 3: Diachronic Identity (Story: 'Marley and Marley')

Before discussing the story, I find it best to begin with a survey of the major theories of time (eternalism, presentism, growing block). This is because arguments about time travel tend to quickly get confused. Having presented the options about time it is then natural to ask which one fits the story best. Debates about identity over time and the problem of temporary intrinsics then follow. It is worth distinguishing perdurantist theories from both endurantism and stage theory. Students are also apt to talk about free will in this context. Note that David Lewis' paper 'Survival and Identity' (1976) is one of the classics, but rather technical for undergraduates. It is also directly responding to Parfit's famous paper which I only introduce later in the course. For this reason, I don't recommend that students read Lewis' paper yet. The summary I provide should be sufficient to get the idea across.

## Week 4: The Soul (Story: 'Edward the Conqueror')

I use the soul theory to introduce the metaphysics of essences. Discussion of the story should fairly quickly get into the nature of the soul, and brainstorming what features it could have. Only after this point is it worth introducing the difference between a thing's essence and its accidents. This could lead to a discussion about Socratic style conceptual analysis using necessary and sufficient conditions. More ambitiously, I use the issue of essences to introduce theories of modality and identity across possible worlds. That is, counterfactual versions of me need only share my essential features. Teachers with a philosophy of mind background may be interested in discussing materialist versus non-material theories of the soul/mind. Plato's discussion of the soul in the *Phaedo* is mentioned in my commentary and could be usefully discussed. I also make some points about probabilistic reasoning in my commentary that teachers may wish to dig into.

# Week 5: Memory (Story: 'Life Sentence')

Psychological continuity is central to debates about personal identity and my commentary summarizes the initial moves in that debate. Locke's analysis in Chapter 27 of *An Essay Concerning Human Understanding* is a classic, and quite approachable. It is important to clarify what we mean by memory, its various types, how long it persists, and its potential reliance on external resources. For instance, in the story, Wash has a sense memory of eating chocolate. What kind of memory is that? I save the issue of quasi-memories for my discussion of teleportation cases. Meanwhile, it is worth discussing Locke's claim that every conscious experience is self-conscious. A related epistemological issue is the extent to which the 1st person perspective has authority over the 3rd person perspective when judging identity over time. Debates about what justifies punishment are also highly relevant in this context.

# Week 6: Narrative Theory (Story: *The Affirmation*)

A classic reference point for the narrative theory is Chapter 13 of Daniel Dennett's *Consciousness Explained*. Marya Schechtman has a chapter on narrative views in *The Oxford Handbook of the Self* edited by Shaun Gallagher (2011) – which is a good general source. Galen Strawson also articulates the anti-narrative view in a 2015 *Aeon* article called 'I Am Not a Story'. Teachers may be interested in debates about the construction of character by means of engaging with narratives. I have a paper 'Narrative and Character Formation' (2014) that is relevant here. Alongside the narrative theory of personal identity it is interesting to discuss the metaphysics of fictions and fictional truths. Brock and Mares' volume *Realism and Anti-realism* (2010) has a good chapter on this, amongst others. Students may be interested in what makes a narrative part of the same story as another (considering things like reboots, spin offs, fan fiction, canon versus non-canon, etc.). The pragmatist approach to truth also gets mentioned in the commentary.

# Week 7: Teleportation (Story: 'Think Like a Dinosaur')

Apart from issues of identity, I like to use this session to return to overarching question of whether thought experiments can establish metaphysical claims. As I mention in my commentary, the teleportation thought experiment seems to be one of the few cases in which a slam dunk demonstration is provided. Nevertheless some philosophers disagree! (the 2020 philpapers.org survey has the statistics on this and several other relevant issues). Do philosophers who think that teleportation is survival simply fail to understand the case? There is an interesting blog post by Eric Schwitzgebel called 'The Envy Argument against the View that Teletransportation is Death' (28 July 2023). Schwitzgebel confirmed to me that he has given up on numerical identity for persons. Meanwhile, *Contemporary Debates in the Philosophy of Science* (2004) edited by Christopher Hitchcock has duelling chapters on the argumentative role of thought experiments, including a comparison to visual proofs in mathematics. *The Routledge Companion to Thought Experiments* (2018) edited by Michael T. Stuart, Yiftach Fehige and James Robert Brown is also a good resource. Parfit often gets credited for the teleportation thought experiment, but an earlier philosophical source is Dennett and Hofstadter *The Mind's I* (1981). Duplication via teleportation was also turning up in science fiction stories in the 1960s. Science-fiction legend Stanislaw Lem anticipates many of the philosophical issues in chapter 6 of his *Summa Technologiae* (1964), although this was only translated into English in 2013.

# Week 8: Brain Transplants (Story: 'The Extra')

Brain transplantation and splitting is another core issue in the personal identity debate. Before turning to Parfit's rich and nuanced paper 'Personal Identity' (1971), Shoemaker's non-branching condition should be discussed. Lewis' solution to splitting via temporal parts can also be reintroduced. My view is that philosophers have treated brain transplantation far too glibly and that given the complexities of the procedure, the intuition of survival in non-branching cases is not reliable. Eric Olson also argues against survival in chapter 3 of *The Human Animal* (1997). Bernard Williams' classic (1970) paper 'The Self and the Future' can be discussed in this context, though since it is a brain state transfer case, it could alternatively be paired with a separate session on mind-uploading (see below).

# Week 9: Animalism (Story: *Sirius*)

Animalism is a good place to consider the nature of personhood in detail. Dennett has a useful chapter on the conditions of personhood in *Brainstorms* (1981). There is also plenty of contemporary work on the legal personhood of animals, providing an interesting practical application of the issue. Given its emphasis in Stapledon's story, the role of the hand in human intelligence is worth discussing, and the general idea that cognition is embodied. There are also hints in the story that Sirius prefers different conceptual metaphors, relevant to Lakoff and Johnson's *Metaphors We Live By* (1980). Once Sirius' personhood is explored, one can then turn to the arguments in favour of animalism. It seems to me that non-dreaming sleep holds a more powerful argument for animalism than has been recognized. Eric Olson summarizes his argument for animalism in Martin and Barresi (eds) *Personal Identity* (2003). Stephan Blatti and Paul Snowdon (eds) *Animalism: New Essays on Persons, Animals, and Identity* (2016) is a useful collection.

## Week 10: Two Persons, One Body (Story: 'Through the Window Frame')

I like to start this session by summarizing Thomas Nagel's classic 1971 article 'Brain Bisection and the Unity of Consciousness'. Tim Bayne has a detailed analysis, in which he defends the necessary unity of consciousness called 'The Unity of Consciousness and the Split-Brain Syndrome' (2008). Returning to personal identity, Olson has a 2014 article, 'The Metaphysics Implications of Conjoined Twinning', in which he denies that the Hensel twins are distinct beings. The thought experiment by Mark Reid which I discuss in my commentary and which inspired Sean Williams' story can be found in the Blatti and Snowdon (eds) *Animalism* volume. These cases more generally raise the issue how exactly we draw the boundaries of what physical stuff is part of a given person, or part of a living thing. This is a special case of the problem of the many, which is usefully summarized in a *Stanford Encyclopedia of Philosophy* article.

## Week 11: Constitution (Story: 'Constitution')

I tend to begin this session with a detailed presentation of the metaphysical theory of constitution. I recommend Chapters 2 and 4 of Lynne Rudder Baker's book *Persons and Bodies: A Constitution View* (2000). Eric Olson's book *What Are We?* (2007) also has an introductory chapter on constitution. Students may well have heard of the Ship of Theseus thought experiment and this is often a source of strong disagreement. It is worth considering if the metaphysics of constitution applies beyond organic beings and human artefacts. For instance, a body of water may only constitute a river given a certain context. Teachers may also explore what the difference is between living and non-living systems. Leonardo Bich's Cambridge Element *Biological Organisation* (2024) is a useful source on this and the related concept of teleology. Besides this, the story is a good opportunity to explore issues about using tools and prostheses to extend or regulate our cognitive and emotional capacities as in Andy Clark and David Chalmers' famous paper 'The Extended Mind' (1998).

## Week 12: Group Minds (Story: 'Social Dreaming of the Frin')

In addition to offering a counter-example to animalism, the possibility of group mindedness is interesting in its own right. The theory of collective intentions is summarized in my commentary. I also have a special interest in the Hogan twins' case which I discuss in detail in a paper called 'A Case of Shared Consciousness' (2021). The ethics of group mindedness is also fascinating, especially given the potential applications of neuron-level sensors. Luke Roelofs and Jeff Sebo have an article on 'Overlapping Minds and the Hedonic Calculus' (2024) that raises interesting points about shared pains. Teachers may also use this opportunity to discuss socially constructed entities more generally.

## Week 13: Social Identity (Story: 'Remedy')

As mentioned in the commentary, issues about authenticity can be usefully discussed in connection with this story, including the existentialist perspectives of Sartre and de Beauvoir. Following on from the discussion of group minds, the construction of social reality can be more deeply investigated. Students may consider what would happen if one's qualities were systematically denied by others – one's sex, one's race, one's very personhood. It seems that some of one's personal qualities (including survival) should persist, but others may rely on social endorsement. Students may also be interested in discussing the authenticity of using pharmaceutical treatments for depression and other psychological disorders.

## Additional Issues

Some US universities run 16-week courses, so here are some additional issues that could be addressed.

*Mind Uploading*: I claim in my commentary that teletransportation is metaphysically equivalent to both mind-uploading and brain-state transfers. However, this might be disputed. It may be worth having a separate session on these possibilities and there are a number of relevant science fiction stories (see Appendix B). Peter van Inwagen discusses the metaphysics of brain-state transfers in 'Materialism and the Psychological-Continuity Account of Personal Identity' (1997). He also offers a materialist take on Christian resurrection in 'I Look for the Resurrection of the Dead and the Life of the World to Come' (2018). General issues about artificial intelligence and whether a purely software person is possible might also be raised. Eric Olson has a paper 'The Metaphysics of Artificial Intelligence' (2018) that comments on this.

*The no-self view*: In my commentary on 'The Barbie Murders', I discuss the no-self view. Teachers may wish to save this issue for a separate session, drawing more widely on Buddhist metaphysics and ethics. The main reason I do not have a separate session on the no-self view is that it is extremely hard to find a story that presents it. One possible example is the 'faceless men' in George R. R. Martin's *Song of Ice and Fire* series of books (e.g. *A Feast for Crows*, Chapter 22 'Arya') but it is not a very clear case. This issue could raise a debate or a challenge. Why is the no-self view so rare in fiction? How might students approach writing a story that captures this theory?

*Why am I me*: I have not addressed in this volume the disconcerting question: Why am I me? It can feel arbitrary that of all the billions of conscious entities, I am *this* one rather than another. Does this question reflect a philosophical confusion? It has not been much addressed in the professional literature, although there's an unpublished paper by Tim Klaassen on philpapers.org that is helpful. My sense is that Arnold Zuboff's (somewhat bizarre) theory that we are all the same person is also addressing this question. In fiction, a relevant story is Greg Egan's 'The Safe Deposit Box' (1990) since the protagonist switches from person to person each day.

# Appendix B: Literature and Films on Personal Identity

Below is a very incomplete list of stories, novels and films relating to issues of personal identity. Where a novel has been made into one or more films, I list only the novel but mark the entry with a +.

## Clones and Doppelgangers

Edward Ashton, *Mickey7* (2022) +
Matthew Baker, 'The President's Doubles' (2016)
John W. Campbell, 'Who Goes There?' (1938) +
Jack Finney, *Body Snatchers* (1954) +
Kazuo Ishiguro, *Never Let Me Go* (2005) +
Ursula Le Guin, 'Nine Lives' (1969)
Stanislaw Lem, *Solaris* (1961) +
Iain Reid, *Foe* (2018) +
José Saramago, *The Double* (2002) +
William F. Temple, 'The Four-Sided Triangle' (1949) +
Sean Williams, 'The Lives of Riley' (2016)
Gene Wolf, *The Fifth Head of Cerberus* (1972)

## Film

Wes Craven, *Shatterday* (Twilight Zone episode) (1985)
Timothy Greenberg, *Living with Yourself* (2019)
Duncan Jones, *Moon* (2009)
Joseph Kosinski, *Oblivion* (2013)
Jordan Peele, *Us* (2019)
Harold Ramis, *Multiplicity* (1996)
Roger Spottiswoode, *The Sixth Day* (2000)

## Temporal Parts of Individuals

Matthew Baker, 'Parenthetical' (2024)
Jorge Luis Borges, 'The Other' (1972)

Ray Bradbury, 'A Touch of Petulance' (1980)
Ted Chiang, 'Story of Your Life' (1998) +
Philip K. Dick, 'The Skull' (1952)
David Gerrold, *The Man Who Folded Himself* (1973)
Robert Heinlein, "—All You Zombies—" (1959) +
Stanislaw Lem, 'The Seventh Voyage' (1976)
Audrey Niffenegger, *The Time Traveller's Wife* (2003) +
Kristine Kathryn Rusch, 'Red Letter Day' (2010)
Norman Spinrad, 'The Weed of Time' (1970)
Kurt Vonnegut, *Slaughterhouse-Five* (1969) +

## Film

Eric Bress and J. Mackye Gruber, *The Butterfly Effect* (2004)
Shane Carruth, *Primer* (2004)
Terry Gilliam, *12 Monkeys* (1995)
Rian Johnson, *Looper* (2012)
Nacho Vigalondo, *Timecrimes* (2007)
Robert Zemekis, *Back to the Future* (1985)

# Souls and Reincarnation

Douglas Adams, *Life, The Universe and Everything* (the character Agrajag) (1982)
Matthew Baker, 'Lost Souls' (2020)
Fonda Lee, 'Old Souls' (2017)
H. P. Lovecraft, 'The Tomb' (1917)
Richard Matheson, *What Dreams May Come* (1978) +
David Mitchell, *Cloud Atlas* (2004) +
Edgar Allan Poe, 'Morella' (1835)
Edgar Allan Poe, 'The Facts in the Case of M. Valdemar' (1845)
Kim Stanley Robinson, *The Years of Rice and Salt* (2002)
Pu Songling, 'Three Incarnations' (c. 1740)
Sean Williams, 'The End of the World Begins at Home' (2004)

## Film

Warren Beaty and Buck Henry, *Heaven Can Wait* (1978)
Jonathan Glazer, *Birth* (2004)

Gaspar Noé, *Enter the Void* (2009)
Jerry Zucker, *Ghost* (1990)

## Amnesia and False Memories

Philip K. Dick, 'Imposter' (1953)
Philip K. Dick, 'We Can Remember It for You Wholesale' (1966) +
Philip K. Dick, *Do Androids Dream of Electric Sheep?* (1968) +
Umberto Eco, *The Mysterious Flame of Queen Loana* (2004)
Daryl Gregory, 'Second Person, Present Tense' (2005)
Joe Haldeman, *All My Sins Remembered* (1977)
Dennis Lehane, *Shutter Island* (2003) +
Yōko Ogawa, *The Memory Police* (1994)
John Varley, 'Just Another Perfect Day' (1989)
Sean Williams, *Saturn Returns* (2007)

## Film

Michel Gondry, *Eternal Sunshine of the Spotless Mind* (2004)
Christopher Nolan, *Memento* (2000)
Alex Proyas, *Dark City* (1998)
Andrew Stanton, *Finding Dory* (2016)

## Narrative Identity

Elizabeth Bear, 'Erase, Erase, Erase' (2019)
James Patrick Kelly, 'Selfless' (2019)
Marcel Proust, *Time Regained* (1927) +
Sean Williams, *The Grand Conjunction* (2009)

## Film

Nick Cassavetes, *The Notebook* (2004)
Charlie Kaufman, *Synecdoche, New York* (2008)

## Teleportation

Algis Budrys, *Rogue Moon* (1960)
Thomas M. Disch, *Echo Round His Bones* (1967)
George Langelaan, 'The Fly' (1957) +
Edward Page Mitchell, 'The Man without a Body' (1877)
Frederik Pohl, *Farthest Star* (1975)
Christopher Priest, *The Prestige* (1995) +
Sean Williams, *The Resurrected Man* (1998)

## Brain State Transfers and Mind-Uploading

Thomas Anstey Guthrie, *Vice Versa* (1882) +
Matthew Baker, 'The Transition' (2016)
Grace Chan, *Every Version of You* (2022)
Greg Egan, *Permutation City* (1995)
William Gibson, *The Winter Market* (1985)
James Patrick Kelly, 'And No Torment Shall Touch Them' (2017)
qntm, 'Lena' (2021)
Robert J. Sawyer, 'Mindscan' (2005)
H. G. Wells, 'The Story of the Late Mr. Elvesham' (1896)
Roger Williams, 'The Metamorphosis of Prime Intellect' (1994)
Sean Williams and Shane Dix, *Orphans of Earth* (2003)
Robert Charles Wilson, *The Harvest* (1993)
Chelsea Quinn Yarbro, 'Into My Own' (1975)

## Films

James Cameron, *Avatar* (2009)
Brandon Cronenberg, *Possessor* (2020)
Owen Harris, *San Junipero* (Black Mirror episode) (2016)
Spike Jones, *Being John Malkovich* (1999)
Wally Pfister, *Transcendence* (2014)
Tarsem Singh, *Self/less* (2015)
Lana Wachowski and Lilly Wachowski, *The Matrix* (1999)

## Brain Removal and Transplants

A. A. Attanasio, *Solis* (1994)
Charles Bukowski, '(swastika symbol)' (1983)
Edgar Rice Burroughs 'The Master Mind of Mars' (1927)
Lena Coakley, 'Mirror Image' (2001)
Roald Dahl, 'William and Mary' (1959)
Alasdair Gray, *Poor Things* (1992) +
H. L. Gold, 'Man of Parts' (1954)
Norman Elwood Hammerstrom and Richard F. Searight 'The Brain in the Jar' (1924)
Robert Heinlein, *I Will Fear No Evil* (1970)
C. M. Kornbluth and Frederik Pohl, 'The Meeting' (1972)
H. P. Lovecraft, 'The Whisperer in the Darkness' (1931)
H. P. Lovecraft and Duane W. Rimel, 'The Disinterment' (1937)
C. L. Moore, 'No Woman Born' (1944)
Robert Sheckley, 'The Body' (1956)
Curt Siodmak, *Donovan's Brain* (1942) +
Louis Ulbach, 'Prince Bonifacio' (1860)

## Film

Jordan Peele, *Get Out* (2017)
Carl Reiner, *The Man with Two Brains* (1983)

## Animal Uplift

David Brin, *Star Tide Rising* (1983)
Mikhail Bulgakov, *Heart of a Dog* (1925)
Robert A. Heinlein, 'Jerry Was a Man' (1947)
James Patrick Kelly, *King of the Dogs, Queen of the Cats* (2020)
Dick King Smith, *Harry's Mad* (1984)
H. G. Wells, *The Island of Dr Moreau* (1896) +

## Film

James Gunn, *Guardians of the Galaxy Vol. 3* (2023)
Rupert Wyatt, *Rise of the Planet of the Apes* (2011)

# Divided Minds

Wyman Guin, 'Beyond Bedlam' (1973)
Robert Heinlein, 'The Unpleasant Profession of Jonathan Hoag' (1942)
Kwak Jaesik, 'I Meet Her' (2015)
James Patrick Kelly, 'Crazy Me' (2011)
Stephen King, 'Secret Window Secret Garden' (1990) +
Edward Lazellari, 'The Date' (1999)
Ursula Le Guin, *City of Illusions* (1967)
Stanislaw Lem, *Peace on Earth* (1986)
Howard L. Myers, 'Partner' (1968)
Chuck Palahniuk, *Fight Club* (1996) +
Edgar Allan Poe, 'William Wilson' (1839)
Arula Ratnaker, 'Babirusa' (2022)
Robert Silverberg, 'In the House of Double Minds' (1974)
Robert Louis Stephenson, 'The Strange Case of Dr Jekyll and Mr Hyde' (1886) +
Roger Zelazny, 'No award' (1977)

## Film

Peter Docter, *Inside Out* (2015)
Richard Fleischer, *The Boston Strangler* (1968)
Carl Reiner, *All of Me* (1984)
M. Night Shyamalan, *Split* (2016)
Ben Stiller, *Severance* (2022)

# Bionic Replacement

Isaac Azimov, 'The Bicentennial Man' (1976) +
Max Barry, *Machine Man* (2011)
L. Frank Baum, 'The Tin Woodman of Oz' (1918)
Greg Bear, 'Blood Music' (1983)
Daniel Dennett, 'Where Am I?' (1981)
Greg Egan, 'Learning to Be Me' (1990)
James Patrick Kelly, 'The Promise of Space' (2013)
Damon Knight, 'Masks' (1968)
Stanislaw Lem, 'Are You There, Mr Jones?' (1955)

Edgar Allen Poe, 'The Man that Was Used Up' (1839)
Frederik Pohl, *Man Plus* (1976)
Alastair Reynolds, 'Diamond Dogs' (2001)
Reiko Scott, 'Phantom Limb' (2018)
Masamune Shirow, *Ghost in the Shell* (1989) +
Marc Stiegler, 'The Gentle Seduction' (1989)
Sean Williams, 'Salvation' (1995)
Robert Charles Wilson, 'The Cartesian Theatre' (2006)

## Film

Paul Verhoven, *Robocop* (1987)

# Mental Fusion and Group Minds

Brian Aldiss, 'Let's be Frank' (1957)
Matthew Baker, 'Discrepancies' (2023)
Greg Egan, 'You and Whose Army?' (2020)
David H. Keller, *The Human Termites* (1929)
James Patrick Kelly, 'In The Dark' (2024)
Damon Knight, 'Four in One' (1953)
Ann Leckie, *Ancillary Justice* (2013)
George R. R. Martin, 'A Song for Lya' (1974)
Ramez Naam, The *Nexus* Trilogy (2012–15)
Alaistair Reynolds, 'Great Wall of Mars' (2000)
Olaf Stapledon, *Star Maker* (1937)
Theodore Sturgeon, *The Cosmic Rape* (1958)

## Film

Jonathan Frakes, *Star Trek: First Contact* (1996)

# Loss/Radical Change of Social Identity

Matthew Baker, *The Sentence* (2024)
Thomas M. Disch, 'The Asian Shore' (1970)

Eugie Foster, 'Sinner, Baker, Fabulist, Priest; Red Mask, Black Mask, Gentleman, Beast' (2009)
Franz Kafka, *The Metamorphosis* (1915)
Claire North, *The Sudden Appearance of Hope* (2016)
Robert Silverberg, 'To See the Invisible Man'+ (1963)
Sean Williams, 'The Cuckoo' (2014)

## Film

John Frankenheimer, *Seconds* (1966)
John Landis, *Trading Places* (1983)
Carl Tibbetts, 'White Christmas' (Black Mirror episode) (2014)

# Index

**Bold** numbers indicate most important entries

abortion 113, 198
abstract object identity 151
amnesia 110, 299
anātman, *see* no self
animal autonomy theory 263–4
animal cognition 196
animalism 174, **195–200**, 221–4, 245–6, 260, 264, 293–5
animal uplift 196, 301
artificial intelligence 296, *see also* bionic replacement
authenticity 284–6, 295

bad faith 285
Baker, Lynne Rudder 246–8, 294
bionic replacement 2, **243–9**, 302–3
body-brain interaction 160–1, 170, 184, 195
brain bisection, *see* divided minds
brain transplantation **170–5**, 197, 293, 301
branching identity 172–3, 293, *see also* transitivity of identity
Buddhism, *see* no self

cell replacement 57, 243
character 57, 111, 113, 126, **129**, 174, 220
cloning, *see* duplication
collective intentionality, *see* group agency
collective minds, *see* group minds
conjoined twins 221–2, 259, 294–5
consciousness 175, 262–3, *see also* mind-body interaction

constitution theory 200, **246–9**, 263
corpus callosum, *see* divided minds

death 33, 151, 198, 263–4, 286
dementia 129, 196
depersonalization 129, 283
Dennett, Daniel 5, 60, 125–9, 152, 244, 291, 293
Dissociative Identity Disorder 221
distinctness of beings, *see* identity > synchronic identity
divided minds 171, **219–24**, 302
dreams 198, 259
duplication 33, **149–53**, 170, 297

ethics of identity, *see* self-interest
embodied cognition 195, 293
essence 2, 78–9, 197, 224, 290–1
extended mind thesis 244, 294

false memories, *see* memories > quasi-memories
fiction theory of self, *see* narrative identity
fictions, metaphysics of 152, 292

Gendler, Tamar 3, 289
God 151
group agency 262
group minds 37, **259–64**, 295, 303

hemispherectomy, 171, 223
Hume, David 37

identity
    diachronic identity **56–60**, 78–9, 109, 150, 221, 223, 246, 263
    numerical identity **33–5**, 56, 199, 283, 290
    qualitative identity 33, 35, 109, 290
    social identity 33, 35, 285, 295, 303–4
    synchronic identity 34–5, 222
identity over time, *see* identity > diachronic identity
illusion of self 36, 152
immortality 79, 249, 263–4
interaction problem, *see* mind-body interaction
intuitions 4–5, 58, 60
is-ought gap 286–7

linguistic ability 196
living beings, metaphysics of 113, 248–9, 264
Lem, Stanislaw 292
Lewis, David 59–60, 110, 172–3, 290, 293
Locke, John 34, 83, **109–10**, 112–13, 125, 174, 291

machine parts, *see* bionic replacement
materialism about identity 153, 198
memories
    as a tool 174
    brain based 153, 170
    different types distinguished 86–7, 110
    episodic memory 110
    procedural memory 110–12, 170
    quasi-memories 152, 299
    selectivity of 126
    semantic memory 110–12
memory criterion, *see* psychological continuity
mental fusion, *see* group minds
mind-body interaction 81, 200, 219–20, 243
mind-reading 260
mind swaps 150–1

mind uploading 151, 295–6, 300
moral responsibility 34, 78, 110–11, 113, 195–6, 221, 263

Nagel, Thomas 294
narrative identity **125–30**, 291–2, 299
no self 36, 296

Olson, Eric 199, 224, 245, 247, 293, 294, 296

Parfit, Derek 172–3, 290, 292–3
Plato 79, 259, 293
persistence, *see* identity > diachronic identity
persistent vegetative states 198, 247
persona 284
personality, *see* character
personhood 109, **195–7**, 199, 248, 260
philosophical method 1–2
physicalism, *see* materialism about identity
pregnancy 264
probabilistic reasoning 80
psychological continuity 82–3, **109–13**, 152–3, **170–4**, 197–8, 291–2
punishment, *see* moral responsibility

Reid, Mark 220–2, 294
Reid, Thomas 112
reincarnation 79–83, 298
resurrection 151, 296
Rousseau, Jean-Jacques 284

Sartre, Jean-Paul 285–7, 295
science fiction
    advantages of 4–5, 150, 175
    aesthetics of 4, 37, 170, 245–6, 259
    characterization of 3, 78
    realism 4–5, 33, 56, 151, 171, 195, 243
    writing as discovery 244–6
science fiction authors authority 3–4
Schechtman, Marya 129, 291
schizophrenia 129–30

Schwitzgebel, Eric 292
self-consciousness 109, 112, 125, 173–4, **195–7**, 199, 224, 247
self-interest 36, 57–8, 111–12, 287
sense of self 129, 152–3, 173, 199, 245
ship of Theseus 294
Shoemaker, Sydney 293
skills, *see* memories > procedural memories
sleep 198, 293
social norms 283–5
souls **78–83**, 286, 290–1, 298
survival, *see* identity > diachronic identity

teleportation **149–53**, 170, 292, 295, 300
temporal parts, 59–60, 172–3, 223, 290, 297–8
thought experiments
    deceptiveness 5, 60
    definition 2–3
    effectiveness 150, 175, 222, 243, 289, 292
    realism 4–5, 56, 60, 151, 222, 243
Time, debates about 59, 173, 290
Time travel 3, 56, 60
transitivity of identity 113, 171, 221
truth 126–9, 292

unity of consciousness 294, *see also* divided minds

van Inwagen, Peter 296

why am I me 296
Wiggins, David 171
Williams, Bernard 293

Zuboff, Arnold 296